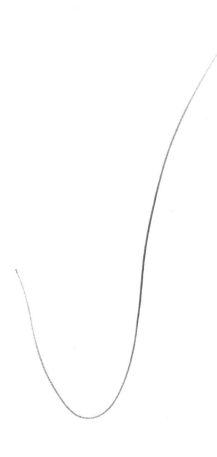

BERTRICE SMALL

THE BORDER VIXEN

 NEW AMERICAN LIBRARY

New American Library
Published by New American Library, a division of
Penguin Group (USA) Inc., 375 Hudson Street,
New York, New York 10014, USA
Penguin Group (Canada), 90 Eglinton Avenue East, Suite 700, Toronto,
Ontario M4P 2Y3, Canada (a division of Pearson Penguin Canada Inc.)
Penguin Books Ltd., 80 Strand, London WC2R 0RL, England
Penguin Ireland, 25 St. Stephen's Green, Dublin 2,
Ireland (a division of Penguin Books Ltd.)
Penguin Group (Australia), 250 Camberwell Road, Camberwell, Victoria 3124,
Australia (a division of Pearson Australia Group Pty. Ltd.)
Penguin Books India Pvt. Ltd., 11 Community Centre, Panchsheel Park,
New Delhi - 110 017, India
Penguin Group (NZ), 67 Apollo Drive, Rosedale, North Shore 0632,
New Zealand (a division of Pearson New Zealand Ltd.)
Penguin Books (South Africa) (Pty.) Ltd., 24 Sturdee Avenue,
Rosebank, Johannesburg 2196, South Africa

Penguin Books Ltd., Registered Offices:
80 Strand, London WC2R 0RL, England

ISBN 978-1-61664-907-4

 REGISTERED TRADEMARK—MARCA REGISTRADA

Set in Goudy
Designed by Alissa Amell

Printed in the United States of America

PUBLISHER'S NOTE
This is a work of fiction. Names, characters, places, and incidents either are the product of the author's imagination or are used fictitiously, and any resemblance to actual persons, living or dead, business establishments, events, or locales is entirely coincidental.

The publisher does not have any control over and does not assume any responsibility for author or third-party Web sites or their content.

The scanning, uploading, and distribution of this book via the Internet or via any other means without the permission of the publisher is illegal and punishable by law. Please purchase only authorized electronic editions, and do not participate in or encourage electronic piracy of copyrighted materials. Your support of the author's rights is appreciated.

For Aneta, who keeps me sane

A note for my readers: *Aisir nam Breug* is pronounced: Asher nam Breg.

THE
BORDER
VIXEN

Prologue

*M*ad Maggie Kerr could outride, outrun, outfight, out-drink, and outswear any man in the Borders. These were not, however, the virtues a gentleman looked for in a wife. But if a man liked a tall lass with dark chestnut brown hair, hazel eyes, and a fat dower, then perhaps Mad Maggie could be considered acceptable—for those reasons and the fact she was Dugald Kerr's only heir, and Dugald Kerr controlled the Aisir nam Breug.

The Aisir nam Breug was a deep, narrow passage through the border hills between Scotland and England. No one could recall a time when this transit had not been managed by the Scots Kerrs at its north end and the English Kerrs at its south end. Payment of a single toll gave the traveler the guarantee of a safe trip from one side of the border to the other. Merchants and messengers, bridal parties, and other voyagers all used the Aisir nam Breug. Warring factions did not. It had been an unspoken agreement for several centuries that the Aisir nam Breug could be used only for peaceful travel.

Management of this resource had made the Kerr family wealthy over the years. They did not, however, flaunt their wealth, but their home, set upon a low hill, was more a small castle than a tower or manor house. And the village at the foot of that hill had an air of comfortable prosperity about it that was unique in the Borders. They were loyal to the king and always ready to aid a neighbor. The Kerrs of Brae Aisir were considered both honorable and trustworthy.

But the old laird was certainly in his final days. He was the last legitimate male in his line, with a stubborn girl just turned seventeen as his only heir. And despite her reputation, which had earned her the sobriquet of Mad Maggie, Dugald Kerr needed to find his granddaughter a husband—a man who would be strong enough to hold the Aisir nam Breug for the son he would sire on Mad Maggie. It would not be an easy task, but the laird of Brae Aisir knew exactly the kind of man who could tame his lass. Finding him was another matter, however, and this man would also have to win her respect, for Maggie was proud.

"He must be able to outride, outrun, and outfight her," Dugald Kerr declared to David, his younger brother, who was the family's priest.

"I suppose yer right, Brother," David Kerr said with a small smile, "but 'twill nae be easy finding such a man. I shall have to pray mightily on this."

The laird gave a snort of laughter. "Aye," he agreed, "ye will."

"How will ye go about it, Brother?" the priest inquired.

"I'll give a feast and invite all the neighbors. Then I'll announce my intentions to them. I know Maggie frightens many of them, for she is outspoken and headstrong, but surely the lure of the Aisir nam Breug will tempt them to overlook these faults."

"She's nae as bad as she pretends," Father David said. "Yer household runs smoothly because of her. She knows how to direct the servants and care for the sick. She's nae fearful of hard work. I've seen her myself in yer fields, and working with the women salting meat for the winter, and making jams."

"She'd rather hunt the meat than prepare it," the laird said with a chuckle.

"Aye, Brother, she would," the priest agreed. "But she can do what a woman with a large household needs to do. She will make the right lad a fine wife. But I don't believe you'll find that lad among the Borders, Dugald."

"I must begin my search somewhere," the laird of Brae Aisir said.

Chapter 1

"The hall is full, I suppose," Maggie Kerr said to her tiring woman, Grizel.

"Aye," came the tart reply. "All come to stuff themselves and get drunk at yer grandfather's board," Grizel snorted. "Armstrongs and Elliots, Bruces and Fergusons, Scotts and Bairds who are forever telling the story of how their ancestor saved the life of King William the Lion and thus gained their lands. There are a few Lindsays, and Hays too, and nae one of them fit to wipe the mud from yer boot, my darling lass."

"Maybe I'll nae join them," Maggie said. "I dislike being presented as Grandsire's prize mare." She reached for the cake of scented soap on the rim of her tall oak bathing tub and rubbed it slowly over her arm. "I don't want to marry, and I am more than capable of holding the Aisir nam Breug myself without interference from a stranger calling himself my lord and master. Jesu, why wasn't I born a lad?"

"Because ye were born a lass," Grizel said matter-of-factly. "Now finish yer bath. Ye have to get down to the hall sooner than later. I'll nae let you shame your grandsire, my dearie. Nor would ye do it. Ye know yer duty better than any."

Then Grizel went and laid out the burgundy velvet gown that Maggie would wear that evening. It was high-waisted and had a low scooped neckline that revealed most of her shoulders. The tight-fitting sleeves and the hem of the gown were trimmed in dark marten. The servant set out a pair of round-toed sollerets covered in the same velvet as the gown and burgundy silk stockings with matching garters.

As Maggie stepped out of her tub, Grizel hurried to wrap her in a warmed towel. "Sit down, and let me prepare you. Then we'll put on your chemise, and you can choose the jewels you would wear. You should show to your best advantage, my dearie."

"God's balls!" Maggie swore. "Ye too, Grizel? I don't care if one of those fools asks for my hand or not. I don't want a husband, and I shall make it very difficult for any man to please me enough to win my favor." She pulled on her soft linen chemise.

Smiling to herself, Grizel gently pushed the girl down on a stool and began to brush out her hair while Maggie dried her feet. "Yer a Kerr," she said as she plied the boar bristles through Maggie's thick chestnut-colored tresses. "Ye'll do what ye must for the good of the family."

Maggie snorted at her tiring woman's words. Grizel was like a mother to her, as her own mother had perished giving birth to her, and her father had died in a border clash six months before she was born. Grizel had lost her husband in that same fray, and her own infant son about the time Maggie entered the world. Grandsire had brought the nineteen-year-old widow up from the village to wet-nurse his new granddaughter. She had been born strong, Dugald Kerr said. There had been no doubt she would survive.

And when she no longer needed nourishment from Grizel's teat, the wet nurse had remained to raise the child for the laird of Brae Aisir. Maggie loved Grizel dearly, and she hated to disappoint her. She would go into her grandsire's hall the coming evening and be shown to prospective buyers as if a blood mare at a horse fair, but she would wed no man who could not gain her respect. And there was none among the young men she knew who had ever even been able to command her attention. They were a rough-spoken lot, and she knew their only interest in her was the Aisir nam Breug. Maggie pulled on her silk stockings, fastening the ribbon garters to hold them up.

"Let's get yer gown on," Grizel said, and she helped Maggie into the rich, soft velvet, seeing that the tight fur-cuffed sleeves fitted without a wrinkle, then lacing up the garment. The high waist of the gown forced the girl's breasts up so that they were quite visible above the low neckline. The fabric of the skirt fell in graceful folds.

"Give me my rope of pearls," Maggie said.

Grizel opened the jewel casket and drew out the pearls as her young mistress picked out several rings, which she put on her fingers. The tiring woman slid the pearls over Maggie's head. "They look just lovely," she told the lass.

"Braid my hair now in a single plait," Maggie instructed.

"I will nae do it!" Grizel said vehemently. "Yer grandsire said ye were to leave yer tresses loose this evening. I've a gold ribbon band with a small oval of polished red quartz for ye to wear as a headpiece."

"Christ Almighty! The mare is to be presented as never mounted," Maggie swore.

"Well, ye never have," Grizel said sharply, "though yer wild behavior has left many wondering. So ye'll do as yer told, Maggie Kerr, and nae shame yer grandsire or yer clan's good name this night."

Maggie laughed. Grizel rarely scolded her so severely. "Oh, very well. My hair shall fall about me like that of a fourteen-year-old lass, for not only am I willful, at seventeen I am fast growing out of my breeding cycle," Maggie teased the older woman. "So let my suitors think I am a helpless creature. If they would delude themselves."

Now it was Grizel who laughed. But then she secured Maggie's long hair with the gold ribbon band. "Put yer shoes on, and yer ready to make yer entrance," she said.

Maggie slipped her feet into the pretty slippers, then stood up. "You realize," she said to Grizel, "that I will frighten all those clansmen in the hall with my grand entry. I'm not the usual border woman in her one good gown trying to please. I'm the heiress to Brae Aisir, and I won't let them forget it."

"Dinna," Grizel replied. "The man who wins you will love you and respect your position. He must be worthy of you, my lass. You must nae accept a lesser man. Beware, however, of those who will try to seduce you to gain an advantage over you."

Maggie laughed. "I have managed to hold on to my virtue for seventeen years, Grizel. I will continue to hold it from those lusting after my wealth, my body, and my family's power. I can tell you that I know the man I must eventually wed is nae in Grandsire's hall this night." She reached out to take the hand of the older woman. "Come along now, Grizel. To the hall! It should prove an amusing evening."

They left the girl's rooms and descended the winding stairs. Maggie's apartment was in the southwest corner of her grandfather's home. They entered the great hall, Grizel shoving the men crowding the large room aside so her mistress might get through to the high board, where her grandfather was awaiting her arrival.

Dugald Kerr watched her come. There was pride in his brown eyes, and his mouth quirked with his amusement. The wicked wench had dressed to intimidate, and by the open mouths he could now see as he looked out over his hall, she had been successful in her attempt. She was fair enough to evoke lust in not just a few of the men there. But she did not come eyes downcast, shrinking away from his guests. She strode with the sureness of who she was—Margaret Kerr; his only heir, and closest blood relation other than his brother, David.

He was proud of her, especially because he had never expected that his frail, weak daughter-in-law, dead with Maggie's birth, could have given him any heir, let alone such a strong lass as Maggie. His youngest son, Robert, had married Glynis Kerr, one of the Netherdale Kerrs. After several centuries, they were but distantly related. Unfortunately Glynis had proved frail. She lost two sons before Maggie had been born. When Robert had been killed in the early days of Glynis's confinement, Dugald Kerr had despaired.

His two older sons, their wives, and their children were dead. The eldest of his three sons, like the youngest, had died in the border wars. He had been newly wed, and his wife had not yet borne a bairn. She had returned to her family and made another marriage. His middle son had succumbed with his wife, and two little boys, to a winter epidemic. Robert had been sixteen then. A year later he was wed, and three years later he was dead. His wife, however, understanding the gravity of the family's situation, had forced her sorrow away from her until she could birth her child safely. But seeing her father-in-law's face when the child slid from her body, Glynis had whispered but two words, "I'm sorry," loosened her hold on life, and died.

Watching Glynis's daughter now make her way to the high board, Dugald Kerr wished Glynis had lived to see the magnificent heiress she and Robbie had given Brae Aisir. He smiled broadly as Maggie stepped up and, greeting her great-uncle David first, bent and kissed Dugald Kerr's ruddy cheek. Then she settled herself into the high-backed oak chair at his right hand and gazed out over the assembly.

"Is there anyone in the Borders not eating at your expense tonight, Grandsire?" she asked mischievously, her hazel eyes dancing wickedly.

"Yer husband might be among that pack of borderers, lass," he replied, smiling at her. Maggie was, he had to admit to himself, his weakness. It was why he had allowed her to run rampant throughout the Borders. Her daring and independence delighted him, although he was wise enough to know it would not have in any other woman.

"There's nae a man in this hall tonight whom I would wed and bed, Grandsire," she told him candidly.

"It's a woman's place to marry," David Kerr said softly to her.

"Why? Because we are weak and frail vessels, Uncle? Because we are told that God created man first, and therefore we are less in his eyes? If we are less, then why is it our responsibility to bear new life to God's glory?" Maggie demanded of him.

"Why must ye always ask such damned intelligent questions, Niece?" the priest asked. His eyes, however, were dancing with amusement.

"Because I love stymieing ye, Uncle. I refuse to fit the church's mold that women are lesser creatures, fit but to keep house and spawn new souls. I do not want a husband taking precedence over me at Brae Aisir. I am perfectly capable of managing the Aisir nam Breug, and need no stranger to do it for me," Maggie said firmly.

"And when ye have left this earth, who will be left to care for the Aisir nam Breug, Maggie?" the laird asked her quietly.

She caught his hand up and kissed it. "We will be here forever, Grandsire," she said to him. "Ye and I will look after the Aisir nam Breug together."

"That is a child's reasoning," Dugald Kerr replied. "Yer no longer a child, Maggie. Ye need a husband to father a child upon ye. A child who will one day inherit what the Kerrs of Brae Aisir have kept safe for centuries. I will not force ye to the altar, but sooner or later ye must choose a man to wed. And I will help ye to find the right man, Granddaughter. One who will respect ye. One whom ye can respect."

"Nae in this hall tonight, Grandsire," she answered him.

"Perhaps ye are correct, but before we cast our nets afield, Maggie, we must give our neighbors the opportunity to woo ye," the laird said.

Maggie picked up the silver goblet studded in green malachite by her hand, and drank a healthy draft of the red wine in it. "I cannot gainsay ye, Grandsire," she told him. "Very well; let us see what we may find from this showing of lads all eager to win my hand, spend my fortune, and take my inheritance." And she laughed.

"God help the man who finally pleases ye," David Kerr said dryly.

The laird laughed and signaled his servants to begin bringing the meal. They streamed into the hall, bearing steaming platters, dishes, and bowls of food. The trestle tables below the high board where the three Kerrs sat had been set with linen cloths, polished pewter plates, and tankards filled with good strong ale. There were round loaves of bread upon the tables, small wheels of hard cheese, and crocks of sweet butter. The servants offered poultry, fish, boar, and venison, which the male guests greedily ate up. Few of the vegetables offered were consumed by the clansmen, who were content with well-cooked meat, fish, game, bread, and cheese.

At the high board the dishes were more varied, and while it was meat, game, and seafood, it was more delicately offered. Trout braised in white wine and set upon green watercress was offered along with a bowl of steamed prawns. There was a roasted duck stuffed with dried apples and bread, and roasts of lamb, boar, and venison. Bowls of peas and a salad of lettuces were presented. The high board had a large round cottage loaf, butter, and two cheeses—one from France that was soft and creamy, the other a good hard yellow cheese.

Maggie watched as the guests wolfed down everything offered to them and quaffed tankard after tankard of brown ale. Some of the men had more delicate manners than others. The clansmen barely mingled, sitting at their own tables and eyeing one another suspiciously. She wondered how long it would be before a fight would break out, but she knew her grandsire's men-at-arms now lining the hall could handle any unpleasant situation. The high board was cleared, and a sweet was brought for Maggie. Cook had made for her a custard with jam, which Maggie very much favored.

Her grandfather waited for her to finish the treat before he stood up. Instantly the hall quieted. "'Tis good to have ye all here with us tonight," Dugald Kerr said, and he smiled down at them. He was a handsome man in his sixties not yet bowed by his years. He was clean shaven and had a full head of white hair cut short, a long face and nose, and sharp brown eyes. He wore a long dark tunic brocaded in gold and trimmed with marten. No one would have ever mistaken the laird of Brae Aisir for anything other than what he was—a wealthy man.

"As you must surely know, I am growing older," he began. "My only heir is my granddaughter, Margaret. I hope to find a husband for her among ye. However, I will not give her to another lightly. To win her hand ye must be able to outride, outrun, and outfight Maggie. Ye must win her respect. Now, should any of ye wish to put yerselves forth as a possible husband for my granddaughter, come and speak with me before ye depart on the morrow. The man who weds and beds my Maggie will one day control the Aisir nam Breug. But if I can find none among ye who suits her or me, know that I will look elsewhere, but the same conditions will apply. Now drink up, and let my piper entertain you all." Dugald Kerr sat back down.

A murmuring arose in the hall now, and Maggie almost laughed as speculative glances were cast in her direction by the men below. As it had been guessed that the laird of Brae Aisir was seeking a husband for his granddaughter, many of the other clan lords had come with the sons they had of marriageable age. And several of the lairds themselves were unmarried, or widowers seeking a second or third wife.

"'Tis a goodly selection," her priestly great-uncle murmured. "Lord Hay's brother looks a possible match for you."

"I prefer a younger man whom I may control," Maggie said low.

"One who will be content to let me do what needs doing while taking all the credit. I care naught for recognition. I just want the Aisir nam Breug managed properly. If I spawn a son I can teach, then I will do so. But none out there looks to possess any wits at all."

"Ye cannot judge by just looking at them," her grandfather remarked. "Let the piper play, and dance with a few of them. Perhaps you will be surprised."

"More likely I will be disappointed, but I will take your advice, Grandsire," Maggie replied. Then rising, she called out, "Who will dance with me, my lords?" And she stepped from the dais to be suddenly surrounded by a group of eager males. Looking them all over with a bold eye she smiled, then addressed a young man with pale blond hair. "Ye will do to start with," she said, holding out a graceful hand.

He eagerly grasped the hand and said almost breathlessly, "Calum Lindsay, Mistress Maggie." His other arm slipped about her waist as the piper began to play a lively tune. He was unfortunately not a good dancer, tripping first over his own feet, and then hers. He looked to be no more than sixteen, and his Adam's apple bobbed nervously up and down in his throat as he concentrated on the quick steps of the country dance. Not once did he dare to meet her glance, for he found he was intimidated by the beautiful girl.

Maggie's chestnut brown hair was tossed about as they danced. It was impossible to engage Calum Lindsay in conversation, as she could see if he had to speak with her, he would lose his concentration with the dance. She was relieved when an older man stepped in to partner her, cutting the lad out to the boy's obvious relief. Maggie looked directly at the gentleman, recognizing the red plaid of Clan Hay. "And ye are?" she asked.

"Ewan Hay," he replied shortly as they capered across the hall with quick steps and turned sharply. He lifted her up, swinging her about before returning Maggie's feet to the floor. "I am twenty-eight, have never been wed, am a third son, and will speak with your grandsire on the morrow."

"Indeed," Maggie replied. "And think ye that ye can outride, outrun, and outfight me, Ewan Hay?"

"Yer a woman, for Christ's sake," he responded. "Oh, I've heard of yer reputation, but 'tis certainly bragging, madam, and nothing more."

Maggie laughed. "God's balls, sir, what a fool ye be if ye believe that! Still, ye are welcome to speak with my grandsire. Nothing will give me greater pleasure than to beat ye in all three contests."

Ewan Hay's face darkened with anger. "We will see, madam, just how ye fare in a contest with me. And when I have put ye in yer proper place, and wed ye, I shall on our wedding night take a sturdy hazel switch and whip the pride out of ye. Ye will learn how to behave like a proper wife in my charge."

"I would nae wed ye if ye were the last man on the face of the earth," Maggie said angrily. "Remember my words when I blood ye with my blade." When the music stopped she pulled away from him and returned to the high board.

"Yer flushed," Dugald Kerr noted. "Did Lord Hay's younger brother say something to distress ye?"

"He will sue for my hand, beat me in all three contests, and whip me with a hazel on our wedding night so I learn my proper place," Maggie told her grandsire and her great-uncle.

The laird's head snapped up. He looked about until he could find Ewan Hay, then glared at him. "I shall nae accept his suit," he said angrily.

"Nay, let him try to best me," Maggie said in a cold, even voice. "He is a man who wants public humiliation, and I shall enjoy giving it to him. Let the bastard try to beat me in fair combat. I shall enjoy shaming him before the rest of them."

"Be careful, Niece," David Kerr said warily.

"I will, Uncle," Maggie replied. She rose again. "Now, sirs, if ye will excuse me, I have had enough tonight and would beg yer leave to depart the hall."

"Ye have it," her grandfather said. "Rest well, my bairn."

Maggie departed the great hall, moving quickly through and past the tables below the board. She had eaten sparingly and drunk little. Tomorrow, when Ewan Hay sought to gain her hand in marriage, she intended pressing him into the battle immediately. Under the best of conditions she could beat him, but he had poured a lot of ale into himself tonight, and she didn't doubt for one moment that after their meeting he had been tempted to swill more like the pig he was. She smiled wickedly to herself. She must get to bed immediately. A good night's rest was necessary to teaching Lord Hay's younger brother the lesson he needed to learn.

Grizel was waiting for her, and she listened as Maggie shared the details of the evening with her. "That Hay laddie is too bold for my taste," she said.

"He won't be quite so bold by this time tomorrow," Maggie said grimly.

"Be careful, my lass. A fellow like that is not to be trifled with, I fear," Grizel said. "They are said to be hard men, the Border Hays."

"Wake me at first light," Maggie said as she finished undressing. She washed her face, hands, and teeth before climbing into her comfortable bed hung with rose-colored velvet curtains.

"I will," Grizel promised as she put her mistress's clothing away. Then she hurried from the bedchamber while behind her Maggie blew out the taper by her bed.

As morning began to lighten the sky some hours later, Grizel returned to awaken the girl. Maggie jumped from her bed at once, rested and ready for her challenge. Instructing her serving woman, she pulled on a pair of dark-colored breeks, tucking her chemise into the pants and donning a white linen shirt that she carefully laced up. Then she sat pulling on a pair of light woolen stockings, and her worn leather boots. "I'll go to the kitchens and get some hot oats," she said to Grizel, and ran off.

The cook filled a bowl with oat stir-about. Maggie shaved some sugar from the sugar cone the cook offered over her oats and poured heavy cream atop it. Then taking up her spoon, she quickly ate the porridge.

"A slice of fresh cottage loaf, mistress?" the cook asked.

"Just the oats. I think I will be running this morning," Maggie said.

The cook cackled. "The server says Lord Hay's brother is engaging the laird in conversation right now. I saw him last night. He has a handsome face, but he used one of the serving lasses hard. His heart is a cruel one."

"Dinna fear," Maggie answered the woman. "I'll nae have him." Then finished with her oats, she hurried up the stairs to the great hall where Lord Hay and his brother, Ewan, were speaking with the laird. Maggie bounded right up to her grandfather's side, where she stood looking boldly down at the two men.

"Ewan Hay would have yer hand, lass," Dugald Kerr said.

"Is he willing to meet our terms, Grandsire?" Maggie asked quietly.

"He says he is," came the reply.

"*Today?*" Maggie said pointedly. "I dinna like him, Grandsire, and I would quickly put his hopes to an end."

"Today? Are ye mad?" Ewan Hay burst out. "Ye indulge the wench, my lord, far too much. When we are wed I will nae indulge her so."

"If ye wish to try to win me, sir, it will be on my grandsire's terms, and nae yers," Maggie said coldly. "Today, tomorrow, next week. Ye will nae overcome me, and frankly I should just as soon be quit of ye today as tomorrow."

"My lord?" Ewan Hay turned to the laird.

"She's correct, young Hay. So if ye want her, ye will take up the challenge this day. If ye canna win her today, ye will nae be able to win her another day—believe me."

Ewan Hay turned to his elder brother, but Lord Hay shook his head, saying, "The laird knows whereof he speaks. If ye really want her, then best her this day and be done with it, Ewan. If ye choose nae to, ye canna be blamed if ye dinna want to face this challenge. There are other lasses more biddable for ye to wed than this one."

"I will nae be beaten by a woman," Ewan Hay snarled, his face darkening when Maggie laughed aloud.

"We will run barefoot," she said sweetly.

"*Barefoot?*" His voice went up a full octave.

"'Tis my way, sir." Then she sat down at the high board, swiftly removing her boots and stockings.

"Decline the challenge, and let us go home," Lord Hay said to his brother.

"*Never!*" Ewan Hay almost shouted.

The course they would race both on foot and by horse was to be the same. They would go across the drawbridge, down the hill, run straight through the village, turn about, and come back up the hill again to circle the little keep once before crossing the drawbridge once more. As soon as they returned, they would mount up and redo the identical route a-horse. There would be no stopping.

"And if ye survive the races," Maggie said, "I will engage ye in swordplay. The match is over when one of us draws blood. Do ye agree?"

"Aye!" Ewan Hay said through gritted teeth. When he had met her challenge and won, he would beat her black and blue on their wedding night for her boldness this day. He yanked off his shoes and stockings.

"Ye hae small feet," Maggie noted. "They say a man with small feet has a small cock, sir."

Lord Hay swallowed back his laughter as his younger sibling's face darkened again with outrage. The lass was baiting him nicely into anger. If he succumbed to that anger, he would drain his energy, but then that was precisely what the girl intended.

He did not expect he would be welcoming Mad Maggie Kerr into their family.

The hall emptied out into the yard and to the drawbridge. Grizel hurried up to her mistress to tie her hair back with a red ribbon. Then Dugald Kerr asked both combatants if they were ready. Gaining their acquiescence, he raised his hand up and dropped the white napkin he had been holding. It fluttered to the ground as Ewan Hay and Maggie Kerr sprinted off to the cheers of the onlookers.

But it was obvious from the beginning that the man could not outrun the girl.

She was almost out of sight before he reached the end of the drawbridge. He winced with each pebble that his foot struck, swearing softly as he tried to run to catch up with her. At the end of the village were two Hay clansmen waiting to verify that both parties had gone the full length. Maggie passed him going in the other direction.

"Bitch!" he shouted at her as she dashed by, and he heard her laughter.

Maggie gave it her all. She wanted this over and done with. Regaining the courtyard, she did not even pause to put her boots back on, although she had more than enough time to do so. She leaped upon the back of her dapple gray stallion and raced from the courtyard, leaning low upon the beast, her bare heels digging into the animal's side. She passed Ewan Hay as he stumbled up the hill to encircle the castle. It was over, and she knew it, but she knew he would not admit defeat until she blooded him with her blade. She was actually looking forward to it, but she was denied the pleasure, for when she rode back into the courtyard, Ewan Hay was seated upon a step, Grizel tending to his bleeding feet. He had not even bothered to mount his horse.

Maggie slid from her horse and walked over to him. "Do ye admit defeat, sir?" she asked him coldly. "Ye completed but one of the three challenges."

"Madam, despite yer wealth, and the power ye will hold, I would nae hae ye for a wife if ye were the last woman on the face of God's green earth," Ewan Hay said grimly. "Yer a border vixen, and I pity the man, if he even exists, who will tame, wed, and bed ye. Is that a stallion ye were riding just now?" He stared, surprised.

"Aye," Maggie drawled, smiling. She bent to pull her stockings and boots back on.

Ewan Hay shook his blond head. "A woman who rides a stallion is nae the lass for me," he admitted to her, briefly humbled.

"Ye ran a good race," Maggie said generously.

He looked up at her and shook his head. Then he said to Grizel, "Can ye help me get my boots on, woman?"

"Yer feet are too swollen, sir," Grizel said. "I'll wrap them for ye, but ye'll nae wear yer boots for the next few days."

Ewan Hay swore beneath his breath. "How am I to ride?" he asked of no one in particular. He stared at his neatly bound feet.

"We'll get ye on yer mount," Dugald Kerr said. He did not invite either Lord Hay or his brother back into the keep. "See to it," the laird told the captain of his men-at-arms. Then he turned to his granddaughter. "The men yer training are waiting, lass."

"Aye, Grandsire," Maggie said, going off to drill a small squad of lads awaiting her in the courtyard. She tossed the reins of her stallion to one of the stable boys as she went.

Dugald Kerr gave a final glance to the Hays. "I thank ye for coming," he said. Then he turned away and returned to his hall where throughout the morning he bid his guests farewell. Most of them had watched as Ewan Hay had been humiliated and soundly beaten. None of them stepped forward to speak with the laird other than to thank him for his hospitality. When the last of them had departed, Dugald Kerr sighed, saying to his priestly brother, "I know Maggie is a formidable lass, David, but are all of our border lads such weaklings that they would not even attempt to meet the challenges set forth?"

"Nae after seeing the Hay beaten so thoroughly," David Kerr said. "Why must ye insist on a husband for Maggie meeting such a challenge?"

"She will nae love or respect a man who cannot best her. Her husband will need her help, her guidance, in managing the Aisir nam Breug. There isn't a man in my house, in my ranks, on my lands, who does not respect Mad Maggie Kerr. There are some who even fear her, David. And they are right too. What a pity she was not born a lad!"

"She's more lad than lassie," the priest said dryly, "but I suppose yer right. She'll need a strong man by her side. But after today's exhibition, I dinna know who'll have her. I will pray on it, however, Dugald."

In the weeks that followed, several of the border lords sent to the laird of Brae Aisir; some even returned to speak with him face-to-face in an effort to negotiate a marriage contract between one of their kinsmen and Mad Maggie Kerr. But Dugald Kerr remained firm in his resolve. The man who married his granddaughter had to vanquish her, and earn her respect. Turned away, the lairds finally met at a small inn in the border hills to discuss the matter of Dugald Kerr, Mad Maggie, and the Aisir nam Breug.

"If the old man dies," one laird said, "what will happen to the traverse? It can't be left in the hands of a flighty lass."

"We all know the girl must be wed," another laird said, "but who is brave enough to force the lass?"

"David Kerr knows enough to hold the Aisir nam Breug," a voice spoke up.

"He's a priest. Do we want the church controlling the passage?" another said.

"Dugald Kerr looked sound of both body and mind to me," a man remarked.

"Aye!" several voices agreed.

"Perhaps we hae best leave things as they are right now," an Elliot clansman said.

"The lass is ripe for marriage, and if some of the younger lads were to court her, mayhap she would forget her foolishness and choose one of them."

There were murmurs of assent from the majority of the men in the small inn. They drank a toast to their decision, then scattered in different directions. But Ewan Hay sat brooding over his tankard. He had considered kidnapping the vixen while she was out riding, forcing her to his will, and impregnating her. She would have to wed him then or suffer the shame of bearing a bastard. She would be ruined for any other man and have no choice but to accept him. But such an action was apt to cause a feud between the Hays and the Kerrs. His elder brother had warned him against such an action. He would more than likely end up being killed himself, he said to Lord Hay in an attempt to reassure him that he would not act in a precipitous manner.

"I'll kill ye myself, Ewan, if ye shame the Kerr lass," Lord Hay warned. "Find another way if ye really want her. I'm not averse to the Hays controlling the Aisir nam Breug. It's made the Kerrs wealthy. I should enjoy a bit of that wealth."

"I could go to the king," Ewan Hay said to his brother. "I could tell him how old Kerr is coming to his end. Of how a man is needed to watch over such a valuable resource, and the laird has but a frail granddaughter for an heir."

Lord Hay considered his younger brother's reasoning. "Aye," he said slowly. "'Tis just possible ye might gain an advantage if ye went to the king. The rest of them are trying to figure out how to get around old Dugald Kerr. This might be the way, and the first man to the post is likely to gain the prize. Aye! Go to the king, Ewan."

So Ewan Hay took his horse, and a dozen men-at-arms, and rode to Linlithgow where the king, James V, was now in residence.

James Stewart was twenty-four. He was a tall big-boned man with short hair, and icy cold eyes. His features were sharply drawn and fine with a narrow long nose much like an eagle's beak. Still, he was considered an attractive fellow by the women of the court and already had several mistresses, for he had charm. His charm, however, did not run deep. He was known to be ruthless when he wanted his way. James V was not a man who excited loyalty. The earls and the lairds did not like the king, for he was a hard and greedy man. His common folk loved him. At the moment, the king was contemplating taking a queen, considering candidates from Italy, France, and even Denmark, from where his paternal grandmother had come.

Lord Hay had warned his brother to tread lightly, but Ewan Hay was eager to take his revenge upon Mad Maggie Kerr. He could think of nothing but her fury and frustration when the king ordered her to marry him. And so, having managed to gain a few moments of the king's time, Ewan Hay went to court, dressed in his finest tunic.

"Who is he?" the king asked his page as Ewan approached him confidently.

"The brother of Lord Hay, a border lord. He's unimportant, my liege."

"Then why am I speaking with him?" the king wanted to know.

"He said the matter is of great importance to Scotland," the page murmured.

Ewan Hay had reached the chair where the king sat. He smiled toothily and then bowed low. "My liege, I appreciate your seeing me," he began. His eye, however, shifted briefly to the beautiful woman who leaned against the king's chair. She had fine big breasts and full, lush lips. He forced his gaze away from her.

"What is so important to Scotland that you would ride from the border to Linlithgow to speak with me, Ewan Hay?" the king asked. He had seen the man's gaze shift to his mistress, Janet Munro.

"The future of the Aisir nam Breug is in terrible danger, my liege," Ewan began.

"What is the Aisir nam Breug, and why should I care if it is in danger?" James Stewart wanted to know.

"Why, my lord, it is a passage between Scotland and England that has for centuries been used as a safe traverse between England and Scotland. It is controlled on our side of the border by the Kerrs of Brae Aisir and on the other side by their English cousins, the Kerrs of Netherdale. These two families have kept it free of warring parties so commerce and honest folk may travel between the two countries in safety. The Kerrs have become rich over the years from this passage," Ewan said.

"Indeed?" the king replied, now interested. How was it he had not known of this?

But then his border lords were very difficult and independent men. He had only just gotten firm control of them in the past few years. But, curious now, he said, "What is the problem, then, Ewan Hay?"

"The laird of Brae Aisir is in his dotage, my liege. His only heir is his granddaughter, Margaret. The lass is of marriageable age, but the old man will nae part with her. If Dugald Kerr dies, what will happen to the Aisir nam Breug with no strong man to oversee it? The girl can be given a dower for a husband, but she canna control such a valuable asset to Scotland, my liege. And what if she takes an English husband? They are a close family, Brae Aisir and Netherdale," Ewan lied, for he didn't really know.

"Are they?" the king said. What was it about this young man? From the moment he had opened his mouth, James Stewart hadn't liked him. "Would ye wed the lass?" he asked, curious as to the answer he would receive.

"Nay, my liege. She refused my suit, and I would nae hae a wife who did not want me," Ewan said. But he would have her, he thought, if only to crush her spirit.

"But ye want her inheritance," the king remarked.

"Aye . . . nay, my liege! 'Tis my brother and all the local lairds who fear for the fate of the Aisir nam Breug. They sent me to bring this situation to your attention." He lied again, hoping it was not obvious.

"And now ye have," the king said with a small smile. "Go home, Ewan Hay. I must think on the information ye have brought to me, but rest assured that I will see the status of the Aisir nam Breug solved so that the laird of Brae Aisir may go to his God knowing that both it and his granddaughter are in safe hands."

Ewan opened his mouth to speak further, but the king waved a dismissive hand at him, and the king's page was immediately at Ewan's elbow escorting him from the royal presence before he might say another word. It had not gone at all as he had intended, but the king had not refused his subtle request. He would go home and tell his brother that the Aisir nam Breug was near to being in their hands.

James Stewart watched him go. "A dishonest fellow, I have not a doubt," he said.

Janet Munro slid into his lap. "I didn't like him, Jamie," she said.

"There is more to it than he is admitting or telling." She nuzzled his ear.

He slid a casual hand into her bodice, cupping one of her gloriously large breasts. "What would ye do, Jan?" he asked her as he caressed the soft flesh absently.

"Ye need to send someone ye can trust into the border to learn more about it before ye decide. Ye canna take that man's word for anything, I am thinking," she said.

He nodded. "Aye, but whom shall I send?"

Janet Munro thought for a long moment. Then she said, "What about yer cousin, Lord Fingal Stewart?"

"Do I know him?" the king asked. He didn't think he knew a Fingal Stewart.

"Nay, ye do not. Like ye, he descends from King Robert the Third through his elder son, David, whose bairn was born after that prince was killed and was protected by his mother's Drummond kin. He was one of the first who swore loyalty to James the First when he returned from his exile. James the First gave his nephew a house in Edinburgh. The family are called the Stewarts of Torra because their house is near the castle beneath the castle rock. They have always been loyal without question, to James the Second and Third, and then to yer father, James the Fourth."

"How do ye know all of this?" the king asked his mistress.

She laughed. "Fingal's grandmam was a Munro. We're cousins. He's a good man, my lord. Honest and loyal to the bone. Tell him what ye want of him, and he will do it without question." She gave him a quick kiss on his lips.

The king withdrew his hand from Janet Munro's bodice and gently tipped her from his lap. "Send to yer cousin," he said. "I am interested to meet this relation I never knew I had. If this Aisir nam Breug is all Ewan Hay claims it is, we cannot have it fall into the wrong hands."

And it will provide me with a new source of income, he thought to himself. A king could never have too much coin in his treasury.

Janet Munro curtsied, her claret red velvet skirts spreading out around her as she did. "Aye, my lord, I will do yer bidding," she said. And then she left him.

Chapter 2

ᔈ

*I*n the company of six of the king's men-at-arms Janet rode to Edinburgh, going to the stone house with the slate roof that sat off the street known as the Royal Mile, below the walls of Edinburgh Castle. She had sent a messenger ahead, and Fingal Stewart was waiting for her. His serving man ushered her into a small book-filled chamber.

"I bring you greetings from yer cousin, the king," Janet said, kissing his cheek.

"I wasn't aware my *cousin*, the king, was even mindful of my existence," Fingal Stewart said wryly. "And what, pray, my pretty, does he want of me? Sit down, Jan."

"Today a border clansman came to him with an interesting tale," Janet Munro began, seating herself as she spread her skirts about her. Then she went on to tell Fingal Stewart of Ewan Hay's visit. When she had finished she said, "Neither Jamie nor I liked the fellow. He isn't telling the whole story. It's obvious the fool hopes the king will gift him with this old laird's holding because this pass is said to be valuable."

"And the heiress," Fingal Stewart murmured. Land and a woman, he considered, were always the makings of a volatile situation. There would be wealth to be gained by whoever got the lass.

"Nay! He said he didn't want the girl. He claimed she had refused his suit," Janet Munro replied. "I think he lies. He wants the lass."

"But his true interest lies in this Aisir nam Breug," Fingal Stewart said slowly. "He would get the king to disinherit the lass who turned him away for his own benefit. A prince of a fellow indeed. But what has this to do with me?"

Janet shook her head. "I'm not sure, Fingal, but I believe the king would have you go into the border to reconnoiter the situation and bring him back the truth of the matter."

"Why me?" Fingal Stewart was curious. Although he was Lord Stewart of Torra, he was but distantly related to the king. They had shared a thrice-great-grandfather, and the royal Stewarts had rewarded their small loyalty when James I came to the throne with their name, a title, and this undistinguished house. They were not wealthy, nor influential, and had no place among the court or the powerful. Fingal Stewart hired his sword out when he needed funds. His father had done the same.

The rest of the time he lived quietly, gambling with a few friends now and again and enjoying the favors of one of the town's pretty whores for a night or two. His funds did not extend much beyond that. He had been decently educated, but he had no pretensions, for there were plenty of others bearing the name Stewart who kept him from thinking he was someone special. He wasn't, and he didn't want to be.

"The king wants someone not associated with him, but he also wants someone he can trust, Fingal," Janet Munro told her cousin. "Ye are nae just his kin. Yer mine too."

He thought a moment, and then grinned. "Aye, I am related to ye both. Maire Drummond gave David Stewart, Duke of Rothsay, heir to King Robert the Third, a son. She was enceinte with the bairn when Rothsay was murdered by Albany, so James the First followed his father after his exile in England."

"The Drummonds protected the bairn whose mam died birthing him," Janet said.

"And Albany was so busy with his plotting to supplant his nephew, he forgot all about the child who grew up, married an heiress, and sired two sons and two daughters before dying in his bed at the age of fifty-four," Fingal said.

"Which of the sons do you descend from?" Janet asked, curious.

"The elder, who was christened Robert after his father. He had a son, David, who wed Jane Munro, and sired James, who sired me at the advanced age of fifty-six."

"God's mercy," Janet exclaimed. "I did not know that! How old was yer mam?"

"Sixteen," Fingal Stewart said. "She was the granddaughter of an old friend. Her entire family was wiped out in a winter plague. She had nothing, so she sent to my father, begging his help. There was nothing for it but to marry her, for she had virtually naught to bring any man for a dower. Even the church did not want her. I was conceived on their wedding night. My father wanted to be sure that my mother was safe if he died because, while he was hardly a wealthy man, he did have this house and a small store of coin with the goldsmith. He believed if they shared a child, none would dispute her rights. And she loved him, strange to say. She died when I was ten."

"But your father lived to be eighty," Janet Munro said. "I remember my father remarking upon it. He said he had never known a man to live that long."

"Do ye love him?" Lord Stewart asked her, suddenly changing the subject entirely. "Do you love James Stewart, Jan?"

.Janet Munro thought a moment, and then she said, "James Stewart is nae a man who inspires love, but I like him well enough, and he is good to me. He wants a lover who pleases him and asks little of him. Actually he is more generous that way." She laughed. "My influence with him is coming to an end, for he plans to go to France in the autumn. He wants a queen, and Marie de Bourbon, daughter of the Duke of Vendôme, is available. I have just discovered I am enceinte, and so I will retire to my father's house when the king leaves, and only return at his invitation, which is unlikely. He will nae offend his new queen, nor would I make an enemy of her."

Fingal Stewart nodded. "When would he see me?" he asked.

"Come back to Linlithgow with me today," she said.

He nodded. "Very well," he agreed. "I suppose today is as good a day as any. But first I must see if Archie can find me more respectable garb in which to meet the king."

"I'm not sure ye have a good enough garment to go to the court," Archie said dourly when asked. Turning to Janet Munro, the serving man complained, "I keep telling him he must keep one fine thing, but he says the expense is not worth it." He sighed. "I'll see what I can find for him, my lady."

"He's quite devoted to you," Janet noted with a small smile.

"He fusses like an old woman with one chick," Fingal replied.

Archie managed to dress his master in a pair of brown and black velvet canions, which were tight knee breeches. The stockings beneath them were brown, and his leather boots almost covered them. The matching black velvet doublet was embroidered with just the lightest touch of gold breaking the severity of the garment.

Standing before his cousin, Lord Stewart, now fully dressed, said, "I have no idea where he managed to obtain such garb, or keep it so well hidden from me."

Archie grinned and handed his master a dark brown woolen cloak and a pair of brown leather gloves. "I dinna steal it," he said. "Ye paid for it, my lord."

"I'm sure I did," Fingal replied.

"I had forgotten what a handsome devil ye are," Janet said. She pushed a lock of her cousin's dark hair from his forehead. "Do ye have a hat for him, Archie?"

"No bloody hat," Lord Stewart said firmly, "and especially if it has one of those damned drooping feathers hanging from it."

"I saved no coin for a hat, as I know how ye feel about them," Archie said.

Together the two cousins rode the distance between the city and the king's favored palace, the men-at-arms surrounding them. The summer day was long, but it was close to sunset when they arrived. Janet Munro sent a page for the king and brought her cousin to her lover's privy chamber to await James Stewart. It was close to an hour before he came. Outside the windows of the small room the skies grew scarlet with the sunset, and then darkened. A serving man came and lit the fire in the hearth, for the evening was cool and damp with a hint of a later rain.

Finally James Stewart entered the chamber. He was a tall young man with the red-gold hair of his Tudor mother, and eyes that were gray in color but showed no expression at all. He held out his hand to Fingal Stewart, and a quick glance at Janet Munro told her she was dismissed. She curtsied and departed. "So," the king said, "I am to understand we are cousins."

"Like you, my lord, I trace my descent from Robert the Third through his elder son, David," Fingal Stewart explained. "You descend from his younger son, King James the First."

"I was not aware David Stewart had any offspring," the young king replied.

"Few were, my lord. His mistress was a Drummond. When Albany murdered him, her family protected her and the son she shortly bore. Albany was too busy consolidating his position, and frankly, I believe he forgot all about her. When King James the First returned home as a man, his cousin came and pledged his loyalty."

"A loyalty my great-great-grandfather certainly needed," the young king remarked.

"My ancestor was well schooled in loyalty to his king, and that king saw that he was legally able to take the surname of Stewart. He also gave his cousin a house in Edinburgh near the castle," Fingal told his royal companion.

"Where do the Munros come into your family tree?" the king asked.

"My grandfather married a Munro who was the sister to Janet's grandfather. I believe Jan was named for her, my lord."

The king nodded. "We are but distantly related now, you and I, Fingal Stewart, but blood is blood. Jan tells me you are loyal to me. Is that so? I am not so well loved by my earls, though the common folk revere me." He looked closely at his companion.

"I am loyal, my lord," Fingal Stewart said without a moment's hesitation.

"When my father pushed his father from the throne," the king wanted to know, "which side did Lord Stewart of Torra take then?"

"Neither side, my lord. He remained in his house below Edinburgh Castle until all was settled. He had been loyal to King James the Third and was equally loyal to King James the Fourth," Lord Stewart explained.

"A prudent man," the fifth James noted with a small chuckle. He had liked the candid answer he had received. "And ye, Fingal Stewart, are ye a prudent man?"

"I believe such can be said of me, my lord," came the quiet answer.

The king looked Lord Stewart of Torra over silently. He was a big man, taller than most, with dark hair like the Munros, clear gray eyes like his own that engaged the king's gaze without being forward, but a face like a Stewart with its aquiline nose. The king would have easily recognized this man in a crowd as one of his own family. He trusted his mistress's advice in this matter. Janet Munro was the most sensible woman he had ever known. And he had known many women despite his youth. His stepfather, the Earl of Angus, had seen to that in an attempt to debauch him. Angus was now in exile, and his flighty Tudor mother wed to Lord Methven. However, this man now seated with James in his privy chamber was not just his kin, but kin to his reasonable and judicious mistress as well. He was not allied with any of the king's enemies. If Fingal Stewart could not be trusted, then who could be? "Jan has told you of my visitor earlier today?"

Lord Stewart nodded. "She has, my lord. She said she believed you wanted me to go into the Borders to see to the truth of the matter if it could be done discreetly."

"Aye, I had thought that was what I desired, but while Jan was gone to fetch you, *Cousin*, I thought more on it. I am not well beloved by certain families in the Borders—families allied with Angus and his traitorous Douglas kin. My justice towards them has been well deserved, but harsh, I know. If I send you into the Borders to reconnoiter the situation, someone is certain to guess why you are there.

"The situation into which I am sending you is fraught with danger if I do not strike quickly and decisively. So I have decided you will travel with a dozen of my own men-at-arms at your back who will remain with you. You will present yourself to Dugald Kerr, the laird of Brae Aisir, and tell him I have learned of his difficulties. Then you will hand him this." He held out a tightly rolled parchment affixed with the royal seal. "I have written to the laird that I have sent him my cousin, Lord Stewart of Torra, to wed with his granddaughter,

Margaret, and thus keep the Aisir nam Breug safe for future generations of travelers. The marriage is to be celebrated immediately. I
dinna nae trust the laird's neighbors, especially the Hays. If the lass
is wed, the matter is settled, and peace will reign. I want it settled
before I leave for France in a few weeks' time."

Fingal Stewart was astounded by the king's speech. He had expected to travel cautiously into the Borders and carefully ferret out
the truth of whatever situation the king needed to know about. But
to be told he was to go and wed the heiress to Brae Aisir? He was
briefly rendered speechless.

"Ye aren't already wed, are ye?" the king asked him. "I did not
think to ask Jan." God's foot, if Lord Stewart were wed, what other
could he choose? Whom could he trust?

"Nay, my lord," Fingal managed to say.

"Nor contracted?"

Lord Stewart shook his head in the negative. He was trying hard
to adjust to being told to marry. How old was she? Was she pretty?
Would she like him? It didn't matter. It would be done by royal command. No one disobeyed a royal command and lived to brag on it. He
dared say naught until he heard more of this, and why.

"Do ye have a mistress ye will need to placate?" James Stewart
wanted to know.

"I canna afford a mistress," Fingal Stewart answered the king. "I
am nae a rich man, my lord. My parents are both dead. Nor do I have
siblings. I have my house, but naught else. I hire out my sword to earn
my living, and possess but one servant."

"So ye are free to leave Edinburgh quickly," the king said almost
to himself. It was perfect. It did not occur to him that Lord Stewart
might turn him down. He couldn't. This was a royal command, and
to be obeyed without question.

"Aye, my lord," Fingal Stewart replied. He was agreeing to this madness because he had no other choice. It was his family's tradition to be loyal without question to their kings. Still, he made a small attempt to reason with James Stewart and learn more of what was expected of him. "Why must this lass be wed quickly, my lord? May I know what more is involved in this situation? What will the laird of Brae Aisir think of your sending a cousin to wed his heiress? What if he says nay?"

James Stewart barked a short laugh as he realized in his eagerness to solve this problem he had told Fingal Stewart little or nothing of it. "The Kerrs of Brae Aisir possess control of a pass through the Cheviots into England. The pass is called the Aisir nam Breug. Their English kin, the Kerrs of Netherdale, control the other end. The pass has always been used for peaceful travel; never for war nor raiding. The Kerrs on both sides of the border have defended it against such use. The laird is old. He has one heir, his granddaughter. She will not choose a husband from among their neighbors. Indeed, she is said to be called Mad Maggie, for she is willful and wild.

"The laird fears his neighbors will attempt to wrest his control of this crossing from him, or from his granddaughter when he is gone, but the lass has him at an impasse. He'll nae refuse my command that she take ye for a husband. If old Kerr had his own choice for the lass, the matter would have been long settled. He obviously did not. His neighbors are already eyeing the Aisir nam Breug, I'm told. If this Hay fellow had the stones to attempt to steal a march on them, and come to me in an effort to gain an advantage, then he fears someone else gaining what he covets. Ye'll be the answer to Dugald Kerr's prayers, Cousin. Now get ye into the Borders before there is bloodshed over the matter. I have only just gotten the lairds there settled down after years of running roughshod over my authority," the king said. "Return to Edinburgh on the morrow to fetch yer servant. Shut up yer house. Then go south, Fingal Stewart. Hopefully the lass will be pretty enough to please, but if she isn't, just remember that all cats look alike in the dark." And James Stewart laughed. "Bring her back to court when I have returned with my queen."

"Yer taking me from relative obscurity, gifting me with a wealthy wife, and giving me control of an asset that is valuable to you, and to Scotland. I will be a man of power, my lord," Fingal Stewart said quietly. "Other than my undying loyalty, what will ye require of me in return for this bounty?" His candid gaze met the king's eyes, and James Stewart laughed aloud.

"Yer a canny fellow, Cousin," he complimented his companion. "I will take half of the tolls ye collect from travelers, payable on Michaelmas each year in hard coin."

"One-third," Fingal Stewart dared to counter. "The pass must be maintained in good condition, and the laird I am certain supports his people with these monies. Remember I am a stranger coming at your behest to wed its heiress, and take control no matter whether the old laird welcomes me into their midst. Nothing must appear to change for the Kerrs of Brae Aisir other than a husband for the heiress. Remember, my lord, I have naught but my sword and yer word to recommend me. My purse is empty."

James Stewart nodded. He was known to be tightfisted, but he was also no fool. A third of the yearly tolls from this traverse was a third more than he had previously had.

He held out his hand to his cousin. "Agreed!" he said as they shook.

Lord Stewart rose from his chair, recognizing that he was now dismissed.

"Thank ye, my lord. My sword and my life are yers forever." He bowed low.

The king nodded his acknowledgment of the words, and with a wave of his hand he dismissed his cousin from his presence.

Fingal Stewart turned and left the privy chamber. He found Janet Munro awaiting him in the dim corridor, and he told her of what had transpired.

"Yer a man of property now," she said in a well-satisfied voice. So many royal mistresses enriched themselves and their families during their tenure. She had not, accepting only what was offered. She knew her parsimonious lover would see her and her child comfortably supported. She was satisfied now to have done something for the cousin she had always liked. He was a good man and deserved a bit of good luck.

Digging into her skirt pocket, she pulled out a small pouch. "Ye dinna have to tell me the condition of yer purse, Fin. And ye canna travel without coin. The king wanted ye to have this." Janet thrust the purse at him. "Yer men-at-arms are just paid for the year. Ye may retain them for yer own, but next Michaelmas ye must pay their wages yerself. Ye have a house in the town, gold in yer purse, a servant, and twelve men-at-arms. Ye will nae appear a poor man when ye come to Brae Aisir, *and* yer the king's own blood to boot." Then standing on her toes, she put her arms about him and kissed his cheek. "God bless ye, Cousin."

He returned her embrace. "Thank ye, Jan. I know 'tis ye who have brought me this good fortune. Should ye ever need me, ye have but to send for me," Fingal Stewart said. He suspected the gold in the purse she had given him was from her own small store.

"Come along now," she said briskly. "There is food in the hall, and I've found a place for ye to lay yer head this night."

He followed her and while he ate at a table far below the high board in the king's hall, he looked about him. The chamber was filled with the mighty. Before she left him to join her lover, Janet Munro pointed out the Earl of Huntly; the young Earl of Glenkirk; Lord Hume, who was now warden of the East March; the provost of Edinburgh, Lord Maxwell; and George Crichton, bishop of Dunkeld, among others. Fingal Stewart watched the panorama played out before him, listening to all the gossip spoken.

He was, he decided, glad to be a simple man.

When the evening grew late, Janet Munro came to him again and brought him to the stables where his horse had been taken. "Ye can sleep here, Cousin," she told him, "but be gone by first light. Yer men will join ye at yer house tomorrow before ye depart."

He thanked her a final time, noting she did not reveal aloud to where he was traveling, for she was wary of being overheard. His mission was after all a clandestine one; a preemptive strike to be carried out before anyone could prevent it. He slept several hours before rising in the pale light of the predawn, saddling his stallion, and riding back to Edinburgh. It was a chilly ride beneath the light rain now falling.

His manservant, Archie, was awaiting him anxiously. There had been no need for him to go with his master the previous day, but he had been concerned when six men-at-arms had arrived with Lady Janet to conduct Lord Stewart to Linlithgow. "My lord!" The relief in Archie's voice was palpable. "Yer home safe."

"Pack up all our personal possessions, what few we have, Archie," Fingal Stewart said. "I'm to have a wife, and a great responsibility that goes with her."

"My lord?" Archie's plain face was puzzled.

His master laughed. "Is there something to eat?" he asked.

"I'm just back from the cookhouse, my lord. Aye, come into yer hall," his servant said. "I've fresh bread, hard-boiled eggs, a rasher of bacon."

"Then let's eat, man, and I'll tell ye all," Lord Stewart said.

They went into the small chamber that served as the house's hall. The fresh food was already upon the high board, for Archie had taken the chance his master would return sooner rather than later. He quickly served his lord, poured him a small goblet of watered wine, and was then waved to a place by his side. The two men ate silently, quickly, and as the last piece of bacon disappeared from the plate, Fingal Stewart spoke.

Fingal explained all to Archie, concluding, "So, Archie, we are leaving Edinburgh and settling down with a wife, and a real home, and probably a covey of bairns eventually. Do ye think yer ready for such an existence?" Lord Stewart chuckled.

"I am!" his manservant said without a moment's hesitation. "'Tis a blessing, it is, my lord, to have been given such a bounty. We're not getting any younger, either of us."

As big as his master was, Archie was a wee bit of a man, short and wiry with stone gray hair and sharp blue eyes. His family had served the Stewarts of Torra for many years, and but for his master, he was alone in the world now.

"Perhaps we'll find ye a nice plump lass to warm yer bed on those cold border nights," Fin teased, and he laughed aloud.

Archie laughed with him. "Aye, my lord, 'twould please me greatly if we did."

"My cousin, Lady Janet, has given me a purse, and the king has supplied us with twelve men-at-arms to go with us. They will be here shortly to escort us into the Borders, Archie. Ye had best hurry and pack us up now," Fingal Stewart said with a smile. "Can we leave within an hour or two? And shall I send for Agent Boyle and rent the house?"

"Nay, keep the house empty for now, my lord. What if ye want to bring yer lady to court once we have a queen? There's never any room at court for unimportant folk."

"The king prefers Linlithgow Palace to Edinburgh Castle," his master replied. "But yer right. I should not be hasty. Still send for

Boyle and see what he says. We'll need the house watched so nothing is stolen while I am in the Borders."

Archie hurried from the hall, and opening the front door of the house, gestured to one of the lads always about the small street. "Go and fetch Agent Boyle to Lord Stewart. He must come immediately," Archie said. "There's a copper in it for you when you return with him."

The boy pulled at his forelock and ran off. The rain was beginning to fall more heavily. Archie then went about the business of packing up what they would take. Less than half an hour had passed when a hammering came upon the front door. Archie ran to open it, admitting the house agent. He flipped the lad his copper while ushering Boyle inside. He led the man to the hall where Lord Stewart was packing up his weapons.

"Boyle's here, my lord," he announced.

Fingal Stewart looked up, beckoning the man to a seat by the fire. "Sit down, Boyle," he said. "Sit down. Archie, a dram of whiskey for Master Boyle."

"Thank ye, my lord, thank ye. 'Tis damp outside." He accepted the dram cup, and swallowed down its contents. Then he looked to Lord Stewart. "How may I serve you, my lord?" he asked politely.

"I have to leave Edinburgh for some months," Lord Stewart began. "I will need you to find someone to watch over the house so it not be burgled. Someone reliable who will not sell off my few possessions while I am gone," he told the house agent.

"Ye don't want to rent, my lord?" Boyle inquired.

Fingal Stewart shook his head in the negative. "What if I return before I anticipate? If I have no house, where can I lay my head and stable my horses?"

"I was nae considering a rental to a family, my lord. Men of importance come to Edinburgh, wealthy merchants, those high up in the church, among others. They are nae asked to the castle. They do not choose to house themselves at some inn. Their stays are brief. A few days, a few weeks, a month. And they pay well for their privacy and the discretion that a house like this can provide them, my lord. They bring their own servants and require naught but a secure shelter."

"And how much commission would you want for providing such a service, Master Boyle?" Lord Stewart inquired.

"But ten percent of the rental fee, my lord," Boyle answered him.

"I will want a woman in to clean before any come, and after they go," Lord Stewart said. "And you will pay her from your ten percent for I have nae a doubt that you will also collect ten percent from your clients as well."

The house agent's eyebrows jumped with his surprise.

"How much will you charge per day?" Fingal asked, and when Boyle told him, he nodded. "Do not consider you can cheat me by paying me for four days when the guest remains seven," he warned. "I have eyes that will watch ye. I will expect a proper rendering of my account every other month. You may deliver it to Kira's bank in Goldsmith's Lane. They will be informed to expect it, and will advise me if they do not get it, Master Boyle. If this is satisfactory to you, I will allow you this rental."

"Will ye be visiting the town yerself, my lord?" the agent asked.

"I will send to you when I am and will expect the house available to me when I come," Lord Stewart said sternly. "I will attempt to give you enough notice that your clients not be inconvenienced by my coming. Is this agreeable to you?"

Master Boyle nodded. "Quite, my lord."

Both men stood up and shook hands.

"I am departing today," Lord Stewart said. "Archie will give ye a key."

The house agent bowed and exited the hall where Archie was

waiting for him. The manservant handed Master Boyle two keys on an iron ring. "Front door, and door from the kitchen into the garden," he said. He opened the front door, ushering the man out.

Master Boyle hurried out, and down the street to the Royal Mile, stepping aside as he came to the congested wider way to allow a party of mounted men-at-arms to enter the small lane. He stopped, watching to see what business they could possibly have on such an undistinguished lane. His bushy eyebrows jumped as they halted before Lord Stewart's stone house. He peered down the dim street to see the badges on their jacket arms. The bushy eyebrows jumped again as he recognized the king's mark.

Well, well, well, Master Boyle thought. *What brings the king's men here? And what business could they have with my client?* Was he being arrested? Was that his reason for leaving Edinburgh for several months? But then he considered that Lord Stewart was undoubtedly related to His Majesty and was probably being sent on an errand for his master. Thinking no more about it, he hurried on his way through the rainy morning.

The men-at-arms in the lane dismounted, one of them pounding on the door to the house. Archie answered the summons with a few pithy words. "Is this how ye ask to enter the dwelling of the king's cousin?" he demanded of them. "Wipe yer booted feet, my lads. Come into the hall and warm yourselves. His Lordship is waiting for ye."

The dozen men followed Archie, several of them chuckling at the feisty little man as they entered the chamber. It was hardly an impressive room, but they knew from a servant of the king's mistress that the man awaiting them was the king's own kin. They stood in respectful silence waiting for whatever instructions this lordling would give.

Lord Stewart looked up. It was time to face his future. He took a deep breath and, rising from his chair by the small hearth, greeted the men-at-arms. "Good morrow, lads. Warm yerselves by the fire. We are almost ready to depart. Do ye know where we are going?" Lord Stewart asked the men.

The soldiers murmured in the negative.

"Choose a leader from among ye," he told them. "I need one of ye in charge of the others. Be ready with yer choice when I return." Then he left the hall to find Archie, who was just finishing packing up their possessions on the second floor of the house.

"They're a rough-looking bunch," Archie said as Lord Stewart entered his bedchamber. "I wonder if they're to be trusted."

Fingal Stewart shrugged. "We'll see soon enough, won't we?" he replied. Seeing his traveling garments laid out for him, he quickly stripped off the clothing he had worn to Linlithgow along with his leather boots. "I slept in a stable last night," he said ruefully, sniffing the velvet doublet.

"It can be aired out," Archie responded pragmatically. "I'll pack it with some clove to overcome the scent of the king's barn. Ye'll not be wearing it until yer wedding day." He carefully folded the garment and placed it with a few nails of the spice with the other clothing already in his master's small trunk. Before closing the lid, Archie reverently laid his master's plaid on top. Its background was green with narrow bands of red and blue, and slightly wider bands of dark blue. It was the ancient family tartan.

Fingal Stewart pulled on a pair of sturdy dark brown woolen breeks over his heavy knitted stockings, yanked his boots back onto his big feet, and pushed his sgian dubh into the top of the right one. The weapon had a piece of green agate sunk into its top, and its scabbard had Lord Stewart's crest set in silver. He tucked his natural-colored linen shirt into the pants, fastened a leather belt about his waist, drew on a soft brown leather jerkin with buttons carved from stag horn, and picked up his dark woolen cloak. He looked to Archie. "Are we ready?" he asked his serving man.

Archie nodded. "The fires are all out in the house except in the hall."

The two men left Lord Stewart's chamber and descended back down into the hall where the men-at-arms now stood about the fire getting the last bit of warmth they could before their long ride. Archie went immediately to the hearth and began extinguishing the low flames and coals with sand from a bucket set near the fireplace.

"Have ye chosen a captain from among yerselves?" Lord Stewart asked them.

A man stepped from among them. He was almost as tall as Fingal Stewart. His features were rough-hewn, his hair a red-brown, his eyes, which engaged the taller man's fearlessly, blue. He had a big nose that had obviously been broken once or twice. "I am Iver Leslie," he said. "The lads have chosen me." He gave a small but polite bow.

Lord Stewart nodded and offered his hand to Iver, who took it in a firm grasp and shook it. "You'll ride next to me," Fingal Stewart said. Then he brought Archie, who had completed putting out the fire, forward and introduced him. "This is Archie, my servant. Sometimes he will speak for me, so listen when he does, and obey him. He's a wee bit of a fellow, but be warned he's handy with both his fists and a knife."

Archie nodded towards the men-at-arms, who nodded back. "There's a bit of whiskey left in the keg at the end of the hall," he said. "Drink it, or put it in yer flasks, while I get our horses, lads." He grinned as they made a beeline for the keg; all but Iver remained by Lord Stewart's side. Archie's wise eyes spoke their approval of Iver.

"I'll bring the beasts around to the front, my lord," he said. Then he hurried from the hall.

"Go and get some whiskey for yerself," Fingal Stewart said quietly.

"Thank you, my lord."

Iver quickly went down the hall, and seeing him, his men made way for him. He filled his flask and came back to stand by Lord Stewart's side. "May I ask where we are going, my lord? We were not told."

"We are traveling into the Borders to a place called Brae Aisir," Fingal Stewart said.

"I'm being sent to wed the old laird's granddaughter, his only heir. The laird is Dugald Kerr, and with his English kin on the other side of the Cheviots, they control a passage through the hills called the Aisir nam Breug that for centuries has been used only for peaceful travel. King James wants to keep it that way. The laird's neighbors have of late been showing signs of impatience, for the lass will not choose a husband, and if Dugald Kerr should die too soon, there is no male heir to look after this valuable asset."

Iver nodded. "Aye, a lass canna guard such a treasure without a husband."

"Yer not from the Borders," Lord Stewart said.

"Nay, I come from a village near Aberdeen," Iver informed his new master.

"Good! Then ye'll have no loyalties but to me, and to the king," Fingal Stewart remarked. "Are any among yer lot borderers?"

"Nay, I know them all, my lord. They all come from Edinburgh or Perth or somewhere in between. None are from the Borders," Iver replied.

Lord Stewart nodded. "Tell them where we are going, and why. We are not invaders but the king's representatives. I expect good behavior. Any man who can't behave will face punishment at my own hand. I'm a fair man, and expect the truth from every mouth. I'll not punish a man for the truth, but if I catch him in a lie, 'twill go hard on him. Do ye understand, Iver?"

"I do, my lord, and I'll see the lads understand too. Might I ask if the laird is expecting us?"

"He is not, but the king believes he will welcome us nonethe-less."

"The king would know," Iver replied pragmatically.

Archie returned. "I've got the horses, my lord."

Lord Stewart flung his cloak about his shoulders. Iver called to the men to come. Archie brought up the rear, and locked the house door behind him. He then climbed up onto his horse, taking the lead rein from the horse serving as a pack animal for them. The rain was falling steadily as they clattered down the lane and out onto the Royal Mile. The serving man hunched down. It was late summer, and while the rain wasn't cold as it might have been in another season, it was still uncomfortable. He hoped the weather would turn for the better by nightfall or at least on the morrow. It didn't.

They rode until it grew too dark to ride. There was no shelter but a grove of trees when they stopped. It was too wet to light a fire. They pulled oatcakes and dried meat from their pouches, washing them down with some of the contents from their flasks. The horses were left to browse in the nearby field while their riders huddled beneath the greenery with only their cloaks to keep the rain from them. The next day and night were no better. They avoided any villages along their way so as not to arouse curiosity.

"Yer captain has explained where we are going. A troop such as ours would cause chatter if we passed through them, or sheltered in them," Lord Stewart explained to his men on the second night. "We don't want the laird's neighbors becoming inquisitive. We'll reach Brae Aisir tomorrow sometime, if that is any comfort to you. It will be warm, and ye'll get some hot food in ye then."

They all held on to the thought that night, their backs against a rough stone wall, the thunder booming overhead, the lightning crackling about them. The horses had to be staked out and tied to prevent the frightened animals from fleeing. The rain poured down.

The next morning, however, dawned bright and sunny. Lord Stewart instructed his men to change their shirts and stockings if they had the extra clothing. He was relieved that they all did. He wanted his men looking smart, not hangdog, when they entered Brae Aisir. The dry garments would help to raise their spirits.

Brae Aisir. He didn't know what to expect, but with its dark stone, a moat, a drawbridge that was up, and obviously fortified, it certainly wasn't what looked like a small keep upon a hillock. He wondered whether the king knew of this structure; perhaps he assumed that a prosperous border laird lived in a well-kept tower house or manor. Fingal Stewart was suddenly aware that the Aisir nam Breug was more important than just a traverse between England and Scotland. How had they managed to keep warring factions from using it? He obviously had a great deal to learn about his new responsibilities. He hoped old Dugald Kerr was up to teaching him. They had stopped to observe the keep.

Now Lord Stewart turned to Iver. "Send a man ahead to tell them I come for the laird on the king's business. We'll wait here until we are asked to proceed. I don't want the village below put into a panic fearing that we are raiders."

Iver gave a quick order, and a single man detached himself from the group, galloping down the hill, through the village, and up to the keep. He stopped before the raised drawbridge, and waited. Finally a wood shutter on a window to one side of the entry was flung back. A helmeted head appeared.

"What do ye want?" a voice shouted down to him.

"Messenger from Lord Stewart, who waits on the other side of the village. He comes to the laird bearing greetings and a message from King James. May he have permission to enter?"

"Wait!" the voice said, and the shutter slammed shut.

After several very long minutes the shutter banged open, and the voice called, "The laird bids your master come forth. He is welcome to Brae Aisir."

"Thank ye," the messenger said politely and, turning his mount, headed back down the hill, through the village, and up the hill on the other side. Behind him he heard the creaking of the drawbridge as it was being lowered. "Yer welcome to enter the keep, my lord," he told Fingal Stewart when he had reached the place where his party of horsemen awaited his return. "They were lowering the drawbridge as I returned to ye."

Lord Stewart turned to his men. "We will ride through the village sedately. These borderers are a prickly lot. I don't want anyone, child or creature, trampled with our coming. We are welcomed, and 'tis not a race." Then swinging about, he raised his hand and signaled his party forward.

Villagers going about their daily chores stopped to move from the road and stare at the riders. A fountain and well were in the center of the hamlet. Several women were there getting water. They turned to stare boldly at the strangers. One pretty young lass even smiled at the men-at-arms and was immediately smacked by an older woman, obviously her mother. There was a small chapel at the far end of the village that they passed as they began to ascend the far hill to the keep. A priest stood before the little church, watching them, unsmiling, as they passed him by.

Reaching the keep, they clattered across the wooden drawbridge. As they did, the iron portcullis was slowly raised so they might pass through into the keep's yard. Fingal looked carefully about him, drawing his mount to a halt. Within the walls was a large stone house with two towers, a stable, a well, and a barn. The courtyard was not cobbled but had an earth floor still muddy with several large puddles from the past days' rain. As he dismounted, a man hurried forth down the stairs from the house.

"My lord," he said with a bow. "I am Busby, the laird's majordomo. Ye are most welcome to Brae Aisir. The laird is waiting for ye in the hall. Yer men are welcome to enter as well. The hearths are blazing, for the day is cool despite the welcome sunshine. Summer is coming to an end, and I imagine yer travels have been wet." He led the visitor briskly up the steps, into the house, and down a broad passage into the great hall. "My lord, Lord Stewart," Busby said, bringing the visitor to his master.

Dugald Kerr stood up and held out his hand. The laird was tall, but not nearly as tall as the man before him. He had a full head of snow white hair, and his brown eyes carefully assessed Fingal Stewart. "Welcome to Brae Aisir, my lord. Sit down! Sit down!" He indicated a settle opposite his high-backed chair as he sat once more.

A servant hurried up, tray in hand, and offered a goblet of wine first to his master, then to his master's companion.

The laird raised his goblet. "The king!" he said.

Lord Stewart reciprocated. "The king!" he responded.

The two men drank in silence.

Then the laird said to his guest, "Yer messenger said ye come from the king with a message for me, my lord. Yer James Stewart's kinsman?"

"I am," Fingal replied. He reached his hand into his jerkin, and drew out the small rolled parchment he had been given to bring to the laird, handing it to him.

"Do ye know what is in this?" Dugald Kerr asked candidly.

"I do, my lord," Fingal replied.

Nodding, Dugald Kerr broke the dark wax seal on the parchment and unrolled it. His sharp eyes scanned the writing, and then he looked up. "How did the king learn of my *difficulties*?" he asked.

"A man named Ewan Hay came to him with a story the king believed to be but a half-truth," Fingal said. "But learning of the Aisir nam Breug, the king became concerned for yer safety, the safety of yer granddaughter, and the safety of this traverse, my lord."

The laird nodded again. "And yer willing to wed my Maggie, my lord?"

"I do not believe that either of us has a choice in this matter," Fingal replied, "but I swear to you, my lord, I shall treat yer granddaughter honorably and fairly."

"Nay, neither ye nor I has a choice," the laird said. "But Maggie will be a different story altogether, sir. I dinna envy ye yer courting." And Dugald Kerr chuckled richly, his brown eyes dancing with amusement. "'Twill be a rough wooing, I fear."

Chapter 3

As the laird enjoyed his mirth, Maggie Kerr entered the hall. "I am told we have a visitor, Grandsire," she said, coming forward.

Fingal Stewart watched her come. She was dressed in woolen breeks, boots, and an open-necked shirt. A wide leather belt encircled her waist. The skin of her neck and face was damp with obvious exertion. The lass was more than pretty, he realized, but the confident stride as she walked, the open curiosity in her hazel eyes, the set of her jaw, told him she would be neither biddable nor easy. He stood politely as she came forward.

"The king has sent ye a gift, lassie," the laird chortled. He was truly enjoying this.

"*The king? A gift?*" She looked genuinely puzzled. "The king has never set eyes upon me. Why would he send me a gift?"

"Ewan Hay went to visit His Majesty. He told him ye needed a husband, lass," the laird cackled. "And so the king has sent his own kinsman to wed ye." The laird waited for the outburst that was not long in coming.

"Ewan Hay told the king I needed a husband? Why would that pox-ridden donkey's ass do such a thing?" Then her eyes widened. "God's balls! He thought to steal Brae Aisir out from beneath us, Grandsire, didn't he? He thought the king would order me to wed him, the imbecile!" Then her eyes fixed themselves on her grandfather's companion. "Who are ye, sir?"

"Lord Fingal Stewart, madam," Fin answered her.

"And yer the king's kin sent to wed me?" she demanded.

"I am," he replied.

"And what, my lord, have ye done to win such a prize?" Maggie wanted to know.

"I have been loyal, madam. The Stewarts of Torra have always been loyal to the Stewart kings since the days of James the First. The king knows he may trust me to do as I have been bid," Fingal Stewart answered her in a hard voice.

"Torra? *Of the rock?*" Maggie was curious in spite of herself. "Where do ye come from, my lord?"

"Edinburgh, madam. We are the Stewarts of Torra because our house sits below the castle rock itself," he told her.

"Ye have no lands then," she said scornfully.

"I have a house, a manservant, twelve men-at-arms gifted me by the king, some coin with Moses Kira, the banker, a modest purse of gold I've brought with me, and James Stewart's favor. Naught else," Fingal Stewart responded honestly.

Maggie had not expected a candid answer. She had never met a man before who was quite so direct. Usually men struggled to please her, to win her over—even that obnoxious simpleton Ewan Hay. "So ye've come to wed me for my wealth," she said, contempt tingeing her voice.

"I've come to wed ye because I have been ordered to it," he replied as insultingly.

"If ye think to wed me, my lord, ye will have to comply with the same rules all my other suitors have faced. And none has succeeded to date. I'll wed no man, particularly a stranger, whom I cannot respect. If ye can outrun me, outride me, and outfight me, I'll go to the altar willingly, but not otherwise."

"There's no choice here, lass," the laird told his granddaughter. "This man has been sent by the king, and I tell you truthfully that I am happy to see him. Ye'll wed him, and that's the end of it. Will ye let a man like Ewan Hay dispossess ye when I'm dead? Make no mistake, lassie, without a strong husband to follow in my path, our neighbors will be fighting ye and one another for control of the Aisir nam Breug."

"But Grandsire, if he does not compete against me, those same neighbors will rise up against the Kerrs for having imposed our conditions upon them, but not upon the king's kinsman," Maggie argued. "Ye swore before them that all suitors must conform."

"The lass is right," Fingal Stewart agreed. "If I am to have the respect of yer neighbors, my lord, I must accept the lady's challenge. 'Twill not be difficult to overcome her. I'm surprised this Hay couldn't."

Maggie suddenly grinned wickedly. "I can outrun, outride, and outfight *any* man in the Borders, my lord," she repeated, "and I will, I promise ye, outrun, outride, and outfight ye."

"I am not from the Borders," Lord Stewart reminded her with an answering grin.

"Ye can have yer contest, Maggie," her grandsire said, "but first I will have the marriage contract drawn up. Ye and Lord Stewart will sign it. When the contest is over, win or lose, ye must accept the marriage and have yer uncle bless it in the chapel."

She hesitated.

"Are ye afraid I'll beat ye?" Lord Stewart taunted her.

"I'm just concerned with having to live with a weakling," Maggie said sharply.

He laughed. "Madam, have ye ever been spanked?" he asked her. She turned an outraged face to him. "Nay, never!"

"Ye will be, and soon, I have not a doubt," he told her.

"Lay a hand on me in anger, my lord, and I'll gut ye from stem to gudgeon," Maggie told him fiercely, her hand going to the dagger at her waist.

The laird's face grew grim at her combative words, but before he might admonish her, Lord Stewart laughed aloud.

"Marrying a stranger cannot be easy for either bride or groom, madam," he told her, grinning. "I can but hope this passion of yers extends to the marriage bed, for then we will suit admirably, and there will be no talk of murder, I promise ye."

Though Maggie was tall for a woman, he towered over her. She gasped and blushed at his blunt speech. No man had ever spoken so suggestively to her. For a moment she was at a loss for words. Then she said, "I'll sign the marriage contract, for in law that will make ye my husband. And I'm certain that will convince the greedier among our neighbors that the Aisir nam Breug's future ownership is settled. Particularly after they have met ye. Ye would appear to be reasonably intelligent and competent, my lord. But ye will nae bed me until ye have fulfilled my terms."

"*Maggie!*" Her grandfather almost shouted her name. "Ye cannot set the terms of this matter. The king has said ye will wed him, and ye will!"

"Aye, I will, Grandsire, but for the reasons earlier stated, he must best me," she replied. "The king said I must wed him—not lie with him."

"I will best ye, lassie," Fingal Stewart told her quietly. "Here's my hand on it." He held out his big hand to her, smiling.

She took his hand, watching almost mesmerized as his long thick fingers closed over her smaller hand, enclosing it completely as they shook. Then he shocked her by yanking her forward. An arm clamped about her waist, pulling her close against him. His chest was hard, and she could smell a mixture of male and the damp leather of his jerkin. A hand grasped her head, those same fingers wrapping themselves in her chestnut hair to hold her steady as his mouth descended upon hers in a fierce, quick kiss that left her breathless and gasping with surprise. He released her as quickly as he had taken her. Maggie stumbled back, but then, swiftly recovering, raised her hand to slap him.

The big hand sprang forth to wrap firmly about her wrist. "Nah, nah, lassie," he warned her softly. "I have the right now."

"Yer hurting me," Maggie said through clenched teeth, "and ye have no rights yet, my lord."

The laird watched the interaction between his granddaughter and Lord Stewart, fascinated. He would have to thank the king for sending him such a strong man to take on his responsibilities, not that he was quite ready yet to relinquish them. Fingal Stewart had a great deal to learn about the Aisir nam Breug. But he obviously was already skilled at handling a woman. Dugald Kerr chuckled.

"Are ye going to allow this ape to manhandle me, Grandsire?" Maggie demanded. She was utterly outraged. He had kissed her! Made her feel weak, and she wasn't weak. *She wasn't!* And her grandfather had done nothing to prevent it. Indeed, he had laughed.

"I'm going to call for David to come and meet Lord Stewart. I want yer marriage contract signed by the morrow. What date will ye fix for the challenge, lassie?"

"I'll sign the contract, for I have already given ye my word, but the challenge will have to wait, Grandsire. We are only just past Lammastide. We have late crops to harvest, and the fields must be opened for gleaning. When this is done, we will set a date, Grandsire," Maggie said.

"I am content with that," Lord Stewart quickly said, for he could see the laird was eager to have the matter settled and ended. "Send for the priest I saw in the village as we passed through, and let us make a beginning to it."

"Busby," the laird called. "Send for my brother to come to the keep immediately, and tell him to bring parchment and pen."

"I must go back to the yard, Grandsire," Maggie said. "I was train-ing the new lads when I was told of Lord Stewart's arrival." Without waiting she made a quick curtsy to both men and hurried out of the hall.

"She trains the recruits?" Lord Stewart was surprised.

The laird nodded. "In archery, and other combat skills," he said. "Do ye now see why I have acquiesced to her demand that a husband be able to outrun, outride, and outfight her? She is beautiful, and she is clever, but she would rather be outdoors than in the hall. She has been that way since she was a wee lass. And from the moment I taught her how to use a bow, her pursuits were more those of a lad than of a lassie. She governs the house as well, for Grizel, her tiring woman, made her learn the things she must know to manage it. I pray God that you can overcome her, my lord, for Brae Aisir will be all the safer for an heir or two. I wish she were not so difficult, and I too old to control her."

Lord Stewart sat down again and sipped from his goblet. "She is a strong woman—she must be to survive here in the Borders," he began. "She has become formidable, I suspect, to protect ye and the Aisir nam Breug. The signing of the contracts on the morrow makes us legally man and wife. Beneath her brave heart and fierce will, yer granddaughter is still a woman. She knows she cannot escape the king's will, but she is afraid, though she would deny it. The moment my lips touched hers, I knew she had never been kissed. Let her have the time she needs to accustom herself to our marriage. Let us learn to know each other before I bed her. Ye need have no fear. I will beat her in whatever challenge she puts forth. And when I do, she will do her duty, for I know ye have raised her to accept her responsibilities."

"The king cannot possibly know the great favor he has done for us in sending ye here, Fingal Stewart," the laird said. Then his brown eyes twinkled mischievously. "How much is it costing Brae Aisir?" he asked.

Lord Stewart laughed. "I see my cousin's reputation extends into the depths of the Borders," he replied. "He wanted half of the yearly tolls paid each Michaelmas in coin. I argued for a third. When the contracts for our agreement reach me, I shall ask they be paid on St. Andrew's Day beginning next year. I believe that is fairer as I have no idea what ye collect, although judging from yer keep, I must assume it is a goodly sum."

"It is," the laird said, but gave no further details.

"Perhaps tomorrow the lady will ride out with me so I may see the pass," Lord Stewart suggested.

"Aye, before the winter comes there is much you will need to see and learn about Brae Aisir. And tomorrow I shall send one of my own men to the king with my thanks for sending ye. If ye wish to write to him, my messenger can take yer letter too."

Father David Kerr, robes swaying, hurried into the hall, his servant behind him carrying the priest's writing box. "What is so important that I must come posthaste, Dugald?" he asked his older brother. The priest's eyes went to Lord Stewart.

"This is Fingal Stewart, Brother. The king has sent his cousin, Lord Stewart of Torra, to wed with Maggie," the laird began. Then he went on to explain.

The priest listened, nodding as his elder brother spoke. When the laird had finished he said, "'Tis as good a solution as any, Dugald." He held out his hand to Fingal. "Welcome to Brae Aisir, my lord."

The two men shook. Then David Kerr looked back to the laird. "And what, pray, does my niece think of this? I saw her when I came into the courtyard working her lads hard. I think she is not pleased to be told what she must do."

"She will sign the marriage contract tomorrow when it is drawn and ready," the laird assured the priest.

"And the blessing?" the priest asked.

"He must fulfill the conditions any other suitor would before the blessing," Dugald Kerr said. "She is determined, and Lord Stewart says he can beat her fairly."

"You would let her have her way in her foolishness?" David Kerr asked Fingal.

He nodded in the affirmative. "Aye. She needs to feel she has some control over her life even if she doesn't. Some men might not care, but I want my wife to respect me. She will not if I cannot best her. And yer neighbors will not feel so slighted by this match when I do."

The priest looked thoughtful, and then replied, "Yer a clever fellow, my lord. And I think ye could be dangerous, given the opportunity. If yer willing to indulge the lass, then so be it. When will yer contest take place?"

"After the gleaning," Lord Stewart replied.

"Well, 'tis not so long to wait," the priest said. "I'm pleased to see yer a disciplined man."

"Remain here tonight, and draw up the contracts," the laird said. "I want them signed after morning Mass, Brother."

"Agreed!" David Kerr said. He turned to his assistant. "Tam, go and put my writing box in the laird's library. Then go home. I'll not need ye again till the morrow."

"Aye, Father David," the boy said, and hurried off to do as he had been bid.

A servant brought the priest a goblet of wine, and the three men sat talking before one of the hall's two large hearths. Seeing them there as she came in, Maggie slipped up the stairs to her bedchamber where Grizel awaited. The serving woman had had her young mistress's tub set up, and the steam was rising from the hot water as Maggie entered the room.

"I didn't ask ye for a bath," the girl said.

"Yer not going down to the hall for the meal stinking of yer sweat like some man-at-arms," Grizel said firmly. "What will yer husband think of ye?"

"He's not my husband yet," Maggie said, irritated.

"He will be on the morrow," Grizel snapped back.

"Does everyone in Brae Aisir know my business now?" She pulled off her boots and garments impatiently.

"Fourteen mounted men ride through the village and up the hill to the keep, and ye think it will go unnoticed? Get in the tub before the water cools. A hall full of servants, and ye think no one is listening? This is the most exciting thing that has happened at Brae Aisir in years, lassie."

Maggie climbed into her tub. Taking up the washing rag, she soaped it and began to scrub herself vigorously. "The contract is to be signed tomorrow, and that's an end to it," she said. "I will have obeyed the king's command. There will be no bedding until he can prove himself worthy of me and earn my respect."

Grizel shook her head. "Yer the most stubborn lass in the Borders," she said.

"Aye, I am," Maggie agreed. "But if after proclaiming I should wed no man who could not outrun, outride, and outfight me, it would be Lord Stewart who would suffer if he did not rise to my challenge. There would be some like that boob Ewan Hay who would challenge his right to the Aisir nam Breug and cause a feud between the Kerrs and half a dozen clan families in the region. Let this *husband* the king has sent me prove to them all that he is worthy to take on this responsibility *and me*."

"He's a big bonnie man," Grizel said. "He'll beat ye and show the others he can be the true master of Brae Aisir after yer grandfather relinquishes his authority."

"We'll see," Maggie replied to her tiring woman.

"Have ye decided when ye will issue the challenge?" Grizel asked her mistress.

"What? Has that information not been spread from the gossips in the hall yet?" Maggie teased her companion.

Grizel laughed. "Nay," she said.

"After the gleaning," Maggie told her, but she was already considering other ways to avoid doing what was really her duty. She would do this in her own time, not another's. She finished bathing, and after drying herself thoroughly, she dressed in the garments that Grizel had laid out for her—a plain gown of medium blue velvet brocade with a low square neckline, tight-fitting bodice, and tight sleeves. She wore her clan badge as a pendant on a gold chain. It showed the sun in its splendor with the motto *Sero sed servio*, meaning *Late, but in earnest*.

Grizel brushed out her mistress's beautiful warm brown hair. Then she set a French hood with a short trailing veil that fell just as far as Maggie's shoulders. The hood had a carefully pleated linen edge. "Put on yer slippers and yer ready to go down," Grizel said. "Ye look respectable and like a young lady should now."

"He wouldn't care what I looked like," Maggie said. "The Stewarts of Torra do their duty by the king, he told me. He's marrying me because the king said so and for no other reason, Grizel. He was insulting."

"It's yer own fault," Grizel told her bluntly. "Ye refused to get to know any of the marriageable men in the vicinity. Yer heart is nae engaged, lassie, so what does it matter whom ye wed now? Yer grandfather is sixty-three. He could wait no longer for ye to settle on a husband, especially as ye had no intention of doing so."

"But I can take care of the Aisir nam Breug, Grizel," Maggie said. "I don't need a husband to do it for me. Why do ye think I learned to ride, to run, to fight, to do accounts? It was so I could take over for Grandsire one day."

"*And after ye?*" Grizel said. "Who would care for the Aisir nam Breug after ye? Do ye think ye'll live forever, lassie? Ye need a husband, and bairns to follow ye."

Maggie sighed. "I know," she admitted. "I had just hoped to have more time."

"Yer seventeen, lassie," Grizel reminded her.

"Only last April," Maggie said.

"Yer mother birthed ye when she was sixteen," Grizel replied.

"And died in the process," Maggie answered.

"She was a sweet lass, but English, and weak," Grizel remarked. "Now get ye down to the hall, lassie. Ye know how yer grandsire dislikes it when yer late."

Maggie nodded, then hurried from her bedchamber. In the hall she found her grandsire, the priest, and Lord Stewart much as she had left them, talking by the hearth.

She silently signaled Busby. "Is the supper ready?"

"It is, mistress. Shall I have it brought?"

"Aye. I imagine our guest is hungry at this point, and the rest in the hall as well. Was Cook able to find enough to feed the extra mouths?"

"She's using the extra bread she had, added more vegetables to the pottage, and sent her lad to fetch a new wheel of cheese to cut for the trestles," Busby informed his young mistress. "There'll be cold meats for the high board as well."

At a nod from Busby, the servants hurried from the hall to quickly return with the meal. Wooden bowls were set before each man at the trestles below the high board. They were filled by those same servants with a pottage of carrots, onions, leeks, and rabbit in a thick gravy. Bread and cheese were put on each table, and the tankards were filled with ale.

"My lords," Maggie said to the three men by the fire, "come to table." She ascended to the high board and seated herself in her place next to her grandfather's high-backed chair. Pewter plates, spoons, and silver goblets had been laid at the four places for the diners. There were bread, cheese, and a platter of cold meats along with the pottage, the main meal having been served hours earlier. Wine was poured into the goblets.

Lord Stewart looked about the hall as he ate. The chamber would be considered small by some; yet it was far larger than the hall in his house. It had two hearths, and four tall arched glass windows, two on each side of the room. It had a stone floor. A large tapestry hung behind the high board. Flag staffs with hanging battle flags had been set into the stone walls on the window sides of the hall, which had an arched roof with carved and painted beams. The room easily held five trestles and their benches. They were filled tonight. The chamber gave the appearance of prosperity not always seen in some halls.

And when he had ridden through the village earlier, it had looked comfortable as well. The cottages were well cared for, unlike in many villages. Their slate roofs were in good repair. He had seen no broken windows, and the doors were actually whitewashed. There was a large round fountain with a Celtic cross in the village's square. He had seen no garbage in the street, and the people appeared well fed. Brae Aisir was unique in that.

Maggie watched Lord Stewart from beneath her lowered lashes. What was he thinking? she wondered.

"I want ye to take Lord Stewart through the Aisir nam Breug to-morrow," the laird said. "Not all the way, just a half-day's ride, lassie. Explain to him how the defenses work. Don't go over the border, how-ever. No need for the Netherdale Kerrs to know ye have a husband yet. We'll talk with them before the snows fall, or in the spring."

Maggie nodded. "I agree," she said. She turned to Fingal Stewart. "Their former patriarch, Edward Kerr, who was also my grandfather, thought I should wed one of my English cousins. I would not, for an English master at this end of the Aisir nam Breug would have been unsuitable. His loyalties would have been to whichever English king was in power, and not to our King James. And if the English con-trolled both ends of the pass, they might be cajoled into violating our long-held principles of only peaceful traverse. My mother was a Netherdale Kerr, but she was fragile and no Scot. I am a Scot, my lord, and I am not fragile. I am strong," Maggie said proudly.

Strong, proud, and beautiful, Fingal Stewart thought as she spoke. What a wife she was going to be! "I will be honored to be your hus-band, madam," he told her.

Maggie colored, her cheeks taking on a most becoming shade of pale rose. She dipped her head in silent response to his compliment, and reaching for her goblet, sipped her wine. Then she began to eat again with good appetite, he noted.

"She is not used to being courted," Father David Kerr said softly.

"I am surprised she is not wed," Lord Stewart responded in equally low tones.

"Her reputation is an honest one, my lord," the priest answered. "She is as fleet of foot as a deer being pursued by a pack of hounds. She rides astride, and like a demon."

"What is her weapon?" Lord Stewart asked.

"What isn't her weapon, although she will battle you with a clay-more. She is an excellent archer. She can use a lance astride as well as any knight. She is skilled in hand-to-hand combat. To be candid with ye, my lord, my grandniece scares the very devil out of those who know her. Especially the young men, which is why none but Hay's fool of a younger brother attempted to meet her challenge. She was a-horse before the lad had even finished their footrace and was back in the keep courtyard, her ride finished as he sat with bloodied feet complaining. He gave up then. Lord Hay held no animosity towards the Kerrs. He had warned his sibling against making an attempt to vanquish Maggie."

"So that's why he went sub rosa to the king," Lord Stewart said aloud. "His pride had been badly damaged. He hoped James would hand over to him what he could not fairly win." Fingal Stewart laughed. "He misjudged my cousin badly."

"Could the king not have made a similar arrangement with the Hays as he made with ye?" the priest asked.

"Nay. Ye borderers are a fierce lot," Lord Stewart said with a smile. "Did he not spend some months subduing your earls? The king trusts few men, good Priest."

"But he trusts ye," David Kerr said. "Yer his blood."

"Even blood cannot always be counted upon," Fingal Stewart said wisely. "I am an exception not just because of my blood tie to the king, but my maternal grandmother was sister to the grandfather of the king's current mistress, Janet Munro. So the king and I are doubly bound. It was Janet Munro who informed the king of my existence, and how the Stewarts of Torra have never betrayed their kings. Until that day, the king had no knowledge of me at all despite our blood tie."

"I have heard stories both positive and negative about the king," Father David replied. "Yer tale is most interesting, my lord. It is a good thing that James Stewart acknowledges yer kinship, but also a good thing that ye have never been involved in any of the conspiracies that have surrounded him since his unfortunate childhood."

"I am six years the king's senior," Lord Stewart said.

"Then ye are thirty years of age, or thereabouts," the priest noted.

"Thereabouts," Lord Stewart agreed.

"Yer late to wed, or have ye been wed before?" the priest inquired.

"I have not been wed prior, nor to my knowledge do I have any bastards, and while I have known several women, I could not afford to keep a mistress," Lord Stewart said. "Is there anything else ye would know, good Father?"

The priest chuckled. "Ye understand why I ask, my lord. Ye are unknown to us, but ye come with written instructions from the king to wed our heiress. We cannot refuse the king's command, but we would know the kind of man into whose keeping we are placing our Maggie. One day when ye give yer daughter in marriage, ye will remember this day and understand."

"I descend from King Robert the Third through his murdered son, David, who got a son on his mistress, Maire Drummond. When the first James Stewart returned from an eighteen-year exile in England, his nephew came to pledge his undying loyalty. In return that king saw his nephew was permitted to use the surname Stewart; and he gave him a stone house with a fine slate roof below Edinburgh Castle, which is how we became the Stewarts of Torra. When the first James was foully murdered, that same nephew was one of the men who got the queen to safety and saw her son secured upon his throne. Since that day we Stewarts of Torra have never deviated in our loyalty," Fingal told the priest.

"We have never had the authority or the wealth to be involved in the battles to control the boy kings James the Second and James the Third. Nor did we take sides when the fourth James saw his father overthrown. We have simply remained loyal to the Stewart kings in power in any way we might. We have never broken faith with our kinsmen. So when our king told me to wed the heiress to Brae Aisir, I could give but one answer. Aye, my lord. My family's motto is *Ever faithful*. Our clan badge is a greyhound lodged in front of a crown proper. Is there anything else you need to know, Priest?"

"Ye have no siblings?"

"Nay. My father was content when I was born that he had a son. He had thought his line to die with him, for he was not a rich man and had not wanted to take a wife to share his poverty. He wed my mother, the orphaned kin of a friend, to keep her safe. She was sixteen and he past fifty when I was born. But he loved her, and she him. She died when I was ten, and my father just a few years ago."

"He would have been very old," Father David said.

Fingal chuckled. "He was eighty and had a strong constitution."

"Now I know what ye can tell me, my lord. The rest I shall learn as I come to know ye better. My brother, the laird, will not be unhappy with what you have told me."

Maggie had listened as Fingal had spoken to her great-uncle. His family might have had no wealth, but it would seem to be respectable with good clan connections—Munros, Drummonds, and Stewarts. She snuck a quick look at him from beneath her lashes. He was fair to her eye with his long face and shock of short, coal black hair. And his form was strongly built, and well muscled. She was tall for a woman, but he had topped her by at least half a foot. Could he overcome her fairly in the challenge? Would she let him? Or would she beat him as she would any man who attempted to best her?

Only time would tell, and Maggie needed to get to know Fingal Stewart better.

The following day they signed the marriage contracts drawn up by Father David, then met in the courtyard of the keep. They would ride with several men-at-arms, and she would show him the Aisir nam Breug. A late-August sun shone down on them, and above the skies were clear blue. They rode down the hill and through the village of Brae Aisir. A half mile from the village, Maggie turned her horse to the right, and Fin realized they were on a narrow and very ancient paved stone road. He was surprised when the hills suddenly rose up around them.

Seeing the look on his face Maggie said, "Aye, it comes upon ye suddenly, doesn't it. This is the beginning of it. Our part runs for just over fifteen miles before the border is reached, and ye can cross into England."

"How do ye know when ye've reach the border?" he asked her.

"There is a cairn of stones topped by an iron thistle. A few feet farther on the other side of the pass is a second cairn of stones topped by a rose. Pass by it going south, and yer in England. Pass by our cairn going north and yer in Scotland. 'Tis that simple, my lord," Maggie explained patiently.

"I can see the road is too narrow for an army or group of raiders to travel with any urgency," Fingal Stewart noted, "but do ye have any defenses at all?"

Maggie smiled mischievously. "Look up and about ye, my lord."

He did, and it was then he saw the low stone watchtowers set at intervals, and carefully staggered on both sides of the pass. Lord Stewart was impressed.

"We keep three men in each tower," Maggie told him. "In case of an emergency, one man is sent to Brae Aisir or Netherdale, whichever is closer, to give the alarm."

"Yer English kin keep faith with ye first?"

"As we keep faith with them," Maggie replied. "The welfare of our folk is paramount for us all. Without the tolls we collect, how could we care for our people? We are not disloyal to our kings, and the pass has in its time prevented a tragedy or two because it has been a safe traverse through the Borders when there was no other way."

He nodded. It had all been carefully thought out, and it had been done several centuries ago. He was astounded that the Kerrs had been able to keep the Aisir nam Breug neutral and free of strife for all these years. Would he be able to successfully carry on the tradition? And what would the English Kerrs think of a Stewart marrying the last of the Brae Aisir Kerrs? They traveled that day to the border and back. And in the weeks to come Fingal Stewart took several of his men and rode the pass himself, familiarizing himself with the landscape, the watchtowers, the road itself.

August and September were over. The fields had been completely harvested, and the villagers were allowed to glean in them, gathering up what remained of the crops for their own families. The hillsides were bright with their autumn colors. One evening as October began, Dugald Kerr spoke to his granddaughter.

"It is time for ye to set the date of the marriage challenge," he said to Maggie.

"Och, Grandsire, we must bring the cattle and sheep from the summer pastures first," Maggie said. "I have no time for racing now. Just yesterday one of the shepherds thought he heard a wolf in the far hills. I'll not lose good livestock to those beasties."

"I agree with her," Fingal Stewart said quietly.

The laird and his brother looked at each other. Finally Dugald Kerr said, "Well, 'twill not take long, and as yer already legally man and wife I suppose a few more days cannot matter." And the priest nodded in agreement.

So the sheep and the cattle were brought down from their summer pastures to browse in the fields near the keep during the day, and be penned safely within the village with their dogs at night. Again the laird asked his granddaughter to set the date for the challenge between her and Lord Stewart. But Maggie demurred a third time.

"Grandsire, we have not filled the larder with enough meat to get through the winter," she said in reasonable tones. "How can I rest and take my own pleasure if I permit this keep to go hungry come the snows?"

"I agree," Fingal Stewart murmured. "I commend your constancy to duty, madam. We will hunt together every day until we have enough meat to sustain us in the months ahead." He smiled pleasantly at her. "And then I will meet your challenge so our union may be blessed. The winter is as good a time as any to make an heir for Brae Aisir."

The old laird and the priest both chuckled at this, for Maggie's face had taken on a look of annoyance at Fingal Stewart's words.

"An excellent plan," Dugald Kerr said. "I'd like to be holding my great-grandson in my arms by this time next year," he said.

"And I'd like to be alive to baptize the bairn," Father David said.

Maggie's temper exploded. "I'll not be thought of as some damned broodmare to be bred for fresh stock," she told them.

"'Tis yer duty, lassie," her grandfather told her. "Yer duty to Brae Aisir."

"I know my duty to Brae Aisir," Maggie said fiercely. "I have done that duty since I was a wee lass, Grandsire."

"Aye," he replied. "Ye've done duty by this family, and ye've done it well, but yer the last of us now, lassie, and yer duty is to give us a son. Ye've been given a good man for a husband. Now let him get a child on ye for Brae Aisir."

She ran from the hall, shocked by his words. Yet why should she be shocked? Her grandfather had only spoken the truth to her, and Maggie knew it. But still, to give up her authority to a stranger; to be nothing more than a creature to be bred? She did not know if she could bear it. She was close to tears. And then as she stood in the dimness of the corridor outside the hall, an arm went around her. Maggie stiffened her spine.

"He is eager to see an heir," Fin said quietly.

"Are ye?" The arm about her was more comforting than constraining.

"Aye, but not until yer content with this," Fin told her.

"Do ye want to bed me because ye must?" she asked.

He laughed softly, the warm breath soft against her neck as he bent down so only she might hear him. "I know ye have a mirror," he said. "Yer beautiful, lass."

"So bedding me will not prove too onerous a duty because I am beautiful," Maggie said testily.

"Lass, we are already wed by royal command. We must bed each other eventually. Am I to be distained because I appreciate that yer fair of face and form? As I come to know ye, I find that I like ye, Maggie Kerr. I admire yer honor and faithfulness to duty. Set the date for yer challenge so Father David may bless our union," Fin said.

"Ye think ye can beat me?" Her tone was irritable.

"No one remains a champion forever, lass, and I am the man who will defeat ye," he said with surety. "Why are ye afraid of that?"

It had been comfortable leaning back against him, but now Maggie pulled away. She pushed his arm from her waist, pivoting about as she did. "I am Mad Maggie Kerr of Brae Aisir, and I fear no man," she said. "But before I set the date for this contest between us, the larder will be filled with meat. When that is done, I will set the time for our contest; ye have my word on it." She spit into her right hand and held it out to him.

He was surprised by the gesture, for it was not a woman's, but he spit into his right hand in return and shook her hand. "Done, madam, and done again!" he said.

Her gaze met his. "Yer a puzzlement to me, Fingal Stewart," she told him.

"Why?" he asked her. He puzzled her? 'Twas interesting, Lord Stewart thought.

"I am used to the society of men, but I have never known a man with such patience as ye have," she admitted. "Ye could lure a doe onto the spit."

"Is that why ye work at trying my patience, lass?" he queried, a small smile touching his mouth.

Maggie laughed. It was a loud sound, and filled with genuine amusement. "If there is a limit to yer patience, my lord, I have yet to find it," she admitted.

"There is a limit," he warned her. "But if I am indeed to lure the doe onto my spit, then I must exhibit great forebearance else it flee me into the hills."

"I will not run," she told him, blushing at the innuendo. I will leave ye now, my lord. We must be up and away before the dawn if tomorrow's hunt is to be successful."

He bowed to her. "Good night then, lass," he said. "I'll be up on time."

Maggie picked up her skirts and ran up the narrow stone stairs. She sensed he wanted to follow, but he did not, nor did she look back. He did puzzle her. If he was not an intimate part of the king's coterie, then what was he? He had been very candid with Father David about his past. And he had been equally candid with her. How had he lived? If he hired out his sword, where had he fought, and for whom? In France? She wanted to know more, but would her curiosity ever be satisfied? Or would she have to accept Fingal Stewart for what she saw, and what he had told her? Was there even more?

She thought there might be, but perhaps he needed to be more certain of her before he would tell her. Had the king investigated his kinsman, or had he just accepted the suggestion and the word of his mistress, who would, of course, want to aid her cousin?

"So," Grizel said when Maggie had closed her bedchamber door behind her, "yer grandfather is pressing ye again, or so says the gossip from the hall."

Maggie smiled. "First we fill the larder for winter," she replied.

"And after that?" Grizel asked, her brown eyes curious.

"I've given my word to set the date then for the contest between us," Maggie said.

"I know yer word is good." Grizel nodded. "Well, perhaps we'll have an early snow, and ye won't be able to settle the matter till spring."

Maggie laughed as she stripped off her garments. "I'm afraid Grandsire won't wait that long. I've been told he would hold his great-grandson in his arms by next autumn. And the priest concurred."

"I'll wager ye didn't like being told that," Grizel said as she shook out her young mistress's gown, and hung it in the wardrobe.

Maggie sighed. "They're right, Grizel, although I will deny it, should you repeat my words. Lord Stewart seems to be a strong man, and he will hold the Aisir nam Breug as well as any Kerr before him. I can advise him until he is more certain of himself, but the truth is, other than keeping the accounts, my duty is to give Brae Aisir an heir."

"There is bound to be trouble when the Netherdale Kerrs learn ye've wed," Grizel said. "Lord Edmund has not been unhappy that ye've turned away all possible suitors."

"Edmund Kerr cannot believe that the English could manage the Aisir nam Breug alone. They control but eight miles of it to our fifteen. Those fifteen are Scots soil, not English. This cannot be Berwick all over again with the two sides wrangling over it. The pass would be useless then," Maggie pointed out.

"I think Lord Edmund hoped to wed ye himself," Grizel put forth.

"He's put two wives in the ground already, but has been slow to seek another."

"He has nine sons, which should be enough for any man, and half a dozen are already wed with bairns of their own. Not to mention the bastards he sired on both sides of the border. The Netherdale Kerrs have no lack of heirs," Maggie remarked. "Besides, he's my uncle and close to fifty if he is a day. The rumors say he has a very devoted and jealous mistress. There is even speculation that she hurried his last wife to her death in order to become Lord Edmund's third wife. He can't seriously have any expectations of wedding me, and if he does, it is simply to get his hands on the entire Aisir nam Breug. I honestly doubt he could outrun, outride, and outfight me, Grizel." Now in her nightgown, Maggie undid her plait and began brushing out her long chestnut brown hair.

"Will ye hunt tomorrow?" Grizel asked her mistress as she finished putting away all of her garments. She picked up the girl's boots and polished the dust from them with a cloth she pulled from her skirt pocket.

"Aye, I want the larder filled by Martinmas," Maggie said. "I'll take us to that wee loch near the pass entrance tomorrow early. There have been geese overnight there.

"We'll catch them as they rise from the water to begin their southward flight. If everyone's arrow rings true, we will come back with a dozen or more."

"Lord Stewart's Archie says the villagers have seen a boar in the wood lately," Grizel told her mistress.

"I had heard," Maggie answered. "Aye, I'd like to get that boar. If he's young, he'll be tender and make a fine feast on Christ's Mass day." She climbed into her bed, drawing the down coverlet up and settling back into her pillows. "I love hunting in the autumn the best," she said. "Good night, Grizel."

"Good night, my lady," the tiring woman answered as she departed her mistress's bedchamber.

As the door clicked shut behind Grizel, Maggie closed her eyes. Tomorrow would be a wonderful day, she decided. She would show Fingal Stewart that she was more than just a female upon whom he would breed up sons. She would take more game than he did, if only to irritate him. He said his patience had limits. She wondered whether that patience would come to an end if she pricked his pride hard enough. With a smile upon her face, Mad Maggie Kerr fell into a sound and most contented sleep.

Chapter 4

She was up before Grizel even came to awaken her the following morning. She could see the dark sky with a narrow shaft of waning moon through the half-open wood shutter. Maggie lay briefly enjoying a few last minutes of warmth before throwing her coverlet back and getting up from the bed. Pulling the night jar from beneath the bed she peed, leaving it for Grizel to empty. Then, going to her small hearth, she added some bits of kindling, coaxing her fire up from the dark red coals. As it lit, she added more wood, then pulled the ceramic pitcher from the coals where it had sat the night long keeping the water in it warm.

Maggie stripped off her simple white cotton nightgown. Pouring some water into a pewter basin, she picked up the washing rag, soaped it with a sliver of soap that had the fragrance of woodbine, and washed herself thoroughly. Then, using her most prized possession, a small brush with short, hard boar's bristles set into a piece of carved horn, Maggie scrubbed her teeth. Her ablutions concluded, she opened the trunk at the foot of her bed and drew out a cotton chemise that came only to her midthighs. It was lined in rabbit's fur. Putting it on, she added a white linen shirt over it, lacing it up. Next she pulled on a pair of woolen stockings and dark woolen breeks, which she secured with a wide belt. Next came a fur-lined soft doeskin jerkin and her leather boots.

As Maggie sat back down upon her bed to brush out her long hair and braid it into its single plait, Grizel came into the chamber. "Good morrow," Maggie said cheerfully, affixing a small bit of scarlet ribbon to hold her braid.

"Ye should have waited," Grizel said.

"I awoke and couldn't lie there. Besides, I'll want to eat before we go."

"I'll go fetch something," Grizel said.

"Nay, I'll go to the kitchens," Maggie said as she hurried from her bedchamber. She ran down the stairs to the hall and from there down another short flight of steps to the warm kitchens, where the cook and her helpers were busy at work. To her surprise Lord Stewart was already there, seated at the table where the cook and her staff usually sat.

"Good morrow, my lord," Maggie greeted him as she sat down. Immediately a bowl of oat porridge was put before her. Maggie spooned a bit of honey into it and poured in some heavy golden cream before she began to eat enthusiastically.

"Yer up early," he remarked.

"We're hunting," she said matter-of-factly. "The beasties are up too, my lord."

The cook plunked a hot cottage loaf on a wooden board between them with a knife and a tub of butter. She cut two wedges, handing them each one.

"Have ye some hard-boiled eggs and bread for us to take?" Maggie asked the cook.

"Aye, my lady, and a bit of cheese and apples as well," the cook answered her. "Iver took it to pack up in the saddlebags."

"Iver?" Maggie looked confused.

"My captain," Lord Stewart said as he smeared butter across his bread with his big thumb.

"Oh, aye," Maggie said, remembering. "We've got to do something more to integrate your men with our men, my lord. They have kept apart from each other since ye arrived."

"Aye," he agreed. "'Tis a knotty situation, madam, but it must be corrected. The captain of this keep's men-at-arms is not a young man, but I have already seen he has earned his position by being good at what he does. Would he consider accepting Iver as his second in command? Or does he have a man in that position already?"

"Nay, he does not," Maggie said. "The problem for Clennon Kerr is that he is related to almost every family in Brae Aisir. He has several nephews among his men. They are his two sisters' sons. How can he choose from between not just them but the rest of the men without offending someone among his kinsmen? So he has kept the authority to himself. I will speak with my grandfather when we have returned from the hunt today. If it pleases him to do so, he will appoint your man, Iver, to be Clennon Kerr's second in command. Will that suit you, my lord?"

"It will," Lord Stewart replied. Then he turned and looked sternly at the cook and her helpers. "There will be no gossip should you have overheard our conversation. If word gets out before the laird is consulted, and Clennon Kerr is consulted, I will know where to lay the blame. My justice will be harsh and swift. Do ye all understand me?"

The cook nodded. "I'll keep all here as silent as the grave," she promised.

He nodded, satisfied, and gave her a smile of approval.

They had finished their meal and now walked upstairs to the hall where those accompanying them were gathering. Some of the men were eating oatcakes and drinking from their flasks. It was the kind of meal they could finish a-horse. Seeing Lord Stewart and his companion, Iver signaled the men to move out into the courtyard.

It was still dark outside, but the edges of the sky were showing signs of light as they mounted up. With Maggie and Fingal Stewart leading them, they exited forth from the keep's courtyard. The horses' hooves made a soft *clop clop* as they went. A pack of dogs ran by their side, yapping softly.

"Where are we going?" he asked her.

"There's a small water near the pass entrance. The geese overnight there on their way south this time of year. They fly at dawn. We'll be there in time," Maggie assured him. "And there's a boar that has been seen in the the nearby wood."

They reached their destination. The sky above them was considerably lighter than it had been when they left the keep. Tethering their horses, they crept through the underbrush to see a large flock of birds floating upon the placid water. They could hear the soft cackle of bird talk as they prepared their bows, carefully notching their arrows, and then waiting patiently for the moment when the birds would instinctively fly.

The horizon began to show signs of blazing color. The scarlet and gold spread out along the edges of the sky. And then as the sun burst forth over the purview of the blue, the flock of geese rose up from the water, their cackling and the sound of their flapping wings making a great noise. The hunters stood up, and the arrows from their bows being loosed flew towards the birds. Some quicker than others rearmed and shot a second time. A rain of geese fell into the water while the birds that had escaped flew up and southward.

"Loose the dogs!" Maggie cried.

The water dogs among the pack dashed into the small pond, swimming towards the dead geese. Finally when all the birds had been gathered up and brought ashore, Maggie instructed one of the younger men among them to take them immediately back to the keep, where they would be hung head down in the winter larder until they would be needed for a meal. They counted twenty-seven geese among their kill.

"'Twas nicely done," Fingal Stewart said to Maggie.

"If I couldn't outthink a goose, what kind of a chatelaine would I be?" she asked him, grinning broadly.

"Still a beautiful one," he told her, grinning back as she colored prettily.

"Now we have a boar to find," Maggie replied, quickly changing the subject. "He'll be more difficult, but if he's young, not so wily as an older boar."

They rode away from the little water now devoid of birds, directing their horses' steps towards a woodland bordering the village. But though they hunted the morning long, they could find no game at all. Just before dark, they took a young stag. Maggie was not at all satisfied. She wanted that boar.

"We'll hunt every day until we find him," she said to Lord Stewart.

They returned to the keep where the stag was butchered and hung in the winter larder, which was a little more than half full. If the weather remained decent, they should be able to fill it by month's end, for there was plenty of game in the vicinity, Fingal Stewart thought to himself. Though they had missed the main meal of the day, the cook had provided them with trenchers filled with hot lamb stew that they consumed immediately. Afterwards Maggie spoke with her grandfather, Lord Stewart by her side.

She explained to the laird the necessity of combining the keep's men-at-arms with the men who had come with Fingal Stewart. "The two groups should be blended into one underneath the command of Clennon Kerr, Grandsire. But since our captain has never been able to choose a second in command, I would suggest that Lord Stewart's captain, Iver Leslie, fill that position. Clennon Kerr must be consulted, of course, but it needs to be done sooner than later," Maggie told her grandfather.

"Aye," the old man agreed. "It will also help my new grandson to be accepted by all here if we make the two groups one."

"Your new grandson?" Maggie said sharply.

"He's yer legal husband, lassie, which makes him my grandson," the laird answered her pleasantly. He signaled to Busby, and when he had come to his master's side, the laird said, "Fetch Clennon Kerr to me."

"Aye, my lord," the majordomo said, hurrying off.

Several minutes passed in silence, and then Clennon Kerr came bowing to the laird, to Lord Stewart, and to Maggie. "Ye wish to see me, my lord?"

The laird explained, and when he had finished, his captain nodded in agreement.

"Aye, my lord, 'twill suit me well. I have watched Iver Leslie in the weeks he has been here. He is a disciplined soldier," Clennon Kerr replied. "And now that ye have made this decision, my sisters will have to cease nagging at me to promote this relation or that," he chuckled. "And no one can claim I have favored my close kin over any other."

"Busby!" the laird called, and when Busby came, he was sent for Iver Leslie.

Iver, who had been dicing with his Edinburgh companions at the end of the hall, gathered up his small winnings and hurried to the side of the laird of Brae Aisir. "Ye wished to see me, my lord?" he asked, bowing politely and casting a quick look at Lord Stewart.

"With yer master's permission, and that of my own captain, Clennon Kerr, I have decided to make ye second in command of the keep's men-at-arms."

Iver's face showed genuine surprise. "My lord, surely one of yer own could fill this position better than I," he said. "I am honored, and will of course accept, but I should not take another's legitimate place."

"I am related to everyone in Brae Aisir," Clennon Kerr told Iver. "How can I pick one of my relations over another without causing offense? The laird has made his decision, and I am frankly relieved." He held out his big hand to Iver Leslie, whose equally large hand clasped it in friendship.

"Busby!" the laird called. "Drams of whiskey all around." Then he looked at the two soldiers. "'Tis settled then. The decision was mine, Clennon Kerr. Yer sisters cannot blame ye, and the rest of yer kin will be relieved, I'm thinking."

Busby himself brought the tray with the dram cups of whiskey. A health was drunk to the laird's wisdom. The matter was settled but for one thing.

Going to stand at his place at the high board, the laird called out, "Hear me all within this hall and the sound of my voice. I have appointed Iver Leslie to be the keep's second in command after Captain Clennon Kerr. Now let's have a round of ale to celebrate, laddies."

And the serving men were at the trestles filling the tankards. A health was drunk to the two captains. Then the hall settled back down into its usual evening routine. The laird questioned his granddaughter as to the hunt that day and the state of the larder.

"The larder is filling nicely. A few more weeks and we'll have it done," Maggie said. "By the beginning of December for certain, Grandsire."

"Set the date for yer contest, then, for December," Dugald Kerr said. "The sooner, the better, my lass."

"And if it snows?" she asked him mischievously.

"We'll clear the road for ye, lass," he promised her.

There was no point in arguing with him any longer, Maggie

thought. Fingal Stewart was already her husband under the laws of Scotland. To put him off any longer was to put Brae Aisir in danger. She already suspected this was the man who could beat her fairly. He was neither afraid of her nor intimidated by her. But she would do her very best, and he would not find it easy to overcome her.

"December fifth," she said.

The laird's face was immediately wreathed in smiles. "Done!" he replied. "Ye heard her, David. She said December fifth."

"I heard her, Dugald," the priest responded.

"I agree," Lord Stewart said.

Maggie laughed aloud. "You always seem to agree with me, my lord. You would, it appears, be a most reasonable man. I hope it continues after we are fully wed."

"I cannot promise, madam, for you are not always a biddable woman," he said.

Maggie nodded. "That is indeed true, my lord," she agreed. "I am not always easy, but I am usually right." She smiled sweetly at him.

Now Lord Stewart laughed.

Dugald Kerr was pleased by what he saw. His granddaughter seemed to be accepting of this marriage of the king's will. It all boded well but for one small detail.

Maggie and Fingal were rarely alone, if ever. They needed more time together, but how was he to accomplish it? And then he knew, and the solution was simple. "Maggie, lass," he said to her, "take Fingal to my library, and show him yer accounts. She's a clever girl, my lord, as you'll see when ye look at her books. No one can manage the accounts like my granddaughter."

"Och, Grandsire, I doubt Lord Stewart is interested in numbers," Maggie responded, but she was smiling at her elder.

"Nay, nay, I am quite interested," Fingal Stewart assured her. He understood what the old laird was about. He and Maggie did need some time alone, and it was unlikely they would get it in the hall filled with Brae Aisir's men-at-arms not yet gone to their barracks for the night. Ordering them out of the hall would but give rise to talk.

Maggie stood up. "Very well," she said. "Come, and I will show you how I work my magic with numbers."

They departed the hall, and she brought him to her grandsire's library. It wasn't a particularly large chamber, but it was cozy with a small hearth that was already alight, and a row of three tall arched windows on one wall. Surprisingly there was a wall of books, some leatherbound, others in manuscript form. There was a long table that obviously served as a desk facing the windows, and a high-backed chair behind it at one end. Upon the desk were several leather-bound ledgers. Maggie opened one.

"I keep an account of every expenditure made," she said. "This is the account book for the household expenses. We are, of course, like most border keeps, self-sufficient but for a few things. The servants are paid for the year at Michaelmas as are the men-at-arms. The other books are records of the livestock bought and sold, the breeding book, and the book of the Aisir nam Breug," Maggie explained. "Since the beginning, a careful record has been kept of all those going south into England, and coming north into Scotland. The Netherdale Kerrs keep a similar record."

"And ye do this yourself?" he asked.

"Aye. Grandsire says 'tis best we handle our own business," Maggie told him.

"How do ye fix the rate of the toll charge? Or is it simply a set rate?" he asked.

"'Tis one rate for a single traveler or a couple, male and female. A merchant with a pack train of animals pays according to the number of animals he has. A peddler riding with everything on his back pays a set rate. There are fixed rates for wedding parties, families traveling together, messengers," Maggie explained.

"'Tis well thought out," Lord Stewart remarked. "You note travelers in both directions though you collect tolls only one way," he noted. "Why?"

"To keep use of the traverse honest," Maggie said. "Over the centuries there have been times when some sought use of the Aisir nam Breug for less than peaceful purposes. We have caught the few and ejected them. Once we blocked the way. The watchtowers above the pass know who is in each party. We allow travel north from dawn in the morning, and south from the noon hour until sunset. In the dark months, travel alternates days going north Monday, Wednesday, and Friday; and south Tuesdays, Thursdays, and Saturdays. Sundays the pass is closed but for emergencies such as a messenger."

"How long have the Kerrs on both sides of the border held this responsibility?" Lord Stewart asked.

"For more than five hundred years," Maggie told him.

How sad, Lord Stewart thought, that Maggie should be the last of the Kerrs of Brae Aisir. Perhaps he should add the Kerr name to his own. Others had done it in similar situations. Yet he was proud of his name. He would think on it.

"That is all I have to show ye," Maggie said, breaking into his thoughts. "Do ye have any questions to ask of me, my lord? If not, I should like to go to my chamber and bathe. We have another day of hunting ahead of us on the morrow."

"Stay," he said to her. "Can we not talk together?"

Maggie looked puzzled. "Talk? About what? Have ye questions?"

"Aye, questions about the girl who is my wife, yet not my wife," Fingal Stewart answered her. "Sit by the fire with me."

"There is only one chair," Maggie told him.

"Then sit in my lap," he said. "Or I can sit in yers," he teased.

She eyed him warily. "Sit in yer lap? Can I not answer yer questions standing? And what can ye possibly want to know about me? Why should it matter, for yer wed to me by the king's command, my lord."

"Aye, I am," he agreed pleasantly, "but what I know of ye so far, Maggie Kerr, I like. I would know more. And I would have ye like me."

"It doesn't matter," Maggie said bleakly. "We're wed."

"I was told ye had no other ye preferred," Lord Stewart said. "Have I taken ye from another who has engaged yer heart?"

"Nay, I don't," Maggie answered, "but I have never liked being told what I must or must not do, my lord. 'Tis childish, I know. Even if I might control the Aisir nam Breug alone, I canna bear an heir for Brae Aisir without a husband. Had there been a man among our neighbors who pleased me, I might have taken him as such, and shared the responsibilities of the traverse with him. But there was none. The young men fear me, for I am not a maid willing to sit by the hearth, and murmur yes, my lord, to a husband I canna respect, or one who does not respect me. I have said it often enough. None of them wanted me for myself, but only for my wealth and power. So I chose none among them. They thought my grandfather was so desperate for a husband for me he would do whatever he had to do. But my grandsire knows me well, and he loves me. He understands my needs. But now King James has interfered in this matter." She sighed. "I will not let you win, Fingal Stewart. Ye must overcome me fairly."

"I will," he promised her.

"I know some think me selfish that I would have my way. I am not. I have controlled the Aisir nam Breug for almost three years now by myself. Grandsire is not well enough to do what must be done. I need a man who is willing to learn from a woman. That fool Ewan Hay was hardly the man."

"I have heard you beat him badly," Fingal Stewart remarked.

"I did!" Maggie admitted, restraining a wicked grin that threatened to break out upon her face. "I had to so he would give up and go away. I never expected the wretched weasel to go crying to the king. The damned fool had not a chance of outrunning me. Even if I had loved him, and I certainly did not, I could not have thrown the race, for everyone in the Borders knows there is none who can run as fast as I do. I outran him and rode the course a-horse as he sat nursing his bloodied feet, the fool!"

"Yer a hard lass," Fingal Stewart said, his tone grudgingly admiring, "but to carry all the responsibility ye have carried, ye must be hard. But I can beat ye, Maggie Kerr, and I will." He sat down in the chair by the fire, and surprising her, reached out and yanked her into his lap. "That's better," he said. "Now tell me more about yerself, and I will tell ye about myself. I'd like us to at least be friends before I bed ye."

Maggie made a quick attempt to bolt, but Fingal Stewart pulled her back, his arm tightening about her.

"Nah, nah, lassie, yer my wife. A husband has the right to cuddle with his woman." His gray eyes caught her hazel eyes. "Have ye not cuddled with a sweetheart?"

"I've never had a sweetheart, my lord. Do ye think me wanton? I have more important things to be about," Maggie told him angrily. She was not comfortable. She didn't like being imprisoned by his arm. Her head had no place to go but his shoulder. She could smell the damp leather of his garments. It was strong, and it was too masculine. He reeked of power, and it frightened her. "Let me go," she said, attempting to keep her voice level and without fear. "Please release me, my lord."

"Yer afraid," he said, surprised. "Why are ye afraid?"

"I don't wish to be constrained," Maggie answered him.

He was silent a moment and then said, "I am but attempting to know my wife, lady. If I loosen my arm, will you remain in my lap for the interim? I know your word will be good."

"Ohh, that is so unfair!" Maggie cried softly.

"Why?" His tone was innocent of any deception, but they both knew better.

She laughed. She couldn't help it. "So you either hold me within yer embrace, or trust me to remain within it by my own choice," Maggie said. "And ye do not think it an unfair preference ye put before me?"

"Nay," he replied in the same bland tone. "Ye are too used to gaining yer own way, Margaret Jean Kerr. Now there will be times in the future when it will amuse me to let ye run headstrong as yer grandfather has done these seventeen years, but ye will not always have yer way with me. I'll be wearing the breeks in this family."

She stiffened. First with the use of her full Christian name—how had he known it?—and then with her outrage at his speech. "Ohh, yer an arrogant man!" she told him. She was actually more at a loss for words than she had ever been. Never had she been spoken to in such a manner. She was Maggie Kerr, the heiress to Brae Aisir, damn it!

"Excellent!" he praised her. "Yer beginning to understand me. I am Fingal David Stewart, Lord of Torra and one day laird of Brae Aisir. I am arrogant, but not without cause. I descend from kings, lass, and the master of Scotland himself has sent me to marry ye, get bairns on ye, and keep the Aisir nam Breug as it has always been. My family has ever been faithful, and I will not shame them or their memory. Now will ye let me court ye, or will this be a war between us?"

His arm had loosened from about her. Maggie jumped from his lap. She had made him no promises, and she would make him none. "I don't know," she said in answer to his question. Then she ran from the library.

Fin sat before the small chamber's little hearth for some time after she had gone.

He had had enough experience with women to know she was confused and frightened. *God deliver me from skittish virgins,* Fingal Stewart thought to himself, but he knew that her fear of intimacy between them wasn't really the problem. Once he could kiss and caress her, he would win her over, and their bedsport would be pleasant, not that that mattered. Her duty would be to produce bairns for Brae Aisir; sons and daughters to ally them with other border families. But that wasn't the true difficulty between them.

It was control of the Aisir nam Breug that stood between them. The old laird had been wrong not to impress upon his heiress that it would be her husband controlling the pass, and not Mad Maggie Kerr. Still he had a great deal to learn about that traverse, and it was Maggie who would have to teach him for her grandfather was old. He had already turned his duties over to the lass. Oh, Fingal Stewart could beat his bride in the physical challenge she demanded. Of that he had no doubt, though others had failed. But it was his education regarding the Aisir nam Breug that would win Maggie's heart once she realized he could manage the responsibilities involved.

Martinmas came, and they still had not enough meat to last the winter. They hunted each day from dawn to dusk as the days shortened. Slowly the cold larder began to fill up. The meat from the deer they took was butchered. It hung alongside strings of rabbits, geese, and ducks. The boar, however, continued to elude them, but Maggie didn't care now that she was satisfied the keep and village were safe from starvation.

Like many border keeps, the Kerrs had royal permission to fish in the streams, rivers, and lochs in their area. They smoked and salted their catch, storing them in barrels. Dugald Kerr was a kindly man. He allowed the head of each household in his village to trap two coneys a month for their families and to lay away a small keg of salted fish. It was considered a generous gesture, especially given that the laird allowed them to grind in his mill the little grain they grew each growing season. The miller, of course, was allowed to take a tenth share for his trouble.

On St. Andrew's Day, Maggie pronounced the larder was filled to capacity. The weather was growing colder each day, and the nights were much longer now than they had been in September. The moat beneath the drawbridge was covered by a thin sheet of ice most mornings. It melted away during the daylight hours, but re-formed each night. Eventually it would not melt until spring. The stone walls of the keep began to show rimes of frost except in the few chambers where the hearths blazed. The men-at-arms began to sleep in the hall most nights now, for their barracks just within the walls had no hearth. In the stables and barn, those caring for the beasts slept with them in the hay for warmth.

The first day of December dawned sunny and unnaturally mild. A peddler asked shelter for the night. He would be traveling through the Aisir nam Breug in the morning. He had come from Perth via Stirling and Edinburgh. The peddler brought with him a large fund of gossip he was only too willing to share with the hall. He was surprised to learn the heiress to Brae Aisir had a husband, and one who had been sent by the king himself.

"Our Jamie has gone to France to seek a bride," he began, and he chuckled. "He's well funded to go courting, thanks to the church."

"What has the church to do with it?" the old laird asked.

"Why, sir, with these Protestant heretics rising up all over across the water, and even in England, our king's allegiance to Holy Mother Church is a valuable commodity for the pope to have. The king needs an income, and the church is wealthy. I heard he is to have seventy-two thousand Scots pounds over the next few years. 'Tis a fortune!

And three of our most important abbeys and three priories of great consequence are to be given to his bastards for their income. He has six, and I'm told his latest mistress, Janet Munro, is with child." The peddler chortled. "Why, this fifth Jamie is every bit the man his da was, God bless him!" The peddler raised his tankard, drank to the king's health, and continued on with his gossip.

"They say he can have his choice of a wife from among the noble and royal families in Italy, France, and Denmark. That devil who rules England, King Henry, has even suggested a match with Princess Mary, his daughter," the peddler said. "And our Jamie has been presented with many diplomatic honors by those wooing him."

"The king prefers a French match," Lord Stewart said quietly.

"Aye! Aye! So he does," the peddler agreed. "They say the Duke of Vendôme is offering one hundred thousand gold crowns as a dower for his daughter, Marie. But the king turned the lass down."

"How on earth could you know that?" Lord Stewart demanded.

"Ah, sir, I passed through Leith recently. Word had just come that the king visited the court of the Duke of Vendôme in disguise. Despite her great dower, 'tis said he found the lady deformed and crippled. He left the duke's household quickly without making an offer for the lass. He has, it is said, fallen in love with Princess Madeleine, King François's daughter. It is reported she is a bonnie lass. The king offered for her, and the betrothal has been made. The marriage will be celebrated in January at the great Cathedral of Our Lady in Paris. We'll have a new French queen when the king brings her home," the peddler said, pleased to have been able to deliver this news to Brae Aisir.

But he had also gained some excellent gossip to pass on to the Netherdale Kerrs. It would gain him a night's lodging and a few meals in their hall on the morrow when he had traveled through the Aisir nam Breug. While he had told his tale standing before the high board, he had not, of course, been invited to be seated there. He was, after all, only a humble peddler. He had sat below the board with a trestle full of men-at-arms. It was there he had learned that the heiress to Brae Aisir's bridegroom was a cousin of King Jamie himself and had been sent by the king to wed Mad Maggie Kerr.

The contracts, he was told, had been signed weeks ago, but the couple had not yet bedded because Lord Stewart had yet to fulfill the famous challenge issued by the bride that was known throughout the Borders. The challenge was to take place on December fifth. The peddler wished he had an excuse to remain at Brae Aisir so he might relate firsthand what transpired. Looking at Fingal Stewart, however, he already knew. The man stood at least eight inches taller than the lass. He was muscled and in prime condition. If he couldn't outrun, outride, and outfight Mad Maggie Kerr, he didn't deserve to bed her.

The next day, however, dawned cold and rainy. The old laird invited the peddler to remain until the weather cleared. He accepted. He was in no hurry for he was on his way home to Carlisle where he would spend the winter months with his wife making another bairn. The peddler had plans. One day he intended to open a shop in the town, and it would be his sons he sent out to spend the spring, summer, and autumn months on the road while he remained behind in his shop. Word that he was in the keep had spread to the village. The women came to purchase ribbons, threads, needles, pins, and the fine lace trim he was known to carry. It turned into a profitable day, and when the peddler departed the following morning, he was in an excellent mood. The day might be cold, and the north wind had begun blowing, but he had a plump purse, and his wife was waiting for him at the end of his journey.

It took him the daylight hours to ride through the pass, leading his pack horses behind him. But as a weak sun was setting, he came in sight of Netherdale Hall where he was warmly welcomed by Lord

Edmund. "Let me eat first, my lord, and then I shall bring you all the news I have gathered along my way," the peddler said. "I have some that will be of particular interest to you."

"Eat," Lord Edmund Kerr said, curious, but hardly anxious. The peddler was an unimportant fellow, but amusing, and the quality of his merchandise was excellent. "News of King James, I expect," he said.

"Aye, and of the Kerrs of Brae Aisir," the peddler replied as he dug a spoon into the wooden trencher of hot rabbit stew.

Lord Edmund raised an eyebrow but remained silent. To appear eager would make him look foolish. He would wait for the fellow to eat his meal. An imperceptible nod of his head brought a servant to fill his goblet. He sipped it slowly, thoughtfully, as he waited to learn the latest news. Had his cousin Dugald died? He doubted it. The old man for all his frailty was going to outlive them all.

Edmund Kerr had lived a half century. He had buried two wives. The first had given him six sons and three daughters. The second had borne three sons before she died in childbed with a sickly daughter. He was a handsome man with nut-brown hair just now being sprinkled with flecks of silver. He had the hazel eyes so many of the Kerrs on both sides of the border had. He stood six feet in height and was stocky with his age. And while he had a very satisfactory mistress, he wanted another wife.

Dugald Kerr would have to wed his granddaughter sooner than later. And who better to husband the wench than Edmund Kerr? He might even get a son or two on her, for a woman without children was prone to mischief. He had fathered several bastards. His mistress, Aldis, had given him a fine little daughter just a few months back. With nine legitimate sons to his credit, a new female child was more than welcome.

As for Maggie Kerr, his niece, he had seen her several times. She was a beauty, and his cock tightened in his breeks just thinking about her. A strong lass, she would make a fine wife for a man entering his old age—a young wife just like the king's, he thought. But more important was that she was the heiress to Brae Aisir. That he was her uncle and that the Church might object meant nothing to him. She was only his half sister's child. He would have the lass no matter. When he wed her, the Aisir nam Breug would belong to him. He would use this new power to his own advantage.

The peddler finished his meal and, rising, went to stand before Lord Kerr's high board. He recounted all the gossip about King James while all in Netherdale Hall listened. Then clearing his throat, he delivered the newest tidbit in his arsenal. "The heiress to Brae Aisir has a husband," he said.

Edmund Kerr grew pale and then flushed with anger. "Say on, peddler," he commanded the man in a hard, tight voice.

"One of the lass's rejected suitors went to the king, complaining. 'Tis thought he believed King Jamie would order his marriage to Mad Maggie to protect the Aisir nam Breug. Instead, the king sent his cousin, Lord Fingal Stewart, instructing him to wed the lass, and take charge of the pass himself. Though he has not bedded her yet, the contracts making them man and wife were signed weeks ago," the peddler concluded.

"How do ye know he hasn't bedded her?" Lord Edmund asked.

"The old laird has insisted Lord Stewart meet the conditions his granddaughter has set out. He must face her challenge to outrun, outride, and outfight her," the peddler explained to his host. "He'll win too, I expect. He's a big man with long legs."

Lord Edmund cursed softly beneath his breath. Why couldn't his life be simple? Now he would have to kill Lord Stewart, and widow the heiress. She could have no love for this stranger sent by her king. The death of an unwanted husband wouldn't matter to her at all. But it was hardly an auspicious way to begin a courting. "When will this challenge take place?" he asked the peddler. "Do ye know?"

"Oh, aye, my lord, I do. 'Twill be in three days time on the fifth of the month," answered the peddler. "I only wish I could be there to see it, but the weather is closing in, and I want to get home to Carlisle," the peddler said. "My wife and bairns are waiting."

Lord Edmund smiled and nodded with apparent understanding of the peddler's desires. "Of course," he murmured. "Travel with St. Christopher's blessing come the morrow. The news you brought has been most interesting and entertaining." Then the master of Netherdale Hall departed for his privy chamber.

His eldest son, who had been in the hall, heard the peddler's tale too. He knew his sire had planned on attempting to convince old Dugald Kerr to give him his heiress as his third wife. Unlike his father, however, Rafe Kerr was more of a realist. He doubted that the old laird would have so easily complied with his English relation's demand, and there was no love lost between the two family patriarchs. He almost laughed aloud at the thought of his father attempting to tame Maggie, his cousin.

Rafe had met up with her out on the moors several times and knew her for a hard woman. But Lord Edmund Kerr wasn't used to hard women. He liked meek, compliant wives, although one could hardly call his mistress, Aldis, meek. She was a hot-tempered bitch who usually managed to get her way with his father. And the old man positively doted on the wee bairn Aldis had birthed recently. She had done it, of course, so she might dig her claws deeper into Edmund Kerr, and while he might not realize it, she had succeeded. But while he didn't like Aldis, she kept his father occupied and away from trouble. But recognizing his father's ire, Rafe followed him into his privy chamber.

The older man whirled about. "What the hell do you want?" he snarled.

"What are you going to do?" Rafe asked. He was a younger, slender version of his sire. "If James Stewart is interested enough in the Aisir nam Breug to have sent blood kin to wed my cousin, then that's an end to it."

"Accidents happen," Edmund Kerr said ominously.

"Don't be a fool," Rafe said. "As long as the Scots kings knew little or nothing of the passage, you had the chance to take it all for us. That opportunity is gone now."

"James Stewart is interested in only one thing," Edmund Kerr said. "What he can gain from the Aisir nam Breug. I'm sure I can make the same arrangement with him that he has made with his cousin."

"You will cost us everything with your greed," Rafe said bluntly to his father.

Edmund Kerr went to strike his eldest a blow, but Rafe blocked him, his own thick fingers tightening about his father's wrist. His elder grew bright red in the face, his eyes almost popping from his head. Then he said, "Give over, my son, and hear me out."

Rafe loosened his grip, releasing his sire's hand. "Nay, you hear me out, Da. But a third of the passage is in England. There is no argument or doubt about it. Yet our kinsmen in Scotland have shared the largesse of this traverse equally with us for centuries. If you succeeded in taking it all for yourself, you would be at the mercy of King Henry, who could force the use of the Aisir nam Breug for ulterior purposes. Then the Scots would retaliate, for the Kerrs' neighbors would certainly complain to their king. And then our most comfortable living would be gone, Da. It isn't worth it. My cousin has been wed by royal command. There's an end to it."

"But not bedded yet, which means there is no new heir in her belly," Edmund Kerr said. "If her husband were to die before he planted his seed, then she would need a new husband. There is nothing wrong with my taking her for my own wife if she is widowed. And I would have our son manage their part of the road when he was old enough. Nothing wrong with a father guiding his son, Rafe, is there? I guided and taught you."

"If you think the Scots king, now knowing of the Aisir nam Breug and its value, will let you marry my cousin and then take over the pass until a son you give her is grown, you have lost your wits, Da. And what if the bairn died? Maggie Kerr is like no woman you have ever met. You don't know her. All you can remember is a pretty lass you've seen now and again over the years. But I've seen her grown, Da. They don't call her *Mad Maggie* because she's a sweet young flower. She really can outrun, outride, and outfight any man in the Borders. And she's proud of it. Who the hell wants a termagant like that for a wife? And there is that little matter of consanguinity to consider."

"A couple of good beatings would cure her temper," Lord Edmund said.

"You wouldn't survive the first blow you aimed at her," Rafe said candidly. "She's a proud woman, Da." He noted his father's avoidance of the consanguinity.

"You sound as if you admire her," his father remarked.

"I do," Rafe replied. "I wouldn't want her in my bed, or birthing my bairns, and I especially would not want my daughters to be as independent as she is, but aye, I do admire her. I don't quite understand why I do. I think perhaps 'tis because she is like some magnificent wild creature, a falcon, an eagle, that cannot be tamed."

His father looked at him. "You're a damned romantic fool like your mother was," he said coldly. "However, you do not put me off the lass. Everything you have said intrigues me. With a woman like that by my side, we could make our own terms with both England and Scotland. We don't have to belong to either."

"What do you think Aldis will say to what you're considering?" Rafe asked wickedly. "She is hardly apt to stand by while you court and wed another. She'd kill you first. She gave you a bairn so she might bind you to her more closely."

"Wee Susan's a bastard just like a dozen or more others I've sired on various women hereabouts," Lord Edmund said. "Aldis is no fool. She knows her place."

Rafe Kerr laughed harshly. "Nay, Da, 'tis you who are the fool if you actually believe that. Aldis would be your wife. Marry her. She's a young wife for your old age."

"I want to go to Brae Aisir tomorrow," Lord Edmund Kerr said. "And I want you with me, Rafe. Let us meet this kinsman of Jamie Stewart, and see his mettle. And I want to be a spectator to this challenge between him and old Dugald's wench."

"That I will enjoy seeing myself," Rafe said enthusiastically. "The last man who attempted to win her was beaten so badly he has yet to raise his head from his shame, or so 'tis said. He was a Hay, I am told."

"We'll start out at first light," Lord Edmund said. "We should reach Brae Aisir by late afternoon. I doubt old Dugald will be glad to see me, but hearing of the wedding from our peddler friend, I could not resist coming to add my good wishes as the lord of the Netherdale Kerrs; especially as our two families will be working together to ensure the Aisir nam Breug remains the safe and peaceful route through the Cheviots it has always been." He smiled toothily at his oldest son, and Rafe laughed.

"You're a clever old devil, Da," he said. "Very well, let us go and size up the enemy. But I will wager you'll never get control of the whole road."

"We'll see," Lord Edmund Kerr replied to his eldest. "First things first, however, Rafe. Now I must go and have Aldis make certain I show at my best."

Rafe laughed all the harder. His father would have his mistress dress him in his best finery so he might go and court another man's wife. Aldis would hardly be pleased. Edmund Kerr was certainly a brave fellow, his son thought, amused. Brave or foolish, perhaps a bit of both; Rafe Kerr wasn't entirely sure which.

Chapter 5

he day dawned dry and cold. A weak sun hung low in the winter gray sky. Late the previous afternoon Brae Aisir had unexpected guests when Edmund Kerr and his son, Rafe, arrived. The sun had already set. Maggie welcomed them graciously, although she was suspicious of this sudden visit from their English kin. The old laird was less tactful than his granddaughter. Seated at the high board he glared down the hall as the visitors were announced and entered. His mouth was flint-thin with his disapproval of his English kin's arrival. His brown eyes grew hard with mistrust.

"Good evening, Cousin Dugald," Edmund Kerr said by way of greeting, though they were related in several ways. He bowed along with his son, smiling.

He wants something, Maggie thought. The smile showed too many teeth. She had never liked Edmund Kerr on the few occasions they had met when she was a child. This uncle reminded her of a fox, always looking at her as if she were something to eat, and he was just waiting for her to ripen and fall into his mouth.

"This is unexpected," Dugald Kerr replied to his kinsman's greeting. "What the hell brings ye to Brae Aisir on a winter's night, Edmund?"

"Bad news, Dugald," the Lord of Netherdale replied. "Bad news. I hosted a peddler a few nights past who said your heiress was wed by royal command. I cannot believe such a thing is true. Certainly you knew I would be offering for Margaret now that I have been widowed once again. With no male heir to follow you, a match between us is the perfect solution to keeping the Aisir nam Breug in the hands of the Kerr family. You would let strangers have our heritage, Dugald?"

The laird of Brae Aisir stood up, glaring down at his kinsman as he leaned over the high board, his broad hands flat upon its smooth surface. "Brae Aisir is Scotland, Edmund, not England. I was glad to give Maggie into the keeping of a good Scots husband, the king's kinsman, I might add. Besides, ye don't need a wife. Ye've had two. Ye've a quiver full of bairns. Ye've a mistress the gossips say is jealous of any female who casts an eye upon ye. There's even a rumor she helped yer last wife to her death. Yer Maggie's uncle, for God's sake! She is wed to Fingal Stewart, and that's an end to it. I'll give ye and yer lad shelter tonight, but on the morrow I expect ye both gone back through the Aisir nam Breug. I dinna hope to see ye again." Dugald Kerr sat back down.

"The marriage hasn't been consummated," Edmund Kerr said boldly. "It could be annulled by the archbishop in York."

The laird leaned back in his chair. "Yer balls are as wizened as yer brain, Edmund," he said. "Yer too close in blood for me to have ever considered such a match. For sweet Jesu's sake, her mam was yer half sister. The marriage will be blessed tomorrow by the keep's priest, and consummated soon after. Why the hell would I turn away King James's own kinsman, a strong vital Scot, for an ancient Englishman?"

A snicker rippled through the hall from the men at the trestles.

"I'm young enough to have just sired another child," Edmund Kerr said angrily.

"I'm sure ye labored mightily to get that bairn, if indeed it's yers," the laird replied.

Now there was open laughter among the men-at-arms.

"My father is disappointed, as would any man be to lose such a lovely young woman as the lady Margaret," Rafe Kerr said in an attempt to ease the situation. His father was looking more foolish with each word he uttered.

"Are ye the eldest?" Dugald Kerr asked the young man.

"Aye, my lord," Rafe responded.

"The heir?"

"Aye, my lord. I am Rafe Kerr."

"Ye look to have more sense than yer sire, laddie. This is Fingal Stewart, Maggie's husband," he said, indicating with a wave of his hand Lord Stewart, who sat on his right. "Ye two will be doing business together eventually. Ye should get to know each other. Busby! A goblet of wine for young Rafe Kerr, and his sire too. Come up and join us at the high board, laddie." He looked to Edmund. "Sit down, Edmund. I don't like ye, and never have, but yer heir looks to have promise."

"Go on," Edmund Kerr hissed at his son, and then he seated himself on a bench at the nearest trestle, taking the goblet offered and drinking deeply.

The younger man joined those at the high board, seating himself next to Lord Stewart. The two men began talking.

The old laird chuckled.

"I almost feel sorry for Lord Edmund," Maggie said to the laird. "Ye were very hard on him, Grandsire."

"Pompous fool," Dugald Kerr muttered. "And the nerve of him to think I would ever consider giving my darling lass to him to wife."

"He doesn't want me, Grandsire. He wants to control the entire

Aisir nam Breug," Maggie replied. "You know that's why he has hot-footed through the traverse this day."

"Even if ye were a perfect match for him, I wouldn't have allowed it," Dugald Kerr said. "This is Scotland. We may be in the Borders, but the boundary between Scotland and England has always been clear in the pass. Ye needed a Scots husband, and ye have one now."

"Only if he beats me on the morrow," Maggie said.

The laird nodded. "He will," he said with surety.

Maggie laughed. "Have ye lost faith in me then, Grandsire?"

"I'll never lose faith in ye, lass, but this man is the man for ye."

Maggie was not about to agree with her grandfather. At least not yet. But she had to admit that the past few weeks had been a revelation to her. They had hunted together, and he had not treated her like some delicate creature. He had treated her like an equal. But once the marriage was blessed and consummated, would he behave the same way? He was learning the business of the Aisir nam Breug from her quickly. Her grandfather noted it and was pleased.

She and Fingal had visited every one of the watchtowers along the miles under Scots control. He spoke with the men, and the men liked him. He saw where repairs were needed for both the towers and the narrow stone road. He had asked her who originally built the road, and she had told him no one was really certain, but it was probably a people known as the Romans who had built the wall that was the divide between England and Scotland. He wanted to know how the Aisir nam Breug became the Kerr family's responsibility.

Maggie had explained that the family traced its roots to an Anglo-Norman family who sent several of their number north in the eleventh century. Two brothers had discovered the stone road deep within the hills. They had divided it, the elder taking the larger section and settling in Scotland, and the younger taking the small section and settling in England. Lord Stewart had nodded. Those were the days when a man could go forth and make his own fortune, and found a dynasty.

Seeing her grandfather, her husband, and Rafe Kerr deep in conversation, she slipped from the table to seek out Busby. "See two bedspaces nearest one of the hearths are made ready for Lord Edmund and his son," she instructed the servant. "And send Clennon Kerr and Iver Leslie to me in the library."

"Aye, m'lady. Is there anything else I can do for ye this evening?" Busby inquired solicitously. "I know the race will be run on the morrow."

"Make sure the breakfast served afterwards is hearty," Maggie said with a twinkle in her hazel eyes. "I imagine his lordship will be quite worn-out attempting to win the challenge."

Busby chuckled. "Aye, my lady," he said. "I'll tell Cook to make it a festive meal for ye." Then he asked with the familiarity of a man who had known her since her birth, "Do ye think he can beat ye, my lady?"

"Perhaps," Maggie said slowly. "Dinna say I said it, Busby, but the man has long legs." Then with a grin she hurried off to the library.

Clennon Kerr and Iver Leslie quickly joined her.

"I want a hearth built in the barracks," Maggie told them. The hall isn't large enough to comfortably hold all the men at night, but the barracks are too cold now that winter is about to descend upon us. Before the weather becomes bad, the hearth and its chimney must be built. The hunt is over. The cattle and sheep are in the home meadows. The men have more than enough time on their hands. Have them gather all the materials they will need before they open the wall up. And be certain they cover the opening at night so the weather doesn't get into the barracks."

"Yes, m'lady," Clennon Kerr said. "Is there anything else?"

"Nay, and I'm off for bed. I need my rest before tomorrow's race," Maggie said.

Iver Leslie grinned. "He's fast, m'lady," he told her.

"God's toenail, I hope so," Maggie answered him. "My last suitor ran like a lass." And then she left the two men who were guffawing loudly at her remark. She had told Grizel no bath this evening, but she would surely need one after tomorrow's race. She had sent Grizel to her own bed; Maggie had no need of her, being perfectly able to wash and undress herself.

Tomorrow, she thought as she finally lay abed. Fingal Stewart was the first man she had ever considered having the ability to beat her in fair combat. She had been running the hills about Brae Aisir for so long, she couldn't remember when she had first begun. Her grandsire said she was just past two when she had disappeared over the drawbridge one day, giving them all a terrible fright until she came running back up the path from the village. It was quickly observed that Maggie Kerr could run very fast. By the time she was four, the village lads were running with her, and by the time she was six, it was acknowledged that no one could run as fast as she could run.

Tomorrow, however, her reign as the fastest person in the Borders could easily come to an end. And if it did, then she would have to accept Fingal Stewart as her husband. She had to admit to herself that he had been very patient with her waiting to consummate the marriage. She had put all thoughts of consummation from her mind these past weeks ever since the marriage contracts had been signed, making her legally his wife. She felt a bit guilty about that day, for she had not dressed herself in a beautiful gown for the signing. She had the Aisir nam Breug to show him, and signing the documents that would make them man and wife was but a bit of legal business to be swiftly concluded. She had dressed as she usually did, but then so had he.

And on the morrow they would both be dressed for their combat.

But afterwards, she promised herself, she would dress herself properly for the blessing of their union, and the feast to come. Mad Maggie Kerr might be considered a hoyden by most who knew her, but she did know how to dress like a lady. There was that wonderful burgundy velvet gown trimmed in marten in her wardrobe she might wear, or perhaps the dark green velvet with the gold trim. To her surprise, she fell asleep considering her gowns, but she had awakened before dawn, her head clear. Climbing from her bed, she ran to the window to see what kind of a day it would be. It was gray, but on the horizon a weak sun was just struggling to rise. To her relief there seemed to be no wind as the bare trees stood black in stark relief against the light sky. The water in the moat was liquid, not ice. It hadn't frozen the past night, which meant it was warmer despite the month.

Without waiting for Grizel, Maggie opened the trunk at the foot of her bed and pulled out a pair of breeks. They were soft with age, and she always wore them when she ran. Yanking off her night shift, she dressed herself quickly. First came a cotton chemise that just reached her midthighs. Then came her shirt and breeks with a leather belt to hold them up. She ran a brush through her hair, then tied her rich brown locks back with a scarlet ribbon. "I'm ready!" she said aloud as Grizel entered her bedchamber.

"Yer eager then," her tiring woman said. "Well, so is everyone else. The laird is in the hall with Father David and the Netherdale Kerrs. I passed yer husband on the staircase coming down as I was coming up for ye."

"Then 'tis time," Maggie agreed.

"I'll bring yer boots and stockings for the riding," Grizel said, picking up the items as she spoke. Then she quickly followed her mistress downstairs.

"Good morrow, all," Maggie greeted them, bounding into the hall.

"Good morrow," they greeted her back.

"Are ye ready, Granddaughter?" Dugald Kerr asked her solemnly.

"I am, my lord."

"And ye, Fingal Stewart, are ye ready?"

"I am, my lord."

"Then let us go out to the courtyard where the race will begin and end," the laird said as he led the way. Once outside, he spoke to them both. "This will be a harder challenge. A footrace across the draw-bridge, down the path into the village, through the village, around the kirk at the end of the village, and back the same way. The second part of the challenge is a horse race that follows the same path as the footrace but for one exception. Before ye may recross the drawbridge, ye must ride about the keep once. The final part of the challenge is a combat with claymores to be held here in the courtyard.

"When first blood is drawn, the match is over. If either of you cannot finish any part of the challenge, your opponent is declared the winner. Do ye both understand the rules of this competition?"

"I do, my lord," Fingal Stewart said.

Maggie nodded. Then she looked at Lord Stewart and said in an almost defiant tone, "I run in bare feet, my lord."

Fingal smiled at her. "I don't," he said in a pleasant voice.

"Do ye not think that gives ye an advantage?" she demanded of him.

"Nay, I think 'tis ye who has the advantage, madam, but 'tis a cold morning. I prefer to keep my boots on," he answered. "But I'll be happy to wait to begin this contest between us if ye decide ye will wear yers."

"She's clever," Rafe Kerr said softly to his father.

"How so?" Lord Edmund wanted to know.

"She's used to the track she'll travel in her bare feet. In boots the road would not be familiar. She could stumble, and lose time. But her bare feet know the path very well." Rafe said. He shook his head admiringly. "She's a braw lass, Da."

"Are ye ready then?" the laird asked the two combatants, and when they nodded in the affirmative he said, "Then we begin. On yer marks. Get set. Go!"

Maggie leaped forward. The wood of the drawbridge felt firm and sure beneath her bare soles. Her feet knew the way well, and with each pump of her legs her speed increased. She breathed rhythmically, and knew she would not begin to feel even slightly winded until she was crossing the drawbridge again. Head high she ran, and before long she felt the ribbon holding her hair begin to loosen, and then it flew away. As her long hair blossomed about her, she heard the triumphant cry of the lass who had caught the ribbon. It was an unspoken rule that when Mad Maggie Kerr's ribbon blew off during a race, only a woman might have it. The single street of the village was lined with Kerr clansmen and women watching the lady meet her latest challenge.

She was about to turn her head to see how far behind her he was when a movement by her side caught her eye. Maggie swiveled her head slightly and to her astonishment found herself looking into the face of Fingal Stewart. And she realized he was running as easily as she was. He grinned wickedly at her. As they raced around the kirk at the end of the street, Maggie increased her speed; however, to her surprise, he kept up with her. As they raced back down the village street, she began to feel a burning in her lungs. She was racing, she realized, faster than she had ever raced before.

They were both breathing hard as they struggled up the path to the keep. Maggie forced a final burst of speed as she reached the drawbridge and pounded across it. But Fingal Stewart would not be beaten, meeting her speed with his own. Together they raced into the courtyard, shoulder to shoulder and gasping for air as they did.

"'Tis a tie!" Dugald Kerr shouted. "Well done, Maggie and Fin! Well done!"

But Maggie wasn't listening to her grandsire's praise. In a final sprint, she dashed across the courtyard barefoot, and leaped upon her stallion's back, urging the beast from the keep's enclosure. At first surprised that she would not take a moment to accept the congratulations of those assembled, Fingal Stewart followed her lead, exhorting his stallion to follow and catch up with her.

Maggie flattened herself as she leaned forward on the stallion's neck, goading him onward. No man had ever beaten her in a foot-race. None had ever come close. Yet Fingal Stewart had tied her, and done it fairly. Worse, she suspected he could have even done it in his bare feet, though he chose to wear his boots. Had he worn them to give her the advantage? God's foot! Now she would always wonder, and she could hardly ask him because had he tried to give her the advantage, it would seem a paltry thing to do.

Then her ears caught the sound of hoofbeats as his stallion caught up with hers. The two beasts screamed at one another rearing up, teeth bared, their hooves striking out as their riders sought to get them under control and racing again. It had been madness to pit two ungelded males against one another, but neither Maggie nor Fin was willing to ride another horse.

"I told ye this would happen," he shouted at her as the villagers scattered away from the half-battling stallions.

"Do ye want to admit defeat?" she taunted him as she yanked her horse's head around, and kicked it into a gallop again.

His laughter was her answer. They raced down the village street, around the kirk, and back towards the keep. He kept his animal just a pace behind her to avoid another battle between the two stallions. He fully intended pushing his horse ahead of hers as they reentered the courtyard. They reached the top of the path again, and dashed about the stone keep. Maggie was certain the victory would be hers, and when it was, it wouldn't matter who won the combat by sword. There would be no clear-cut winner, for to win this challenge, one combatant had to win all three contests. Her stallion clambered onto the drawbridge again, his hooves pounding against the wood of the bridge. But to Maggie's surprise, Fingal Stewart's stallion was suddenly once again head to head with hers as they galloped into the yard and came to a screeching halt.

"'Tis a dead heat once more!" the old laird declared delightedly.

The two sweating stallions stood with wild eyes, foam about their mouths, and heaving sides as their riders slid from their backs. They were too tired to renew the fight between them as the stable lads led them away to separate ends of the stables to recover.

"Will ye be battling me with yer claymore in yer bare feet?" Fingal Stewart asked her, grinning.

"Will ye take off yer boots too, or are yer dainty feet still too cold?" Maggie mocked him, returning the grin.

"Put yer socks and boots on, lassie," the laird told his granddaughter. "Ye should have done so before ye mounted that big beast of yers to race."

"It didn't affect my riding," Maggie said, seating herself upon the stone steps into the house. She pulled on the warm knit stockings Grizel handed her, and then her boots. Upon standing she said, "I'm ready now."

Clennon Kerr, the keep's dour captain, handed Maggie her claymore. It was a fine weapon, fifty-five inches in length with a cross handle. It was a plain sword with no fancy or decorative embellishments about it. The captain handed Fingal Stewart an identical weapon. "They're the same blade, my lord," he said.

"So I see," Lord Stewart answered. He had quickly come to trust Clennon Kerr, for Iver liked him, which he would not have had the captain been duplicitous. And an almost imperceptible nod from Iver told him all was well.

A chair, brought from the hall, was set upon the top step leading to the hall. The laird settled himself into the chair, his English kinsmen standing by his side. He would be able to clearly see everything from his position. Below them the keep's men-at-arms formed a circle, and the two combatants stepped into it. They were garbed as they had come from the hall that morning, and wore no mail to protect them.

"Remember," Dugald Kerr said in a stern voice, "this contest between ye both ends when first blood is drawn. Try not to injure each other seriously. It is a battle of skill between ye. Naught else. I will stop it if either of ye displays undue roughness. Ye may now begin."

Their weapons required that they fight with two hands. Grasping the hilts of their claymores, they raised them in a salute to each other, and then metal met metal with a horrific clanging. Fingal Stewart was not surprised by Maggie's skill with her claymore. With any other woman he might have been, but he had found her to be a woman not given to bragging. If she said she was proficient in something, he accepted that she was, and she had said she could wield a claymore as well as any. She could. It took all his skill to keep from being blooded by her.

He didn't know why he cared other than the fact that a man, especially one who would one day control an important ingress into Scotland, should not be vanquished by a woman; yet he was uncomfortable with the reality that to win this contest between them he must blood her. If he could wear her down eventually perhaps she would yield to him without the necessity of it. But Maggie was a stubborn woman. Unless he won all three challenges, Fingal Stewart knew she would not respect him. Of course, the first two contests between them had ended in a tie, so if he had not beaten her, he had at least equaled her, which should gain him a modicum of her respect.

But he knew that this last battle between them must yield a clear winner, and he had to be that winner.

He had spent the past few minutes keeping her at bay. Now he began to fight her in earnest, raising his claymore with two hands, the blade striking hers fiercely as she blocked his attack. The clash of the two blades reverberated through her entire body, and Maggie staggered, surprised. She suddenly found herself on the defensive against him, and she realized he meant to win here unequivocally where he had not won before. She stiffened her spine, and fought hard driving him back, back, back, step by step by step.

"Jesu, she fights like a man," Lord Edmund said, not realizing until his son laughed that he had spoken aloud.

"Still want her for a wife, kinsman?" the laird of Brae Aisir asked mockingly of his Netherdale cousin. "She's more woman than any ye have ever known."

"She's magnificent," Rafe said. "I hope we never meet in battle."

"Yer a wise man, laddie, unlike yer sire," Dugald Kerr told him.

"A lass belongs in the hall directing her servants," Edmund Kerr said, finally speaking. "Not in the yard in breeks fighting with a man. Ye've let her run wild, Dugald. I don't envy her husband. I hope he can successfully bed that wildcat of yours. He'll have to if yer to get a male heir."

"Tonight," the laird told him. "Look closely, Edmund. My Maggie is beginning to tire. Fingal Stewart is a strong opponent. And his patience is coming to an end."

"Aye," Rafe noted softly, "she's tiring. I'm sorry to see it, for she's a brave lass."

She was his wife, damn it! Fingal Stewart thought as he realized that Maggie was not going to give up. And he wanted her, not because a king had matched them to serve his own needs or even because it was his right, but because he was coming to love the stubborn wench. She was everything a man could want in a wife—noble, brave beyond measure, and loyal. She was honest to a fault, firm but kind to her servants, and the villagers would not have been so devoted to her had she not had all of these virtues. And with a modicum of total honesty he had to admit she was a beauty. Aye, Mad Maggie Kerr was everything a wife should be. *His wife.*

There she stood. Her capable hands gripped the hilt of her claymore as she fought him. Her shirt was wet beneath the arms, sticking to her back and breasts. She was gasping for breath, and near to falling on her face with her exhaustion, but she would not give up. The marriage was fact. The contest before the consummation had been to satisfy any discontent among the Kerrs' neighbors that the king's kinsman had had his bride dishonestly. His forbearance at an end, Fingal Stewart raised his claymore even as Maggie raised hers against him. With a mighty blow, he knocked the sword from her hand, over the heads of the men-at-arms encircling them, and across the courtyard.

Maggie fell to her knees, the force of the two weapons meeting having gone right through her. She knelt there in the dust, unable for a moment to arise, for her legs seemed unable to function at all. Everything ached—her shoulders and her arms, her neck, the palms of her hands. Her fingers were suddenly weak. She heard Grizel's cry of distress.

As she raised her head, her eyes suddenly filled with tears. She looked to her grandfather, ashamed to have failed, and Maggie knew she had indeed failed.

"My lord?" Fingal Stewart's calm voice queried. Then he said, "I know the rules ye have set for this contest, but I will not, cannot blood a woman in combat. We have both fought fairly, and the only blood I will take from Maggie Kerr is that which belongs to her maidenhead and is rightfully mine. If there is a winner to this swordplay, then ye must declare such, my lord." Then he bent, reaching out to draw Maggie to her feet, his strong arm going about her waist to hold her against his side. "Yer a braw lass," he said low so that only she could hear him, "but I'm not as young as ye are, and ye've fair worn me out, madam. Give over now, and let there be peace between us, Maggie mine."

Unable to help herself, Maggie nodded, giving him a weak, cheeky grin in reply.

"Enough!" Dugald Kerr responded in a surprisingly loud and strong voice. "I declare this challenge over. Both contestants have won in the footrace and the riding, but 'tis Fingal Stewart who has won the battle of the claymores. I name him the winner, and let none say otherwise." He looked straight at his granddaughter as he spoke. "Margaret Jean Kerr, will ye accept this man, Fingal Stewart, as yer true husband in every way a man is husband to his wife?"

"I will!" Maggie declared loudly so that all heard her. "He has even before this day gained my admiration, but today he has gained my respect. I will be his wife proudly and gladly in every way in which a woman is wife to her husband."

Fingal Stewart turned Maggie so she faced him, bending down to give her mouth a long and hot kiss as cheers erupted about them. He would have carried her off this moment had he not known more was expected of them that day than just a coupling. Jesu! Her mouth was the sweetest he had ever known, and he couldn't stop kissing her.

Her head spun riotously with the kiss. She had known a stolen kiss on her cheek here and there to which she had always responded by smacking the bold lads, yet never but once before had she known a kiss like this one. Their lips locked together seemed to engender a ferocious heat. She slid her arms up about his neck, pressing herself against him with a need she didn't quite understand at all. Was it lust? Was it love?

He felt his cock swelling within his breeks. Jesu! She was going to love as fiercely as she had lived. The thought was intoxicating, and he held her even closer, wanting her to know his need. Pulling her head away from his, Maggie's surprised eyes met his. "I think they all know we have made our peace now, madam," he said to her in a level voice. "If we kiss any more, I fear yer grandsire will have to throw a bucket of cold water over us, Maggie mine."

"I've never known a man, for all that's said of me," she responded softly. "Ye'll be gentle, Fingal, my lord?"

"'Tis December, Maggie mine, and the nights are long," he replied for her ears alone. "I'll be gentle, and we'll love at our leisure, for we have a lifetime ahead of us."

"I'll want to bathe and change my battling clothing for wedding finery before Father David blesses our union," Maggie told him.

"Then I shall do the same," he said as the circle of grinning men surrounding them broke open to allow them to pass through.

They walked up the stairs to where her grandfather still sat. Dugald Kerr was smiling broadly at them both. "Well done, both of ye," the old laird said. "I'm proud that my great-grandchildren will come from such strong stock. Make me a lad first."

"With yer permission, my lord, we will want to bathe and change into more suitable garments before the blessing," Fin said to Dugald Kerr.

The laird nodded. "Go along then," he said as with his consent they turned and left him. Dugald Kerr stood up now. He looked at his English kinsmen. "Go home," he told them. "There is nothing for you here at Brae Aisir."

"I'd prefer to remain until the morrow," Lord Edmund told his kinsman. "Surely ye will want yer relations at the blessing, the feast, and to attest to the honesty of the bride," he said in silky tones.

"Da!" Rafe was not pleased, for he realized his father had not yet given up on his impossible dream of uniting the two families and thereby putting the pass under the control of a single person, namely himself.

Dugald Kerr laughed harshly. "Jesu, Edmund, was being party to the challenge not enough for ye? Very well then, stay. But fair or wet, ye'll go on the morrow if I have to escort ye myself." Then turning, he stamped back into his warm hall.

"Are ye mad?" Rafe asked his parent. "'Tis over and done with, Da. They'll bed tonight, and from the look of them both, Brae Aisir will have an heir in less than a year."

"Aye," his father said. "But a bairn is a fragile creature, Rafe. I've fathered enough of them and buried enough of them to know that."

Rafe Kerr looked hard at his father. "If I thought you would dare such a thing, Da, I'd kill you myself," he said.

Lord Edmund looked at his eldest son in surprise. "We could control the whole Aisir nam Breug. Why would you not want that? Our power in the Borders, both sides, would be enormous. We would collect the tolls going both ways. What do you find repugnant about that, Rafe?"

"Everything," his son replied. "Have you no wisdom about this, Da? We borderers own but scant loyalty to our kings. We rule ourselves on both sides of the border. The traverse has been kept honest and free of strife because the *two* branches of our family have controlled it over the centuries. No king has told us what to do. We decided *together* long ago that the pass would be used only for peaceful travel. We set the tolls *together*. *Together* we built the watchtowers that oversee the route. We have stood *together* against any who would use the Aisir nam Breug for illicit purposes.

"Do we not have enough strife among our families here in the Borders, Da? One family on either side of the march controlling the pass would open it to all manner of evil. A king could interfere and claim the land for his own. They dare not do it with two families in control. Bribery would ensue, and not necessarily with the lord ruling the pass, but among the men guarding it who would look the other way if paid to do so. They would open the Aisir nam Breug to smugglers and raiders. But with the two families ruling the road, it is too difficult for such dishonesty to flourish. It might have been us, Da, whose direct line expired. Would you have wanted old Dugald Kerr to take your responsibilities away from your designated heir?"

"We could be richer than we are if we had the entire traverse," Lord Edmund said.

"I am your heir, Da, and I will not support you in this foolishness," Rafe said. "I like Lord Stewart, from what little I have learned of him in our conversations. When old Dugald dies or decides to give up his responsibility, Fingal Stewart will manage his end of the road well. He's an honorable man."

"You're a fool," his father replied. "How fortunate that I have other sons."

Rafe Kerr laughed. He was the most capable of all Edmund Kerr's sons, legitimate and born on the wrong side of the blanket. When they were all children, his father had made it a point to teach the younger of his siblings unquestioned loyalty and obedience to Rafe, for Rafe—as his father was constantly pointing out to the others—was the heir. And Rafe had enforced their sire's teachings as he had grown. Each of his brothers had his trust and loyalty in return. And if there was one thing of which he was entirely certain, it was that not one of them wanted all the responsibilities that went along with being the heir to Edmund Kerr, and overseeing their part of the Aisir nam Breug. "Give over, Da, and enjoy the day," he said. "The laird's wine cellars will be open wide today." Then putting an arm about his father's shoulders, he walked with him back into the hall.

Around them the servants were dashing about setting the high board. The trestles and the benches were brought from an alcove of the hall where they were stored when not in use. Barrels of October ale were rolled in. Small wheels of hard yellow cheese were placed on each trestle. A linen cloth edged in lace was laid over the high board. A large silver gilt saltcellar in the shape of the sun in its splendor, which was the Kerr family's crest, was set upon it. Silver goblets studded with green agate were placed at the six places being set with round silver plates, spoons, and forks. Each guest had his or her own knife.

"Old Dugald has forks," Lord Edmund noted. "Why don't we have forks in our hall?" he grumbled.

"Aldis suggested them, but you wouldn't pay the cost," Rafe reminded him. "You said the Florentine merchants were smiling thieves in silk clothing."

"Humph," Lord Edmund said. "Tell her she can get them. And I want a dozen. Dugald probably has a dozen. We can't be lacking."

A servant brought them wine, and they joined their host by the fire as they awaited the bride and bridegroom.

Maggie had hurried to her chamber to find her large tub set up, the serving men just bringing in the last buckets of hot water. When they had poured it into the oak tub, Grizel shooed them out. Then she pulled off Maggie's boots and socks. The girl stood, slipped her breeks down over her hips, and, kicking them away from her, unlaced her shirt, drawing it off, and finally her short chemise. Then without a moment's hesitation she stepped up the wood steps and down into the tub. "God's blood!" she swore softly. "I ache in every joint, Grizel. I must soak a moment or two before I wash."

"Ye fought hard," Grizel said proudly. "It was a grand contest and will be spoken of in the Borders for many years to come."

"Few saw it but our own," Maggie reminded her tiring woman.

"They'll repeat it to their kin who were not here today, and they will pass it on to others throughout the Borders," Grizel said.

"God only knows how the tale will end up, for it will be embellished by each person who repeats it," Maggie said, laughing softly.

"He's a fine man, and will give ye strong sons and daughters, mistress," Grizel said. "Is there anything ye would ask of me now that ye face yer wedding night?"

"Nay," Maggie replied, a faint blush touching her cheeks. "I've seen enough lasses and lads in the hay and out on the moors to know just enough to make a beginning of it. And what I don't know I expect that my husband will tutor me in to make up for my deficiencies."

"Aye," Grizel agreed. " 'Tis better that way, for ye'll learn to please him. And ye'll get yer way more often than not pleasing a husband than displeasing him."

"Help me wash my hair," Maggie said, changing the subject. "My scalp is soaked wet with all my efforts this morning."

Grizel brought her mistress a small stone jar filled with scraps of soap that had been melted soft in a bit of water. Taking a small pitcher, she dipped it into the tub and poured the water over her mistress's head. Then Maggie dipped her fingers into the jar, bringing up a handful of the mixture, which she rubbed into her head. The sweet-smelling mixture foamed up quickly as she scrubbed her head. Grizel rinsed the soap away, and the two women repeated the process. When all the soap was finally erased from Maggie's hair, she took her tresses into a hank, wringing it out. Then Grizel pinned the wet hair atop the girl's head so she might continue her bath.

"I can't decide whether to wear the burgundy or the deep green velvet," Maggie said to her companion as she scrubbed herself.

"Neither," Grizel surprised her by replying. "I've been working for weeks on a gown for ye to wear on this day, my lady." She chuckled, well pleased by the look of excitement that bloomed on Maggie's face. "Finish with yer bath," Grizel said, smiling.

"Do ye think my lord has bathed too?" Maggie wondered aloud.

"Aye, he has," Grizel answered her.

"How can ye know?" Maggie inquired.

"Archie is a man who enjoys a bit of chatter," Grizel said, chortling. "He said he was putting sandalwood oil in his master's bathwater today."

"My lord's manservant likes ye," Maggie teased her tiring woman.

"Do ye ache less now?" Grizel asked, avoiding the subject of Lord Stewart's man.

"Aye," Maggie replied, but her hazel eyes were twinkling. "I don't think I have ever in my life fought so hard as I did this day. My husband is very skilled with his claymore. Not once did he give me the opportunity to slip beneath his guard and blood him," she said admiringly.

"Did ye want him to?" Grizel inquired slyly.

Maggie smiled almost to herself. "Nay," she admitted. "I didn't."

"He's a bold man, and an honorable one too," Grizel said, nodding approvingly.

Maggie finally emerged from her tub. The water was cooling, and she was beginning to ache again. She dried herself thoroughly, wrapping the cloth about herself. Then she sat down by her hearth to get warm again while she toweled her hair with another cloth and began brushing it out before the fire.

" 'Tis past noon," Grizel said at last. "Ye must dress, and then go to the kirk for the blessing. The Netherdale Kerrs haven't left. They're staying for the blessing and the feast. Lord Edmund is not happy about yer marriage, but Rafe, yer cousin, seems a good lad. Not at all like his da. Imagine the old fool telling yer grandsire that he wanted to wed ye and bring the two families together," Grizel said indignantly.

"He wants to control all of the Aisir nam Breug," Maggie said. "I seem to be the answer to his desire. I'd nae wed him if he were the last man on earth, and as fair as a May morn," Maggie said. "I've never liked him, even as a child."

Grizel took the hairbrush from her mistress, and running it through the girl's hair said, "Yer dry now. Let's get ye dressed, my lady."

Maggie could see her undergarments laid out upon her bed, but there was no sign of a gown. Grizel handed her mistress a pair of soft woolen stockings that were pale in color and came just below her knee. She drew them on, affixing them with a plain ribbon garter. Standing, she next put on a chemise. It had long sleeves trimmed with gold lace, and a low square neckline also edged in gold lace that would match her gown's neckline. Next Grizel added two silk petticoats that tied in the back with ribbon.

The tiring woman went to the wardrobe and drew out the bodice, which already had its sleeves affixed, and the skirt that made up the gown that Maggie would wear. The lower half of the gown was a funnel skirt of orange tawny velvet brocade edged in brown fur. The matching velvet bodice had a square neckline edged in gold embroidery, and the sleeves had deep turned-back cuffs of rich brown marten, the gold lace from her chemise sleeves just barely visible. "Well?" Grizel said, smiling.

"It's beautiful!" Maggie exclaimed. "It's perfect!" She threw her arms about the older woman. "Thank you, Grizel! Thank you!"

"I want the king's kinsman to see what a fine lady ye are," Grizel said. "I want him to know yer the kind of wife he can take to court one day when the king takes a wife. I want him to be proud of ye as all here at Brae Aisir are proud of ye." She wiped a tear or two from her warm brown eyes.

Maggie was close to tears herself after Grizel's declaration. "Help me finish dressing," she said, a catch in her voice. What on earth was the matter with her today? She supposed it was the shock of actually losing the contest. Before this day no one seeking her hand who had dared to take up the challenge had ever gotten past the footrace, although she had raced her stallion just to make a point with Ewan Hay. The contracts had been signed weeks ago. She was already wed to Fingal Stewart. But now he had gained her respect. He had proved himself worthy to be her husband this day, to inherit control of the Aisir nam Breug eventually, to sire bairns upon her.

She stood silently as Grizel fastened the skirt of her gown. It fell in graceful folds over her petticoats. She slid her arms into the bodice, waiting while Grizel carefully laced it up the back with gold ribbon. She sat carefully, letting her tiring woman brush out her long rich chestnut brown hair. It would be worn loose, attesting to her virginity. A gold ribbon embroidered with tiny glittering bits of gold quartz was fastened about her forehead to hold her tresses in place. Maggie stood and took the soft leather gloves Grizel handed her. They would be riding to the kirk. Her servant slipped a fur cape about her shoulders.

"Yer ready," Grizel said.

Maggie descended into the great hall where the men of her family awaited her. Her grandfather was dressed in a long, dark brown velvet coat with full-puffed sleeves, and a large fur collar. She smiled at him, but then her gaze went to her husband, and her eyes widened with both approval and surprise. If as Grizel had said, she was fine enough to appear at the king's court, then so was Lord Fingal Stewart.

Chapter 6

~

She had always thought him passing fair for a man, but looking at him now, she realized how handsome he truly was. At five feet ten inches, she was considered extremely tall for a woman, but he topped her by at least half a foot. His thick wavy black hair was cropped short. His gray eyes looked out at her from beneath thick bushy black eyebrows. He had a long face with an aquiline nose, and while his mouth was big and thin, when he smiled it changed the severity of his countenance. He smiled at her now, and Maggie smiled back.

"Ye are beautiful, madam," he gallantly told her, taking her hand up and kissing it.

"As are ye, my lord," she said, admiring his deep green velvet doublet with its bit of gold embroidery, padded sleeves, and fur cuffs. He had matching slashed breeches, silk stockings that showed his shapely calves, and embroidered shoes.

"Archie seems to have some magic that grants him proper garments for me when the occasion demands it," Fingal Stewart answered. He had fully expected to wear the black and brown canions he wore to court. He tucked her hand into his arm.

"Can we get to the kirk for the blessing?" the old laird asked impatiently.

"I could do it here, Brother," Father David Kerr said.

"Nay! I want the blessing pronounced in the kirk," Dugald Kerr replied. "The kirk is full of Kerrs now waiting for this."

"We should not keep them waiting another minute then, my lord," Fingal Stewart said. Then he turned to Maggie and said mischievously, "Do ye want to race?"

She laughed loudly. "Nay, my lord. We shall proceed through the village upon our mounts at a docile pace as is suitable for this day."

In the courtyard a fine chestnut gelding and a cream-colored mare with a dark mane and tail stood waiting patiently. Lord Stewart lifted Maggie onto the mare, waiting while she pulled on her riding gloves and adjusted her skirts; she did not ride astride this day. Then he swung himself up on the gelding next to the laird and the priest, who were already mounted. Slowly they descended the hill path and into the village. The street was lined with villagers who then fell in behind the riders escorting them.

The priest hurried into the church building with the villagers behind him eager to find places among the keep's servants where they too might watch the ceremony. Lord Stewart lifted Maggie from her saddle. When her feet had touched the ground, she found herself flanked by her grandfather on one side of her and Fingal Stewart on the other. Together the two men escorted her into the kirk and up the aisle where Father David Kerr stood awaiting them. Without a single word, Dugald Kerr, laird of Brae Aisir, placed his granddaughter's hand into the hand of Lord Fingal Stewart. Then he stepped back and aside to watch the proceedings as Edmund Kerr glared, angry to have been foiled.

"Kneel," the priest said. When they had, he pronounced the church's blessing upon the union of Margaret Jean Kerr of Brae Aisir and Lord Fingal David Stewart of Torra. A hand rested upon the head of the bride and of the groom as he spoke. Then Mass was celebrated for all within the small kirk. When it concluded, David Kerr announced, "Fingal Stewart and Maggie Kerr are now man and wife in the eyes of the church as well as the laws of Scotland."

"Huzzah! Huzzah! Huzzah!" those within the church shouted with one voice.

"Long life and many bairns to our Maggie and her man!"

They arose from the velvet-cushioned kneelers. Fin swept Maggie into his arms and kissed her quite thoroughly to the delight of the clansmen and women. Then they hurried from the church together, the old laird coming behind them, accepting the congratulations of his folk. Rosy with blushes, Maggie was already seated upon her mare.

Fin aided Dugald Kerr to clamber upon his horse, then mounted his own animal, and they returned to the keep, the Netherdale Kerrs and the village coming behind them.

In the courtyard Maggie and Fin greeted each Kerr, giving them a small but useful gift; honing stones for the men, a small basket of colored threads for the women, and a sugar plum for each child. There were ale and sweet cakes for everyone. A health was drunk to the bride, the groom, and the laird. Then the clan folk departed back to their own cottages, allowing the wedding party to reenter the hall where the celebratory feast would now be enjoyed by the family and its retainers.

It was midafternoon now. The day had cleared. As the sun set and the fires blazed in the hall hearths, the food was brought forth to the high board. Fresh trout and salmon were served on platters of peppery wild cress. This was followed by a roasted goose, a leg of lamb, a ham, and a rabbit stew with tiny onions and sliced carrots in a rich brown gravy flavored with red wine. There was a bowl of late peas from the kitchen garden, and some lettuces braised in white wine along with fresh bread served with both butter and two cheeses. The cups, studded with green agate, were filled with dark red wine that tasted sweet to Maggie's tongue.

Below the high board the men-at-arms and the family's retainers enjoyed trout, ham, rabbit stew, bread, and cheese, while their cups were never empty of the laird's good ale. There was much camaraderie and laughter between the trestles, for the men of Brae Aisir and Lord Stewart's men were now one and the same.

Lord Edmund glowered out over the small assembly. He had lost his chance to gain the whole of the Aisir nam Breug today. But there was always tomorrow. Maggie could prove infertile. She might die in childbed or birth only daughters. Discord could be sewn among the Kerr clan folk when old Dugald died. Did the Kerrs really want a Stewart overlord and master? Despite his son's warning, Edmund Kerr wasn't ready to yet concede his loss. His fist tightened about the stem of his goblet, and his lips narrowed.

"We're leaving immediately on the morrow," Rafe Kerr said quietly to his sire. "The head groom in the stable says there's a storm coming in another day or two. I'd just as soon be home in Netherdale Hall when it does."

"Aye," his father agreed. "No need for us to remain here any longer. My cousin will be glad to see the back of me, I'm certain."

Rafe laughed. "Aye, Da, he will, 'tis truth. Old Dugald doesn't like you at all. He told me he holds you responsible for not telling him that Glynis was frail."

"I had hoped my half sister would produce an heir for Brae Aisir whom I would one day influence and match with one of my daughters," Edmund Kerr said.

"So you've meant to have it all along, Da, have you?" Rafe was surprised, but then once his father got an idea he liked stuck in his head, it was difficult, if not impossible, to move him in another direction. He was his father's heir, and he certainly did not want the entire responsibility of the Aisir nam Breug to fall upon him. Their eight miles were enough for him. His father hadn't managed his responsibility in years. It was Rafe who had overseen their part of the pass since he was sixteen. He was now past thirty. Some years were more difficult than others depending on whether England and Scotland were quarreling. And if they were, keeping the Aisir nam Breug safe was harder.

But from the looks of Lord Stewart, his cousin's bridegroom was a strong man and would sire strong sons on Maggie. She was nothing like her mother had been. Glynis Kerr had been beautiful, but a wise man would have seen she was frail. Sadly, Dugald Kerr's son was not wise, and Rafe was frankly amazed she had lived to birth three bairns despite the fact the only one surviving was a lass. Dugald Kerr had blamed Edmund Kerr for not pointing out that Glynis was delicate, and for the sake of them all discouraging the match between his half sister and the laird's son. But Dugald had had three sons then, and several other grandchildren. Who could have anticipated all that had happened, and that a lass would end up the last of the Kerrs of Brae Aisir?

"Ye hae a serious look about ye, lad," the laird said. "'Tis a happy occasion we celebrate today. Do ye have a wife?"

"Aye, sir, I do. And two little lads and two little lasses," Rafe said with a smile.

"Then the succession of yer family is assured," the laird remarked. "I hope by this time next year the succession of ours is as well."

"The bairn won't be a Kerr," Edmund said meanly.

"What matter?" Dugald snapped back. "The bairn will have *my* blood. No family's male line goes on forever, ye sour fool! Yers will end one day too. The name of Stewart is a proud and noble one. Can I complain that one of that royal line will take my place eventually,

Edmund? I know that Fin will keep our portion of the pass safe, and so will his sons and sons' sons. And yer Rafe is a reasonable man. He will work well with my granddaughter heiress's husband. Kerr and Stewart together keeping the Aisir nam Breug as it has always been. A safe traverse for honest travelers. Now shut yer mouth, and cease yer carping, for what's done is done, and what is, is."

Rafe hid his smile. He knew of no other who would dare to speak with his father in such a manner.

The laird's piper now came into the hall and began to play. Maggie and Fin danced a country wedding dance in the space between the high board and the trestle tables. It was a simple stately dance that had been executed for centuries in Scottish halls throughout the land. Fin's arm about Maggie, they moved slowly and sensuously to the deep rhythm the piper, a drummer, and a clansman playing upon a flute performed.

Her head back against his shoulder, she looked up into his handsome face and recognized the look of longing upon it. Maggie's heart beat a little faster. Her velvet skirts swirled about them as they danced. He lifted her up and swung her about. His eyes never left her face, and she found she was unable to turn away from him though her cheeks grew pink. And then as the dance slowly came to an end, Fin bent to brush her lips with his. Maggie sighed audibly, then blushed with the realization of it. He smiled down into her face and led her back to the high board. To her surprise, she found herself breathless.

Then Clennon Kerr and Iver Leslie arose to dance amid two crossed swords in the same expanse. In their stocking feet they stepped agilely and gracefully between the sharp blades as the music grew more and more spritely. The efforts of the dancers were much appreciated by the onlookers. As the two men finished, those at the trestles arose, clapping and shouting their approval. Another round of ale was suggested. When the kegs ran dry, the evening would end for the guests.

Grizel arose from her place at a trestle and slipped up to the high board to whisper in her mistress's ear. Maggie nodded. She leaned over, saying to her grandfather, "I shall depart the hall now, Grandsire." He nodded silently. Maggie reached out to touch the arm of her cousin Rafe. "I know you will leave even before dawn," she said to him. "Thank you for coming. I wish you a safe passage home, Rafe Kerr."

"And I wish you and Fin happiness and many sons, Cousin," he replied. "I'll tell Da you bid him farewell. As you can see, he is in his cups now." His head nodded to Lord Edmund, who had fallen asleep still clutching his goblet, which was now empty.

Maggie couldn't help but smile. "His head will hurt the whole way home," she said. "I doubt he'll come again soon to Brae Aisir."

Rafe chuckled wickedly as she arose and hurried from the hall to the cheers of the men-at-arms who watched her go. Rafe spoke now to Fingal Stewart. "It's unlikely I'll see you on the morrow, my lord, so I will bid you farewell tonight. For the sake of the Aisir nam Breug, put no trust in my father. He's a devious man, and he would control the entire traverse. He will use any means to gain his way, I fear. If it seems disloyal to you that I speak thusly, know that my concern is for the Aisir nam Breug and our family's safety. The two families working together to maintain and protect the pass over the centuries has kept it safe and free of political influence. But we need both families in this endeavor. I am not disloyal, and will attempt to keep my father's meddling to a minimum, but he is still Lord of Netherdale, and I can only do so much. So beware of him, and his schemes," Rafe Kerr concluded.

"I understand," Lord Stewart replied, and he held out his hand to Rafe, who took and shook it. "Thank ye."

"I wish you happiness, and strong sons," Rafe replied. "And while I see a gleam of eagerness in your eye, you must wait a while longer. Brides need time to prepare themselves for the first coming of their husband. A bit more wine may be in order."

The two men grinned companionably at each other.

Upstairs, however, Maggie had been divested of her wedding finery, and she now sat quietly as Grizel brushed her mistress's long chestnut hair. "Ye were a beautiful bride," Grizel said fondly.

"I ache in every joint," Maggie complained. "My shoulders and arms are so painful, and yet I have fought with my claymore before."

"Not as hard as ye did this day," Grizel responded. "Ye were fierce, lass."

"But he overcame me," Maggie said as she sat while her tiring woman slicked the brush through her thick hair. "I've never been overcome before. Am I really a good swordswoman, or have my opponents been allowing me to win to humor me?"

"Nay, nay," Grizel responded. "No one at Brae Aisir has been yer equal until today, my bairn. But did ye really want to be victorious over him? He did not crow with his triumph, for he has too much respect for ye."

"But he won," Maggie said again.

"Aye, he did. He was tired of the contest, and did not wish to blood ye. He simply knocked the claymore from yer grasp, lass, but I could not say that he overcame ye." She gave her young mistress a mischievous grin.

"Nay, he didn't, did he?" Maggie suddenly felt better about the day's events. She grinned back at Grizel and chuckled.

"But dinna torment him about it, lass," Grizel advised the younger woman. "Sometimes 'tis better to allow a man to think he has the upper hand. And this is yer wedding night. Certainly ye dinna want to quarrel with yer lord." She had finished brushing Maggie's long tresses. Putting the hairbrush aside, she said, "Time to get into yer bed now. I'll be returning to the hall to tell him yer waiting." She helped the girl into bed, plumping the pillows up behind her. Then Grizel bent and kissed Maggie's cheek. "May ye have many healthy sons, my bairn," she said, and turning, she hurried from the bedchamber, closing the door firmly behind her.

Maggie sat almost frozen, her heart beating faster, it seemed, than it usually did. She was very aware of the ache in her shoulders, neck, and arms. More than anything else she wanted a good night's sleep. She wouldn't get it, of course. *He* would come, and they had one more duty to perform this night for the good of Brae Aisir. Her grandfather would want the bloodied sheet proving her virtue to fly from the roof come the morrow.

It was going to hurt. That much she knew for she had heard enough of the servant lasses complain of their first time with a man. But what was it *really* like to be with a man? Was there pleasure after the pain? She didn't know enough about what was to transpire between her *husband*—God's toenail, that word sounded so strange in her mouth and to her ears—and herself. She knew he would cover her body with his and that his cock would find an entry into her body. What more to it was there? Well, she supposed it was as much as many lasses knew, but bloody hell she wished she could avoid it all tonight and just sleep her aching muscles away. He had been a fierce opponent today, and he had given her no quarter at all other than avoiding wounding her.

Grizel reached the hall, and going to the high board murmured in Lord Stewart's ear, "Yer bride awaits ye, my lord." Then she returned to her place at the trestles.

Fin nodded, and leaning over so Dugald Kerr and Rafe Kerr might hear him said, "Good night, my lord, Rafe." Then he arose, and stepping down, made his way from the hall. About him the men-at-arms chuckled softly, and nodded to one another, smiling. Each man had the single thought in his head. Brae Aisir would now be safe. Fingal Stewart would do his duty tonight, and Mad Maggie would birth a future generation for them. They had waited a long time for this moment to come.

He sprinted up the stairs, then stopped suddenly. Where would she be? In his chamber? In hers? Then he heard Archie's voice.

"I'll help ye undress, my lord. Grizel says yer wife awaits ye in her chamber."

Fin breathed a sigh of relief. What a fool he would have looked going from door to door seeking Maggie. He stepped into his own chamber, and with Archie's aid stripped off his wedding finery. "Should I ask where these garments came from?" he said dryly as he pulled off his doublet.

"Honestly come by, my lord, I swear it," his serving man assured his master. He handed him a rag with which to wash. Lord Stewart had bathed fully after the challenge.

Fin washed himself and scrubbed his teeth with the rag. He debated whether to wear the white cotton nightshirt. Probably best he wear it into her bedchamber tonight as she was hardly used to the naked male form. He didn't want her shrieking with fright, and he would have to go through the narrow corridor both coming and going. He turned to go to the door, but Archie's hand stopped him.

"Nay, my lord, this way," the serving man said, and he opened a small curved top door in the wall that Fin had not noticed before, so well was it hidden in the paneling. "Press the carved rose on the other side when you wish to return to your own chamber," Archie murmured in a low voice.

Lord Stewart stepped through into another bedchamber. He turned to carefully close the door behind him, seeking and finding the rose first. The room was dim but for a fire in the hearth, and a taperstick on a small table next to the bed where Maggie now sat up in her bed, straight as a poker, the look on her face a combination of nerves and fear.

Maggie had stiffened as the wee door had swung open and her husband stepped through into the chamber. When he turned to come towards the bed, she swallowed hard.

Fin sat down on the edge of the bed. "Well, madam," he said, "here we are at last as God, the king, and the laws of Scotland would have us."

"I am ready to do my duty," Maggie said primly.

Fin laughed. "Oh, Maggie mine," he replied, "it may be a duty we do for Brae Aisir, but I want it to be a pleasurable duty for us both."

"How many women have you loved?" she asked, surprising him.

"I have loved none, but I have *made love* to enough to know what is pleasing to lovers," he said. "There are men who believe a woman's body is for their pleasure alone. They take what they want from women and care nothing but for their own enjoyment. I have learned that a man's greatest pleasure comes from giving his woman pleasure too. You are a virgin, of course. Tell me what you know of lovemaking so I may correct the misconceptions first, and then add to your knowledge."

"Could we not just do what needs doing, my lord?" she asked nervously. "I ache in every joint from today's challenge, and want nothing more than sleep." Her cheeks were pink at having said the blunt words just spoken.

Fingal Stewart laughed aloud. "Oh, Maggie mine," he said, "never have I known a woman of such candor as ye are. But what we do this night is more than just a duty." Reaching out, he took her hand in his. It was cold, but her slender fingers curled about his. That was good, he thought. "You aren't afraid of me, are you?" he asked her.

"Nay," she responded. "I know ye now and believe ye to be a good man."

"Are ye afraid of the coupling?" he queried.

"Nay!" Maggie quickly said. Then blushing, she admitted, "Mayhap a little, but only because I am not certain what is expected of me." She sighed. "I do not like being so wretchedly ignorant, my lord."

"Ye must trust me, Maggie mine," he said, "and I have learned these past months that your trust is not easily or quickly given."

"To not be in control of my life is difficult, my lord. I know these are words a man does not often hear from the lips of a woman, but I trust you enough to utter them to you without fear of a beating."

"I will never beat you, my lady wife. A man who beats a woman is admitting his own defeat, and I have never admitted defeat in all my life. Now we both know what needs doing this night, and we shall do it. Then we shall sleep, for I tell you truly that my body aches even more than yers. Ye were not an easy opponent to overcome, Maggie mine." He smiled warmly at her as he spoke.

The words came out before she might stop them. "Ye dinna beat me, my lord."

"I disarmed ye, lass," he replied with a grin, appreciating the fine line of distinction she had drawn and not in the least offended. "And then yer grandsire declared me the victor. Do ye really want to disagree with the old man?"

"And break his heart?" she replied. "Nay, I do not. But ye did not really beat me, my lord. My silence allowed ye the victory, but I am not unhappy with the outcome."

"I am very relieved to hear it, lass," he told her softly. Then he brushed the back of her hand with his lips, slowly kissing each finger upon it. He turned the hand over and placed a deep kiss upon her palm as he looked into her lovely face.

Maggie's hazel eyes grew wide with surprise as she felt a ripple of excitement race through her. She had never known the palm of one's hand could be so sensitive.

"Take off yer night garment," Fin's voice instructed quietly, his eyes meeting hers.

"Will ye take off yers?" she countered, her heart beginning to thump in her ears.

In response, he loosed her hand and pulled his night garb off, tossing it carelessly to the floor. "Turnabout is fair play, madam," he told her.

Unwilling to play the shrinking virgin, Maggie yanked her gown over her head and tossed it bravely onto the floor next to his, but she grasped the coverlet up with one hand to cover her naked breasts, not daring to look at him now.

Then to her surprise Fin stood up. "Look at me," he said to her. "Look and see how a man is fashioned. If you have questions, I will answer them."

This certainly had to be the oddest wedding night any couple had ever had, Maggie considered. Then, raising her gaze, she looked at the naked man before her. He was surely the most magnificent male creature ever created, she decided, despite her lack of sources for comparison. Oh, she had seen men in the fields naked from the waist up. She had seen others, their lower torsos wrapped in linens as they labored on the few hot days of summer. She had even seen glimpses of male buttocks as they eagerly used a lass in the hay or the hedges. But never had she seen a fully naked man, or one of such perfection.

He was wonderfully tall, and his limbs were in perfect proportion to his trunk. His arms, his chest, and his back were muscled, but not overly so. His calves were exceedingly shapely, his thighs strong. He was not a hairy man like some she had seen. There was the lightest covering of down on his legs and arms. His broad chest, however, was smooth. His buttocks were firm, and she was certain she saw a dimple where his spine split the flesh into twin moons. His feet were large, suiting his size. A thick thatch of black curls sprang forth from his mons. His manhood hung long and relaxed amid it. It didn't look at all particularly dangerous, Maggie thought. In fact it seemed rather indifferent. What if her body didn't excite it? After all, he had said he was marrying her because the king had told him to wed her. It had hardly been a flattering commentary.

Fin had turned himself slowly so she might observe him at her leisure in his entirety. Now he held out his hand to her. "Come, madam," he said. "Ye've now seen me. I would see ye." He gently peeled the coverlet from her hand and drew her forth from the bed onto her feet to stand where he might view her as freely and as frankly as she had viewed him. She was statuesque for a woman, taller than many men, but he still towered over her. She was beautifully formed with shapely arms and legs, a light ripple of muscle across her smooth shoulders that eased into a long back. Her buttocks were surprisingly round and plump. He wanted to kneel then and there to nip at them, but he didn't. Her breasts were round but not overly large. The nipples upon them could be called dainty. Her slim torso boasted a narrow waist that flowed into well-proportioned hips and trim, but firm, thighs. Her mons was covered in chestnut-colored curls, the hue of which matched her long hair. Unlike some women, she did not pluck her curls. His eyes fell at last to her feet, which were slender and long in keeping with her height.

"Yer a beautiful lass," Fin finally said.

Maggie colored. She had hardly breathed as his gray eyes had slowly explored her female form. But now unable to help herself, she sneezed.

"Into bed with ye, lass," he said, quickly pushing her toward the furniture in question and as swiftly climbing in next to her.

It had been done so quickly, Maggie didn't have time to consider it, but suddenly she was lying side by side with this man who was her husband. He put his arms about her, and she gave a little cry of surprise. *"Oh!"* He was wrapped about her, and the sensation of his flesh touching her flesh was amazing to her.

"Yer chilled," he said with understatement. " 'Twas selfish of me to keep ye from our warm bed, feasting myself on yer fair form, Maggie mine," he apologized.

"Yer my husband, and ye may do as ye please with me," Maggie said.

"Nay," he replied, surprising her. "It was thoughtless, lass, but yer so beautiful."

"So are ye," she murmured back. She was beginning to feel warm again.

Fin chuckled. "I dinna think I've ever been called beautiful, but I thank ye."

His arms tightened about her, and he kissed the top of her head. Maggie winced.

"What is it?" His voice was filled with concern.

"If ye might not hold me so tightly, my lord," she said to him. "My neck and shoulders really do ache. I don't ever recall being so sore."

He loosened his grip upon her. " 'Tis difficult not to hold ye tightly, lass," he admitted to her. "It seems as if I've waited forever to hold ye."

"Ye but came to Brae Aisir less than four months ago, my lord," she said.

"But I knew then ye were to be my wife, and when I saw ye, how could I not want to hold ye in my arms?" Fin felt her firm young body cradled against him, and a frisson of desire raced down his spine. He knew what was expected of them that night, and she knew too, but he didn't want this first experience with him to be unpleasant. And he realized that until Maggie was with child, he would be expected to be with her each and every night but for a few. He wanted to prepare her for what was to come, and he wanted her content when it was over. Whether her passions could be fully engaged by him he didn't know, but their couplings should be enjoyable, and she should not dread them.

Could they love each other? Did such a thing as love even exist? Was it possible for them to find it together? Fingal Stewart really had no answers to his own questions. But he did know if they liked and respected each other, if they could enjoy the coupling of their bodies and produce bairns for Brae Aisir, the marriage would be a good one. It was the best he could hope for now. The time for talk had ended.

"My lord," she began, but he stopped her mouth with a quick kiss.

"Enough, lass. Let me lead ye, Maggie mine. And while it pleases me to hear ye call me *my lord* in public, in private I would prefer ye spoke my name." His lips met hers once again in a deep passionate kiss.

Maggie almost swooned with the sweet pressure of his mouth on hers. She didn't know if she would ever love him. Was love even real? But a man who kissed her as he was now kissing her certainly could be liked. She kissed him back, feeling his big palm cupping her head as his lips worked against hers. She felt a need to open her own lips to him, and his tongue slid between them to touch, to caress her tongue. Maggie shivered, for she had never imagined such a thing. It was exciting, thrilling, and without her even being aware of it at first, her tongue caressed his back.

When she realized what she was doing, Maggie wasn't certain she should be shocked by her own behavior, but Fin certainly didn't seem to mind. Indeed, he seemed to encourage her actions. Her heart jumped in her chest when his other hand fastened itself about one of her buttocks to bring their bodies into seriously close proximity. The warm hand on her bottom made her briefly faint with excitement. The sensation of their bodies, breast to chest, belly to belly, thigh to thigh, caused her to pull her head away from his delicious kisses, gasping with pleasurable shock. "*Oh my!*" she whispered. The feel of his skin against hers, the scent of him in her nostrils, was utterly and amazingly intoxicating. "I don't know what to do," she said, softly surprised by the sound of her own voice, and that she was able to speak at all.

"Nay, Maggie mine, remember that I will lead ye tonight," Fin said as he now laid her back among the pillows. He sighed audibly. "Ye have the most delicious mouth, love. I could kiss ye all night long but that we have other business to attend to first." His fingers brushed against one of her breasts. Then bending, he ran his tongue slowly between the two round globes. "These are two sweet fruits to be treasured," he told her.

His fingers brushed a breast, slipping beneath it to cup it in his hand.

No one had ever touched her breasts. For that matter, no man had ever touched her body at all. Maggie wasn't a simpleton. She knew he was beginning to make love to her, but the reality compared to the servant lasses' gossip was totally different. She hadn't known her heart would beat so quickly, or that ripples of ice would race down her spine followed by a fiery heat that made her want to cry out. Everything he was doing to her was unfamiliar, but it was wonderful. She heard herself saying to him, "I know ye must lead me, my lord, but instinct makes me want to do something other than lie like a log."

"Let yer instinct be yer guide, lass," he told her. Then his dark head dipped to take one of her nipples into his mouth.

"*Sweet Jesu!*" Maggie cried softly. Her fingers dug into his shoulders as she felt the tug of his lips on her breast because at the same time she had felt a tug in her nether regions. How was this even possible? But as he suckled on her, the sensation didn't go away. Indeed, it increased her rising excitement. She sighed, her delight obvious to him.

He released the nipple and began to press kisses down her torso. He could feel her body quivering beneath his mouth, but she had shown him no fear to his actions so far. She would naturally have a virgin's anxious moments, but so far she was taking to his mouth and hands easily. He ceased his kissing and lay back. She needed to see the havoc she was causing to his body.

"Dinna stop," she said softly. "I like what yer doing."

"I like it too," he replied, "but ye have wanted to participate in our first passion, so I shall instruct ye in what to do, Maggie mine. Sit up and touch my cock. I know ye have not touched one before. This one will pierce yer maidenhead soon, and afterwards it will find its home in yer sweet sheath. It will water yer hidden garden and give ye my seed. Touch it, and know it, love. It is more fearful of the advantage ye will soon hold over it than ye can be of its small power in releasing yer virginity."

She sat up, amazed to see the formerly lean and lank flesh was swollen hard. Reaching out, she wrapped her hand about it, surprised to see that her fingers did not quite meet. Its former length was even longer now. 'Twas a most impressive weapon indeed.

Releasing it, she let her fingers stroke it briefly, then reached beneath to cup his pouch in her warm palm. "Yer balls are cold to my touch," she said to him. "Should they not be heated with yer lust as yer cock is, my lord?"

"Ye must call me Fin, Maggie mine. I know not why a man's balls are chill, but they always are. 'Tis a mystery." He was close to flinging himself atop her, for the hand now playing with him had set his blood aboil.

She nodded as her fingers teased innocently at him. "Yer cock is quite upstanding now, my . . . Fin." She gave it a little squeeze that almost destroyed him.

"Aye, it is. I think we must now consider the removal of yer maidenhead," he replied in what sounded like a calm voice. He gently pushed her back as she released her hold on his manhood. Then he began kissing her again as his hand stroked her torso, moving slowly lower and lower until he reached the nest of chestnut curls. He crushed her mons gently but firmly several times as she gasped with surprise into his mouth. A single finger ran along the slip separating her nether lips, pressing through them to find her little love bud. Fin was pleased to find she was already moist with her rising desire.

He had not been wrong. She was going to be a passionate woman.

Maggie lay as still as a doe in the brush waiting for what was going to come next.

When his finger touched a hitherto unknown place between her nether lips and began to worry it, gently at first, and then with more urgency, she cried out in surprise. He silenced her with more kisses as the tip of that terrible finger played harder. Her head spun, and when a burst of utter pleasure overcame her, she pulled from him, crying out again. "*Sweet Jesu!* No more, I beg ye. 'Tis too delicious."

He did not answer her, instead stroking her flesh into ease, and then moving lower.

Maggie was tightly shut to him. His finger tenderly coaxed the flesh barely enough to begin the gentle pressure that would open her first to his finger, and then to his manhood.

Fin felt her body begin to resist him. "Nah, nah, sweetheart, ye need to be readied for what is to come," he murmured to her.

God's toenail! Why didn't he just mount her and be done with it? Maggie wondered to herself. It had to be better than all this anticipation he was causing to build up within her. She tried to be at ease, and felt the tip of his finger slip into her. "*Oh!*"

Again he said nothing. Instead, he pushed his finger to the second joint.

"*Oh!*"

And finally Fin sheathed the digit in its entirety. He let it remain there so she might get used to the pressure of it. Then he began a slow rhythm with the finger, moving it back and forth. He was painfully aware as he did so of the ache in his own cock.

"*Ohh!*" Maggie half whispered. Then she felt herself relaxing and enjoying his sensuous actions. She wanted more. To her great surprise, she realized a primitive instinct made her want that big cock of his pushing inside her. Was she wanton? Or was it natural for a wife to desire her husband so greatly? "Fuck me," she whispered. "Not just with your finger, Fin. I am ready to take you within me. *Please!*"

The invitation was more than welcome. It was a relief, for his cock was throbbing mightily. Now he needed to take her without spilling his seed too quickly. Nudging her thighs apart with a knee, he covered her body with his. Slowly he guided his aching need into her. First its head, then inch by slow inch until he reached the barrier of her innocence. It was tight, and she winced visibly as his manhood touched it. There was only one way of doing this, Fin knew. Looking into her face, he saw her eyes were squeezed tightly shut. He almost smiled with the sweetness of it. "I'm sorry, lass," he told her, pulling back slightly, then driving himself fully into her sheath.

The shock of it, the burning pain that filled her, caused Maggie to scream. She began to beat at him, her fists thrashing beneath him in an attempt to dislodge him.

And when she couldn't, Maggie, to her embarrassment, began to cry.

Fin kissed the tears from her cheeks, murmuring soothing sounds.

"'Tis done now and 'twill not hurt ever again, Maggie mine," he assured her. Did no one tell her it would hurt? Her maidenhead had been lodged tightly. He continued kissing her tears, which, to his relief, had now ceased. He kept himself very still for a few brief moments.

"I knew it would hurt," she whispered, "but not like it did. Are we done?" She did not open her eyes to look at him.

Fin laughed softly, brushing her lips with his. "Nay, love, we've but begun." Then he began to move gently upon her, struggling to hold back the explosion of passion that was threatening to overcome him.

The pain had disappeared almost as quickly as it had come. Now the sensation of his cock thick and hot within her engulfed Maggie. Her whole body seemed to be deluged with sensation as he thrust to and fro. She was overwhelmed with languor. Her body, so tense but a few short moments ago, was alive with a plethora of new sensations.

She could divine that he was being careful, gentle with her. Would another man have been so? She couldn't imagine Ewan Hay taking such care with her.

Maggie suddenly wrapped her arms about Fin, drawing him closer to her. His rhythm began to increase. His strength made her absolutely breathless with what she suddenly realized was her own excitement. "*Yes!*" she breathed into his ear.

Fin groaned as her hot breath whispered against his flesh. He wanted her to know some pleasure from this first coupling, but it was becoming more and more difficult to hold back the lust boiling inside him. Then he heard her make a small mewling sound, and looking at her face, he saw the touch of ecstasy glowing. "Aah, Maggie mine," he cried out as his body stiffened, then jerked hard several times.

Somewhere in the delicious haze that had briefly overcome her Maggie felt his cock spasming, and she knew he was releasing his seed into her. Would it take root tonight, or would they have more nights to create an heir for Brae Aisir? She hoped the latter as he fell away from her, lying upon his back and breathing hard.

"I meant for ye to have more pleasure," he said, his tone filled with regret. "I wanted yer first time in my arms to be something ye would remember, but God's toenail, lass, I was like a lad unable to control my lust for ye."

"But I liked it, Fin," Maggie told him. "Except, of course, for the pain. Ye made me feel as I never had before. I know I will enjoy our future couplings."

He laughed low, rolling onto his side to look at her. "Ye found a bit of delight, for I saw it momentarily in yer face," he told her. "But one day perhaps I will be able to make ye cry out with joy as we couple. I want that for ye, Maggie mine. I never cared about it with the women I used to slack my lust. Their bodies were for my delectation. I paid for them, and while I liked giving them pleasure, it didn't matter if it was nothing more than a quick coupling. But with ye, my wife, 'tis different. I want perfection for ye, and I shall keep trying to attain it until I can give it to ye." Leaning over, he kissed her mouth, pleased that she eagerly kissed him back.

She was surprised by his revelation. Was it possible if she used her body to please him that she would hold a certain small power over him? He had said something similar earlier, but she had not understood it then. Now she thought she did. Reaching out, she caressed his face. "Ye were careful with me, and I thank ye for it."

"We are wed until death," he responded. "I want us content with that. I want our bairns to grow to man- and womanhood in a happy home with parents who honor and respect each other. Had I simply satisfied my lust, ye should not have enjoyed this first coupling. Ye might have grown to fear our couplings, and I didn't want that to happen."

"I will not fear them now," Maggie reassured him. "Will ye mount me again tonight? I still ache from our contest today, but I should not mind at all if ye wished to have me once again."

Fin laughed again. Would he ever grow used to Maggie's candid tongue? And it had proved a delicious tongue. Eventually he would teach that facile little tongue new uses that would surely surprise her at first. "Nay," he said. "The deed has been done. On other nights I will enjoy making love to ye the night long, but tonight I think we both could use our rest. Look beneath ye, lass, and see the proof yer grandsire will be proud to display come the morrow."

Maggie shifted herself, and was astounded to see beneath her the bloody stain of her virginity now turning brown upon the fine linen sheet. And she could see her thighs were smeared with dried blood too. She fixed her gaze on Fin. "Aye, we have done well, my lord, and Grandsire will not be shamed."

He arose from her bed, gathering up their two night garments. Handing her hers, he put on his. Then he climbed back into bed with Maggie.

"Ye are not returning to yer own bed?" Many men preferred visiting their wives, and then sleeping in their own beds.

"Tonight I would be with ye," he said as he gathered her into his arms. The delicious feel of her bottom pushing into him was intoxicating. Reaching around, he captured one of her breasts, and burying his face into her scented hair, sighed contentedly. Very quickly he was snoring lightly.

Maggie, however, remained awake a bit longer digesting this evening. This man she had been ordered to wed was turning out to be a better bargain than she had ever anticipated or even imagined. He was intelligent, and he was swiftly learning the ways of the Aisir nam Breug. He had quickly settled into the keep, and he had been easily accepted by all. The Kerr clan folk were usually not so quick to countenance strangers, but they had taken to Fingal Stewart as if he were one of them for all his life.

She snuggled against the sleeping man, enjoying the sensation of his hand clasping her breast. The coupling had been good. His restrained passion had opened a whole new world to her. Maggie could not help but wonder what that passion was going to be like when it was fully unleashed. And would she be able to match his ardor? She very much wanted to match it. Aye! She did! Her eyes were growing heavy, but before she fell into a contented sleep, Mad Maggie Kerr considered that she had never before pondered such a thing. Why was she contemplating it now? The coupling was for the purpose of creating heirs for Brae Aisir. That's what the church taught. There certainly was nothing more to it than that. *Or was there?* She realized as she finally tumbled into sleep that she couldn't wait to find out.

Chapter 7

⟡

To their mutual surprise they slept late, and no one came to disturb them. Maggie was amazed to find him still in her bed. His eyes were closed, his breathing even. She took the opportunity to look down at him. She had been correct in her observation the past night. He was handsome—not pretty like a lass, but in a masculine way, with his long straight nose, high cheekbones, and long thin mouth. He had shaved his face yesterday, but already a shadowy veil of black beard was beginning to show itself. His eyelashes were certainly thick for a man's, Maggie thought. His eyes suddenly opened, and she found herself staring into molten silver.

"Oh!"

"May I assume ye like what ye observe, madam?" he teased, and the long mouth turned up in a smile.

"Aye, yer a bonnie lad, Fingal Stewart," Maggie answered back pertly. She wasn't going to blush and simper like some little fool, although his open eyes had surprised her.

"Yer a bonnie lass," he responded. "We'll make pretty bairns together."

"The sun is way past dawn," she said. "Why did no one come to awaken us?" She made no move to arise from the bed.

"I believe they were being discreet," Fin replied. "They are giving

146

me time to ravage ye again, for all here are eager for an heir." The gray eyes were twinkling.

"Should we do *it* again now?" Maggie asked curiously. "'Tis morning, and the sun is shining brightly."

"Aye, it is," he said. "But yer newly opened, love. I think we may wait until tonight to continue with our endeavors, madam. Unless, of course, yer feeling particularly lustful for my body," Fin teased her further.

"Yer a fool," she told him, but she laughed.

"Did ye enjoy the coupling?" he asked candidly. She had said last night that she did, but he wanted to be certain now in the light of day that he had not repelled her.

"Aye," she answered him. "I did. After the pain. I must ask ye, husband, for I have no knowledge of these things prior to last night, but there was something more than just the linking of our bodies, Fin. For a brief moment I sensed something I had never felt before. Do ye know what it was? Did ye feel it too?"

"'Twas pleasure, Maggie mine," he said. "Virgins do not usually have much pleasure, if they have it at all. The sweetness of passion comes with time. As to men, if they are with a lover who pleases them, they too gain delight from their togetherness."

Maggie nodded. "I suppose we should get up. Hopefully the Netherdale Kerrs are already gone into the pass."

Flinging back the coverlet, he climbed from the bed. "I'll see Grizel comes to ye," Fin said as he pressed the little rose carving on the wall. The door sprang open, and he was gone through it, leaving her alone in the bed.

It was almost an hour before Grizel appeared. "Ye look rested," she said brightly.

"His lordship has gone down to the hall. I've had the tub brought to his chamber so ye can bathe before going down. Come along with ye now, my lady." She quickly helped Maggie from the bed, hurrying her through the hidden door and helping her into the tub.

"Now ye just soak a bit while I take the evidence of yer virtue lost to yer grandsire," she told her mistress before she bustled out, leaving Maggie in the tub.

Returning to her mistress's bedchamber, Grizel pulled back the coverlet and stared down at the stained bed linen. Nodding with satisfaction, she pulled it from the bed. Then she hurried down to the hall, the sheet gathered to her ample bosom. Dugald Kerr was still seated at the high board. He was engaged in conversation with Maggie's new husband. Grizel stepped before the board. "My lord," she said to the laird, curtsying.

Dugald Kerr looked up.

Grizel flung open the sheet to reveal the bloodstain.

The old laird looked, nodded, and then said, "Have Clennon Kerr fly it from the battlements, and tell my granddaughter she has done well."

Grizel curtsied again. "Aye, my lord." Then gathering the linen back up, she left the hall.

"She was braw," Fingal Stewart told the laird.

Dugald Kerr nodded. "Aye, she's always been a brave lass." Then he looked closely at the younger man. "Ye like her, don't ye?"

"Aye, I do," Fingal answered without any hesitation. "She makes me laugh with that sharp tongue of hers. She has no fear of speaking her mind."

"That's why I let her have her way in this matter of marriage," the laird responded. "Maggie has always known what she wants. I suspect if the king hadn't sent ye, and ye had been a lesser man, my granddaughter would still be a maid."

"If the king had sent another?" Fingal asked, curious as to what the laird would say to his query.

"She would have eventually killed him rather than wed him," the old laird said bluntly. "Ye gained her respect quickly, but for the honor of the Kerrs, she had ye meet the challenge she had set forth for all of her suitors. And that has gained ye credibility with our neighbors, particularly as ye beat her."

"We were equal in both races," Fingal said, "and she would not have given up in the swordplay had ye not declared me the victor. I cannot say with complete honesty that I overcame her. I am frankly astounded at her skills."

"Ye disarmed her fairly," Dugald Kerr said. "She is a braw lass, Fingal, but in truth she could hardly stand any longer, let alone wield her claymore. My judgment was a fair one. Maggie knew it too, for if she had disagreed with me, she would have shouted it to the high heavens for all of Scotland, and not just the Borders, to hear."

Fin laughed. "Aye," he agreed with the older man, "she would have."

Upstairs, Maggie soaked in her tub. The water felt wonderful, and the wretched soreness she had felt in her muscles the past night was almost gone as was the soreness between her thighs she had awakened with this morning. Would she be sore each time they coupled? He had promised her there would be no more pain after the first time. Well, she would learn if it was truth tonight, for he had said they would sleep together again each night until she was with child. It was fair.

When she went down to the hall, she found her grandsire alone. "Where is Fin?" she asked him. "And please tell me the Netherdale Kerrs are gone."

Dugald Kerr chuckled. "Aye, at first light, and Edmund complaining as they departed. As for yer husband, he's gone out to make certain the men in the watchtowers have what they need to weather the snowstorm old Tam says is coming."

"How long ago did he leave?" Maggie wanted to know.

"Too long for ye to catch up with him," the laird said. "The hall is yer province now, lass."

"Ye know if I don't get out of doors I will suffer for it, Grandsire," Maggie said reasonably. "Once the storm sets in, I will be forced to remain in the hall until it passes."

Dugald Kerr sighed deeply. "Margaret Jean," he said, and she knew when he called her by her full Christian name that it was serious. "The Aisir nam Breug is no longer yers to watch over. That's what yer husband is for, lass. Let him do his duty so he may gain the respect of the men who serve him now. Dinna go trailing after him. If ye would ride out, take a man with ye, but stay away from the pass. Go out and visit the far cottages. 'Tis yer place to see to our clan folk now as the lady of Brae Aisir."

Maggie thought a long moment. As much as she hated to admit to it, to face it, her grandsire was right. The Aisir nam Breug was Fin's obligation now, not hers. A sense of great loss overcame her. She had known with a part of her being that this day would come, yet she had not expected it to really happen. But it had, and she would have to make a new place for herself in the scheme of things. "Yer right, Grandsire," she said. "I'll ride out to the far cottages, and aye, I'll take a few of the men with me."

" 'Tis hard, Maggie lass; I know, for I can see it in yer eyes. But yer a woman, and a woman's place is different from that of a man," Dugald Kerr said. His tone was a kindly one, but Maggie felt a flash of bitterness at those words.

"My sex mattered little these past years when I controlled the traverse for ye, Grandsire. Think if ye will that others thought ye were just indulging me and allowing me to play while it was ye who really held the reins to our heritage. Well, perhaps some did believe it, for there are still enough men in this world who think a woman is not capable of anything other than hearth and bairns, but others knew better. They knew ye lay ill, and I was in charge. The Aisir nam Breug has never been managed better than when I was managing it, so do not, I beg ye, tell me that my place is in the hall at my loom while I wait for my big belly to ripen." Then turning abruptly, Maggie departed the hall.

Dugald Kerr watched her go. She was right, of course, but what did that matter? She was a woman, and the rest of the world would refuse to see her for anything other than that. It saddened him, for he did not want his granddaughter unhappy, but had he died before she wed, their neighbors would have been upon her like a wolf on a lamb.

Out in the stables, Maggie saddled her stallion, calling to Clennon Kerr to bring a few men and ride out with her. Finished, she climbed upon the animal's back and rode him out into the yard.

"Where are we going?" Clennon Kerr asked her.

"To the far cottages. I should see that all is well for the cottagers," Maggie said.

"Take Iver Leslie then," Clennon Kerr replied. "He's nae been that way, and he should have some familiarity with the path. Yer not going to the pass?"

"My husband is there now," Maggie said shortly.

"Aye," Clennon Kerr said. "'Tis right he should be, my lady."

"Get the men going with me," Maggie told him sharply. "I'll not dally this day, with the coming snows."

The keep's captain said nothing more. He understood why she was in a black mood today, but 'twas past time she took her rightful place as the lady and gave Brae Aisir some bairns. He went off to fetch Iver, calling to several men as he did to get their horses and mount up. Several minutes later, Maggie and her party of men-at-arms rode across the drawbridge and out into the hills.

They rode in silence for some minutes, Iver at Maggie's side. Finally she turned to him, saying, "The cottages we're visiting are at the edge of our lands. We've made them very secure for the inhabitants.

They're stone, the windows have thick shutters, the doors are bound in iron, and each of the three dwellings has a small well inside so they may be self-contained in the event of attack. There are no families there. Only men, and three older women who take care of them. They are shepherds, and cattle herders."

"They're helpless in case of attack, however," Iver said.

Maggie laughed. It was a hard sound. "Nay," she told him, "but ye'll see."

The day was fair, but cold. There wasn't a cloud in the bright blue sky, nor was there the faintest puff of wind. They rode for more than an hour, and then Iver saw ahead of them in the distance on the low hills a grouping of three cottages. Maggie sent one of the clansmen ahead to warn the cottagers of her coming.

"The sheep and cattle are now at Brae Aisir, but in the summer these are some of the meadows in which they browse."

"What do these men do when the beasties are at the keep?" Iver asked, curious.

"They patrol the border between us and our neighbors," Maggie said. "They make repairs to their equipment and warn us of any undue activity in the region."

"Why are we here then?" Iver persisted.

"I'm the lady of the keep," Maggie said. "It's my duty to see to their well-being. The women who look after these clansmen look to me. My visit allows them to know they are not forgotten out here."

Iver nodded. He was admiring of his mistress, although he would have never admitted to such a thing. It wasn't his place to approve or disapprove of her.

Reaching the cottages, they dismounted. A large-boned woman was waiting to greet them. "My lady!" she said, curtsying. "Ye honor us, and with the storm coming."

"Good morrow, Bessy Kerr," Maggie greeted the woman. "I wanted to be certain ye had all ye need for the winter."

"Oh, aye, my lady, everything is in order as you would wish it. Clennon saw our supplies delivered several days ago when Tam told him of this earlier than usual storm. But there is one small difficulty."

"What is that?" Maggie wanted to know.

"Mary's daughter is near her time. 'Tis a first bairn, and Mary desperately wants to be with her, my lady. The lass never told her mam she was almost five months gone when she wed last summer, or Mary would have asked sooner. She learned it from her son-in-law, who brought our supplies, when the bairn was due."

"Can ye manage with just the two of ye?" Maggie asked.

"Oh, aye! Mary's burden is the lightest. She cares for just four lads. We can close up her cottage until the spring when she returns to us. Sorcha and I have more than enough room for two each," Bessy Kerr said cheerfully.

"Tell Mary she can ride back with us," Maggie said.

"Thank ye, my lady!" Bessy curtsied again. Then her eye went to Iver. "And who is this fine laddie?" she asked him.

"Iver Leslie," was the short answer, and he reddened slightly.

"He came with my lord from Edinburgh and is Clennon Kerr's second in command," Maggie explained. "My union with Lord Stewart was blessed yesterday."

Bessy's eyes grew wide. "He overcame ye, my lady? I never thought to see the day when anyone could outrun, outride, and outfight ye, but . . ." she said, hesitating.

"'Twas past time," Maggie, chuckling, finished the sentence for Bessy.

Bessy nodded, grinning back at her lady. "Aye," she agreed. "Now, will ye come into my cottage for some cakes and ale?"

"See to the others. I want to show Iver about, and then we'll join ye," Maggie answered the woman. Then looking at her companion she said, "Come along, Iver."

He followed her while she led him about the small settlement, pointing out what he might need to know one day. "Ye still haven't told me why these clan folk of yers are safe in an attack. Aye, the cottages are strong, and the slate roof on each will prevent their being destroyed by fire, but eventually they have to give in," Iver said.

"Nay, they don't," Maggie told him. "In each cottage is a small dovecote. In the event of an attack, three pigeons are released, one from each cote, with a message attached to one of their wee legs. They come home to Brae Aisir entering the keep into their own special cote. There is always someone watching that cote for them. No one has figured out how we so quickly repel an attack on our borders," she laughed. "There are two more places on our lands where cottages with pigeon cotes exist. We'll visit them in the spring, for there is no time today."

Iver nodded. "'Tis cleverly done," he said.

"I've shown ye all ye need to know here," Maggie told him. "Let's go and get some cakes and ale before we return home. Do ye mind riding pillion with Mary?"

"Nay, I'll take the woman," he said, following his mistress to Bessy's cottage. As he ate a fresh-baked oatcake and drank some good October ale, Iver looked about the cottage. It was a well-kept space, clean and neat, with three rooms. The main one, where the men ate and socialized, was the largest. A second room had space for a row of beds. The third was the smallest, and obviously belonged to Bessy. It had a door that could be locked, and no window. It was all very well thought out, he considered. As he drank his ale and ate the oatcake, Bessy flirted with him.

"Yer a fine strong lad," she said, her hand on his arm. "I wouldn't mind having a bit of a tumble with ye." She grinned up at him.

"Yer a shameless woman," he said low. "Ye've got a houseful of lads to play with, Bessy Kerr."

"Nay, Iver Leslie, I would never swive one of them, for it would make the others jealous, and then I should have to fuck them all. There are few secrets kept in a cottage."

And while the others were engaged in speaking with their lady, Bessy reached down and gave his manhood a squeeze. "My lads know me, and they'll keep the lady busy while ye and I have a little fun." Bessy gave him a coquettish grin and pulled him from the room.

She was a woman who wasn't going to take no for an answer, and he suspected they wouldn't get away until he had given her what she wanted. He followed Bessy to her small chamber, and when she shut the door, he surprised her by pushing her up against it and giving her a hard kiss. "Very well, lass, let's give ye what ye need so we may be on our way before the snow starts," he said as her hands yanked his breeks down so she might fondle him to a stand. Iver surprised Bessy by his quick reaction to her touch.

"Yer a big man," she said. "Good! It's been months since I've had a good swiving, lad. Now I'll get through the winter."

His hands pushed her skirts up, clamped beneath her big bottom, and lifted her up to impale her on his manhood. Bessy squealed with excitement, wrapping her arms and legs about him as he began to piston her vigorously. Within moments she was moaning into his shoulder, but he seemed not to be tiring. Bessy was astounded by his vigor. She couldn't ever remember a man using her in so lusty and long a manner.

"Tell me when yer ready," he finally growled into her ear.

Bessy was near to fainting with her excitement and satisfaction. She was going to die if he didn't soon stop. "*Now!*" she managed to gasp.

With a deep chuckle Iver released his own pent-up lust, and when it had drained itself into her, he gave her a hearty kiss, squeezed her plump buttock cheeks hard, and set her down again. Then he pulled up his breeks, fastening them.

She clung to him briefly to keep from falling, for at first her legs would not sustain her. "God's toenail, Iver Leslie, I certainly hope I'll see ye again!" she told him enthusiastically. "Yer the first man who's ever truly satisfied me." Bessy smoothed her skirts first, and then her hair. "We had best join the others," she said. "I don't want the lady realizing what we were doing."

But Maggie hadn't noticed the disappearance of her captain and Bessy. She had been too busy speaking with the men who watched over their borders, and giving the latest gossip to Sorcha and Mary. When they were ready to depart, Iver was relieved to see that Mary was not a big woman as was Bessy. Short and slender, she would not tire his horse unduly. He took her up behind him on his horse, and then, giving Bessy a wink, turned to make the ride home to Brae Aisir.

"The storm is coming in early," Maggie noted as the flakes began to fall when they were but halfway home. "I hope my lord gets home safely."

"The wind is coming from the north," Iver said, "but 'tis barely a breeze."

"It will rise later on," Maggie told him. "Look at how small the flakes are. 'Twill be a serious storm, I'm thinking." She pulled up the hood on her cloak and hunched down as she rode. Even with her fur-lined gloves, her hands were cold, her fingers stiffening and making it difficult to hold the reins.

When they finally reached the village, the snow was coming down harder. The land around them was already covered in white. They stopped briefly to let Mary down at her daughter's cottage. It seemed the mother had arrived in the nick of time, for her child had just gone into labor; the village midwife was hurrying up to the door at the same time as the traveler. "Mam!" They heard the girl's cry of relief as Mary rushed into the cottage.

Through the village and up the rise to the keep they rode. As they clomped across the drawbridge, Maggie could see her husband and his men just ahead of them.

She found herself relieved at the sight of Fin dismounting his stallion as she slid quickly from her own mount, tossing the reins to a stable boy as she did. Maggie smiled at him as he turned about. "I was fearful ye would get caught out in the Aisir nam Breug. The storm came earlier. Tam's old bones aren't quite as accurate as they once were."

"Ye went out in this?" he asked.

"There was no snow when we departed for the far cottages," Maggie told him. "I took Iver and several of the men with me. I don't like staying indoors all the time, my lord. And a good thing we went too. We had to bring back one of the women for her daughter's lying-in. Mary arrived just in time. The lass was already in labor."

They walked together into the hall, brushing the snow from themselves as they came. The old laird looked up, relief upon his face.

"Now, Grandsire," Maggie teased him, "certainly ye weren't worried. I've been out in worse than this, and ye know it."

"Of course, I wasn't fearful for ye," Dugald Kerr prevaricated.

Maggie laughed, and going to him planted a kiss on his forehead.

"Sit down, sit down," the laird said to them both. "Well, Fin, how was the pass this day? Was all well?"

"I rode the hills above the Aisir nam Breug and went to the farthest watchtower first. Then we made our way back. All was as it should be, Dugald. The towers were well stocked with food and firewood, and the men were ready for the storm. From my vantage point I could see the Netherdale Kerrs just passing over the border. They did not see me."

"Good, good," Dugald Kerr said, nodding. Then he turned to Maggie.

"The far cottages are supplied for the winter. Clennon saw to it a few days ago. We brought Mary Kerr back with us, as her daughter was ready to deliver her first bairn.

"Bessy and Sorcha assured us they could manage the winter without her. Mary's lass had just gone into labor, and we reached the cottage at the same time Midwife Agnes did. After the storm passes, I'll send to see all went well, and if it did, we'll bring a gift."

"Well," the laird said, "ye've both had a busy day. The meal is ready, and ye'll want an early bed after yer cold ride."

Maggie laughed again. "Grandsire, ye must never go to court, for subtlety is not yer gift, I fear." But she felt her cheek warming as her eye caught Fin's, and he winked wickedly at her.

The wooden trenchers were set upon the high board and the trestles to be filled with hot venison stew. Father David, who usually ate with them, said a blessing. There was bread, butter, and cheese. They ate heartily, washing their food down with a dark red wine. Maggie wanted something sweet after the meal. Grizel fetched her a small dish of stewed apples and pears. The laird's piper came into the hall and played for them. Dugald Kerr, and his younger brother, David, left the high board to play a game of chess.

Maggie arose from her place. "Give me time to bathe lightly," she said, and was gone from the hall.

He watched her go, thinking that although they had but formally consummated their marriage only yesterday, it felt as if he had been with her and at Brae Aisir forever. He looked forward to going upstairs and spending the evening in her bed. He had never seen himself as a married man, but he realized in a burst of clarity that he very much liked the way his life seemed to be progressing. The hall was warm, his belly was full, his bonnie and braw wife was waiting for him. Could a man really ask for more? Standing up, he stretched himself, stepped down from the high board, and left the hall.

"What think ye?" the priest asked his older brother, watching as Fin departed.

"Oddly, they seem well suited," Dugald Kerr said, and he smiled. "He told me he likes her. That's to the good, Davy."

"Does she like him?" the priest said.

"Maggie has said naught to me but that she respects him. She's not a lass who flirted or teased the lads. She's never been in love even a wee bit. But if she respects him, she will be a good wife to him, and she will do her duty by us all," the laird concluded. He moved his knight piece into an attack position.

"I'll pray for them both," David Kerr said as he studied the chessboard, deciding how he would counter his elder sibling's move.

Fingal Stewart had gone up the stairs into the narrow hallway to his own bedchamber. He found Archie waiting for him. His serving man had put out a cloth, a rag, and a basin of hot water with a little cake of soap for his master. He took Lord Stewart's garments and boots as they were removed.

"Will ye want yer night garment, my lord?" he asked in a bland voice.

"Nay," Fin answered briefly as he quickly washed himself.

"Is there anything more I might do for ye then, my lord?" Archie said.

"Nay, thank ye," came his answer. "Go and see if ye can steal a kiss from Grizel."

Archie chuckled. "She's not an easy woman, my lord," he said. "Good night."

The serving man shut the door behind him and was gone.

Fin smiled at the reply as he pressed the carved rose that opened the door connecting their two chambers. He stepped through into

Maggie's bedroom. She was seated cross-legged and naked upon the bed, brushing her long chestnut-colored hair.

Looking up at his entrance, she smiled mischievously at him. "I see we are of one mind," she said, her eyes boldly sweeping over him.

"Aye, I thought it practical," he agreed, climbing into bed with her and taking the brush from her hand as he seated himself behind her. He began to stroke it through her long locks. "I like yer hair," he said. "It smells of flowers." Bending, he kissed her shoulder and nuzzled the curve of her neck. He set the brush aside.

"Ye have hair as black as a raven's wing," Maggie replied. "I never knew anyone with such dark hair." She had not ever considered a man would brush her tresses, but she had to admit to herself that she very much liked it. The kiss and nuzzle he gave her set her pulse racing, as did the knowledge that they sat together naked in her bed.

His hands slipped about her to cup her two breasts in his palms as he kissed the shallow hollow where her shoulder and neck met. Her nipples immediately hardened.

"We are lovers now, Maggie mine, and as such we should enjoy each other," Fin said.

His rough thumbs rubbed the two nipples. "I don't want ye fretting over what to do. I want ye to follow yer instincts when we are together like this. There is no wrong or right when lovers are together."

Maggie leaned back against him. Until yesterday no man had ever handled her, but strangely she was not shocked by his actions. Her breasts being cradled in the warmth of his palms felt good. *Very good.* She felt the pressure of his belly against her back.

"Ye will instruct me?" she asked him.

"I will teach ye what pleases me, and ye will tell me honestly what pleases ye, or displeases ye. If we are to pleasure each other, it must be that way. Too many men simply take from their women. I would give as well as take, and have ye do the same."

"Who taught ye such courtesies?" Maggie wanted to know, for she had heard enough from other women to know his behavior was unusual.

"My father, who considered it a privilege to enter my mother's bed. He was many, many years her senior. He might have been her grandsire, but to keep an orphaned lass with no dower safe he wed her, and cherished her. After she died, he would say to me over and over again that a woman who gave herself was a sweeter prize than one roughly taken. In my youth I didn't always listen, but as I grew older, I discovered he was right."

"Then ye have forced women to yer will, my lord?" This was a revelation.

"A man who sells his sword does not always behave as a gentleman, Maggie mine," he told her candidly. "Let us leave it at that, but know I shall never force ye."

"And if I said I wanted ye gone from my bed now, would ye go?" she queried.

"I would, but not until I had tried to convince ye otherwise, love," he replied.

One hand released a breast, and smoothed down her torso to her mons. A finger pressed between her nether lips, finding her love bud. He began to play gently with it.

"*Oh!*" Maggie squirmed against his hand.

"Do ye like this, sweetheart?" he asked as he pressed a row of kisses over her shoulder. He could feel the sensitive flesh beginning to swell against his finger.

"Aye, Fin, I like it. I like it very much," Maggie admitted. "Please don't stop!"

"I won't for now," he promised, "but there is another way to please this little bud and give ye even more sweetness. Will ye let me show ye?"

"Ummmm, aye, I'd like that," Maggie replied softly, her voice taking on a dreamy quality as she enjoyed their love play.

He slid out from behind her, saying as he did, "Lie back among the pillows, Maggie mine," and when she did, he drew her two legs up and over his broad shoulders.

Maggie gasped, surprised. *"Fin!"*

"Trust me, love," he told her, and before she might protest, he buried his head between her thighs, his fingers losing themselves among the chestnut curls as he peeled her nether lips open and his tongue found the sensitive swelling bud of her sex. He began to lick at it with gentle, teasing strokes of his tongue.

"Ohh, Fin!" It was as if a fireball had exploded within her. This was surely the wickedest thing that had ever happened to any woman. Coupling was for making bairns. That was what her priestly uncle preached. Why had no one ever said there was such joy in the act? With incredible, wonderful sensations that left every bit of her aflame and ready to burst open, she could indeed feel her juices flowing.

Seeing her ready for even more passion, he covered her body with his own, and guided himself slowly to her entry. With one fluid and smooth motion he pushed into her love sheath. With no barrier to stop him, he filled her completely, and then he began to ride her. Maggie wrapped herself about her husband, half conscious, guided by instinct alone. Every thrust of his cock brought her closer and closer to that elusive something that had escaped her the previous evening on their wedding night. She had no idea what it was she sought, but she moved steadily towards it.

He groaned as he went deeper. She was tight and hot and so very wet. He couldn't seem to get enough of her and almost wept with the pure enjoyment she was giving him so eagerly. He had known some of the finest whores in Edinburgh, France, and England, but he had never known the pleasure that his new wife was giving him.

He found her mouth, and his passionate kisses tried to tell her what he was not ready yet to admit with words.

"*Oh, Fin! I die! I die!*" Maggie cried as she reached the pinnacle of her delight. She soared into a golden unknown while about her stars exploded. Then with a cry she plunged down into a velvet darkness that rose to softly envelop her.

He felt her sheath tightening and spasming about his cock. He groaned deeply, knowing she was tasting true passion. Then, unable to contain himself, he released his lust into her. "*Maggie mine!*" he cried out as the end weakness overcame him, and then he rolled off her body. But quickly he gathered her into his arms, holding her tightly against his chest as his fiercely beating heart slowly quieted itself.

Maggie came to herself slowly. God's toenail! What had just happened to her? Whatever it was had completely taken over and controlled her. She wasn't certain she liked that, although she had to admit the feelings that had pummeled her had been incredible and wonderful. And she was quickly coming to herself again. She felt his arms about her. What was that thumping? Then she realized it was his heart beating very quickly. Her husband had obviously experienced the same wild emotions as she had. She had not considered a man of experience would react in a similar manner.

"Did ye enjoy this better than last night?" His voice pierced her own thoughts.

"Aye! It was wonderful, and ye did not lie," she responded.

"*Lie to ye?*" He was confused.

"It didn't hurt," Maggie said. "Nay, it hurt not at all. It was as if yer cock and my sheath were made for each other, Fin. We fit together nicely."

"As we are man and wife, they obviously were," he replied dryly, "and we did fit well, Maggie mine, I will agree." Then he laughed.

"What is so funny?" she demanded to know.

"Yer honest tongue," he told her. "I've ne'er had a woman I've lain with speak to me in so candid a manner."

"Perhaps they were more practiced and knowledgeable than I," Maggie said. "Seeing servants fucking lustily in the hay or in the heather does not tell you much other than where the parts should go."

He laughed again. "I suppose not," he agreed. "Well, madam, are you pleased with yer lessons so far?"

"Aye," she told him with a grin. "I hope there's more to learn, my lord."

"We'll sleep for a bit, and then if yer willing, we will review what ye have learned so far, Maggie mine," he said to her with an answering grin.

"We should pray that the king finds the same happiness with his bride that we are finding with each other," Maggie said softly as she cuddled next to him, her head on his shoulder. "I don't know if we will find that emotion the poets call love, Fingal Stewart, but I know ye like me, and I surely like ye."

"Aye," he agreed with her. "I hope King Jamie finds his happiness too, for his road is a far more difficult one to travel than is ours." He drew the coverlet over them.

In France the month of December seemed to fly by as James Stewart's wedding day approached. He knew what he was doing was madness, but for the first time in his life he actually cared for another human being. His childhood had not been a happy one.

He had lost three brothers and had but two sisters. His flighty English mother had cared more for her own pleasure and position than for her royal son. He had only been seventeen months old when his father had been killed. He had no memory of James IV at all but what people had told him. Most people had liked his father, and the one trait he had inherited from the previous James was his determination to rule Scotland without any interference from his earls, or from England.

James V had come to France to seek a wife. He would be twenty-five in April, and it was time to marry. He had thought to offer for Marie de Bourbon, the duc de Vendôme's daughter. The girl was more than noble and came with a dower of one hundred thousand gold crowns. Visiting her father's court in disguise, James found the prospective bride small with a hunched back. He departed without revealing himself, leaving his ambassador to explain to the duc that his master was no longer interested.

At the court of King François, however, James Stewart's eye fell upon the king's fifth child, third daughter, Princess Madeleine. Frail from birth, the fifteen-year-old princess had spent most of her life in the mild climate of the Loire region. The French king loved her dearly. When Scotland's king asked for her hand, King François refused.

This child of his heart was too frail to survive the harsh Scottish weather. James Stewart was unhappy to be declined. He wanted a French wife to solidify the auld alliance that had existed for centuries between Scotland and France. He turned his attention in another direction.

Marie de Guise, the duchesse de Longueville, was the daughter of the duc de Guise and his wife, Antoinette de Bourbon-Vendôme. She was three years younger than James Stewart. Marie had recently been widowed, and was the mother of two sons, the second born two months after her husband's death. The Scots king found that he liked her, but she was not ready to be courted or to even consider another marriage.

Late in the autumn, James saw Madeleine de Valois at a court ball again. Drawn back to her, he realized he was in love. And to his surprise, Madeleine admitted her love for him. They went together to King François and pleaded with him for permission to wed. Unable to deny his favorite child her heart's desire, and influenced by his second wife, Eleanor of Austria, the French king finally agreed. The wedding was celebrated on the first day of January at Paris's great cathedral of Notre Dame.

The delicate princess was fortunate in that she did not resemble her father. King François could not under any circumstances be called handsome, his best features being his charm and his power. But his first wife, Queen Claude, had had the same beauty as Madeleine, his favorite daughter. Claude, Duchess of Brittany, had been the daughter of King Louis XII and his wife, Anne of Brittany. Claude was fair to look upon with reddish blond hair and blue eyes. So was Madeleine, but it was her sweetness and firm character that had entangled themselves in James Stewart's cold heart.

For the next few months the young couple were feted and entertained, but their return to Scotland was inevitable. Finally in mid-May the royal couple sailed for Scotland. The young queen had not been well in prior weeks. Exhaustion had been an inescapable result of all the celebrations in their honor. King François knew as he bid his daughter a tender farewell that he should never see her again in this life. He might have regretted his decision to allow her marriage but that she was so very happy, and so very much in love with James Stewart, and he with her.

The voyage was not an easy one, and Queen Madeleine was quite ill by the time their ship reached Leith. Word of the king's arrival spread quickly. The queen could go no farther than Edinburgh. Only the fact that the French king had given his daughter an extremely large dower portion kept the more civilized of the king's lords from complaining aloud of his poor choice of a wife. And plans were already in the works to find a new wife for James Stewart.

When Scotland's king had departed for France the previous summer, he had seen his then-mistress, Janet Munro, married to Matthew Baird, Lord Tweed. James had agreed to acknowledge his child by Janet, and settle a dower portion on it if a female. Lord Tweed had agreed to raise the child as if it were his own. He was not unhappy to have Janet Munro for his wife. Her connection with the king and the generous dower her family provided made her an excellent choice.

And Janet Munro was not unhappy with her new husband. While closer to forty than thirty, he was a satisfactory lover, and told her he expected her to give him bairns eventually. Their home and their income were comfortable. In the very early spring of 1537, Janet gave birth to a daughter who was christened Margaret. Lord Tweed sent word to his king in France of his daughter's birth, but he heard nothing.

"We will travel to Edinburgh when the king returns, for that will be the first place he goes. We will ask for Margaret's portion then," Janet said to her husband. "I want the matter settled before his queen has any bairns."

But when Matthew Baird and his wife, Janet, went to Edinburgh, they found their new queen seriously ill, and the king unable to deal with anything other than his wife. He never left her side, sitting with her for hours on end. Janet Munro was sad for the man who had fathered her child, but she was a practical woman. She wanted what had been promised to her baby daughter. A lass needed a dower to wed respectably.

"I must go to Brae Aisir to my cousin, Fingal Stewart," she told her husband.

"Why?" Lord Tweed asked. "What can he do to help ye resolve this matter?"

"I need to remind the king that it was I who brought Fin to his attention, and thereby gained him another means of support. I want the income James Stewart promised for my Margaret, and only the king can make it so. And if Fin is with me when I ask the king, the matter can be settled immediately."

"What a clever puss ye are, my dear," Lord Tweed said.

"This queen is dying, Matthew," Janet continued. "He is in love with her. Everyone says it. When she dies he will be devastated. Ye don't know him, my lord, but I do. James has never loved anyone in all his life. He is a charming man, but his heart was always a cold one until he met this princess. She is his first, and possibly his only love. He will not be easily amenable to anything after she dies. He will mourn her as deeply as he loves her. He is not a man to do things by halves," Janet said.

"We have not been able to even see him ourselves. Few have," her husband reminded her. "How do ye expect to reach out to him even if yer cousin comes?"

"I'm not certain," Janet admitted, "but I believe I have a way. I have to do this for my wee Margaret's sake. James has not yet received so much as a groat from Fingal. By giving that income to my daughter, it actually costs the king nothing. He will appreciate the subtlety in that, my lord, if I can but point it out to him."

Matthew Baird, Lord Tweed, laughed heartily at his wife's reasoning. "God's nightshirt, Jan, ye are far cleverer than I had realized. Will yer cousin agree?"

"Fingal is a good man," she replied. "He will not refuse me. He will see the wisdom in what I suggest."

"But will the king?" Lord Tweed asked seriously.

Chapter 8

$\mathcal{I}$t was late spring at Brae Aisir, and the hillsides were green with new growth, and white with new lambs. The frost had finally gone from the ground. The few fields were quickly plowed and planted. Traffic through the Aisir nam Breug had picked up with the better weather. In early June, Fingal Stewart was surprised to be visited by Janet Munro, his cousin, and her husband, Matthew Baird, Lord Tweed. They arrived one bright afternoon, traveling from Edinburgh.

Maggie was delighted to have the company, for there had been no visitors to Brae Aisir in months. And particularly as Lady Tweed was her husband's kinswoman, she welcomed the pair warmly. "Grandsire always enjoys company," she said cheerfully. "And especially that of a pretty woman," Maggie complimented Janet.

"Why, ye are far lovlier than I had anticipated," Janet said frankly. "I suspect if the king had known how fair ye were, he might not have been so generous to our cousin. He's always had an eye for a pretty face." She dismounted her horse.

"Come into the hall," Maggie invited the couple. "Are ye traveling with another purpose, or have ye come to see us especially?" She led them inside the stone house, signaling to her servants to bring wine and biscuits as she invited them to sit.

"I see ye've birthed yer bairn," Fin said as he considered why Janet was here.

"A daughter on March third, baptized Margaret as it is a Stewart family name," Janet said brightly. "She's at Tweed House with her wet nurse. It's safer for so young a bairn. The king has returned. His delicate French queen is dying. I have not seen her; few have. But from what I'm told, she'll not last the summer."

"How tragic!" Maggie exclaimed. "Did ye hear, Grandsire? The young queen is dying, poor lass."

"She was frail to begin with, if one can believe the gossips," the old laird said.

"Aye, it has been said," Janet agreed. She looked to Fingal and to the laird. "My lords, I need yer aid in a certain matter." When he nodded at her, she continued.

"The king promised when he saw me wed to my good lord that he would provide for our child, for that responsibility is not my husband's. If a lad, the child would be given a living, a priory or monastery as his other sons have received. The king also swore that if the child were a lass, she would be given a small yearly income and a generous dower portion. Alas, with the queen so ill, his promise has not been fulfilled. Now, with her death imminent, I fear the king will be so deep in mourning that he will not want to be troubled by this matter."

"Yer a clever lass, and a good mother to want it settled soon," Dugald Kerr said.

"How can we help ye, Jan?" Fingal Stewart asked.

"Ye promised to give the king a portion of the revenues ye receive from the tolls ye collect from the Aisir nam Breug," Janet Munro said. "But the king could transfer that right to his daughter to meet his obligation. Margaret would be taken care of at no out-of-pocket expense to James."

"Yer cousin is a bold woman to put her hands in our purse, Fin,"

Maggie said bluntly. She looked straight at Janet Munro when she spoke.

"Ye owe the king in any event," Janet replied stubbornly.

"If he promised yer bairn a living," Maggie snapped, "why not remind him of his promise? While I have heard the king was tightfisted, I was also told he was good to his offspring. Why do ye not solicit him directly and remind him of his promise?"

Janet Munro was surprised that her hostess was so forward, and she wondered why Fingal, her cousin, did not speak up. The look on his face was one of amusement. Did he consider the matter of her child's financial well-being something to be laughed at? But then, to her relief, Lord Stewart did speak up.

"If the king is as deeply in love with his dying wife as has been reported," he began, "he will hardly be in the mood to be reminded of an old obligation to a child born on the wrong side of the blanket. And we do owe him a third of all the tolls we collect to be paid in coin each St. Andrew's Day. That was what was agreed upon when I came to Brae Aisir. Dugald knows it. The king wanted half, only that I bargained him down."

"Why should he have any of our income?" Maggie demanded to know.

"Because he saved Brae Aisir's fate by sending me to be yer husband," Fin told her. "Do ye not think I'm worth a third of the monies we collect each year? I think ye more than worth the two-thirds we retain." He grinned at her.

"Yer a fool, Fingal Stewart," Maggie said. "I'm worth it all!"

"Aye, Maggie mine, ye are," he told her. "Now let us return to Janet's dilemma. I think it an excellent solution that the king's portion from the tolls collected be used to support his daughter. But how can we manage to make such an arrangement? He must be very diverted at the moment with his queen's poor condition."

"He is," Janet said. "Her health is so perilous that she cannot even be moved to Stirling or Linlithgow. She is in the royal apartments in Edinburgh Castle. We can get into the castle. I have a kinsman among the castle guard. And the king's secretary owes me a favor I shall now collect from him. But I need ye with me, Fingal, to assure the king that ye are content with this disposition. Will ye come back to Edinburgh with us?"

"Ye will need *me* as well," Maggie said. "I am the heiress to Brae Aisir."

"But Fingal is yer husband, and surely 'tis his right to make such a decision," Janet Munro said primly. She was a woman of tradition.

Fin laughed aloud. "Nay, Jan, Maggie must come with us, for she is the heiress, and whatever I now possess I possess through her."

"We must leave on the morrow then," Janet Munro said.

"We will depart the day after," Maggie replied. "Ye are barely past childbed, madam, and have raced into the Borders from the city. Ye and yer horses will have a day of rest before we begin our journey. Now I must go and see to yer comfort while ye are with us, and the cook must be informed there will be two more at the high board this day." With a smile she hurried from the hall.

The laird chuckled. "She has had her way since her birth," he said to their guests. "There is no changing her now."

Fin grinned. "The king gave me quite a responsibility, didn't he? It takes a particular skill to manage it, Cousins."

Dugald Kerr laughed aloud.

"She is very forward," Janet Munro ventured.

"A headstrong lady, I can see," Lord Tweed said with understatement.

"She is known as Mad Maggie," Fin murmured, "and is rather proud of it."

"God's foot!" Janet exclaimed. "And ye put up with it?"

Fingal Stewart smiled knowingly. "She is worth it, Jan. I should have never imagined such a wife as I now have."

"He loves her," the laird murmured softly.

"I have not said it, Dugald," Fin quickly replied.

"But ye do nonetheless," the old man answered, "and I'm glad for it. I shall go to my grave content knowing Maggie is safe with ye."

"Yer an old fraud," Fin said. "Ye won't go to yer grave for years, Dugald Kerr, and we both know it. Ye may fool Maggie, but ye don't fool me."

The laird chuckled, giving his grandson-in-law a broad wink. "Ye'll not tell on me, I hope," he said.

Janet Munro smiled at the repartee between the two men. When she had suggested her cousin to the king's service, she could not have imagined the happiness he would have, but she could see it in his face. She saw it when he teasingly reprimanded his wife and saw it in the warm relationship Fingal Stewart had developed with the laird of Brae Aisir in just under a year. Her cousin had a family now, which was something he had not had in many years. All that was missing were bairns. "Is yer wife with child yet?" she boldly asked Fin.

"Not yet," he said, "but neither of us will disappoint Dugald. She is young yet. Will ye give yer lord bairns, Cousin?"

"Aye," Janet replied. "Margaret is three months old now. In another month or two we shall work harder to give her a brother, for it would please my lord, would it not?"

Matthew Baird nodded. "It would please yer lord very much, Jan," he said.

Fingal Stewart smiled. His cousin had found happiness as well, and he was glad of it. He looked forward to the time they would spend together. The rest of the day and the evening were pleasant. The following day Maggie and Fin took their guests on a ride through a portion of the Aisir nam Breug. Lord Tweed was impressed by the traverse and how it was protected. His wife, however, was enchanted by the multi-colored summer flowers that lined the way—yellow and white ox-eyed daisies, common milkwort, Mary's gold, bluebells, and heather.

The following day they departed for Edinburgh, escorted by Iver and a company of a dozen men-at-arms. Fin had sent ahead to Master Boyle, saying that he would expect his house vacated for his arrival and that of his wife and their guests. Two hours before their arrival in the city, and on their second day of travel, Archie and Grizel rode ahead to make certain all was ready. They found Master Boyle eagerly awaiting them.

"I've had the house cleaned, the beds made, and the fires started," he told Archie. "How long do ye think yer master will be here?"

"Two or three days, but no more," Archie answered. "What's yer hurry?"

"I've got two bishops arriving next week, and ye know these churchmen pay well for their lodging. Especially for such a fine house so near the castle."

"We'll be long gone," Archie said. "Lord Stewart wanted to pay his respects to his cousin, the king. We have been told the young queen is failing fast."

"Aye, aye," Master Boyle replied mournfully. "'Tis a great tragedy. Why he picked such a weak little lass is a mystery."

"She brought a large dower with her for the king, and 'tis rumored he loves her," Archie responded. "Even the mighty fall in love with their wives now and again."

"Then 'tis an even greater tragedy. They say some of the lords are already seeking a suitable second wife for him," Master Boyle confided. "Some are pressing for another Frenchwoman, but others say he would do best with a good Scotswoman. Look how many bairns he's fathered on his own. Six fine sons and two daughters—and all healthy. 'Tis hoped they at least allow the king to mourn before they're putting him to bed with another wife by his side." His curious gaze went to Grizel. "Have ye taken a wife then, Archie? I didn't think ye ever would, but she's a fine-looking woman."

"*His wife?*" Grizel said, outraged. "As if I would wed with a bandied-legged old fellow! Indeed! I will have ye know that I am my lady's tiring woman, ye nosy little man. Now, if there is nothing more of import ye need to tell us, get ye gone back to from wherever ye have come. Go on with ye! Shoo! Shoo!"

At first surprised, Master Boyle recovered quickly. With a wink at and a sketchy bow to Grizel, he went off chortling, but not before telling Archie, "Now, there's a fine redheaded woman who could well warm a man's bed on a cold night if he were smart enough, and quick enough, to catch her."

Archie laughed aloud.

"Yer neither smart enough nor quick enough," Grizel said darkly. She bustled off to make certain all was truly ready for their master and mistress but not before instructing Archie to go to the cookshop, and the baker. "Is there wine in this house? And see if ye can find some cheese. We must set out some sort of meal, for my lady will be tired and hungry when they arrive."

The travelers arrived in the late afternoon. Janet Munro sent up to the castle to ask if her cousin, the guardsman, would join them later. When he came, they were able to offer him a joint of mutton, bread, cheese, and wine. He ate and drank the meal gratefully, and when he had finished, he looked at Janet, saying, "Ye wish to enter the castle? When?"

"Tomorrow," Janet said. "We will all come to pay our respects to King James at this trying and terrible time for him."

"I will see ye get in," the guardsman told them, "but it's unlikely ye'll get to see the king. He rarely leaves the queen's side. I saw her, ye know, the other day. She was being carried in a litter to the royal chapel of St. Margaret to hear Mass."

"What is she like?" Janet asked eagerly.

"Pretty as a picture," was the reply. "She looks like an angel and is already halfway to heaven, I'm thinking. I hear ye gave Jamie his second daughter."

"Aye," Janet replied casually. "She's a bonnie bairn."

"Come first thing in the morning," the guardsman said. "I'll leave word at the gate for them to expect ye, and yer husband, and . . . ?" He looked at Fin and Maggie.

"The king's cousin, Lord Stewart of Torra, and his wife, Lady Margaret," Janet told her kinsman. "Actually, I believe the king will want to see Lord Stewart."

"It's not up to me," the guardsman replied. "But at least I can get ye into the royal apartments, Janet. And Lord and Lady Stewart," he added, rising from his place and addressing Fin, "I thank ye for yer hospitality, my lord."

Fin nodded. "I thank ye," he replied.

"Will ye carry a message to the king's secretary for me tonight?" Janet asked.

"Of course."

Janet Munro handed the guardsman the letter she had written earlier to the king's secretary. In it she reminded the man of the favor he owed her and requested that he get them an audience with the king within the next two days. The guard went off with Janet Munro's message tucked in his leather jacket. "I can but hope we are successful," Janet said with a small sigh.

In the morning they dressed carefully, Lord Stewart in black velvet canions, black and white striped hose, and a black velvet doublet lined in white satin, its puffed sleeves slashed to show the white. He had never seen any of these garments before, but all Archie would ever say when he asked was that he had come by them honestly. Maggie wore her fine burgundy velvet gown. Her hair, usually worn in a thick plait, was neatly contained in a gold wire caul this day. They rode out with Janet and her husband early. It was a fine June morning.

Edinburgh Castle sat on a craggy hill that jutted out over the town. It had first manifested itself as a wooden fort, built by King Edwin of Northumbria, in the seventh century. He had named it Edwin's Burgh after himself. The Anglo-Saxon princess, Margaret, who had married King Malcolm III, was considered a saint. She had built the chapel. As she lay dying, the castle was being besieged by an army of Highlanders. Her dead body was lowered down the fortress's west wall and taken to Dunfermline Abbey for burial. The great and newest stone building was a banqueting hall that had been built by James IV. The court, however, disliked this castle, for it was extremely cramped. They preferred Holyrood Palace, which was nearby in the city; a confection of witch's cap towers that reminded one of the great châteaus of the Loire Valley but for the background of rugged hills behind it. Holyrood Palace had charm whereas Edinburgh Castle was what it had always been—a great rough fortress.

They crossed the moat, entering into a great open courtyard where their horses were taken. They followed Janet Munro, who knew her way well, walking to the stone building housing the royal quarters. Maggie didn't like it at all. It seemed a cold, hard place for a queen, let alone a dying woman. Inside, it was cramped, and the furnishings spare due to the lack of space.

"Stay here," Janet said as they came into what was obviously an antechamber. "I must find Master MacCulloch." She hurried off, making her way from the antechamber down a narrow corridor and finally stopping at a small door at its end. She knocked, and then without waiting for an answer, stepped into a little chamber. "Good morrow, Allen," she greeted the man at the high writing table.

Allen MacCulloch looked up. He was a colorless man of medium size and girth who would be indistinguishable in a crowd. He considered this to his advantage. "Good morrow, Janet. Yer up quite early," he said, returning her greeting.

"We must see the king, Allen," Janet said. "I know ye've read my message. Ye never leave anything undone." Her eye went to the comfortable chair by the small hearth. "Do ye sleep here?" she wondered aloud.

"When we are here, aye, I do," he said with a brief smile. "Why do ye want to see him, Janet? 'Twill not be easy, for he rarely leaves the queen's side now."

"'Tis not yer concern why I would see him," Janet Munro said sharply.

"Kinswoman, if ye expect me to work a miracle for ye, and 'twill be a miracle to pry him away for even five minutes, I must know the reason," Master MacCulloch said.

"Remember that I helped ye retain this position when ye were accused of stealing from the privy purse," Janet reminded him. "'Twas I who watched, and I who learned it was Albert Gunn who was the thief. You would have been hanged instead of Master Gunn had it not been for me, Kinsman."

"'Tis true, Janet. I owe ye my life, but I still must have some idea of why yer here if I am to gain the king's ear for ye."

Janet Munro sighed. "Very well," she said. "The daughter I bore him in March was promised a dower and income. My husband sent to him telling the king of Margaret's birth, but he has not replied. I know his love for his queen has driven all else from his mind, but the longer we must wait to settle this matter, the less likely it will be settled. Ye know as well as I do that there are those already seeking a new bride for him. He will mourn, and then be distracted by the search for a new queen. I will never gain what is due my daughter, Allen."

Allen MacCulloch nodded in agreement. "Aye, yer right," he said.

"But it hardly seems so urgent a matter that I must disturb the king over it now."

"I have a way to quickly accomplish the deed, Kinsman. I just need to speak with the king for a brief few moments. I understand that not all that was taken from the king's privy purse was returned," Janet murmured softly.

The secretary flushed, then said, "I will get ye yer audience, Janet. But ye must stay here in the castle until I can accomplish it, for when it is possible, ye must go quickly to him, and state yer case. If ye are not available when the king is, there may not be another opportunity. Do ye understand?"

Janet Munro nodded. "I do, Allen, and I thank ye."

"The debt between us will now be paid in full, will it not?" he asked her.

"Aye, it will be," Janet responded. "I am a mother, Kinsman, and I only want what my bairn was promised, nothing more. I'll have little if anything to do with the court after this. My lord wants a few bairns of his own, and I'm yet young enough to give him some sons, and maybe even a daughter or two."

"Where can I find ye?" he asked her.

"In the first antechamber," Janet Munro replied.

"I'll send to ye when it's time," he told her.

"Farewell then, Allen, and thank ye," Janet said as she left the cramped chamber.

"Well?" Lord Stewart said as she rejoined them.

"The secretary says we must remain here until we are called to come. It may be hours until he can find a moment to get us to James, so we must be patient."

"Will I get to see the king?" Maggie asked ingenuously.

Janet Munro was unable to restrain her smile. "Aye, ye will, but remember ye must not speak to him unless he speaks to ye first."

They waited. And they waited. And they waited. The morning passed. The royal quarters were very quiet, for the king had ordered nothing disturb his queen. Now and again a servant would pass through the chamber in which they waited. The long June afternoon faded into a long twilight. Night came. They had not eaten. They had had nothing to drink but some wine Janet had instructed a serving man to bring them as night finally fell. They spoke little, for there wasn't a great deal to say. Maggie did remark that the hospitality in her grandfather's hall was far better than in the king's.

Finally, two hours past midnight, a page came running into the antechamber. "Are ye Lady Tweed?" he asked of Janet. "Yer to come with me, madam." The page's eyes widened when the two men and the two women got up to follow him. "I was told a lady," he said nervously.

"Ye were not told correctly then," Janet said. "Yer a Leslie, aren't ye, lad? Ye know me, for ye were here when I was last the king's lover. We must all follow ye."

The boy did not argue, for he did indeed know that Janet Munro, now Lady Tweed, had been the king's last mistress before he went off to France to bring back his sickly queen. He led them quickly to a small empty chamber, and then left them.

No one spoke. The door opened suddenly, and James Stewart stepped into the chamber. Maggie followed Janet's lead, curtsying deeply while both men bowed low.

The king raised Janet up by the hand. "A daughter," he said. "Well done, madam. What have ye called her?"

"Margaret, my lord."

James Stewart's glance swung to Fingal Stewart. "Cousin," he greeted him.

Fin bowed again. "'Tis a bad time, I know, my lord, but I would come to pay my respects to ye and yer queen. I have brought my wife to greet ye as well."

James Stewart's eyes turned to look at Maggie, who curtsied again. "Madam," the king said, "I greet ye."

Looking into the king's stern face, Maggie felt tears begin to slip down her cheeks. "Oh, my good lord," she said to James Stewart, "I am so sorry! 'Tis not fair! 'Tis not!" Then she swallowed, trying to control her tears, and catching up the king's hand, kissed it.

Fingal Stewart struggled to find the words to excuse his wife's outburst, but to everyone's surprise, the king put a comforting arm about Maggie and said, "Nay, madam, it isn't fair, is it? But even a king has no choice but to accept God's will. I thank ye for yer concern. I shall tell my Maddie, for she will be touched." He released his hold on her and said to Fin, "I found ye a good wife, Cousin, when all I meant to do was protect Scotland's interests and well-being."

"Ye did, my lord," Lord Stewart agreed, and drew Maggie to his side.

"My lord," Janet spoke up bravely, "there is one bit of unfinished business between us that should be concluded now. 'Tis why I have invaded yer privacy. 'Tis our daughter's care about which I speak."

"Ah," the king replied, understanding.

"I have a solution, my lord, that with yer permission would solve the matter quickly and fairly: Give the income that is yers and comes from the tolls collected from Aisir nam Breug to Margaret, yer daughter. It really costs ye naught as ye will only receive the first of this tribute in November of this year." Janet looked hopefully at the king. "Ye've never had this income, so ye really lose nothing."

A small smile touched the king's lips. "Yer clever," he said, but then he looked to Fingal Stewart. "Will ye agree to this arrangement, my lord?" he asked him.

"There must be conditions," Fin said slowly, ignoring Janet's gasp of surprise.

"Half of yer portion of the tolls will be used for yer daughter's yearly maintenance. The other half will be deposited with the Kira's bank here in Edinburgh. Those monies reserved will serve as Lady Margaret Stewart's dower portion. The arrangement to cease upon her marriage. Should she die before that time, the coin held by the Kiras will be returned to the royal treasury. The arrangement between the royal Stewarts and the Kerrs of Brae Aisir will be concluded for good and all at that time."

"'Tis well thought out, my lord," the king said. "Ye have managed to find a way to regain full control of the Aisir nam Breug one day, Fingal. Well done! And 'twill serve my daughter's interest too. She will have a comfortable income and an excellent dower eventually. I will agree to it, as I am certain Lord Tweed and his wife will too." The cold gray eyes turned to look directly at Janet Munro.

"I agree, my lord," Matthew Baird said. "I would be content if all the monies were set aside for Margaret's dower."

"'Tis generous, my lord," the king remarked, "but I look after my own. Allen MacCullough will see to the arrangement, and I will sign it immediately so ye may all return home knowing the matter is settled. Now I must leave ye, for the queen may be awake again." He dismissed them, but not before taking Maggie by her shoulders and kissing her on both cheeks. "Farewell, madam. I shall always remember your kind heart." Then James Stewart was gone from the chamber.

"Ye might have told me what ye planned, *Cousin*," Janet Munro said sharply.

"Yer daughter needs an income and a dower," Fin said. "I helped ye to see that she got it. But the Aisir nam Breug must have one master in Scotland, and not be passed to a second family and then another and another as these lasses wed. The traverse belongs to the Kerr-Stewarts of Brae Aisir and the Netherdale Kerrs. Now we both have what we need, Janet. Be satisfied with what ye have gotten."

"If I had known ye were so damned clever, I would have considered another kinsman for Brae Aisir," Janet said.

Fin laughed. "He wouldn't have been as strong as I am," he boasted. "Nor could he have outrun, outridden, or outfought her."

Janet sniffed, but Maggie was near to laughing. What a wonderfully clever husband her man was. The Kerr-Stewarts of Brae Aisir. She liked the very sound of it, and she knew her grandsire would too. They returned to the antechamber to wait some more. Finally as the early sun began to stain the horizon, Allen MacCullough came into the waiting chamber with two parchments.

"Can any of ye read?" he asked, and when they all nodded he said, "Read the agreement, and then ye will sign them."

The chamber grew silent as the agreements were read over. Finally they were ready to sign. A page had come into the room carrying a tray with quills, ink, sealing wax, and the king's seal. Fingal Stewart and Matthew Baird signed the agreements as well as a third copy for the royal records. The king's signature had already been written.

The secretary poured a bit of sealing wax on each parchment, stamping the royal seal into the red mass. When all three parchments had been signed and sealed, he rolled them one by one, tying each roll with a thin black cord.

Allen MacCullough put one of the rolls upon the tray, and the page trotted off.

Then he handed the other two copies to each of the two gentlemen. "This business is now concluded, my lords, my ladies. Ye are free to depart the castle. I have already called for yer horses. They await ye in the courtyard. Good day to ye." He turned and left them.

"A very efficient fellow," Lord Tweed noted. "Why did he owe ye a favor, Jan?"

"I saved his life," she said. "But the debt between us is now paid."

"If we had not been up for a full day and a full night," Maggie remarked, "I'd be ready to leave for the Borders this morning, but I am so tired that all I want is my bed right now. And a good meal."

Her companions agreed. They departed the royal apartments, hurrying to find their horses waiting for them as promised. They made their way from the craggy mount upon which the great castle was situated, and back into the town. At an inn called the Thistle and the Rose they stopped to eat a meal. Seated in a corner of the establishment, Maggie was fascinated to see the different people who came into the inn for food, lodging, and drink. It was her first time in the city, and she was amazed by it all.

They ordered and were served eggs poached in Marsala wine, creamed cod, ham, bacon, oat stir-about with cinnamon, fresh warm bread, cheese, butter, and plum jam. Janet Munro was astounded by the amount of food that Maggie managed to eat. She had never seen a woman eat so much nor one who ate with such relish. She didn't know if she felt admiration or shock at her cousin's young wife.

When they had finished their meal, they departed for Lord Stewart's house where Fingal Stewart told his cousin, and her husband, "Stay as long as you wish, but know that Master Boyle, my agent, has two bishops coming next week on a Tuesday, as I let the house out when I am not here. Maggie and I will leave after we have rested a bit. I don't like leaving Dugald alone for too long. It isn't safe."

"I thank ye for the invitation," Matthew Baird said, "but I know Jan wants to get home to little Margaret. We'll depart on the morrow. I thank ye for yer aid."

"Aye, Fingal, thank ye," Janet Munro said. "Even if yer too clever for me by far."

Lord Stewart laughed. "Fair is fair, Cousin." He kissed her cheek. "Travel safely," he told her. Then he joined Maggie upstairs where she was awaiting him.

His wife flung herself into his arms as he entered their bedchamber. She kissed him heartily. "Thank ye! Thank ye!" she said to him.

"For what?" he asked, his arms going about her.

"For regaining what was ours," she told him. "Ye are surely the cleverest man alive, Fingal Stewart. My grandsire will be very pleased."

"It is only ours again when little Lady Margaret Stewart weds, love," he reminded her. "Until then the king's third is hers, half to her dower, the other half to maintain her."

"But then it is ours again with no interference," Maggie said.

"They have no say in how we manage the Aisir nam Breug, but I will tell you truly that I am glad to have James Stewart's fingers out of our pie," Fin said. "Janet will be content as long as her daughter's share is paid in a timely manner, which I will be certain to do, Maggie mine. Now, let us get to bed, for even I will admit to being tired. If we awaken before dark, then we shall be on our way this very day. I am eager to return home to tell Dugald of what has transpired."

They slept until four in the afternoon, but it was high summer, and the sun would not set before midevening. Archie and Grizel having kept reasonable hours, and having been advised by their master, had them ready to depart. By five o'clock they were riding from the town, and on the road to the Borders. They rode until it was almost dark, and after asking shelter of a cottager, slept in his barn for a few hours until the light came again a little after three in the morning. Maggie wasn't unhappy to eat the hard oatcakes and cheese they carried, for she was as eager as her husband to reach home.

Their journey to Edinburgh had taken almost three days' riding in a leisurely fashion with several stops each day. But with hard riding, they reached Brae Aisir just as the dark fell the next evening. Going through the village, Maggie felt contentment at the sight of the lights burning in the cottages and some of the clan folk seated outside gossiping in the mild night air. They had sent a man ahead to advise the keep of their arrival, for the drawbridge had already been raised for the night. But as they rode up the hill road, it was slowly lowered, creaking and groaning mightily until it fell into place across the moat. Their horses clomped across the wooden bridge and into the courtyard.

Dugald Kerr was awaiting them. "Welcome home!" he greeted them.

Maggie jumped from her horse's back and ran to him. "Grandsire, wait until ye hear of our adventures! Fin is the cleverest man alive and has done the Kerr-Stewarts a great service. *Kerr-Stewart!* Is not the sound of it grand? That's what Fin called us in the king's presence." She hugged him, kissing his rough cheek. "Tell me that ye like it."

"I do. I do!" the laird told her. "But come into the hall now so ye may tell me everything that transpired. Ye look tired, Maggie."

"I am, but it doesn't matter. I am so glad to be home, Grandsire!"

Learning they had eaten little since their departure from Edinburgh, Busby, the majordomo, saw that plates containing bread with cheese and meat were brought into the hall along with wine. Grizel and Archie had already disappeared, leaving Maggie in the hall with her husband and her grandfather. Dugald Kerr listened as Maggie recited the news of their adventures.

"Ye didn't see the queen?" he asked.

Maggie shook her head. "Only King James, and he looks so sad."

"Yer granddaughter touched the royal heart by weeping and declaring that the queen's condition was not fair," Fin told the laird. "I never knew James could be touched, but he was. I think she may have gained favor with him, which may be to our advantage one day."

"I didn't do it for that!" Maggie declared vehemently.

"I know, but I also know the king's reputation. He doesn't forget a fault or a slight, but he also remembers a kindness. I imagine all about him have been declaring their false sympathy while at the same time

slyly seeking his opinion on the sort of new wife he would like. Court-
iers say what they know is expected of them in order to gain grace
and favor. Maggie, however, just ushered into the king's presence for
the first time, wept for a king she didn't know, and a queen she will
never know. Her sweetness reached out to him. When we departed
the castle, he kissed her on both cheeks," Fin told the laird. Then
he turned to his young wife. "Someday ye may need a favor from the
king, Maggie mine. I suspect he will remember ye and grant it."

The laird nodded. "Aye, 'tis possible he will."

"I want nothing from the king," Maggie declared.

"Ye may one day, and if not for yerself, for one of yer bairns,"
Dugald Kerr remarked sagely. "Having yer king's favor is nae a bad
thing, lass." He looked to Fin. "Ye did well, my lord. I am now more
convinced than ever that ye will be a good master for Brae Aisir,
and our clan folk. Regaining our full rights when the king's daughter
marries one day was extremely clever. And now that all is settled, I
should like ye both to work harder on giving me a great-grandson. I
am not young and cannot live forever." He sighed, and then seemed
overcome by a bout of severe lassitude.

Fin wanted to laugh, especially as Maggie flew to her grandfather's
side. The laird was a sly old man determined to gain his way in this
matter. Fingal Stewart suspected Dugald Kerr was going to live for
many a long year. He kept his thoughts to himself, instead saying he
thought it was time for them to retire for the night given the lack
of sleep they had suffered over the past few days. The laird heartily
agreed, and so Fin took his wife to bed in order that they might do
their duty by Brae Aisir.

In mid-July, a royal messenger rode to the Borders announcing the
death of Queen Madeleine on the seventh day of the month. She

had died in the king's arms, the messenger confided, on the night he spent in the hall at Brae Aisir. Madeleine de Valois had been a month shy of her seventeenth birthday. They had buried her at Holyrood Abbey next to the palace of the same name where James Stewart had so desperately wanted to bring his bride. The king was in deepest mourning now, and he would speak with no one other than his confessor. But the hunt had begun for a new queen. The king was twenty-five years old, and while he had no shortage of children—six sons and two daughters—he had no legitimate heirs. A new queen was needed as quickly as she could be found, and once again the hunt turned to France. It was important to maintain the French and Scots alliance against the English. There was only one woman whose birth and breeding made her suitable to be James Stewart's queen. He had considered her previously. It was the beautiful widowed Duchess de Longueville, Marie de Guise, who had birthed two sons for her deceased husband. The Scots diplomatic mission set forth to France.

But Henry Tudor, having divorced one wife, and beheaded a second, had just lost his third queen, Jane Seymour, to a childbed fever. In the market for a fourth bride, he sought to block his nephew from obtaining an important French wife. The English ambassador set forth to press King Henry's suit for Marie de Guise's hand. Still in mourning for her husband, the lady was not pleased by either suit. England's, however, she dismissed immediately.

"I may be a large woman," she was overheard saying, "but I have a little neck."

Similar reactions came from other noble ladies being considered by King Henry.

French king François I did approve of a union between the duchess and James Stewart. He sent to the duc de Guise saying he wanted a match between the Scots king and the duc's widowed daughter. Marie de Guise was distressed by the news. She was not against remarrying, but the thought of leaving her country was not pleasing to her. And there was the matter of her sons, who would have to remain at Longueville as they were their father's heirs.

Neither the duc de Guise nor his widowed daughter could refuse King François's wishes. The duc, however, delayed giving the king the expected answer so his daughter might have time to accept what was inevitable. It was then that James Stewart came out of his mourning. His lovely Madeleine had been dead for six months. He had no choice but to take a new queen, to sire an heir for Scotland. He personally wrote to Marie de Guise in his own hand asking her for her advice concerning his dilemma, saying he hoped very much that she would become his queen. They knew and respected each other, which was as excellent a beginning as any for a good Christian marriage, his missive pointed out.

The correspondence was thoughtful and respectful, even tender. It was James Stewart at his most charming, which he could be when he chose to be. Marie was both pleased and touched by the king of Scotland's letter, for she knew how much he had loved her cousin, Madeleine. His offer was an honorable one, and the fact he had come to her personally rather than leaving it all to the diplomats, King François, and her father, was pleasing to Marie de Guise. It showed a modicum of respect for her, for her position as one of France's premier noblewomen. He made her feel as if the choice was really hers.

She acquiesced gracefully. She knew she would be remarried no matter her own wishes. She remembered James Stewart from their brief encounter the previous year. She realized that she actually liked him. He was quite handsome, educated enough, and from what she had heard and been told, he was a king who knew how to rule. Better his wife and his queen than she be wed at her own king's command to some stranger. Scotland might be a rough, cold land, but she would be its queen, and being a queen was no small matter at all. And she would be helping her own native land by keeping the old alliance between Scotland and France a strong one. May 1538 was the date set.

By the time this news had trickled into the Borders, it was past Twelfth Night. Maggie had found herself pregnant late the previous summer, and she now awaited the birth of her first child, who would be born sometime at the end of March. She did not like being with child. She was not allowed to ride or to practice arms in the keep yard. Her grandfather and her husband treated her like some delicate creature. She found them both extremely annoying. The past few months had not been pleasant ones for the inhabitants of the keep as Maggie constantly made her displeasure with them all known.

"The bairn will be born colicky," Grizel said. "Yer dissatisfaction will distress it."

"At least ye don't predict the creature's sex like Grandsire and Fin," Maggie said irritably. "It's the lad this and the lad that. Did it ever occur to either of them that I might birth a daughter? And I suppose if I do, they will both be waiting to see how quickly Fin can get me with another bairn. I hate this! All of it!"

"It's a wife's duty to give her husband an heir," Grizel said as she had said probably a hundred times before. Her mistress had not had an easy time of it, and she wasn't in the least surprised that a girl used to being so active should object to being cocooned as Maggie was being cocooned. She had been horribly sick during the first months of her confinement. When she had felt better, they had attempted to stop her from walking out of doors for fear she would harm the child in her belly. It was ridiculous, and Grizel had said so very firmly. Then she had been allowed this small form of exercise daily, but it wasn't enough for someone as active as Maggie had always been.

"See to yer duties in the hall," her grandsire had advised her.

"The household is under control," Maggie replied in a tight voice.

"And if ye suggest that I sit at my loom one more time, there will be murder done in the hall this day!" Maggie said, glaring.

"I don't remember yer mam being so difficult or yer grandmother," the laird said.

Her belly was enormous to her eye. The little dent in her navel holding the remnants of the cord that attached her to her own mother in the womb was now thrusting forth. The only comfort she seemed to obtain came strangely from the wretched man who had put her in this untenable position. Fin did not sleep with her now, but he would come to her bedchamber each night, sit upon the bed, and rub her feet and ankles for a good hour. His actions were the only thing that kept Maggie from killing him so he could not put her in this position ever again.

One afternoon when Maggie had actually managed to walk as far as the village, Midwife Agnes came to her. She had heard of Maggie's dissatisfaction. "There is something ye can ingest after ye give birth to prevent another bairn until yer ready for one," she said in a low and confidential voice.

"Don't let Father David hear ye," Grizel cautioned. "And what do ye know about such things, Agnes Kerr?"

The midwife barked a short laugh. "I'll keep to my business, Sister Grizel, and ye keep to yers," she said.

"I want it!" Maggie said. "Oh dinna fret, Grizel, I'll give Brae Aisir more bairns. But I don't want to have a big belly every year. My lord is both a potent and an enthusiastic lover." Hearing a creaking noise, she turned. "Jesu!" she swore, for someone at the keep had sent a pony cart to return her up the hill. "I can walk, damn it!"

Chapter 9

The spring equinox came. The days were longer and brighter. On the last day of March, Maggie gave birth so quickly that there was no time, Grizel later complained, for any proper preparations to be made. Not that they weren't ready for the child. The old carved oak cradle had been brought from the attic to be dusted and polished. A new feather and down mattress had been sewn for it. There were swaddling clothes, and tiny gowns ready for the baby.

Maggie had slept fitfully, for her back ached fiercely. Finally as the sun began to rise, she called to Grizel, who had been sleeping on the trundle. "I need wine," she said, "to ease the pain in my back."

"Yer in labor," Grizel replied. "I'll send for Agnes," and she did.

The midwife came to find Maggie, groaning, her pretty face all squinched up. Quickly she whipped off the coverlet and gave a shriek. "The bairn has gotten itself almost out," she cried. "Push down, my lady, and finish it," Agnes said.

Maggie took a deep breath and then pushed as hard as she could, giving a shriek as she did, for she felt her body relieving itself of its burden. And then to her astonishment she heard the cries of an infant. She had been half sitting against her pillows. Now she leaned forward to see what she might see.

The midwife was lifting the bloodied baby up, her face wreathed in a broad smile. "Ye've done yer duty, Mad Maggie Kerr. 'Tis a lad, and no mistake about it," she said.

The door between her chamber and Fin's was suddenly flung open. Her husband stepped into the room. "I heard a cry," he said. "Is all well here?" He looked about him.

"Yer the father of a fine lad, my lord," Agnes said, holding the squalling infant out for him to see. "Let's get him cleaned up and properly swaddled so he may go down to the hall to greet his clan folk."

Fingal Stewart stared at the wet and red infant in her hands. He was not used to children and thought this one rather noisy with his howling. "Maggie?" he said, turning away from the boy and towards his wife.

"For all her troubles these past months," Grizel told her master, "she birthed the bairn easily. I've never seen a quicker delivery, nor has Agnes. If she hadn't awakened me to fetch her some wine, my lady would have had yer lad without us."

"Maggie mine," he said, seating himself next to her, then taking her hand up and kissing it. "Thank ye for our Jamie," he said.

"*Jamie?* We have not yet discussed his name," Maggie responded.

"Why, lovey, have ye not heard yer grandsire and me in the hall these many months talking about what we would name the lad?" he asked her. "He is James Dugald Kerr, and 'twas decided weeks ago."

"And if this bairn had been a lass?" Maggie wanted to know. She was very angry.

"Why, there was never any doubt this would be a lad," Fingal Stewart told his wife in reasonable tones. "We needed a lad. But had my seed been weakened by ye the night I planted it, I'm certain ye would have had a name to give a female bairn."

Maggie couldn't believe what she was hearing. The words coming out of his mouth could have been her grandfather's. She expected the old man to speak such words. But Fingal Stewart? Her husband, who had been so fair with her until this moment? She was outraged. "Leave me," she said in an icy voice.

The delight of his accomplishment in producing a firstborn son now clouding his judgment, Fin said, "In a moment, Maggie mine. I want to take our Jamie down to the hall. Jesu! The lad has good-size balls on him for one so newborn."

"*Get out!*" Maggie shouted. "I'll not have ye parading *my son* about a smoky hall boasting to all who will listen. I will only allow Grandsire in this room to see him. Grizel and Agnes will spread the word as to his birth and health. And when I decide, and only then, will David be taken to the hall."

"*David?* His name is James," Fin said.

"His name is David, after my father, and after my uncle. Add James Dugald to it if ye will, but he is first and foremost David!" Maggie said firmly.

"We'll see what yer grandsire says about that," Fin told her.

"I don't give a damn what Grandsire says," Maggie snapped. "Or ye either for that matter. This is *my* son, *my* firstborn child. Ye did not carry this lad in yer belly for months on end, Fingal Stewart, nor did my grandsire. Yer contribution was to fuck me one fortunate night. And ye enjoyed it as ye always do. The rest of the work was all mine, and I will damned well have a say in naming my son. He will be baptized David James Dugald, and he will be called Davy. Now get out! My son and I need our rest. Yer disturbing us." She waved him away even as Grizel put the swaddled infant into her arms. Maggie looked down at the baby, and was suddenly overwhelmed with a rush of love for her bairn. She had hated the months she had carried him, but seeing him now here cradled against her, she knew she would face a horde of demons to keep him safe.

"Go along, my lord," Grizel told Fin softly. "She'll calm down eventually. Find the laird. Tell him he has a fine new great-grandson, and the Kerr-Stewarts have an heir."

Fin nodded. "The old man will be delighted," he said, and then he left his wife's bedchamber through the same door by which he had come.

"He treated me as if I were some broodmare," Maggie said darkly. "And how dare Grandsire and he choose my bairn's name? And did ye hear him prattling about how I might have *weakened* his seed and produced a lass?"

The two older women burst out laughing.

"Men can be such fools," Midwife Agnes said. "Especially after the birth of a first son. They behave as if they have done it all themselves."

"I want no more bairns for now, Agnes," Maggie said. "Give me what I will need to prevent conceiving. As long as Davy retains his good health, Fingal Stewart and my grandsire will have to wait until a time of my choosing for another heir."

The midwife nodded. "He must keep from yer bed for several weeks while ye heal and recover. If he is randy, then send him to the miller's daughter. She whores now and again to earn a bit of coin to keep her own bairn, as her da will not help her. She was seduced by a passing peddler several years ago, and the miller has never forgiven her. I give her what I'll be giving ye. I'll bring it in two weeks' time to show ye how to use it."

Maggie nodded. "Is there a woman in the village who can serve as wet nurse to Davy? I'll nurse him myself for a month or two, but then I would give him to another for his nourishment, for I need to get back to my own duties in the yard."

"Yer husband and grandsire will forbid it," Grizel warned.

"I'm not some meek stay-by-the-fire," Maggie replied, "and they should both know that. Having a bairn has not changed me one whit."

Grizel watched with amusement over the next few weeks as Maggie behaved with tender concern over her child. Her grandsire was so pleased with her that he acquiesced to her demand that the bairn be named David first.

"Every firstborn son in Scotland is called James for the king," Maggie said. "I would name my son after my father, my uncle, my husband's ancestor. It's fitting for the firstborn of the Kerr-Stewarts to be called David." She cuddled the baby against her.

The laird nodded. "Yer a clever lass," he said.

"I would like the king to be the bairn's godfather," Fingal Stewart ventured. Of late he had become wary of Maggie and her fierce moods.

"I have no objection," Maggie said sweetly.

"I wasn't certain . . ." he began.

"Ye have but to ask me first, my lord," she told him.

A messenger was dispatched to Holyrood, where the king was now in residence, asking if he would consent to be David James Dugald Kerr-Stewart's godfather. The messenger returned with an answer in the affirmative along with the news that James's new queen would be the child's godmother. Of course, little Davy would be baptized immediately for safety's sake with proxies standing in for the king and the queen, who was neither even yet wed to James Stewart nor yet arrived in Scotland.

The old laird nodded, pleased at the king's answer. "He does ye great honor, Fingal," he told Maggie's husband.

"'Tis not me he honors, Dugald, but yer granddaughter. He recalled Maggie's kindness to him before Queen Madeleine died. He repays us now by giving our son powerful connections for his future."

Maggie smiled to herself at his words. The delight at Davy's birth now easing, her husband seemed to be back to being a thoughtful man. The bairn was six weeks old and thriving when Maggie brought Clara Kerr into the hall as Davy's wet nurse. Both Dugald Kerr and

Fingal Stewart were surprised, but Maggie was firm in her intent. As Clara was a respectable woman who had nursed three healthy bairns, but just lost one who was born too early, the laird agreed to the arrangement. If Fingal Stewart was going to disagree, the arrival of a royal messenger put an end to his dissent.

The king would be wed by proxy on the eighteenth day of May at the great cathedral in Paris where sixteen and a half months ago he had been wed to Madeleine de Valois. Robert, Lord Maxwell, would stand in for the king at this wedding. Then after taking time for her farewells, the bride would be escorted across the sea to her new home where she would be wed again, this time with James Stewart by her side.

It was both a happy and an unhappy time for Marie de Guise. She had lost her younger son, the infant Louis, to a childhood illness just a few months prior. She was forced to leave her elder son, three-year-old François, the boy duc de Longueville, behind in France in their family's care. But ahead of her was a new husband, and hopefully other children, one of whom would be Scotland's next king.

At Brae Aisir, Fingal Stewart was surprised to learn that he and Maggie had been invited to the royal wedding, which would take place at St. Andrews several days after the queen's arrival in Fife. Fingal was not comfortable going, but he knew it was a request he could not refuse. The Kerrs of Brae Aisir were not important, and even his kinship with the king would not have necessarily granted them an invitation to such a stellar event. But go they would.

"Is St. Andrews near Edinburgh?" Maggie asked.

"Not near enough for us to stay in our house," Fin told her.

"Then where are we to stay?" she wanted to know. "We must be someplace with accommodation for Grizel and Archie. Someplace where our clothing can be hung so we do not attend the royal wedding looking like rough, uncouth poor relations."

He couldn't give her an answer because he didn't know himself. Archie, however, as resourceful as ever, had gone to Iver to ask whether any of the men who had come with them originally had connections in St. Andrews. To his surprise, Iver Leslie had the answer to their difficulties.

"My late da's brother owns an inn in St. Andrews," he said. "I'll send to him."

"Ye'll need more than just yer kinship," Archie said. "With the king celebrating his wedding there, there will be money to be made. Ye can't ask yer uncle to forgo his share of the profits. Besides, if ye just send to him, he can easily refuse ye. Ye must go yerself and convince him yer master is important to the king, and must have generous accommodation not just for him, his wife and servants, but for ye and yer men-at-arms as well. I know yer a man of few words, but ye must do this for his lordship."

Iver knew Archie was right. His uncle had always been tight with a groat, and Lord Stewart had the coin to pay for what he wanted. It would not cost his kinsman.

Telling his master that he would ride to St. Andrews and obtain the needed lodging, he departed Brae Aisir. Reaching St. Andrews, he found his uncle's inn near one of the the town's three entries, the South Gate. Iver was relieved to learn his childhood memory had not been imagination. The Anchor and the Cross was large and prosperous looking.

Iver's uncle, Robert Leslie, like his own father, had been born on the wrong side of the blanket in a place called Glenkirk. But he hadn't been neglected as a child. Indeed, he had been taught to read and write and knew his numbers. When he was sixteen, he had left Glenkirk, a small purse hidden in his garments, to find his fortune. He had found it by marrying the daughter of an innkeeper in St. Andrews, working hard for his father-in-law, and was now the master of a most prosperous business.

He greeted his brother's son cautiously. "What do ye want?" he demanded to know of Iver. His tone was suspicious. His brother had outlived two wives so far and delighted in spawning bairns like a randy salmon struggling upstream. Most were lads who had to be provided for, and twice he had sought places for his sons, but Robert Leslie had four lads of his own to see to and could not help his sibling.

The captain laughed. "Peace, Uncle. I am gainfully employed and have come to seek accommodation for my master, his wife, and their retinue for the time of the king's wedding. Lord Stewart can pay handsomely for yer best."

"*Lord Stewart*, ye say. Is he close kin to the king?" the innkeeper asked.

"The king is godfather to my master's new son, and our new queen the godmother," Iver replied, although he did not really answer his uncle's question.

"Indeed, is he now?" Robert Leslie responded. "Well, I suppose I can make room although I was holding several chambers for last-minute arrivals who would have paid handsomely for the beds. Still, a kinsman to the king himself, although God knows half of Scotland has been spawned by the Stewarts' loving nature, is a good guest to serve."

Iver smiled, satisfied, drawing a gold coin from his jacket. "This will hold the accommodation for my master until he arrives," he said, turning the sparkling coin over in his fingers several times. "Now show me the rooms you will give my lord and his lady. Then the coin is yers."

"Follow me," Robert Leslie said. He led his nephew up a flight of stairs, and down to the end of a corridor. Opening the door at the end of the hallway he said, " 'Tis the best I have. A chamber for visitors, one for sleeping, and two small alcoves for the servants. It overlooks my garden, not the street, and is quiet."

Iver stepped into the apartment and looked about. Each chamber had a hearth, which was good, for June could have cold nights here by the sea. But it was clean, and he doubted there was a better accommodation in all of St. Andrews. "'Twill do," he said, and flipped the coin to his uncle, who caught it. "They'll arrive on the tenth of the month. I'll be with them. Have ye room in yer stables to sleep the men-at-arms?"

"Aye," Robert Leslie said, "but 'twill cost ye more, for the town will be crowded, and any space that can be rented will be."

"Lord Stewart has lived most of his life in Edinburgh," Iver replied. "He knows the way of the world. We are agreed then?"

"We're agreed, Nephew. How is yer da?" he inquired, unable to help himself.

"I wouldn't know," Iver admitted. "I haven't been back to Glenkirk in at least ten years, Uncle. Yer nearer. Do ye never go?"

"When would I have time?" Robert Leslie said. "A man cannot be the landlord of a successful and busy inn and be somewhere else. If ye haven't eaten, come into my kitchens," the innkeeper said, feeling more jovial now that the transaction had been concluded, and the gold coin rested in his pocket. "And make a place for yerself in the stables tonight if ye will."

"I'll take the meal," Iver replied, "but the day isn't half over, and I can be well on my way back to the Borders by nightfall if I leave afterwards."

"Suit yerself, Nephew," Robert Leslie said. "I'll see ye next month then."

Iver was relieved to reach Brae Aisir several days later and report that he had secured a decent lodging for them to stay.

Maggie, usually so sure of herself, was very nervous about going to St. Andrews. Her earlier enthusiasm had suddenly vanished. "Could ye not go without me?" she asked her husband. "Davy is just getting used to Clara's teat, and my milk only just dried up. I haven't got the kind of clothes one would wear to a king's wedding."

"The king has asked us. I am his kin, and he likes yer kind heart," Fingal said. "This isn't an invitation we can refuse. We will not be among the first rank of guests, Maggie mine. The Gordons of Huntly, the Leslies of Glenkirk, they will be. And while I have avoided the subject for fear of distressing ye, the king has been very hard on several of our border families of late. The Johnsons, the Scotts, the Armstrongs, the Humes, have all suffered his wrath. Anyone he suspects of ties with the Douglases, his hated enemies, is suspect in his eyes. I will not allow the Kerrs to be touched by this behavior. We are asked to the wedding, and we will go. We may not be garbed as well as the earls and their wives, but we shall not bring shame to our name."

Dugald Kerr sat by the hall hearth pretending to doze, but he took in every word Maggie's husband uttered. Fingal Stewart was a blessing to Brae Aisir. He knew that the king, unfamiliar with his kinsman, for Fin had told him so, had had no idea the kind of man he sent into the Borders to wed Maggie Kerr. Nor had he cared. He had only wanted a portion of the revenues from the tolls the Kerrs collected. And he had taken the advice of his current mistress as to whom to send. She, of course, had offered him a member of not only her family, but the king's. It could have been a disaster. And now thanks to his granddaughter's good heart, the Kerrs of Brae Aisir had found favor in the sight of a volatile and fickle monarch. Maggie would go to the wedding if he had to take her himself, the laird decided.

But it was not necessary. When the time came for them to depart for St. Andrews, Maggie's enthusiasm had returned. She bid her grandfather farewell, promising to bring him back a treat of some sort from St. Andrews. "Mayhap a medal blessed in the cathedral to help ease the winter ache in yer bones, Grandsire," she said.

Their trip was relatively uneventful, but as they drew near to the ferry that would take them across the Firth of Forth into Fife, the roads became more crowded with all manner of folk going to St. Andrews. Some were guests, some merchants hoping to sell their wares to the excited folk; others were pickpockets and thieves, and many were going simply to gain a glimpse of the king and the new queen. Summer was almost upon them, and the air hummed with festivity. Iver rode a little ahead of them to secure them places on one of the ferries.

"How many?" the harbor agent demanded to know.

"Lord Stewart, his wife, two servants, fifteen men-at-arms, twenty horses," Iver said. "Official guests for the king's wedding."

The harbor agent nodded. "Yer boat goes out on the hour. Get yer people here." He handed Iver a small slip of parchment. "Don't lose this. Next!"

Iver hurried back to help lead his party to the front of the pushing, chattering crowds. He handed the chit to the seaman seeing to the boarding, and they were waved through, across a gangway, and onto the vessel. Once on board, their men-at-arms saw to the horses, leading them into a sheltered corner on the open deck. The ferry was soon deemed filled, and it was freed from its moorings to slip out into the broad estuary.

Fin was relieved for Maggie's sake that it was a calm sea. There was no strong wind, only enough of a breeze to help them cross the water piloted by the ferry's oarsmen. It was a gray day, however, with a thick canopy of clouds overhead. Lord Stewart knew how both exciting and frightening the trip to St. Andrews was for Maggie. She had never been more than a few miles from her home in all her life. And then suddenly there appeared an impressive fleet of ships making its way towards the same harbor that their ferry was directing itself.

A shout of excitement went up from the captain, and he called down from the small pilothouse where he had been, "My lords! My ladies! 'Tis the king's fleet, and that fine vessel in the middle of it all flying the royal lion pendant is carrying our new queen. Let us have three cheers for our own French Mary!"

And the ferry erupted. "Huzzah! Huzzah! Huzzah!"

And at the same time the ferry full of passengers saluted Marie de Guise, the sun broke through the cloud bank, a golden ray coming forth to seemingly touch the ship upon which she traveled. The ferry passengers gasped, excited, and the talk immediately began to make the rounds of how fortunate an occurrence this obvious show of God's approval was for both King James and for Scotland.

Their ferry reached the other shore before the royal fleet, and the passengers quickly disembarked, for there was still a ride to make to St. Andrews, and if they were not ahead of the queen and her party, they would be delayed for hours. Those in the party from Brae Aisir were swiftly on their way. As they rode to the town Fin told his wife a little about it.

"There has been a town here for as long as anyone can recall," he began. "There are three gates. The North, the South, and the Church. There are two ports. West Port, which opens into South Street, and the Marketgate Port. We're entering through the South Gate. We'll be on South Street, which has many important ecclesiastical buildings."

"Where is our inn?" Maggie wanted to know. "If the queen has set her foot on Scottish soil, then the wedding will be tomorrow or the day after. My gowns need to be hung so the wrinkles are removed. Of course, they will be wed at the cathedral. Is it on South Street too?"

"We'll pass it on the way to the Anchor and the Cross," Fin answered her.

"What an odd name for an inn," Maggie remarked.

"Nay," Fin said. "St. Andrews is the most important church in all of Scotland, and the town is set on the sea."

"Aah," Maggie replied. "I see now. And it is really more dignified than that inn we stayed at last night, the Pig and Pipe," she laughed. "But I loved the sign there with the dancing pig playing on the bagpipe."

"Did ye notice the plaid the pig wore?" her husband said. "It was Hunting Stewart." And then he laughed too.

They passed through the South Gate, moving down bustling and busy South Street. On the north side of the byway they passed Holy Trinity Church, the oldest in St. Andrews, even older than the great cathedral up ahead. Maggie saw why St. Andrews was thought of as the religious capital of Scotland. They rode past the chapel of the Dominican Friary, the Observantine Franciscan Friary set amid a beautiful garden named Greyfriars after the color of the monks' robes.

The cathedral was the most magnificent church Maggie had ever seen or expected she would ever see. Its dark stone spires soared into the partly cloudy skies above the town. It had great windows of what Fin told her was called stained glass. The glass had come along with the craftsmen to make the cathedral windows from France several hundred years prior when St. Andrews Cathedral had been built. It had taken between the years 1160 and 1318 to complete the structure. When it had been consecrated, King Robert the Bruce had been in attendance.

"Where will the king and queen stay?" Maggie asked, curious.

"They will be in the castle at the north end of the town on the Firth of Tay," he answered her. "It's not a particularly comfortable dwelling, I'm told, but the bishop has offered it to them, and there is no other place, aside from a priory guesthouse and an inn."

Used to either making what she needed, or purchasing it from a border peddler, Maggie was amazed by the number of shops on South Street. If there was time, she and Grizel would certainly want to at least look in some of them. Several minutes after passing the cathedral they arrived at their inn. Iver had dashed ahead to make certain all was in readiness for Lord Stewart's party. As they dismounted in the inn's courtyard, Robert Leslie came forth to greet them.

The innkeeper bowed low. "I am honored, my lord, to be able to serve the king's own kinsmen," he told Fin.

"I thank ye for making a place for my wife and me," Lord Stewart answered graciously in return. Iver had told him how impressed his uncle had been with the knowledge that his nephew's master was related to James Stewart. And Fin had understood without the captain saying another word that the depth of that relationship had not been probed, yet was accepted as significant by the innkeeper, who needed to know no more than that the king and Iver's master were related.

"Let me show you to your accommodation, my lord," Robert Leslie said as he led them into the inn and up the staircase, then down the hallway to fling open the door to the guest apartment. "We aired it out this morning, my lord, and the fires are ready to start. Shall I send a maid to do it for you?"

"My man can attend to it, thank you, Master Leslie," Fin replied politely.

"There is a tray on the sideboard here in the dayroom with decanters for yer wine and yer whiskey," the innkeeper said. "Is there anything else I can do for ye now?"

"I want a bath," Maggie said in a firm voice.

The innkeeper looked surprised. "A bath, my lady?"

"Ye have a decent tub, I assume," she continued. "Have it set up in my bedchamber by the fire, and filled with hot water. We have been traveling for several days, and I am covered with the dust of the road."

"Very good, my lady," the innkeeper responded. A tub? Did they have a tub? And if they did, where the hell was it? And how much water would have to be heated to fill such a vessel? Providing accommodation for a lady was not going to be as easy as he had thought. He bowed to Lord Stewart and his wife and hurried from the apartment.

"Do ye have something she can bathe in?" Iver asked, for he had seen the look of consternation on his uncle's face when Maggie had spoken.

"I don't know. I can't ever remember someone wanting a bath while staying here," Robert Leslie admitted. "I'll have to ask my wife. She would know."

Mistress Leslie laughed at her obviously chagrined husband's request. "Of course we have a tub," she said. "My father always said ye needed everything for the unexpected request if ye were to be a well-run inn. Dinna fash, Robert. I'll take care of Lady Stewart, my dear." And she bustled off.

Maggie inspected their little apartment, exclaiming as she went to the windows at the pretty garden below with a view of the sea beyond. Grizel hurried to unpack her few gowns and hang them. When Mistress Leslie arrived to direct the setting up of the tub and saw what Grizel was doing, she insisted the tiring woman bring her ladyship's gowns to the washhouse where they could be steamed free of any wrinkles. Delighted, Grizel picked up the three garments and followed the innkeeper's wife.

"*Her ladyship*," Maggie chuckled. "I don't think anyone has ever called me that before," she said to Fin. "But I am, aren't I?"

"Ye are," he agreed, amused.

"Lady Kerr-Stewart," she mused. "I don't know if I'm up to being Lady Kerr-Stewart. All of this is so strange to me. The town, so many people, the sea beyond the garden windows. And I am here to attend the wedding of a king to his queen. Part of me is excited, and part of me wants to go home right now," Maggie told her husband.

"Yer the bravest lass I know, Maggie mine," Fin told her. "Ye'll do just fine."

"I've never met anyone other than our fellow borderers," she said. "There will be important men and women here. Great Highland lords, a king, a queen, bishops."

"And they will be charmed by yer beauty," he said.

Maggie laughed aloud. "Oh Fingal Stewart, was there ever such a good husband as ye? And do I deserve ye? I am not certain I do." He put his arms about her shoulders, and Maggie leaned against him, feeling a contented warmth fill her. She liked this man who was her husband. Nay, it was more than like. She was coming to love him. She sighed. Was it wise to love one's husband? Love wasn't something with which she was really acquainted, but she knew what she felt now for Fin was more than just a liking.

While Maggie bathed, Lord Stewart sent Iver to the castle so the king would know his unimportant kinsman and his wife were arrived. He expected nothing in return, but at least the king would know they had come. Perhaps the king might even see them at the wedding or in the banquet hall afterwards. It was crucial, however, for James Stewart to know that Fingal Stewart had acted on the royal invitation. He was surprised, therefore, when Iver returned to say the king had sent word he expected to see his kinsman and Maggie this very evening at a reception being held for all the guests.

"He spoke to me himself, my lord!" Iver said excitedly. "I but told a castle servant that I carried a message for the king from his kinsman, Lord Stewart. The next thing I knew, I was ushered into the king's presence. I could hardly speak at first, but then *he* said, 'Why, here is a message from my cousin, Fingal Stewart of Torra.' Those around him pretended they knew who ye were, my lord, and I almost laughed aloud, so eager were they all to please King James. He knew them to be false, and he laughed. Then he asked what the message I carried was, and I told him. 'Tell Fingal, my cousin, that I will expect to see him, and his bonnie Maggie, here tonight,' he told me. I nodded, bowed, and hurried right back to the inn to bring you his message."

Maggie, freshly bathed, and now in the bedchamber, heard Iver's words. "Grizel!" she hissed. "Do ye hear him? What am I to wear?"

"The peach velvet with the gold lace," Grizel said. " 'Twill make a grand first impression on all those fine lords and ladies. Tomorrow all eyes will be on the bride. Tonight is the night to show yerself to yer best advantage, m'lady. I'll tell Archie so my lord's garments match with yers."

"Fin in peach velvet, Grizel? I think not," Maggie teased.

Grizel laughed, and quickly seeking out their master's servant, whispered hurriedly in his ear. Archie whispered back, nodding vigorously. Grizel returned to her mistress and began helping her to prepare for the evening. While she dressed Maggie in the bedchamber, Archie was busily garbing his master in the dayroom. When Grizel had finished, Maggie was wearing a gown of peach-colored velvet with a square neckline edged with gold embroidery. The underskirt of the gown was brocade with gold reembroidery. Her slashed sleeves were tied with gold cords. On her head she wore a gold silk French hood with lace-edged trimming behind which flowed a sheer pale silk veil shot through with gold threads. Beneath her gown her legs were encased in white silk stockings embroidered with gold threads in a vine pattern. Her feet were shod in square-toed flat shoes covered in gold silk and studded with gold beading. She had several rings on her fingers, and her clan badge was fastened to a thick gold chain about her neck.

"Stay here," Grizel said to her lady, "while I see if his lordship is ready."

In the dayroom Archie had just finished dressing his master in light brown velvet. Fin wore slashed breeches, and parti-colored hose of brown and gold. His sleeveless doublet was a brown and gold brocade over which Archie fitted his master into a fine short coat of brown velvet with large padded sleeves. He had brown leather square-toed shoes on his big feet, and a fine gold chain about his neck with the greyhound pendant badge of his family. The hat his serving man gave him had a gold silk-taffeta crown and a stiff flat brim. A single short plume dangled from it.

"Ohh," Grizel said. "Don't he look grand, Archie! Ye've outdone yerself this time, I'll vow."

"Where are the garments coming from?" Fin demanded. "And do not evade answering me this time, you scoundrel. I certainly have no coin for such elegance."

"Tell him!" Grizel said. "He's ever so clever, my lord, he is!"

"Tell me what?" Fin insisted.

"I make yer garments, my lord," Archie said, flushing with his embarrassment.

If ever anything had surprised Fingal Stewart in all of his life, it was his serving man's admission that he made his master's clothing. "Ye sew my clothes?" he said.

"First I make the pattern on paper, my lord. Cut it, and then cut the materials to match. Ye can afford the cloth, and recently ye have been able to bear the cost of a better quality of cloth. Then I sew it all together. Grizel and I worked many a night together fashioning proper garments for ye and the lady. After ye went to Edinburgh to see the king when the little queen was dying, we knew ye would need fine clothing eventually. So we purchased the cloth we needed from the peddlers coming to Brae Aisir, and we fashioned the garments we thought ye would need. Perhaps they are not quite as fashionable as others, for styles change, but ye'll not have to be ashamed."

Maggie had heard all of Archie's explanation through the open door between the bedchamber and the dayroom. Now she stepped forth to stand by her husband's side. "Thank ye both," she told Grizel and Archie. "I don't think either of us has ever had such beautiful clothing. Yer labors are more than appreciated."

Both Archie and Grizel flushed with pride at her words.

"How handsome ye look, my lord," Maggie said to her husband. "The brown and gold of yer garments suits ye, and flatters me."

There was a knock on the dayroom door. Archie quickly opened it.

"The horses are ready, my lord," Iver said. "I've put the proper saddle on my lady's animal."

"God's toenail, I must ride like a proper lady," Maggie grumbled. "I'm always terrified I'm going to fall that way."

"At least you brought the mare, and not that damned devil stallion of yers," Lord Stewart said.

Maggie chuckled. She refused to give up her stallion, nor would he give up his. But to please him, she had ridden her fine white mare from Brae Aisir. She had noticed on the ferry across the Firth of Forth the beast had received many admiring glances, and she had become concerned she could be stolen. But Iver was an excellent captain, and his men were well trained. It was unlikely anything would get past them.

They bid Grizel and Archie good night and descended downstairs. The inn was now full to overflowing, and as they made their way to the door, a voice shouted out.

"Look lads! It's Mad Maggie Kerr, the border vixen herself. She whored herself to an Edinburgh man rather than wed a good borderer." A drunken Ewan Hay planted himself directly in front of them.

Lord Stewart paused only long enough to send the man sprawling. Then turning, he said to a horrified Master Leslie, "See this garbage has been removed by the time we return from the castle, innkeeper."

"Aye, my lord," Robert Leslie babbled. "I want no trouble in my inn. Here, you, Willie, Arthur, remove this man at once!"

Maggie was so surprised, she hardly had a moment to react. Her husband's hand firmly on her elbow, he moved her outside, and lifted her up onto her horse. "Fingal!"

"Not a word, madam," he told her in a hard voice as he lifted her up onto her mare. "The bastard was offensive to ye, to me, to Brae Aisir." He mounted his horse.

"We don't need a feud with the Hays," Maggie told him quietly as they moved off, surrounded by their men-at-arms. But she found herself thrilled that he had behaved so masterfully in her defense. Was it possible he was coming to care for her? Or had it merely been a matter of his pride? She wished she were clever enough to discern which.

"There will be no feud. Lord Hay will understand," Fin responded. "He had really best either send his brother away to fight in someone's war, or find him a wife to settle him down before the man gets himself killed. What a fool he is. Ye would have cut his heart out in short order had ye been forced to wed him, and he is too stupid to realize it."

"Aye, he is, but Ewan Hay is also a man who holds grudges," Maggie said. "And he will wait a long time to avenge a fault. "We don't need him as an enemy, Fin. I'll be the first to agree with you that he's a fool, but he's a dangerous fool."

"He had best remain clear of Brae Aisir. I will not have my wife insulted in a public place. Had he not been drunk, I would have been forced to kill him," Fin said.

"'Twould not have been an auspicious start for our visit, my lord. I do not doubt that whatever small favor we have garnered from the king would be lost by such actions, *and more*," Maggie told him pointedly.

They moved through the town from South Street to North Street and followed along with others who had been invited to tonight's festivities and were also making their way to the castle. Maggie looked about her and decided that she and Fin fit in quite nicely. Reassured their garments were suitable, she felt her courage return; she laughed softly at herself to realize she had been frightened by something as foolish as fashion. She had never been a woman who cared that much for gowns and fripperies. But she also realized that a woman who attended a king's reception before his wedding to a French duchess needed a respectable wardrobe, and she was glad she had one.

They reached St. Andrews Castle, and in the courtyard their horses were taken from them while their men-at-arms found themselves invited to sit at the trestles that had been set up in the large open enclosure. Maggie, her hand on her husband's arm, followed along as they walked with other guests to the great hall of the castle. It was a damp evening, but the big fireplaces in the hall were heaped high with logs, and took the chill from the night. The king and Marie de Guise had not yet joined their guests.

"Every lordling in Scotland must be here," Maggie said, looking about. She saw no one she knew. And the variety of clothing was striking. Many were dressed in the same style of fashionable garments as she and Fin. But others, Highlanders, she immediately realized, came in leather breeches, their plaids pinned with their clan brooches slung across their chests, and over one shoulder. They wore caps with eagle feathers on their heads, and their hair was unfashionably long, some with it tied back, others with it left loose about their shoulders.

"Aye," Fin agreed. "The northerners have come to gain a sense of this man who has barged into their territories, forcing them to his will."

"Do ye know any of them?" Maggie asked, curious.

"Nay," he said. "I have spent most of the last years as a mercenary in France and the Italian and German states. Those Highland chiefs do not venture far from their own lands."

There was a musicians' gallery above the end of the hall where they had entered.

In it a dozen or more musicians sat playing. Servants passed among the crowds, offering small goblets of wine. At the other end of the hall a dais was set up. An awning of wide cloth of gold and royal purple stripes was set over it. On the dais were two high-backed chairs with carved and curled arms. A tufted purple cushion had been placed on the flat seat of each chair. One chair, however, was smaller, and lower than the other. Maggie moved forward to get a better look at what had obviously been set up as thrones.

At that moment the doors at the far end of the hall were opened. A flourish of trumpets sounded from the musicians' gallery, and a stentorian voice pronounced, "My lords and my ladies, the king and the queen." The crowds parted to either side of the hall, making an aisle for the royal couple to move forward to their thrones. Maggie panicked, realizing that in her effort to see the dais better she had become separated from her husband. She stood silently in the very forefront of the crowd, her heart hammering nervously as King James and Marie de Guise came forward.

When the couple had almost reached their destination, James's eye caught Maggie's, and she curtsied lower than she had ever curtsied in her life. "Aah, here is the lady of Brae Aisir, wife to my kinsman, the Stewart of Torra." Raising Maggie, the king said, "Marie, I present to you Lady Margaret Kerr. Where is Fingal, Maggie?"

"I am here, my liege," Fin said, pushing his way through the crowd. He bowed elegantly to the king, and then kissed the new queen's outstretched hand. "I salute ye, madam, and the great house of Guise from which ye sprang. Welcome to Scotland," he said in perfect French.

Marie de Guise broke into a smile. "I thank ye, my lord," she answered him in her own native tongue. "Ye have obviously lived in France."

"I have fought in France, madam," he answered her.

"We must speak again," Marie de Guise said, "and your lovely wife, my lord."

"We will be honored, madam," Fin said.

"My kinsman is not an important man, *ma chérie*," the king told her. "But he is the kind of man you can have complete faith in, for his branch of the family have never betrayed their kings. Not even once. Their motto is *Ever faithful*, unlike many you will meet this night among my great lords." His gaze met Fingal Stewart's. "Thank ye for coming, my lord and my lady." Then, with a bow to them, the king moved on with his new wife to gain the dais and sit upon their thrones.

It was to be the highlight of their visit to St. Andrews, for they did not get close to the king and his bride again. As the king himself had said, they were not important. It made no difference to Maggie. She stood in the great cathedral on the twelfth day of June, watching as the king was formally married to Marie de Guise. She partook of the wedding feast in the castle's great hall that day from a trestle in the back of the chamber.

They had departed the celebration early that night, for in the morning they would begin their return trip to the Borders. Their life was there rather than among the high and mighty who surrounded the king and his new queen. But Mad Maggie Kerr would never forget those few wonderful days she and Fin spent in St. Andrews.

Chapter 10

_E_ wan Hay had never been more surprised in his life than he
was when Mad Maggie Kerr's husband had without a single
word sent him crumbling to the floor. As he sat dazed upon
the floor of the Anchor and the Cross, Ewan tasted the blood in his
mouth, and at least two of his teeth felt loose. But there was no time
to feel sorry for himself, for the landlord's two sturdy sons pulled him
up, and hustled him out the inn door, tossing him rudely into the
street.

"Dinna come back!" the taller of the two said to him.

"Ye have no right," Ewan blustered. "I paid for my accommodation!"

"Ye forfeited it when ye insulted the wife of the king's kinsman,"
the innkeeper's son said. "Begone with ye now!"

"I want my money back!" Ewan yelled as he got to his feet.

"What ye'll get is a beating ye'll ne'er forget if yer not on yer way
by the time I count to three," came his answer. "One! Two! Three!"
The innkeeper's son stepped forward menacingly, his two big fists
balled tightly, his look fierce.

Ewan Hay turned and ran. The laughter that followed him didn't
help his mood. His stomach rolled, and stepping into an alley, he
vomited much of the sour wine and ale he had consumed that day.
Then he stepped out of the narrow passage, straightened his garb,

dusted himself off, and followed along with the crowds headed for St. Andrews Castle. He managed amid the excitement and confusion to gain entry into the great hall before the king and queen arrived.

As he wandered through the jovial crowd of guests, he suddenly spotted Mad Maggie Kerr in her peach velvet gown. He edged himself closer and closer to her. Her husband was nowhere in sight. Ewan had wanted her for years, although she didn't know it. He had first seen her when she was about thirteen, riding across the moors. She had been hell-bent for leather, leaning low over the neck of that great dapple gray stallion of hers, her skirts hiked high, her bare white legs visible to anyone with eyes to see. Her rich brown hair had been blowing in the wind, and Ewan Hay thought she was the most beautiful and desirable girl he had ever seen. She hadn't seen him.

She never saw Ewan Hay as he watched her ride the moors, or at the meetings of the border chieftains when she came with her grandfather and he had been with his brother. He fantasized about seducing her; about riding her down, taking her from her horse, and having his way with her in the heather. She would fight him, of course. And each time he considered it, his cock grew to iron in his breeks. He imagined her clawing at him in a desperate effort to avoid his possession. He imagined her screaming at him, cursing him, as he impaled her and fucked her until she fainted.

He still dreamed of her, the duplicitous bitch! Her breasts rising and falling above the gold edging on her bodice were so damned tempting. That coquettish little French hood that framed her face so perfectly enticed him to creep closer. But then suddenly the king and queen were there. And James Stewart was actually talking to her—talking to that border vixen as if they were friends! Her husband came to stand by her side, and together they conversed with smiles and pleasantries with the royal couple as intimates. Ewan Hay couldn't believe his eyes. How had Mad Maggie Kerr become a king's friend?

Brae Aisir's mistress would become the most powerful woman in the Borders, and Maggie's husband would be the most powerful man. No! It was he, Ewan Hay, who should be that man. And he would have been if James Stewart had given Maggie to him. If only the king had listened to him and then given him the wench to wife, he could have been a happy man. He, instead of Fingal Stewart, would have taken over the Aisir nam Breug. The usurper had no right to Maggie or the land. They should have been his. And they were going to be! Ewan Hay was going to find a way to gain everything that belonged to Brae Aisir—except, of course, Fingal Stewart and his spawn. *But how?*

James V had a good grip on his throne. While not well thought of by his nobility, he was loved by the people and had strong allies in the church. But his determination to eradicate anyone connected with his former stepfather, his mother's second husband, Archibald Douglas, the Earl of Angus, made him enemies. James, however, could not put his wretched childhood in Angus's care behind him.

He had no memories of his father, James IV. But his father had been well liked by all. From all accounts, the fourth James Stewart had been a courtly, educated, dashing prince who had taken his father's throne from him in a coup at the age of fifteen. He had had several beautiful mistresses, a family of bastard sons and daughters, and the devotion of all who knew him. And he had died at Flodden Hill in a battle against the English in spite of having an English princess for a wife. And with him had died more of Scotland's nobility than could be counted. Among the thousands dead were the heads of fourteen important families, a bishop, an archbishop, several abbots, and nine earls.

And James V had been only eighteen months old at the time. His uncle, England's King Henry VIII, wanted physical custody of him. His mother quickly remarried to protect herself and her children. Her choice had been pro-English, but Archibald Douglas, the Earl of Angus, used young James to rule for himself. He did everything he could to see that James was raised ignorant, and debauched. But there were those about the young prince who protected him, and kept him from the worst of Angus's machinations. And his mother found her second husband quickly lost his charm. She divorced him finally, despite her brother's exhortation to remain with him for the sake of her good name, and married a third time to Lord Methven, another error in judgment.

By this time, James V had escaped the clutches of the Douglases, taken up his power, and begun wreaking his vengence. Lady Janet Glamis, sister of the Earl of Angus, he burned at the stake on Castle Hill in Edinburgh for the crime of attempting to poison him. The charges were false. He made the Earl of Morton turn over his earldom to the Crown and pressed the heir to the Earl of Crawford to renounce his claim to that title in favor of the king. He came down hard on the border lords who favored the Douglases, bringing them to their knees and under his thumb. He compelled the lords of the Western Isles to his will. James V was not well liked. But he was feared.

But now happily wed to his beautiful and charming queen, he began embarking upon architectural projects to make over some of Scotland's castles into replicas of the fine châteaus he had seen in the Loire Valley of France. The wealth he had confiscated, the wealth he gained each year, and the generous dowers of his two French queens allowed the king to indulge himself while offering employment to his subjects.

At Brae Aisir life took on a comfortable routine. The Borders were relatively quiet for the moment. Old Dugald Kerr's health seemed miraculously restored. Maggie wondered if her grandsire's former frailty had been a sham to get her wedded and bedded. She had returned from St. Andrews to find that despite her good intentions, she was pregnant once more. A second son, Andrew Robert, was born the following April.

The queen was formally crowned consort in February 1540. In the spring of that same year King James launched a naval campaign against the lords of the northern and western isles who were once again becoming unruly. Late in the previous year, a chieftain in the northwest, one Donald Gorme, had claimed the lordship of the isles, and rebelled. To Fingal Stewart's surprise, the king invited him to join this expedition. Maggie was not happy to have her husband go off to what would surely be a short but nasty war. What did the northwest of Scotland have to do with them?

"What do ye know of the sea?" she demanded to know.

"Naught," he replied calmly. "Archie, pack my things, and tell Iver to choose a dozen men to accompany us."

"Yer going to go?" She was astounded.

"Ye know my family's motto. We've never refused a royal command," Fin said.

"His message is an *invitation*," Maggie pointed out.

"When a king invites ye," Dugald Kerr said, "ye go, lass. It's a polite way of commanding. The king hardly trusts the border families as it is. We're counted among the faithful because of the past behavior of the Stewarts of Torra. Fin has no choice. He must and he will go."

"Yer capable, more than capable, of managing the Aisir nam Breug," Fin said to his wife. " 'Twill be like old times for ye," he teased her.

"I find I like new times better," Maggie muttered.

The two men laughed.

"Never did I think I would see the day when ye would be tamed, lass," her grandsire said, "but ye surely have been."

"I am not *tamed*," Maggie snapped. "But running a household, along with caring for a fussy old man, and two wild lads, is a great deal of work. Now I must add care of the traverse to it? Well, if I must, then I must."

"Ye'll do it, and do it well," Fin told her.

"I'm going to bed," Maggie told him. "I'm going to need as much rest as I can get if I'm to be burdened with all this work."

Fin grinned. "I'll go with ye, madam," he said, following his wife from their hall and up the stairs.

Dugald Kerr chortled, well pleased. Two great-grandsons, and from the looks of it, Fin would get more bairns on his granddaughter.

"Listen to him chuckling," Maggie said as they climbed the stairs. "If he were any smugger, I couldn't bear it."

"He's happy because we're happy," Fin replied as they entered their bedchamber.

"We are happy, aren't we?" Maggie said softly.

"Aye, we are," he agreed, pulling her into his arms. "And why do ye suppose that is, madam?" He kissed her mouth gently. Then he tipped her face up and looked into her warm hazel eyes.

"Because ye love me, of course," Maggie said mischievously.

"I've ne'er said it. I thought it was because ye loved me," Fin responded.

"I've ne'er said it either," Maggie murmured.

"So then we are agreed that we don't love each other," Fin teased her.

"But I know ye love me!" Maggie cried.

"And I know ye love me!" he replied, his gray eyes dancing wickedly.

"Then ye must say it," Maggie told him.

"I will say it if ye will say it," Fin answered.

"Ye first!" she said.

"Nay, ladies first! I am a man of manners, madam," he replied.

"We'll toss for it," said Maggie.

Fingal Stewart burst out laughing. "Ye would decide which of us admits first to loving the other by the toss of a coin?"

"'Tis fair," she said, "isn't it?"

Still laughing, he wrapped his arms about her tightly. "Very well, ye impossible border vixen, I love ye. I probably have since I first laid eyes on ye. Yer bonnie and braver than any woman I've ever known. And while it took some getting used to, I find I like yer quick wit and yer quicker tongue."

Maggie snuggled against him. Then she said provocatively, "I love ye too, Fingal Stewart, and I especially love yer tongue when it plays those naughty games with me."

She felt him grow hard against her as she spoke the taunting words.

He turned her about, his hands reaching up to first unlace her shirt, and then undo the ribbon holding her chemise together. His hands plunged beneath the material to cup her breasts. They were larger now than when he had first known her, but they were still round and firm to his touch.

"Ummmm," Maggie sighed, pressing her buttocks against him.

He groaned, his hands tightening about her flesh, and she rubbed against him more as he pinched her nipples, teasing them to hard little points as she worked to shrug off her blouse and the top of her chemise. But he was not satisfied to have her naked to just her waist. "All of it," he whispered hotly in her ear. She quickly obeyed until she was completely naked. "Now," he said, "on yer knees, wife."

"Yer already hard," Maggie said.

"I need your mouth on me," he told her. "And then I'll put my mouth on you."

Kneeling, she opened his breeches, and his cock burst forward.

Wrapping her hand about the firm pillar of flesh, she squeezed him, smiling as he drew a sharp breath.

Still holding him, she ran her tongue around the swollen head, sliding the tip just beneath to follow its edge. His breathing grew quicker. Her thumb and her forefinger now grasped the ruby head, and she began to lick his extended length with long slow strokes of her tongue. Finally she took him into her warm mouth, sucking upon him in an easy and leisurely fashion. She could feel his hand upon her head, his fingers digging deeply into her scalp as she roused him to a fever pitch.

"*Enough!*" he finally growled, and he pulled her up, his mouth seeking hers desperately as he kissed her until Maggie's lips were swollen and bruised. He was a man who had always been able to prolong his pleasure and that of his partner, but knowing that they would soon be separated made it difficult tonight. He pushed her on her back onto their bed, kneeling between her legs, which hung over the side of the mattress.

"Aye!" she cried to him. "Aye!"

He laughed low. "Beg me for it, border vixen," he said.

"*Please!*" Maggie whispered.

"Tell me what you want," he insisted. "Tell me exactly what you want."

"I want ye to tongue my little jewel until it bursts with delight," Maggie said. "I want ye to suck on it until the sweetness is unbearable. And then I want ye to take that delicious cock of yers and fuck me until I explode with the kind of pleasure that only ye can give me, Fingal Stewart!"

He laughed softly as he parted her nether lips with his thumbs and gave the flesh a slow lick. "Yer certain that is what ye would have me do, madam?" he taunted her.

"I will kill ye if ye don't!" she said fiercely.

"Ye will kill me when I do," he responded, and then he began to obey her instructions in slow and careful detail.

Maggie closed her eyes and let the sensation sweep over her as his tongue licked first the soft insides of her thighs, then the interior of her nether lips, and finally found her little jewel. He flicked his tongue back and forth over the sensitive flesh, his rhythm increasing until she was nearly mindless. And when his lips closed over her jewel and he sucked hard about it, she screamed low as the sensation burst with a ferocity that left her weak with her delight.

Fin stood, pulling her to the edge of the bed, legs raised over his shoulders; he thrust into her as he stood, his swollen length pistoning her with long slow strokes at first, and then increasing the cadence until his cock was flashing furiously back and forth, back and forth, back and forth. Her wet heated sheath tightened about him, causing him to almost lose his control. Maggie's legs wrapped about his neck, encouraging him to bring them both to the pleasure of perfection. And he finally did, roaring his satisfaction as her nails clawed at him. "Jesu, woman!" he groaned happily. "Yer near to killing me with yer sweet loving." He fell on the bed next to her, still fully clothed.

Maggie sighed contentedly, thinking she was glad she was taking Agnes Kerr's remedy now, for he had spilled a great deal of his potent seed a few moments ago.

Davy was two now, and Andrew just past one. She wanted no more bairns for the interim. Reaching out, she slipped her hand into his. "I do love ye, Fin. I don't know when I realized it, but I do. For the love of Sweet Mary, dinna get yerself killed by some northerner. I don't know why men cannot remain at peace."

"I'll not be in the forefront of things, lass," he promised her. "I'm not important enough to be given a command. I'll be remaining as much out of sight as possible, although actually the best place to be will be the king's side. James is no coward, but his lords will not allow anything to happen to him. Especially with his son so small."

"And if yer by his side, he'll know ye've come," Maggie remarked. Then she considered. "Nay, just let him see ye, and then stay in the background. Now take yer clothes off, and let us continue what ye began when ye admitted to loving me."

"Yer insatiable, madam," he said, chuckling, but he arose, and began to pull off his garments, not bothering to lay them neatly aside, but tossing them to lie where they fell, the quicker to return to her warm arms and loving embrace, for on the morrow he would depart Brae Aisir to join the king.

"Take an extra man to send back to me that I know ye've arrived safely and joined the king," Maggie said the next morning as she stood by his horse in the courtyard.

"I'll send Archie back," Fin told her. "I've no need of a serving man, but he's so used to being by my side I could not tell him nay."

Maggie nodded. "Grizel will be relieved," she said low.

"So that's the way it is," Fin replied, smiling.

"We're not supposed to know," Maggie told him, "but I have eyes in my head." She took her husband's gloved hand and kissed it. "Be careful, Fingal Stewart, and do not take chances. I want ye back. I need ye back!"

"I will be back," he promised her.

Father David stepped forward now to bless Fingal Stewart, and his party of men, praying aloud to God and the Blessed Lord Jesu and Holy Mary for their safe return.

Maggie watched him as he rode off, her grandsire by her side. There were tears in her eyes, but she sensed with every fiber of her being that he would be back.

Very little word of the king's expedition seeped into the Borders. Each family had sent some form of representation in order to keep on the king's good side. Ewan Hay had watched his brother ride off, but he would not go. Why would he fight for a man who had taken Mad Maggie Kerr from him? Besides, James Stewart wouldn't care if Ewan Hay was fighting in his war or not. He had Ewan's elder brother, Lord Hay of Haydoun, among his warriors. If Lord Hay didn't return, it didn't matter to him since Ewan was not his heir. His brother had two half-grown sons in good health, and then, of course, Ewan was the youngest of three brothers. Their middle brother had not gone to war either.

The spring turned into summer. There was no word from the north on how the king's war was going. Traffic through the Aisir nam Breug was busy, however, with the groups of merchants headed for Edinburgh, Perth, and Aberdeen, along with family parties and single peddlers. A caravan of gypsies exited the pass one afternoon and asked for permission to spend two nights on Brae Aisir's lands because their leader's wife was about to give birth to her first child. Maggie gave her approval, walking down to personally speak with the gypsy leader. She liked the gypsies, for they had always brought her luck.

"Yer welcome to stay," she told the man, "but dinna steal my livestock. We're just a border family and have nothing to spare but water and a welcome."

"Ye've a king's favor," the gypsy said to Maggie.

"Do we?" Maggie responded, pretending amusement.

"Aye, and ye know ye do," the gypsy responded. "Yer man will be back safe in a short while, but beware, my lady, for ye have an enemy nearby who seeks to claim all that is yers. He hates ye, but desires ye too. He is dangerous." Then the gypsy bowed. "That is all I see, my lady."

Maggie had felt a shiver go down her spine when the gypsy man's eyes had suddenly become unfocused and he spoke. But she respected the sight he possessed. "Thank ye," she told him. "Does yer wife need anything?"

"Nay, but I thank ye for the asking," the man said.

Maggie turned and walked back to the keep. Who secretly desired her, but also hated her? She couldn't begin to imagine an answer, and put the gypsy's prophecy from her mind, concentrating on the fact he had said her husband would be home soon. That meant more to her than some vague prediction that she had an enemy. And how long was a short while? A week? A month? Did the gypsy really know? Or had he just said it, knowing that most every woman in the Borders was without her man right now? More than likely that was it, but she did believe in the sight, and the gypsy seemed genuine.

Then two days after the gypsies had departed Brae Aisir, Lord Stewart, Iver, and their men returned home. Maggie decided under the circumstances not to begrudge the gypsies the lamb that had disappeared when they departed. Their leader's wife had birthed a male bairn. Her husband was unscathed, and none of their men had been injured. Dugald Kerr was eager to learn all that had happened. The entire household and village crowded into the hall that evening to learn of Lord Stewart's adventures.

Fingal took a sip of wine from his goblet, and then looking out into the hall from the high board, began. "Ye all know how independent the northerners have always been," he said. "And Scots kings have gone north to visit, but never before like this. The king set sail to make real to the entire north the power that is his, and every Scots king's. We sailed across the Moray Firth and through the Pentland Firth to Orkney and Shetland. Then we sailed south again around Cape Wrath, down and through the isles. The local chieftains were more than surprised."

Laughter erupted in the hall. They could but imagine the shock the chieftains and the people of the Western Isles experienced as the king's fleet sailed into view with its small army.

"We took a number of captives from the isles," Fingal continued. "They will stand hostage for their chieftains' behavior. They have been taken to Dunbar and Tantallon castles as well as to Bass Rock to be housed. The king has now taken the lordship of the isles for the Crown. I think the northwest will now be peaceful for the interim."

"He's a clever fellow, the king," Dugald Kerr said. "He's given the men in the northwest the same lesson he gave the rebels here in the Borders ten years ago. Aye, they'll be silent for now. And ye brought everyone home safe. 'Tis a good thing."

"I've been a mercenary, as ye know, Dugald. I know fighting. There was little involved in this expedition. A skirmish here and there, but nothing of significance. The chieftains gave up their hostages without a fight. Most of them are tired of all the feuding and quarreling. They have all they can do to survive, but there's always someone now and again among them who will rise up in rebellion. I think they hope the many hostages their families have given will help them to keep that one man, whoever he will be, in check." He looked around the hall at all the familiar faces. "God's foot, 'tis good to be home again!" He lifted his goblet to those gathered. "To Brae Aisir and her clan folk!" he said to them, and they cheered him. They no longer thought of Fingal Stewart as an outsider who had wed their heiress. He was one of them now.

The king came into the Borders that autumn to hunt. He left the queen behind at Linlithgow with his mother. The queen was pregnant with a second child; her first, a son named after his father, had been born in the early part of the year, just before the queen's coronation. The king's mother and wife had become good friends, and Marie de Guise had helped reconcile Margaret Tudor with her son.

Maggie was excited that the king would spend a night at Brae Aisir. Fin was less so. Brae Aisir wasn't the kind of house set up for entertaining a king. It also worried him that the king had no idea that the house was more keep than manor. He hoped this fact would not anger James. Dwellings such as the Kerrs' home usually required royal permission to be built. But Dugald had told him Brae Aisir had begun as a tower house and had just grown from there.

Fortunately, the house had no style, and the chambers were in general small. Fin hoped that the king would not be impressed once he saw this even if the outside of the house set on its hill was impressive. He himself chose a chamber for the king. It had no hearth and only a small wooden-shuttered window. There was barely room to turn around in it, but Fin cleverly saw his servants furnished the space with their best. The bed was hung with homespun linen and red velvet brocade. The springs on the bed had been tightened, and a new mattress and feather bed were laid upon it. There was a fine down coverlet, and pillows, the cases of which were scented with lavender. The taperstick by the bed was silver, and the narrow candle in it beeswax. There was a long narrow table against a wall upon which a tray with a decanter of whiskey and a goblet was placed. The king would be comfortable but hardly envious.

James arrived in midmorning. He came with only one companion, his servant. He was a man who enjoyed going about the land incognito as the *gudeman o' Ballengeich*. His red hair usually gave his identity away, but there were plenty of lasses willing to pretend they were in ignorance of his true identity. Today, however, he was himself, and he was ready to hunt grouse, which was now in season. He met the laird and charmed the old man. Then Fin took him hunting with a party of Kerr clansmen.

"Did ye not want to go?" Dugald Kerr asked his granddaughter.

"I did, but Fin asked that I remain home. The king has not lost his wandering eye or taste for unfamiliar flesh just because he has a queen he likes. Ye know how I am when I hunt, Grandsire. I ride like a devil, and I am very enthusiastic in the pursuit. Fin feared that such behavior would entice the king. Ye can't say no to a king."

Dugald Kerr nodded. "Nay, ye can't," he agreed.

"I shall show the king a mile or two of the Aisir nam Breug tomorrow before he leaves," Maggie said. "And tonight I shall sit meekly at the high board, being a perfect, if dull, hostess." She chuckled. "My husband is very jealous, I find."

"The man loves ye, lass," her grandfather said. "Yer a fortunate woman."

When the hunters returned, the king was in a particularly good mood, for he had bagged a half dozen grouse and killed an antlered stag. He was ready for his dinner and, knowing he would be, Maggie saw that it was promptly served. To begin, there were fat prawns broiled in butter, along with salmon poached in white wine. Then came the poultry, which included duck roasted with a sauce of raisins and apples; a fat capon; and a dish of tiny ortolons in a pie with a flaky crust. This was followed by game, venison, and rabbit, and a pottage of vegetables. Fresh crusty bread, butter, and cheese, both hard and soft, were also offered. The king's cup was never allowed to empty, and the meal concluded with a dish of plump apples baked with honey and cinnamon.

Maggie was relieved that the king barely looked her way. He was enjoying the masculine company of the laird and her husband. He had taken a liking to both Clennon Kerr and Iver Leslie, who had ridden with them that day. And when she decided she might leave the hall, Maggie came and curtsied politely to the king.

"If ye will excuse me now, my lord," she said, "I must see to my bairns. Is there anything ye need that I have not provided?"

The king's eyes flicked over her, and Maggie held herself very still.

"If ye would be kind enough to provide me with someone to warm my bed, madam, I should then be content." His look was questioning.

"Of course, my lord. Someone buxom or more slender?" she inquired politely.

"Buxom and clean, madam," the king responded.

"She will be awaiting ye, my lord," Maggie said with another curtsy. Then she said to her husband, "I'll see to Davy and Andrew and go straight to our bed, my lord, if that would please ye."

"It pleases me," Fin said, looking directly at her. Then he said, "I do believe, Maggie mine, that the king would enjoy Flora Kerr's company."

Now how did he know that? Maggie wondered as she nodded to her husband before turning and hurrying off. Flora Kerr was a pretty widow in the village who earned her living discreetly servicing men whose wives were with child. She kept no man as a lover, nor would she give herself to just any man. He had to have a wife who was with child before she would raise her skirts and offer herself. The women of the village appreciated the service she offered. Flora Kerr didn't want their men. Her late husband had been a controlling man. She was relieved to be free of him. But she did miss the bedsport they had shared.

Maggie sought out Busby, and finding him said, "Fetch Flora Kerr. Tell her the king wants a woman for his bed tonight, and I would be grateful if she would service his needs. I will see she is reimbursed for her time. And tell her to wash. He specifically said the female should be clean. Take a sliver of my soap from the storeroom for her. If she smells of flowers, it will make him remember that we treated him well during his visit to Brae Aisir."

"At once, my lady," Busby said. "I'm certain Flora will be cooperative as well as honored by the king's attentions."

"Put her in his bed to await him," Maggie said.

"Of course, my lady," Busby replied, his eyes twinkling as his mistress turned away and hurried upstairs. He could but imagine her relief that the king had not wanted her to warm his bed. He went himself to fetch Flora Kerr and bring her back to the keep, stopping before he departed to collect the bit of soap from the storeroom.

Maggie told Grizel of the king's request.

"He's a randy fellow, but then, his da was too. Well, Flora will give him a happy time and leave him satisfied," Grizel remarked. "The lads in the village have no complaint. And just how did ye know about Flora Kerr, my lady?"

"She was my husband's suggestion," Maggie said.

"What?!!"

"The whole hall heard him suggest her," Maggie replied.

"Perhaps he visited her when ye were carrying one of yer bairns," Grizel murmured. "He's a lusty man, his lordship."

"Are ye telling me he has visited Flora Kerr himself?" Maggie asked.

"Well, how else would he know of her?" Grizel said. "She will only lie with a man whose wife has a big belly. It gives them surcease from their lust and satisfies hers."

Maggie had undressed and washed herself. Sitting on the bed, she brushed her long hair thoughtfully. "I never would have thought Fin would betray me," she said.

"Och!" Grizel replied. "He's a man, and men will satisfy their needs. He probably hasn't given her a thought since until tonight." She drew the coverlet up and took the brush from Maggie's hand. "Go to sleep. Yer man loves ye, and ye alone."

But Maggie could not sleep at first. She had never considered her husband with another woman. Oh, she knew he had had others before her, but since they were married? She didn't know what to think. Was he tiring of her? Would he, like so many other men, take a mistress eventually? Well, she wouldn't have it! If he couldn't be satisfied with his wife for a lover, then he would have to turn celibate. Or if he would take a mistress, then he could hardly object to her taking a lover. Propped against the cover, Maggie sat waiting for her husband to come up from the hall.

As he entered their bedchamber, Fingal Stewart saw his wife through the haze of all the wine he had consumed this evening. "Mag—gie mine," he slurred the words, smiling at her boyishly.

"Yer drunk!" she said in a hard voice. "And just how did ye know about Flora Kerr, my lord? Did ye tumble the wench when I carried yer sons? How could ye betray me? If I had known now what I didn't know in the hall, I would have gone to the king's bed myself tonight. What's sauce for the gander should certainly be sauce for the goose!"

"Ye think I fucked Flora Kerr?" He was astounded.

"Well, didn't ye? How else would ye know of her?" Maggie demanded.

"Everyone in the goddamned village knows of Flora," Fin replied, the haziness gone to be replaced by a headache. "She's not like Jeannie, the village's whore. She offers herself only to those whose wives are breeding. She's respected for it."

"Ye didn't answer my question," Maggie said angrily. "Did ye fuck her?"

"Nay! I did not fuck her," Fin replied, his temper beginning to rise. "Am I some weakling that I canna abstain from passion when my wife is carrying my bairns?"

Maggie burst into tears, much to her horror and Fin's astonishment. "I couldn't bear it if ye were with another woman," she sobbed. "Yer the only man I've ever loved, Fingal Stewart. I will always be true to ye!"

"What if I died in battle?" he teased her, trying to defuse the situation.

"I'd die too!" Maggie swore dramatically.

"Ye can't die if I die. Who would look after our lads? They can't lose both parents, Maggie mine." Kicking off his boots, he climbed into the bed and gathered her into his arms. "I'm not going to die, love, and neither are ye."

"If ye die before me, I'll never remarry," she told him earnestly.

"And if ye die before I do," he countered, "I'll just take a mistress."

"What?" She began to pound on him with her fists.

Laughing, Fin caught her wrists and pressed Maggie back against the pillows. He kissed her until they were both breathless. His hand slid beneath her night garment and up her leg to give her buttock a squeeze. She began to undress him, pulling off his jerkin, his shirt, then running her hands over his smooth, hard chest. His hands went to the neckline of her gown. He smothered her protest with a kiss as he ripped the garment open to get at her beautiful round breasts. His dark head dipped, his tongue pushing into the valley between the soft yet firm orbs as he struggled from his breeks.

Maggie's fingers threaded themselves through his thick black hair. She teased the sensitive nape of his neck with just the tips of those fingers before she clutched at him, feeling the hard flesh of his torso as her hands caressed him. She moaned as his mouth closed over one of her nipples and began to suckle on her. She loved the tug of his lips on her, and squirmed against him, encouraging him. "Aye, my lord and love! Ohh, that feels so good. Dinna stop."

It was a request he enjoyed complying with, and he sucked on the nipple harder and harder. Then unable to help himself, he nipped at her with his teeth. She squealed, but the sound was more of pleasure than of pain. He transferred his attentions to her other nipple lest it feel neglected, and began to draw deeply on the sentient flesh while her hands stroked him, and she murmured encouragement into his ear between nibbling and kissing it. His cock was already hard, but he wanted more of her than just a quick tumble.

She felt him against her thigh, and reached down to grasp his length, squeezing him, reaching beneath him to tickle his lightly furred balls. He hissed a warning, and she ceased her play, reaching about to squeeze his buttocks instead. After a moment, he slid away from her, rolling onto his side. His hand went to her mons, and cupping it, he crushed it gently several times. A bolt of pleasure shot through her. "Oh, Fin!" she murmured.

He stroked her slit slowly, slowly, with a single finger until he felt the moisture beginning. The finger pressed through the damp folds to find her little jewel. He teased it until he felt it swelling. Then the finger moved to the opening of her love sheath. He pushed the finger into her, smiling when he heard her whisper urgently to him, "*More!*"

Two fingers began to pleasure her, and Maggie squirmed shamelessly upon those fingers, whimpering. And when he sensed she was close, he ceased withdrawing his fingers from her wet sheath as she protested.

"Now, madam, I mean to punish ye for thinking I would consort with Flora Kerr while yer belly was big with my sons," Fingal Stewart said. "Ye will play the whore and beg me for my passion."

"Never!" Maggie cried furiously as he mounted her.

"Aye, ye will. Ye will say, please, my lord, fuck me with your big cock as ye would fuck yer beautiful, foolish, needlessly suspicious wife," he told her, putting just the head of his manhood at the opening of her sheath.

Maggie attempted to buck him off as she swore at him, but she only succeeded in helping him to press a small ways into her sheath. "Nay, you devil! I'll not say it! Ye want me right now as much as I want ye! It's all yer fault I grew concerned."

"My *fault?*" He was astounded. "How is it my fault?" Jesu, he was boiling with desire and wanted nothing more than to plunge himself deep into her, but if he did before she obeyed him, he would lose her respect.

"Because ye knew who Flora Kerr was!" Maggie said with complete female logic. God's toenail! The little bit of him within her felt so good. She wanted him to sheath himself completely and make her scream with delight, but she was not going to grovel. He would lose respect for her.

"For God's sake, Maggie, say it!" he groaned. "Ye know ye want me."

"Say yer sorry first for doubting me," she told him. "Then I'll say whatever ye want me to say, my lord husband, my love."

"I'm sorry I doubted ye, Maggie mine. I was foolish too," Fin told her.

"Please fuck me, my lord, as ye would fuck yer beautiful wife," Maggie told him, and then gasped as he filled her full with himself.

"*Beautiful, foolish, suspicious wife,*" he said.

"Beautiful," she repeated stubbornly.

"I'll not move an inch, madam, until ye say what ye should," Fin told her as stubbornly, and he looked down into her face, his gray eyes intense.

Jesu! Mary! She could feel his hardness—every blessed bit of it. She felt the walls of her sheath tightening and releasing about it. Surrounded by her tight warmth, he could release his juices and gain his own pleasure now. She, however, needed more for her pleasure. Maggie glared back at him. "Beautiful, foolish, suspicious," she said. "Now, damn you, Fingal Stewart, fuck me hard, and fuck me deep. Ye had better soothe the pride ye have just injured or I will never forgive ye!"

He began to move upon her, slowly at first, and then with increasing speed. Maggie soared and experienced starbursts behind her closed eyes. "Aah," she said, but he was not finished with her. His skillful cock seemed to know just where to touch her, how much friction her sensitive flesh could endure. "Ah, ah, aah!" she moaned a second time. It was wonderful; yet he had not released his passions. Still, there was no time for her to think about it, for he was using her harder than he had ever used her before.

She had wrapped her legs about him, hooking her ankles together, but he was growling in her ear to release him. When Maggie did, he pushed her legs straight back over her shoulders while he plunged himself deeper and deeper and deeper into her.

Her head began to spin. Her heart was hammering in her chest, thundering in her ears. Maggie could feel the intense pleasure reaching up to enfold and surround her. Unable to help herself, she screamed with the delight that was overwhelming her. She couldn't open her eyes. She could do nothing except experience the incredible pleasure he was giving her, sharing with her. Her mouth opened, gasping for air, screaming again a final time as her world exploded around her. Maggie felt herself being hurled down into a warm enveloping darkness as every inch of her tingled with satisfaction right down to the soles of her feet. The last thing she remembered was Fin roaring with his own pleasure, and then calling her name.

When Maggie finally came to herself again, she was filled with a contentment such as she had never before known. Fin was sprawled next to her, eyes closed, but his breathing was normal, to her relief. "What happened to us?" she asked aloud, not even knowing whether he was conscious enough to hear her, but he was.

"The French call it *la petite mort*," he told her, his eyes still closed. "Jesu, madam! I hope we can attain it together again. Being beautiful, foolish, and suspicious suits ye."

Maggie laughed. "It seemed to suit ye as well, husband," she responded. "I can only hope our royal guest has as good a night as we seem to be having."

Now it was Fin who chuckled. "How can he have as pleasant a time, Maggie mine? He doesn't have ye, nor will he ever. He may be a king, but kings don't always gain everything in life. Wealth and power, aye. But love? Not often. I think I actually feel sorry for James Stewart." Then he reached for Maggie, pulling her into his arms, kissing her tenderly. "I love ye, Maggie mine. And yer the only woman I have ever loved, or will love."

Maggie sighed happily, then she said, "But what if we had a daughter? Wouldn't ye love her, my lord?"

"Aye," he said, "but I should not love her the way I love her mother. How is it possible that ye have become so important to me? I never knew such a thing could be."

"I know," Maggie replied. "I love ye so much that I should even give up the Aisir nam Breug for ye, Fingal Stewart."

"'Tis fortunate then that ye won't have to, Maggie mine," Fin told her. "Yer stuck with us both till death." And he kissed her again as Maggie sighed, her heart soaring with happiness.

Chapter 11

⌐∽⌐

The queen had birthed her first son on the twenty-second of May in the year 1540. He was James, Duke of Rothsay. Her second son, Arthur, was born on the twenty-fourth of April the following year. For Scotland, 1541 was not a good year. Prince James died two days after his brother's birth, and the baby Arthur died on April thirtieth. James V was now without legitimate heirs once again.

The marriage between James's mother, Margaret Tudor, and his father, James IV, had been made to ensure peace between the two countries. The peace barely survived the death of its maker, James's father-in-law, Henry VII. The fragile peace had been broken several times over the years, the worst example being the battle fought on Flodden Field in September 1513.

James IV was not a man who wanted war. For the first time in years, Scotland was peaceful from the Borders to the Highlands. It was prosperous. But his alliance with France required he attack England if England attacked France. And England's volatile king, James's brother-in-law, Henry VIII, had joined the Holy League with Spain, Venice, and the pope to wage war on France. As the chivalry of the times demanded, James IV sent a message to Henry VIII informing him of his intentions to invade Northumbria. The Scots action wasn't meant to begin a war, and Henry knew it. The Scots meant simply to harass the English and hopefully take some pressure off their French allies.

On the twenty-second of August, James and his army crossed the Tweed into England. Over the next few days they hammered Norham Castle into rubble. Etal Castle surrendered without a fight as did Ford Castle. Lady Heron, the chatelaine of Ford, had a very pretty daughter, and the rumor was that James spent a few days at this castle seducing the girl. And while he did, the Duke of Suffolk, charged by Henry VIII with protecting the north, brought his army to Alnwick. The English had inferior numbers compared to the Scots. They were not as well armed. But King James was no real soldier, nor was he a tactician. The English overcame the Scots. James IV was killed along with the flower of his nobility. And now it was to begin again with his son, and the son of the man who had beaten his father.

Twenty years after Flodden, Henry VIII concluded the Treaty of Perpetual Peace with James V, his nephew. The Reformation had come to England, and Henry felt it was just another excuse for France, Spain, and the Holy Roman Empire to attack him. He wanted no problems from the north's Catholic Scotland. James V's marriage to a French wife did not reassure England's king. Border raids continued with both sides equally guilty.

In 1541, Henry invited his nephew to York to discuss the state of their kingdoms. James did not come. The following winter of 1542, Henry sent James a letter forgiving him for his nonattendance. Henry was now like a beast with a wounded paw. He had just beheaded his fifth wife for her infamous adulteries, and he was already planning to join the Holy Roman Empire in a war against France. That spring he began quietly reinforcing his defenses in the north as the French were already engaged in their new war.

James countered. He called on the Gordon Earl of Huntly to mount a border defense. George Gordon rode into Brae Aisir at the head of a large party of mounted men one summer day. Dugald Kerr welcomed the earl graciously, but he was not pleased by what George Gordon had to say. Lord Stewart stood by the laird listening but remaining silent for the moment. He would not override the old man, for he was still lord of this keep. But he was disturbed by the earl's demand.

"What the hell do ye mean we must close the Aisir nam Breug to all traffic?" Dugald Kerr said. "The pass is operated with our English kin. They won't want to lose income any more than we do."

"The English are preparing to invade us," George Gordon said. His fingers clasped and unclasped the stem of the goblet he had been served.

"It is a known fact," Dugald Kerr told the earl, "that neither side has ever allowed the pass to be used for warfare. We've dealt with King Henry's minions before. The Aisir nam Breug remains safe because the Kerrs of Brae Aisir and the Kerrs of Netherdale never deviate from our centuries-old rule."

"It will be too late when yer English kin allow an English army to ride through it," the earl said testily, and he slammed his goblet down on the arm of his chair.

"If I tell Edmund Kerr I'm shutting off the Aisir nam Breug, he will take it as a hostile act," Dugald Kerr said. "I will not ruin what has been a safe passage for travelers for centuries simply because King James and King Henry are having a pissing contest."

The Earl of Huntly grew red in the face, and before the argument might escalate further, Fingal Stewart finally spoke up. "The English send their armies into Scotland via the eastern borders. And now and again they have come through the western hills. But never through the midsection of the Borders, my lord. The Aisir is too narrow a passage to allow an army to get through it. If you should like, I will take ye there on the morrow so ye may see for yerself. Travelers move single file. There is no way the traverse can be widened to accommodate any army. Lord Kerr is correct when he says to close our end of the passage would be to invite suspicion. Edmund Kerr is a true northerner, and he pays little heed to London. Ye know that is so with the northern English."

"The king fears the pass may be an easy entry for Henry's armies," George Gordon said.

"The king has seen the traverse and should know better," the laird snapped.

"The Kerr families have monitored the Aisir nam Breug for more than five hundred years, my lord. In all that time no invading army passed through it," Lord Stewart said.

"And the king knew naught of this pass until several years ago. The Aisir nam Breug has never presented a threat to Scotland. Tomorrow you shall see for yourself. In the meantime, tell us of what is happening beyond our walls," Fingal Stewart invited their guest. "Aah, I see the meal is coming to the high board. Let us be seated and eat."

"The king would go to war, but he is no warrior. And the memory of Flodden still burns in the hearts and minds of every family who lost sons and fathers," George Gordon said. "We are trying to keep these difficulties under control. There have been raids and counter raids. I'm surprised ye haven't been disturbed."

"We have had one raid recently, and some cattle were driven off, but 'twas no more than usual," Fin replied.

"Yer fortunate," the earl replied. "The English have been marauding and harassing the Tweed Merse. I had to drive them off at Haddon Rig, and now we are burdened with English prisoners. The dungeons at Edinburgh Castle are overflowing."

Maggie sat, the perfect hostess, listening to everything that was said by the men at her table. She knew the keep could sustain a siege provided there were no cannons. Then Brae Aisir's stone walls were as vulnerable as any. She had two sons, and while she had said nothing to Fin, she was certain she was breeding once again. And this time she wasn't certain that being more to the west and middle of the Borders was going to keep them safe. And what if Fin were expected to go to war? He would go, and damn his family's vaunted motto, *Ever faithful!* She needed him here with her, with the bairns, more than James Stewart needed him for cannon fodder. Maggie remembered the tales of Flodden, and how there was hardly a family in Scotland that had not lost men to it.

She was suddenly and inexplicably afraid.

"Yer unusually silent tonight, Granddaughter," Dugald Kerr said. "What are yer thoughts on this new war brewing with England?"

"I don't understand why there must be a war," Maggie said. "England is England, and Scotland is Scotland. We have been so forever. What quarrel can King Henry have with us that he must send an army into Scotland?"

"It actually has more to do with France, Spain, the Holy Roman Empire, and the pope," George Gordon said. "They quarrel with one another over a minutiae of nothing, but they must each have their allies. They would destroy England if they could, but they cannot. We have been allied with France for centuries, and the English do not like it. Now the Reformation has reached England, and it is beginning to creep into Scotland, giving everyone something else to quarrel over. When King Henry isn't defending himself against his enemies over the water, he takes time to harry Scotland."

"It is all quite ridiculous, ye know," Maggie said candidly.

"Aye and nay," the earl responded. "There is much licentiousness in the church today. They preach one thing while doing another. The poor, it would seem, are not stupid or unaware of the religious profligacy."

"There are many faithful priests in villages and keeps like ours all over Scotland who practice what they preach," Father David spoke up.

"Aye, good Father, there are, but it is difficult to see the humble among us when the powerful are blatant in their actions," the earl answered.

"So we are going to war because King Henry is bored right now?" Maggie said.

"Henry Tudor is a man of strong principles. While perhaps not always right in the eyes of the world, he is firm in his own beliefs and behavior," the earl told her. "He would have his nephew listen to his council. When James will not, he believes the French are influencing him through the queen. Remember that one of her brothers is a cardinal of the church—a church that King Henry will no longer allow to exert its authority in England."

"So we will all suffer for the intransigence of these kings," Maggie said slowly. "I dinna like it, my lord. Nor will any woman in Scotland. How many women and bairns will be killed to satisfy the bloodlust of these men? Nay, it is ridiculous."

"I think yer wife is right," the Earl of Huntly said to Fin. "And ye are wise not to have answered the king's call to arms. Many have not."

"We received no call to arms here at Brae Aisir," Fin said. "Had my kinsman called, I would have answered."

"Yer fortunate to be here in this place then, for the call obviously did not reach ye, my lord. It was sent all over Scotland two months ago," George Gordon said.

Maggie knew what was coming. She jumped to her feet and shouted, "*Nay!* Ye were not called, and ye will not go, Fingal Stewart. Ye have responsibilities here."

"The earl says all of Scotland was called, and shame on those who have not answered," Fin responded. "I will not shame my family's name by ignoring this."

"And I will not be widowed nor allow yer sons to be orphaned because yer a romantic fool," Maggie raged at him. "Will this bairn I now carry even know his father? And if I lose you, will I be pressed into marriage again because it is believed a woman cannot manage the Aisir nam Breug? Ye cannot go!"

"Madam, we have an important guest at our board. We will quarrel later," Fin said to her. "Yer with child again?"

"If ye leave me to partake in this foolishness, there will be no later, my lord," Maggie said, furious. "I have a bad feeling about this venture." She turned to the earl. "Tell him he must not go, my lord. He is needed here. Why should he go when others will not?" Her eyes had now filled with tears as she added, "Aye, I'm with child again."

"My lady," the earl replied, "a man's honor is above all else. Yer husband is an honorable man. Now that he knows his kinsman's need, he will answer his call. It can be no other way, else the Stewarts of Torra be dishonored. I will not tell him nay."

Mad Maggie Kerr, who had never in her life wept publicly, now burst into tears. She threw down her napkin, stepped down from the high board, and, sobbing, ran from the hall.

"Shame on ye for making her unhappy, and in her condition," Grizel said from her place at the trestle directly below the high board. She got up and hurried after her mistress.

"Breeding women," the earl said with a smile. "I've seen my own wife behave much the same in her time. Yer lady will calm herself. But, Fingal, if indeed ye received no summons, then ye could remain at Brae Aisir, and none would fault ye. It is possible that because of the sensitivity of the pass, the king did not send to ye. Yer honor must decide."

"Yet he sent ye to suggest we close it," Fin said. "Nay, I must answer the king's call even if others do not. I know he is a difficult man, and sometimes cruel. The incident with the Countess of Glamis was more like his uncle Henry. But he has seen the laws of our land enforced to the gratitude of the commons, and he has kept us prosperous. I should not have my wife and this responsibility were it not for my royal kins- man. My family has ever been faithful to the kingly Stewarts. I will not bring shame upon us by ignoring the royal summons to arms now I have learned of it. I'll show ye the pass tomorrow. Then I will gather my men, and we will follow ye into the king's service."

"God knows I'll welcome any men you can bring. My force is small. I have scarce two thousand men at my command," George Gordon told Lord Stewart.

"I can probably gather no more than thirty," Fin replied. "I can't leave the keep undefended, given the current situation. Brae Aisir is usually safe, but in times like these, ye never really know. A small war party breaking away from a large one could cause us some serious damage. But I will ride with my men."

"And I will be here to see to our defenses, should it be necessary," Dugald Kerr said. "Iver can go with ye, and Clennon will remain with us. And dinna fret over Maggie. She'll calm down and see reason in time."

But while Maggie did compose herself, by the time Fin reached their bedchamber that night, she was not happy at all that he would leave them. "The king should be defending his kingdom," she said, "but instead he sends the Earl of Huntly to do it for him, and he ex- pects ye to leave yer family at his whim."

"I cannot refuse a summons to defend our land," Fin told her. "Be- sides, if it comes to more than border raiding, James will be in the forefront of the battle. He is no coward, Maggie mine. But ever since his mother died the past autumn, the English king has used every excuse he can find to break the peace."

"Convince the earl not to close the Aisir nam Breug," Maggie said to her husband.

"If it comes to real war, there will be no traffic anyway, but if it just remains border raids, then we'll have more traffic going in both directions. I think I'll ride with ye tomorrow."

"Are ye up to it?" he asked cautiously, knowing to suggest she was frail would bring a furious outburst.

"Aye, I am. With each confinement ye and Grandsire grow less restrictive with me. I'm no more than three months gone. I can still ride astride. It's a lass this time," Maggie said to her husband.

"How can ye be certain?" he asked, curious as to her intuition.

"It's nothing like when I carried Davy and Andrew," Maggie told him. "I've barely been sick at all. 'Tis a lass, I'm certain, and I'll name her Annabelle."

"As long as she is as sweet natured as her mother I'll be satisfied," Fin said.

"I'll not let her be one of those sit-by-the-fire-and-sew lasses," Maggie responded. "She's going to learn how to ride, and how to use a claymore."

"Will the man who weds her one day have to outride, outrun, and outfight her?" Fin teased his wife.

"Nay," Maggie said, her tone softening, "but I don't want our daughter helpless to any man when she is a grown woman. I want her to be able to survive on her own if she must. No woman should be helpless without her man."

"Certainly no border woman," he agreed.

The following morning, Fin and Maggie rode out with the Earl of Huntly to show him the Aisir nam Breug. When George Gordon saw the watchtowers above the pass, he was extremely impressed. But when Maggie brought him to the stone thistle markers just before the border with England, she revealed to him the secret of the Aisir nam Breug.

"Ye can see watchtowers on the hillside above each of these markers. This morning messengers rode along each side of the hills, warning our men in each of these little redoubts of the possible war to come, of the battles that have taken place this summer in the eastern Borders. Should an armed party be seen within the pass, the fronts of these large stone markers would be pulled away to release a great torrent of stones that would block the pass, making it impossible to get through. Our kin, the Netherdale Kerrs, have a similar means of protection in place. That is why our markers are a full mile from the true border itself. But above the place delineating the real border are towers, and they would sound the alarm so those above the markers could get to them in time to block the Aisir nam Breug to invaders."

"Have ye ever had to use this system to protect yourselves?" the earl asked.

"Only once. In the time of King Edward the First, who was called the Hammer of the Scots, was it necessary to block the pass; but not since then," Maggie told him.

"Then I see no reason to arouse your English relations' suspicions by closing the pass," the Earl of Huntly said. "Ye have it as well protected as ye can, and 'tis unlikely anyone will attempt to breach it."

"I am told a number of English died the day they tried to come through, for the Kerr clansmen shot at them from their towers," Maggie said proudly. "I wish we could have a small cannon or two to add to our defense, but if we did, it's quite likely that Edmund Kerr, the Lord of Netherdale, would consider it a hostile act," she said with a chuckle.

They returned to Brae Aisir, and the following day the Earl of Huntly, Lord Stewart, and their men departed for Jedburgh, where the earl was quartering his small force. Maggie was not happy to see her husband go, but she stood dry-eyed at his stirrup, offering him a last cup for good fortune. She had managed to get him to take Clennon Kerr's fifteen-year-old nephew, Ian Kerr, with him to act as his messenger. Ian would ride back and forth, bringing Brae Aisir word of what was happening.

George Gordon attempted to reassure her. "It's October, madam, and the English always go home before the snows come."

"I can hope yer correct, my lord, and my husband is home by Christ's Mass," Maggie told the earl. "Godspeed to ye, sir."

He thanked her for her hospitality, then turned to lead his men from the courtyard of the keep.

Fingal Stewart leaned down from his stallion, lifting Maggie up so he might kiss her a final time. It was almost their undoing, for while duty bade him go, for the first time in his life Fin was not eager for battle. He tasted the sweetness of her mouth, felt the single tear on her cheek, and kissed it away before setting her back on her feet. "I'll come back to ye, Maggie mine. If they do not say I'm dead and bring my body home to ye, I will return to ye, and to Brae Aisir. Trust in my word."

"I will!" she told him.

He moved his horse to stop before the nursemaids, who were each holding up one of his sons for his blessing, and gave it to them. Davy, now four, wanted to be taken up on his father's beast, but Fin told the lad nay, for he was off to fight the king's war. Then he turned the stallion about and cantered off to catch up with the earl and their men. Maggie watched him go until all that was left to see was a small cloud of dust.

That night she sat with her grandfather in the hall. "We'll need to double the watch immediately," she began.

"Get the cattle and sheep in from the far pastures," he told her.

"Ye think the troubles will come this way?" Maggie asked him.

"These things always boil over and spread themselves out. If we're fortunate, we'll escape being raided, but there is no guarantee," the laird said.

"I'd better institute an alarm for all to recognize should the English come our way," Maggie said. "I'll put men to watch out on the hills, and the villagers can take refuge in the keep should they have to do so. I'll have the miller grind what grain he has, and we'll store it within the keep. Whatever happens, we have to be able to feed our folk this winter. The hunting has been good this year. The larder is filling."

For the next few days the village and the keep prepared for the worst should it come. On the twenty-eighth of October, Ian Kerr rode into the keep with news. The English had departed Berwick-upon-Tweed where they had been waiting. They had advanced into the Borders, burning Kelso Abbey and Roxburgh Tower to the ground before returning to Berwick. The Earl of Huntly with a little more than two thousand men had been forced to remain where he was, for the English force was twenty-thousand strong. George Gordon wasn't going to allow a slaughter of good Scotsmen. Fingal, Iver, and their men were safe. Ian Kerr departed the next day back to join Fin and their men.

A peddler who came at least twice a year to Brae Aisir arrived from Jedburgh.

He was in a great hurry to get through the Aisir nam Breug and back into England, for he did not wish to be caught in any war between Henry and James. But he had more information to share. The Duke of Norfolk, King Henry's commander, had returned to Berwick. It was said he had not the supplies to support a longer campaign. And King Henry had declared war officially and renewed England's centuries-old claim to Scotland.

"God help us all," Grizel said as she listened.

The peddler hurried off the next morning through the Aisir nam Breug.

The late-year traffic picked up as merchants from England, and from other countries that did business in Scotland, now sought to escape any coming warfare. But they garnered a great deal of news from these men. King James believed that the Duke of Norfolk meant to attack Edinburgh, and he commanded a general mobilization. With a force of twelve thousand men, and some artillery, the king led his forces south. But the English had gone back over the border to Berwick. The weather was beginning to worsen. Supplies were short. James had his men stand down, and returned to Edinburgh to consider what he would do next. False information was spread for the benefit of the many English spies in Scotland. It appeared the king would strike in the southeast; yet a second army appeared to be forming in the west. And then there were no more travelers to pass through the Aisir nam Breug, and all grew silent.

It was now November. Ian Kerr returned once again to Brae Aisir to tell them the king had ordered a muster at Lauder on the twentieth of November. Ian told them that Lord Stewart had said he was to remain at the keep and not return. Clennon Kerr was grim faced when his nephew spoke. He knew there was to be a battle, and Fin didn't want any harm coming to the lad.

And then on the thirtieth of November, as they celebrated St. Andrew's Day, the watch on the keep's height called down that a small party of horsemen was approaching Brae Aisir. As there seemed not enough of them to be a raiding party, the alarm was not rung. The horsemen came closer, and they recognized their own people. Iver Leslie led them, and there were several horses being led that carried bodies.

Maggie watched them approach. Where was he? Why wasn't he

leading his own men? Had he remained behind with the king? She couldn't bear watching the riders come, so went back into the hall to wait. Pacing back and forth, she told her grandsire that Fin didn't appear to be among the returning men and that there were bodies on the horses being led along.

Dugald Kerr's mouth was drawn in a thin line as he said, "Well, at least we have two lads, and perhaps another in yer belly."

It was a harsh comment, but Maggie knew it to be true. She had been wed for the purpose of producing the next generation of males in order that the Aisir nam Breug continue on as it always had. She had never expected to fall in love with her husband. She was only doing her duty. She blinked back the tears. Where was he? He couldn't be dead. She would *know* if he were dead. Wouldn't she? Her heart pounding, she watched Iver Leslie enter the hall and she had to ask. "Is he dead?"

"I don't know," Iver said, and his face showed his desperation.

"Give the man some whiskey," the laird snapped, and when they had, Dugald Kerr said, "Come, Iver Leslie, and sit by me. I would know all that ye can tell me. Maggie lass, sit down. 'Tis no good standing there looking stricken. Let us hear what our captain has to say, and then we may decide what is to be done next."

They both obeyed, and then Iver began to speak. "The king wanted no real battle. The attack was in reality planned for the west, where they would not be expected. They would defeat the small band of defenders who would come to protect the area. Lord Stewart told me King James meant but a brief incursion into England. Once there, a small party of bishops, escorted by a troop of men-at-arms, would find the nearest church, where the clerics would read the papal interdict against King Henry. And that would be the end of it. But the plan, while a good one, did not turn out as had been expected." Iver swallowed down another bit of the laird's smoky whiskey.

"But there was a spy among the king's men, and he managed to alert Sir Thomas, deputy warden of the West March."

The laird nodded. "Sir Thomas is skilled at border fighting," he noted.

Iver continued. "The English managed to bring two thousand men to the field along with at least several hundred light horsemen. But the king had promised the queen, who is near her time, that he would not take part in the fighting. He returned to Lochmaben the morning of the battle. It was left to those of us who had come to his defense. We were no more than a large-size raiding party who fought that day, my lady, and no match for the English, though we knew not the force we would face then." Iver's voice broke slightly, but then with a deep sigh he recovered himself to go on with his tale.

"We expected to dash into England, secure a church for our bishops, and then dash away back into Scotland. The bulk of our army was left to the rear and would have no part in any fighting. They were for nothing more than show. Led by our own warden of the West March, Lord Maxwell, we moved quickly to the mouth of the River Esk, crossed it, and moved onto the Solway Moss. 'Twas there we encountered our difficulties. The land was worse than mire due to all the rains we have had of late. The English army appeared, and it was quickly apparent that we must return as quickly as we could across the Esk back into our own Scotland.

"The infantry was having difficulty moving back across the muddy ground, as was our small cavalry. And then the English light horsemen charged our flank. It was chaos, my lord, my lady. All of our Brae Aisir men were mounted, but some fell from their horses in the fighting. We lost seven, but as it was obvious we were not going to win this battle, Lord Stewart told us to gather up our dead, and their horses, and ride for home.

"Archie was wounded badly, and did not want to leave him. But my lord insisted we take the little man. He's alive, and Grizel is already attending to him. He'll be lucky not to lose his left arm. The gash in it is fearsome, my lady."

"What happened to my husband?" Maggie asked through gritted teeth. It was all she could do not to scream.

"He went off to aid Lord Maxwell, my lady, and that's the last we saw of him. We heard as we rode home that the king's forces surrendered, and many were taken prisoner. Ye'll know if he's alive when the ransom demand comes," Iver said.

"What happened to the king?" Maggie wanted to know.

"He's gone to Edinburgh, I heard, to order a strengthening of the border's defenses," Iver answered her.

"He's alive!" Maggie said in a determined voice. *"Fingal is alive!"*

"We can pray for it," Father David Kerr said. He had come into the hall behind Iver and listened silently as the captain told his tale.

"The keep will need to be fortified more heavily," the old laird said. "God's foot, I would have a cannon on our heights! A cannon is the best defense in times like these."

"I'll go to the brothers at Glenborder Abbey," the priest said. "They have a foundry and cannon of their own."

"Holy priests?" Iver was surprised.

"Glenborder is known for its warrior monks," Father David said. "The English won't burn them out like they did Kelso. That's why they keep clear of Glenborder."

"Ye'll need gold," the laird noted.

"Ye have what we'll need, and more," the priest replied dryly.

Dugald Kerr laughed darkly. "Aye, whatever ye need is yers if ye can convince them to sell me a cannon. Iver, go with him, and take a dozen men with ye. Dragging a cannon, even a small one, back across the moor and hills will be hard work."

"Who is going to go search for Fingal?" Maggie demanded. "Is my husband not more important than yer damned cannon, Grandsire?"

"Nay, he is not," the laird responded in a hard voice Maggie had never before heard him use. "Fingal is either dead and in an anonymous grave, or being held with other Scots nobles in an English dungeon. It will take the English a while to process their prisoners and learn who they are, and where to send the ransom demand. Either way we can do naught, and we need that cannon, Maggie, if we are to defend Brae Aisir."

David Kerr departed the morning of December first for Glenborder Abbey. He returned on the tenth of December successful, the Kerr clansmen bringing the cannon they had purchased with them along with a supply of powder and shot. The laird immediately oversaw its installation upon the narrow heights of his keep. It had cost him dearly, almost an entire year's worth of proceeds from the Aisir nam Breug, but now he knew the keep would be relatively safe from invaders.

On the twelfth of December word came that Queen Marie had delivered a daughter, Mary, on the eighth day of the month at Linlithgow Palace. The king had not been with her. He was ill at his favorite palace of Falkland. Less than a week later came the terrible news that King James V had died. Scotland had a king no longer. It had a queen, and she _was_ ten days old.

"God help us all," Dugald Kerr said grimly.

"God help Queen Marie," Maggie replied. "The great lords will begin to squabble over who should rule in the little queen's name. There will be some sort of civil strife, ye may be certain." Aye, there would be trouble, and here she was with a big belly, an old man, and two lads to look after, along with the Aisir nam Breug. Where was Fingal? Where was the ransom demand from the English? He was not dead. _He wasn't!_

The news of James V's death reached Netherdale when Edmund Kerr found himself host to an unexpected visitor. It was then he also learned that his kinsman's heiress was again without a husband. His eyes narrowed speculatively at the news.

"We can be of help to each other, my lord," Ewan Hay said, smiling a cold smile.

"How could ye possibly help me?" Edmund Kerr demanded to know.

"Ye want to control all of Aisir nam Breug, I am told," Ewan murmured. "If the rumor is true, then I can help ye achieve yer goal."

"Give our visitor some wine," the Lord of Netherdale said.

"Beware this man," his former mistress, now his third wife, Aldis, said softly. "He is dangerous, and wants more than I think yer willing to give, my lord." She offered him a sweetmeat, and he opened his mouth to take and eat it.

Ewan Hay took the goblet offered him, and drank deeply to gain his courage. He had a plan, but he needed the Lord of Netherdale to complete that plan.

"Well?" Edmund Kerr demanded. "And what will ye want in exchange for aiding me?" he asked cynically.

"Only one thing, my lord. I want Maggie Kerr. With yer help I can take control of Brae Aisir and the pass. Without Lord Stewart they are helpless, for yer kinsman is near seventy now, and surely will not live much longer. They need a man to manage it all, and despite your being their blood, yer English. They will not accept yer control especially now after the battle at Solway Moss, and the king's death. They will more easily accept a Scotsman even if his name is not Kerr. Did they not accept Fingal Stewart, my lord?"

"Maggie has two lads, and a big belly that will certainly produce another," Edmund Kerr said. "They are now old Dugald's heirs." As the years had passed, he had given up on the idea of marrying his late half sister's daughter, but he hadn't given up on controlling the Aisir nam Breug in its entirety. Still, given the bitterness of what had recently transpired, he knew Ewan Hay was right. Brae Aisir would not accept him, or any of his sons, or grandsons, as their overlord. He had, however, thought to one day match the daughter he had had with Aldis to one of Maggie's sons. Still, who was to manage until then? "Did Maggie not spurn ye when ye tried to court her years back? What makes ye think she'll take ye now?" Edmund Kerr asked. "Besides, her husband has not yet been proved dead. The traffic through the traverse is done for the year. The snows will soon make the roads impassable, especially the road through the pass."

"Send me to Brae Aisir, my lord, in yer name, with yer men at my back to defend yer rights," Ewan Hay said. "Say with Fingal Stewart among the missing, and yer kinsman elderly and frail, ye want to protect what the Kerrs on both sides of the border have protected for lo these past centuries. Say it is yer familial duty to see to the safety of Brae Aisir's lady, and her bairns."

Edmund Kerr laughed aloud. "Jesu, ye want the wench, don't ye? But why? She doesn't like ye, and will probably kill ye given the opportunity. As for sending my men, nay. It's one thing for me to send a Scotsman to oversee Dugald Kerr's portion of the Aisir nam Breug. That can be counted as familial regard and show a certain delicacy on my part. But to send English men-at-arms makes it a threatening gesture. Ye'll need yer own men. Surely yer brother would be willing to lend you some of his own people. Did he answer yer late king's call to arms? Did ye for that matter, Ewan Hay?" And Edmund Kerr laughed again. "Nay, I'll wager neither of ye did."

"If I have yer assurance that ye support my going to Brae Aisir, then my brother could probably be prevailed upon to give me some of his clansmen to back my actions," Ewan Hay said. "Ye must write it or he will not believe me. And seal it with yer seal."

"I'll sleep on it," Lord Edmund said. Then he left his hall, going to his privy chamber where Rafe, his eldest son and heir, awaited him, for Aldis had sent for him.

"Don't do it," Rafe advised his father. "This Scot is not to be trusted, Da. He will attempt to force Maggie to the altar if her husband is not found among the prisoners to be ransomed and does not return. She'll kill him before it's all over. And what of her bairns? With that man at Brae Aisir, they will be in danger. Dugald Kerr and his granddaughter are strong enough together to manage their portion of the Aisir nam Breug. They, we, need no interference from another."

"If we are canny, Rafe, we can have it all," his father said slowly, his brown eyes gleaming with greed. "The Scots are beaten for now, for many years to come. Their king is dead. Their ruler is a puling female infant sucking at the breast of her French mam.

"Our own king is certainly coming to the end of his life, and his heir's a sickly boy, and two lasses, one whose legitimacy has always been doubtful. And the Protestants are fighting with Holy Mother Church for control of those heirs.

"Think on it, Rafe! We have an opportunity to control all of the Aisir nam Breug! And no one will care in the least what a seemingly unimportant northern lord is doing, for they will all be too busy on both sides of the border trying to control these child monarchs. As long as the traffic flows smoothly through the traverse and none are inconvenienced, no one will know or worry about what is happening to the Aisir nam Breug or who is controlling it."

"Wait at least until spring before you institute this plan, Da," Rafe said. "There is no traffic now in the pass, and we are certain to hear some word of Lord Stewart by the spring. To swoop down on Brae Aisir now is a mistake, and ye will live to regret it. I don't trust Ewan Hay. He wants more than he says he does. Wait, I beg ye."

"If we wait until the spring, Mad Maggie and her grandfather will have reasserted their authority, and we will have no chance of taking it all for ourselves," Edmund Kerr responded. "Now is the perfect time. My kinsman is old and undoubtedly grieving for Fingal Stewart, for he loved him like a son. His granddaughter is heavy with child, concerned for her husband's safety, and in no position to resist. And then there are her sons. We could take both lads from her and bring them here should she attempt to mount a resistance against us," Edmund Kerr said. "Let Ewan Hay have Mad Maggie if he could indeed master her." The Lord of Netherdale wanted nothing but the Aisir nam Breug, the power and the riches having all of it would bring him.

"This is a mistake," Rafe Kerr said. "What if Fingal Stewart hasn't been killed? Possibly he's been wounded, captured. What will happen when he makes his way back to Brae Aisir and finds Ewan Hay in his keep, and trying to mount his wife?" the son asked his father. "He'll not thank us, Da."

"Any ransom demand must come to Brae Aisir. If one does, it will be intercepted, and Mad Maggie will never know. It will allow us to learn where Fingal Stewart is. We'll find him and have him killed," Edmund Kerr said.

"Jesu, Da! Will ye have that man's death on your conscience then?"

"I will do what I must to control all of the Aisir nam Breug, and not just a scant eight miles of it, Rafe," Edmund Kerr told his eldest son. "And if ye attempt to stop me, I will slit yer throat myself. Ye have six legitimate brothers, and I am not without heirs."

"Sons who have been taught unquestioning loyalty to me as yer heir," Rafe countered in a hard voice. He had no doubt his father was capable of killing him.

Edmund Kerr laughed harshly. "I could slaughter ye before their eyes, and not one of them would lift a finger to save ye, and do ye know why? Greed, Rafe. Greed! My second born would become my heir, and the others would live in hope of his displeasing me and moving them a notch farther up."

"I never said I would betray ye, Da," his eldest son said. "And do ye know why? Loyalty. Loyalty to the father who gave me life and has treated me well. But I do not have to agree with yer actions, and I do not. Send Ewan Hay to Brae Aisir in yer name, as yer surrogate, and ye will come to regret it. He'll betray ye in the end, though he uses ye now to gain what he wants. He's a treacherous Scot, and he thinks ye a duplicitous Englishman. Neither of ye can trust the other, and that is a poor foundation on which to build this arrangement," Rafe concluded.

"I'll have ye oversee him and his actions," Edmund Kerr said, nodding. "Ye'll protect the Kerr family's interests." Reaching out, he cuffed his son's head. "I know yer loyal, Rafe, and I trust ye. I've raised ye to be strong, and ye are. It cannot be helped that the old bull and the young bull lock horns now and again. On the morrow tell Ewan Hay that if his brother will give him the men and arms he needs to hold Brae Aisir for me, I will agree to his plan. I don't wish to speak with the fellow again."

"I'll take care of it, Da." His father had asked him to protect the Kerr family's interests—and he would, Rafe thought. He would protect it for Mad Maggie, his cousin, and for her lads, in the event— *God forbid it!*—that Fingal Stewart had been among those killed at the battle now known as Solway Moss. Managing eight miles of the Aisir nam Breug was more than enough for him.

The next day he sent Ewan Hay on his way. The Scot carried with him a parchment upon which Rafe Kerr himself had written the following words:

On this sixteenth day of December, in the year of our Lord 1542,

Ewan Hay has been appointed by Edmund Kerr, Lord of Netherdale, to oversee the interests of the Kerr family at Brae Aisir.

And Rafe Kerr signed his father's name to the brief document, then pressed his father's signet into the hot wax he poured onto the parchment. If Fingal Stewart returned, Rafe would explain his father's concern for his elderly kinsman, Maggie, and her family. He would explain that his father thought a Scotsman preferable, and more acceptable to the folk at Brae Aisir. Lord Stewart was no fool, and he would know what Edmund Kerr was really about, but hopefully as long as old Dugald, Maggie, and the children were healthy and safe, he would pretend to be grateful for the Lord of Netherdale's concern. No harm would be done in the matter. He intended to send his own messenger to the warden of the West March in Carlisle and learn if Lord Stewart was among the prisoners taken up for ransom. Possibly he could facilitate his release if he was. There was more than one way around his father's foolishness and greed.

He saw Ewan Hay off and was glad to see him go. Did Ewan Hay think the Kerrs of Netherdale so stupid that they didn't realize he wanted control of the Brae Aisir Kerrs' portion of the Aisir nam Breug for himself? Rafe shook his head. If it had been up to him, he would have refused Ewan Hay's suggestion and sent him off yesterday. But it wasn't his place. At least not yet. His father, he suspected, would live for many more years. Rafe wondered if Edmund would gain any real wisdom by the time he was Dugald Kerr's age. He somehow doubted it.

"Bobby! Bobby! 'Tis my lad, Bobby!" The old woman ran alongside the litter on which the unconscious man lay.

"Nah, nah, Old Mother," the man-at-arms said. "'Tis one of the Scots we picked up from the battlefield. He doesn't look like he's worth much, but if no one ransoms him, and he lives, he'll be off to the galleys. We'll get some value from him." And the soldier laughed heartily.

"'Tis my son, Bobby," the old woman insisted. "He went off to fight the Scots. 'Tis he. Please let me have him, sir. He's all I have. My man is dead, and who will take care of me if ye take my Bobby from me?"

The soldier, who had some small authority among his ranks, called, "Halt!" to the men carrying the litter. "Yer sure that this is yer lad, Old Mother? Look closely at him. We found him among the Scots dead, wounded and dying."

"'Tis my son, Bobby!" the old woman said again.

The soldier's captain came up to see why the line of prisoners had come to a halt. He listened to the old woman's pleading, and then looked at the man lying on the litter. How the hell did one differentiate between an English borderer and a Scots borderer? He was a Midlands man, and to him these northerners all looked relatively the same. The unconscious man had nothing on him, no plaid, badge, or ring, that would tell the captain the truth of the matter. Whoever he was, he was obviously of no importance. He had an open gash on his head that was still oozing slightly. If he lived, he was likely to bring little to the king's coffers in ransom, and even less being sold into the galleys. It would actually cost more to keep the man alive until his situation was resolved.

"Yer certain this man is your son?" he asked the old woman sharply.

"'Tis my Bobby!" she insisted once again.

"Give him to her," the captain said. He looked to the men carrying the litter. "Take him to wherever she wants," he said, "and now get this line moving again. We're going to be caught in the open tonight as it is."

Touching the unconscious man's face gently, the old woman said, "Yer home now, my son. Yer mother will take good care of ye. I'll heal yer wounds for ye. I thought I should never get ye back again."

Then she led the litter bearers across the marshland following a path they could hardly see until they reached a small neat cottage. She instructed the two men to bring the litter into the dwelling, admonishing them to set it down carefully upon the cottage's single bed. Then she sent them on their way, warning them to follow the path back exactly else they be swallowed up by the mud.

She slammed the door closed behind them and then went to build up her fire, hanging a black iron pot of water on a hook at the end of an iron arm and swinging the arm out over the fire to boil the water. Finding her box of salves and ointments, the old woman waited for the water to boil. When it did, she opened another box, pulling out a clean rag. She began to clean the wound. It had not, praise the Holy Mother, become infected yet. When she could see the shape of it, she was relieved to observe that it was not too deep a cut. Head wounds always bled heavily, giving the appearance of being more serious. Some were. This wasn't. The cut was no more than an inch in length.

But there was a deep indent in his head as if he had been hit by something. She dressed the wound carefully and bandaged it.

Her poor son was filthy. She rolled him from the litter onto the bed proper, then cut the clothing from his unconscious body and washed it thoroughly. Then, puffing and heaving, she managed to get him beneath the warm coverlet. It wouldn't do for her Bobby to get an ague just when she had gotten him back. Jesu and his Blessed Mother had answered her prayers! Well she had prayed to them long enough, hadn't she? She had been faithful, and now she was rewarded. Her son was home with her again. The old woman pulled a stool near to the bed, sat down, and waited for her son to awaken.

Fingal Stewart began to slowly come to himself. He didn't remember a great deal of what had happened. He remembered an English horseman coming towards him and waving his sword. Fin had ducked the clumsy warrior, but the tip of the sword had cut him, and blood pouring from the wound obscured his vision. He was knocked from his horse. When he began to grow conscious once again, it was to find a man with foul breath leaning over him, pulling the ring from his finger. His boots were being yanked from his feet by another man. He protested faintly, trying to rise, but something hit him hard on his head near his wound, and he fell back into an unconscious state.

As he struggled to awaken, he tried to remember where he had been, and what he had been doing. But then the biggest question of all came to him. *Who was he?* He could not, try as he might, remember his name. Or where he had come from. A sudden wave of fear swept over him. His eyes flew open. He was too weak to arise, but he turned his head this way and that, seeking to learn where he was. An old woman, her crossed arms upon his bed making a pillow for her head, was sleeping as she sat upon her stool.

He could remember a battle. It hadn't been a big battle, but it had been a short and a fierce one. Where was he? He moved his head cautiously, his eyes sweeping about the cottage. It was a poor woman's abode, he could tell right away. But it was clean and it was neat. Had this old woman taken him from the battlefield? He was a Scot. That much he could remember. Was this Scotland or England? And what was his name?

"Bobby, my son, yer awake!" The old woman was looking at him with rheumy eyes, her toothless mouth spread in a happy smile. "When I heard the wounded were being brought in from the battlefield, I ran at once in hopes of finding ye alive."

"Where am I?" Fin asked quietly.

"Why, yer home in our own wee cottage in the marsh," she answered.

"The Scottish marshes or the English marshes? And where are my clothes?" He had become aware he was naked beneath the coverlet.

"Yer in England, my son. Aah, I can see the blow to yer poor head has addled yer wits. It will all come back to ye soon enough. Yer safe with yer mam."

"My clothes?" he repeated.

"Why, I cut them off ye, for they were filthy and bloodied, Bobby. Don't worry, my son. I've some breeks and shirts for ye to wear when ye are well enough to get up. Some scavenger must have gotten yer boots before ye were picked up, but there's an old pair of yer da's in the trunk where I put his clothing after he died. Mayhap they'll fit, although yer da had a bigger foot. Are ye hungry?"

"I am," he said, realizing suddenly that he was ravenous.

"Let me get ye a dish of porridge then, Bobby," she said, standing up and going to the hearth where a small pot was now hanging over the glowing coals of the fire.

Bobby. Nay, his name was not Bobby, and this old woman was not his mother. That much he knew for certain. But he was in England, and he was a Scot who had survived a battle. How far from the border was he? And again he tried to remember who he was. He was injured, and because she believed him her son, the old woman was caring for him. What if her real son returned? Or was he more likely lying dead on the battlefield? Whatever the truth of the matter, he would have to remain here for the interim until his wounds were healed, his strength restored, and his memory returned. Or at least enough of it that he could make his way home, wherever that was.

With the old woman's care he began to return to himself physically. He left the bed after several days. His limbs had grown stiff, and he worked each day to return to what felt like normal for him. Looking at his own muscled body, he knew he had been an active man. He suspected he had eaten better too than he was now eating. His diet consisted of oat porridge, bread, and hard cheese. The old woman's tiny kitchen garden was now covered in snow, the ground frozen hard as rock.

She didn't want him to go outside of the cottage. "I'll lose ye again!" she cried the first time he had sought to step out into the cold air.

He had reassured her as best as he could, but she stood in the low doorway of the cottage watching him as he walked about surveying his surroundings. Then he had cut some peat from the muddy marsh where the ground wasn't yet frozen and brought it in for her fire. She had virtually nothing but the few bits of wood she went out to gather each day to keep her fire going. He would gather as much fuel for her as he could as a means of paying her back for her kindness.

The winter set in with heavy snows, short bitter days, and long bitter nights.

Bits and pieces of his memory were beginning to return as the days started to slowly lengthen once again. He remembered he had had a horse, and a sword. One day he recalled a man whose name was Iver. He dreamed of a small stone keep on a hillside above a neat village. There was a priest, and an old laird. And then one night Fingal Stewart awoke suddenly and knew his name.

He arose from the pallet where he now made his bed. He could not take the old woman's only sleeping arrangement once his wounds had healed. Quietly he walked to the small window, opening one shutter to gaze out upon the snowy landscape surrounding the cottage. There was a moon that night. A border moon, he thought. He was Fingal Stewart, Lord Stewart of Torra. That much he knew now, but there was more he could still not recollect. He had to return to his house in Edinburgh and find the man named Iver who could probably help him to unravel the rest of the mystery surrounding him.

"Bobby," the woman called plaintively from the bed where she lay. She coughed a deep cough; she had not been well for several days now and had kept to her bed. He suspected she might be dying, for she had grown very frail with the deepening of winter, and she had lived alone in this marsh for many years, as he had learned from her.

"I'm here, Old Mother," he answered her, turning and walking over to the side of the bed. "Can I get ye something?"

She looked up at him with her rheumy blue eyes. "Yer not my Bobby, are ye?"

Her gaze was sharper, clearer than he had ever seen it.

Fingal Stewart shook his head. "Nay, Old Mother, I am not yer Bobby," he said quietly. "But ye saved my life by insisting to the men of the warden of the West March that I was. For that I am grateful, and I thank ye."

"I thought ye were," the old woman replied. "My Bobby went to fight King James at a place called Flodden. He was just twenty when he left me. His da told me that he died, but I never believed it. I always knew my Bobby would return to me. Ye look so like him," she said. "I was so sure. So very certain . . ." Her voice trailed off weakly, and a tear rolled down her wrinkled cheek.

"Flodden was more than twenty-eight years ago, Old Mother," Fin told her. "King James the Fourth died in that battle. The battle in which I fought was at Solway Moss, and the king now is his son, James the Fifth."

"Yer a Scot," she murmured, shaking her white head. "A gentleman, I think."

"Aye," he said, the tiniest of smiles touching his lips. "I'm a Scot. The head wound I received took my memory, but thanks to yer tender care, I am slowly regaining it."

"Do ye know yer name?" she asked weakly.

"My name is Fingal Stewart," he said, "and I have a house in Edinburgh. That much I remember. I also recall a man named Iver who I hope can help me revive the rest of my memory. I dream of a stone keep and an old laird."

"I am dying," the old woman said matter-of-factly. "Will ye remain with me until I am dead, Fingal Stewart? And will ye see my body is treated with respect?"

"I will not leave ye, Old Mother," he promised her. "I owe ye my life."

"Good! Good!" she said, and her eyes closed as she fell asleep again.

Their positions were now reversed, and it was Fingal who spent his time over the next few weeks nursing the woman who had saved his life by claiming him as her kin. Her spirit was strong though her body grew weaker and weaker. He developed chilblains on his hands from being outdoors in the bitter weather seeking fuel to keep the tiny cottage warm for the woman. He set traps and caught several rabbits he skinned, butchered, and broiled for them to eat. The skins he tanned and dried, making coverings for the old woman's hands, which were constantly icy.

She rallied for a time, and Fin was strangely glad. For now the woman was all he had. They saw no one, for the cottage was in the middle of a frozen marsh, and there was no road visible to his eye leading to it. She told him she had lived in the cottage her entire life. Her late husband has been one of the warden's marshmen who patrolled the area making certain no one poached the water fowl, or the fish. Her father had been one too, which was why the cottage was located where it was.

The old woman had lost two sons and a daughter before her Bobby was born. She had raised him and tried to protect him, but he was a stubborn boy. He might have taken his grandfather's position, but Bobby wanted more adventure than a marshman toiling for the warden of the West March had. When the call had come for men to fight the Scots for King Henry, Bobby had answered that call. When the battle of Flodden had been fought, and the Scots king killed, the old woman's husband had gone to find if their son had survived. He could find no trace of him, and Bobby never came home again. Then several years afterwards her husband had died.

"I lost track of time after that," the old woman said. Then she looked at him with clear eyes and said, "When I am gone, remain here until yer memory is better. No one ever comes here anymore. Ye'll be safe. Yer not so bad a fellow, considering yer a Scot."

Fingal laughed, but then he grew more sober. "We are all just folk," he told her. "It doesn't matter which side of the border we come from, Old Mother. It's the kings and the powerful who cause trouble for us."

She nodded. "There is much truth in what ye say," she agreed.

His rescuer finally breathed her last one early-spring evening. The snows were melting quickly, and bits of green, which would eventually become reeds, were shooting up from the patches of water that just a few weeks earlier had been frozen solid. That morning she had noted the birdsong that had been absent during the winter. Then her eyes had closed. He sat by her side, holding her thin worn hand the day long, and as evening approached, she opened her eyes a final time.

"Ah," she said, smiling. "Here is my Bobby at last." Then with a gasp so faint he barely heard it, the old woman died with a gentle shudder.

Fingal Stewart said a prayer for the woman's soul. He hadn't even known her Christian name though he had lived more than five months in this wee cottage. Because until almost the very end she had believed him to be her son, he had addressed her as *Old Mother*, which pleased her. Now he was forced to pray for her in those terms. The entire time he had been with her she had worn the same dun-colored skirt, a bodice that had probably once been white, and her old woolen shawl. Now Fin searched through the woman's possessions to see if he could find something nicer in which to bury her.

He stripped her scrawny frame, and washed it as best he might with a rag and some warm water from the pot on the fire. Then he redressed her in a clean worn chemise, several petticoats, and a medium blue velvet skirt and bodice he had discovered in a small trunk. Her man had obviously gone raiding as well as being in the service of the warden of the West March. There was no other way a man of his small status could have afforded a velvet gown for his wife. Fin combed the woman's thin white hair, and plaited it neatly. He took a wide silk ribbon he had found with the dress, placing it beneath her chin to tie at the top of her head. It would keep her jaw from falling open. He would bury her on the morrow as it was now dark.

He ate some stale bread and cheese, then lay down on his pallet. Awakening before the dawn, he arose and ate the rest of the bread with what remained of a rabbit he had broiled two days ago; then fetching a shovel, he went outside to find a place he might dig a grave. He found a reasonably dry spot just a short distance from the cottage, and realized another grave was already there—her husband's undoubtedly—but there was room for the old woman. He dug the grave deep, stopping only when he sensed he would hit water. He tossed a shovelful of earth back into the grave to make certain it would be dry. About him the gray of predawn had given way as the coming sun began to stain the horizon, and the birds began to sing.

Returning to the cottage, Fingal Stewart picked up the body of the old woman and, lifting it from the bed, carried it to the simple tomb. Jumping down into the grave, Fin laid the body neatly, the arms over the chest. He placed a small cross he had made from some sticks beneath her hands. Then climbing from the grave site, he began to fill it in, piling the brown soil into a mound. It would flatten out naturally over the next few months, but hopefully the grave would not collapse into itself. Kneeling, Fingal Stewart said a prayer for Old Mother's good soul. Then he returned to the cottage.

He remained there for the next several days. He didn't know if anyone would come to check up on the old woman, but until his memory was fully restored, he didn't want to have to speak with anyone. One word from his mouth and they would realize he was a Scot. He had to go to Edinburgh and find the man named Iver. Oddly, he knew exactly where his house was. But where the man named Iver was he did not know. Still, the first objective was to gain the safety of Scotland, of Edinburgh, and finally of his house.

Standing outside the cottage, he was able to determine north by the placement of the rising and setting sun. Finally, on the third day after the woman's death, Fingal Stewart set out. He had no idea how far he had to travel, but once he gained the border and saw someone, he might safely ask. He had boots on his feet courtesy of Old Mother's late husband. He was clothed respectably, though he hardly looked like a Lord Stewart. His hair had grown to his shoulders, and he kept it tied back. He had a beard, although he knew he did not wear a beard. There had been no means of shaving it; however, he had trimmed it short with a knife. Perhaps at his house in Edinburgh there would be something with which to shave his face and cut his hair.

He had trapped two rabbits, cooked them, and wrapped the pieces along with the last of Old Mother's oatcakes. He didn't think his scant rations would last him as long as it would take to get to Edinburgh, but he had found a small cache of coins beneath the mattress of the cottage's bed. All were dead here. He felt no shame in taking those coins for himself. He had no idea what lay ahead. He walked for at least two hours, finally coming to a river. It was the Esk, his memory prompted him. The force he had traveled with prior to his injury had crossed it on horseback. Scotland lay on the other side of this water, but how was he to get across? There would be no bridge, of course. Neither the English nor the Scots would make it easy for the other to invade. He wasn't certain he could swim across. Sitting down on the bank of the river to rest and consider what to do, he suddenly heard a voice hailing him.

"Laddie! Laddie!"

Looking up, he swiveled his head about.

"Across the water, laddie," came the voice. "Are ye seeking a way to ford yon river? Perhaps I can help ye if ye have the coin."

Fingal Stewart looked over the river to the other side, and saw a man standing by a small boat. "I'm a poor soldier who fought at Solway Moss. I've just been released by the English," he called back to the man. "I have no coin, but I'll give ye a day's labor if ye'll get me back to Scotland so I can get home."

"What can ye do?" the man asked him.

"Whatever ye need done. I'll chop wood, herd yer livestock. I can write if ye need a letter written," Fin answered the man.

"I have two daughters in need of servicing," the man called back. "If I bring ye across, will ye linger long enough to do what needs to be done?"

Fingal Stewart wasn't certain he had heard the man correctly. "*What?*" he said.

The man was already in his boat, and rowing across the Esk. As the river was not particularly wide where they were, the prow of his little vessel slid up onto the English side of the riverbank in short order. The man, of medium height and stocky, climbed out and came towards Fin, holding out his hand. "I'm Parlan Fife," he said. "Let me explain."

Fin shook the man's hand. "Could ye do it as we cross back to Scotland?" he asked. The man looked relatively sane.

"Help me push 'er back into the river, and get in," Parlan Fife said.

Fin complied, but when they were midriver, his ferryman stopped rowing.

"Now, laddie, hear me out. My wife is dead. I've six lasses, and I've managed to get four of them wed respectably. But I have nothing left with which to help the two who remain, and it would take far more than I could earn in a thousand years to find husbands for Lily and Sybil. They're nae ugly or misshapen, but they have another fault that cannot be corrected, nor that a decent man would accept in a wife."

Fin was fascinated. "And what is that?" he asked Parlan Fife.

"They like to fuck," the ferryman answered him.

"*What?!*" Had he heard the man correctly?

"They like to fuck, and they can't get enough of it," Parlan Fife said. "Their reputations are such that some call them witches. It's been a long winter, and they have had no man to satisfy their needs in months. The few families here abouts keep their men away from my lasses for they fear them. Oh, now and again one comes calling, but my lassies wear them out and send them home half dead. Ye look like a strong man, and if ye've been in an English prison since the king's last battle, then ye should be ready for a rough and tumble. I'll take ye the rest of the way across, but ye must agree that ye will service my lasses for at least ten days. After that, yer free to go on yer way again or remain if it pleases ye. I could use the company of another man myself."

"The king's last battle?" Fin said. "What news of the king?"

"Will ye agree to my terms?" Parlan Fife said stubbornly.

Fin considered. To fuck a woman. Aye. It had been months since he himself had satisfied his own lusts. And before Solway Moss? He couldn't remember. "Aye," he said. "I'll give yer two lasses a good ten days to ease their lusty natures. Now, tell me of the king, Parlan Fife."

The ferryman began to row again towards the Scots side of the river. "The king is dead," he said. "Died in mid-December just after his little daughter was born. Scotland has a queen. Her name is Mary. These will not be easy times for Scotland with an infant for its monarch. Already the English king is saying he wants her for his son. That England and Scotland should be one."

The king dead! There was certain to be more war, with the English believing that Scotland was vulnerable, the French Queen Mother fighting to keep her daughter safe, and the powerful lords fighting to gain control of their queen, and thereby ruling Scotland. They would divide into factions behind England, behind France. How he knew this Fin couldn't have explained, but he did. It had happened before.

The little boat finally touched the Scots shore. Fingal Stewart jumped out. He was home again. A few days of servitude to Parlan Fife and his daughters, then he would be on his way again. He followed the ferryman away from the river, walking for several minutes until they came to a stone cottage. There were three small children in the front playing at a game of tag with a large dog that seemed to be watching over them.

"My grandchildren," Parlan Fife said. "Two are Sybil's; one is Lily's."

"Their sires?"

Parlan Fife shrugged. "Who knows," he admitted. "The eldest is a lad, and I'll teach him to man my boat. At least I'll have someone here to watch over me as I grow older. They're good bairns, though I fear for the two little lasses because of their mams."

Remembering Old Mother and her sad, lonely existence, Fin understood.

"Da! What have ye brought home?" A buxom redhead appeared in the door of the cottage. She turned her head back, calling, "Sibby, come and see what Da has brought us." She strutted forth from the dwelling, smiling, hands on her ample hips. "Welcome, laddie!" Her blue eyes surveyed him from the top of his head to his booted feet, lingering thoughtfully on his crotch just long enough to make Fin flush. She giggled. "I'm Lily."

"Ohh, he's a big fellow." A second woman had joined them. She was much like her sibling but that her eyes were gray. She too examined him thoroughly, licking her lips as she did so. "Is he for us, Da?" she asked their father. Her hand reached out to touch Fin's bearded face as the tip of her tongue touched the center of her upper lip.

"The lad will remain for ten days in return for his passage across the river," Parlan Fife told his two daughters. "He's been in prison since the big battle last autumn."

"*Ohhhhhh,*" the two sisters said, looking meaningfully at each other. "What's his name, Da?"

"My name is Fingal Stewart," Fin answered them.

"Is the meal ready?" their father asked them.

"Shortly, Da," Sybil said.

"Would ye like me to shave that beard from yer face?" Lily asked Fin.

"Aye, I would!" Fin replied. Seeing these two women, he wondered if he should have offered the ferryman a coin, but then it was better that Parlan Fife not know he had any coin. He would have to find a place to hide the little purse, for he had no doubt these two wenches would go through his belongings given the opportunity.

Lily led him into the cottage and set Fin upon a straight-backed chair. She removed his shirt, running her hands over his broad chest and back with little murmurs of appreciation. She brought a basin of hot water and a sliver of white soap. Then hiking up her skirts, she sat on his lap, facing him as she shaved the thick black beard from his face. It was not an easy project, and it took time to accomplish. Her bare bottom rubbed and bounced across his crotch. In short order he was hard as iron.

Lily smiled into his face as she shaved him. "Unlace yer breeks, laddie, and take out what I suspect is a fine bit o'cock. No one will know if I sheath ye while I work. How long were ye imprisoned?"

He didn't argue with her. "Five months," he said as he followed her instructions, rubbing himself against the inside of her plump thigh.

Lily put down her razor, reaching beneath her skirts with her hand as she rose up slightly. Her fingers tightened about his length as she guided him to where she wanted him, and then sank down to encase him fully. "Aah, darlin', that is so good. Can ye wait but a moment for me to finish, and then we'll go for a little jog together," she said, smiling. Lily quickly finished, scraping the several months of beard from his face.

She wiped the remaining soap from his skin. Then she leaned forward to kiss him, her tongue plunging into his mouth as her lips parted.

Her shameless aggressiveness surprised him, but Fin quickly gained a mastery of the situation as his hands clamped about her waist. He held her tightly, controlling her movements, for her abstinence had made her too eager. If he had to spend ten days of his time giving pleasure to these two sisters, he would show them what pleasure was truly like. And it was not a quick tumble-and-be-done. Lily's blue eyes began to glaze over as she came close to her pinnacle.

It was at that point Fin ceased all movement. The lass's eyes flew open in surprise, and he said to her, "I will give ye what ye want, sweeting, but ye will remember that both of us must gain pleasure. And pleasure is not gained quickly, but slowly, slowly, and with great patience. Now, are ye ready, Lily?"

She nodded slowly. He watched as her eyes widened. A little moan escaped her lips as the big cock plumbed her depths until she wanted to scream, but he silenced her with a hard kiss, and then with a fierce hard thrust that gave her exactly what she wanted. Lily shuddered several times, and then fell forward onto his shoulder.

"Yer such a slut," Sybil said, coming to tell them the meal was ready. "Could ye not wait until tonight, Lily? Well, I get him first later," the gray-eyed redhead said.

The meal was rabbit stew served in a bread trencher. Fin ate it all. It had been months since he had experienced such a good meal. His host's ale was nutty and flavorful. He was curious as to how the ferryman could keep such an excellent table, but perhaps his daughters' talents accounted for it. Or possibly poaching and thievery supple-mented his income, for traffic across the river right now couldn't be busy. When the meal had been cleared away and the bairns put into their cots, Parlan Fife bid his guest a good night with a grin as his daughters came to fetch Fin.

They brought him into a little chamber that was almost entirely filled by a large bed. A little table was set between the bed and the wall. Upon it was a single short, fat candle that burned with a smoky light. There was a single window, shuttered now with the night. The two sisters wasted no time divesting themselves and Fingal Stewart of their garments. He managed to pull off his own breeks, thereby hid-ing the purse of coins from them, for he had not yet had time to find a place to secrete it.

They ran their hands over his naked body, exclaiming over it as if they were judging a prized stallion. Well, Fingal Stewart thought, amused, he was to be their stallion for the next few days. He turned them about finally, pulling their backs against him, one arm about them, a hand reaching up to fondle their breasts. He liked their breasts. They were round and familiar. He pinched the nipples of the breasts. The two sisters yelped excited, high-pitched squeals. "To the bed with ye," he told them, pushing both women forward. He was re-minded of a similar situation he had found himself in with two ladies many years ago in France. It had been a satisfying time.

Fin lay between Lily and Sybil, an arm about each. "What shall we do, lasses?" he asked them.

"Ye've already had Lily once," Sybil said plaintively. "I want to be fucked!"

"Then make me want ye as yer pretty sister did earlier," Fin told her. "Ye could begin by sucking my cock. That should put it in prime condition to pleasure ye, lass."

Sybil didn't hesitate. She scrambled from his embrace and into position between his legs. "Ohh, even at its rest ye've a fine, big cock," she complimented him. She hoped he knew how to use it, but then, the sounds her sister had earlier made seemed to indicate that he had a talent of sorts. She began to use her own talents licking and sucking upon him; burrowing beneath him to take his pouch into her mouth, and using her tongue to manipulate his stones until his fine cock was upstanding.

Fin's head was spinning with delight. Lily, minx that she was, had placed her cunny directly over his face. Her female scent was intoxicating, he thought as he licked her, tasting her cream. He didn't know which of them was exciting him more. They were both going to be more than satisfied if they kept it up, and he suspected they could. But could he? He pushed Lily aside, growling at her, "Stay wet for me," and then he reached out for Sybil. "Get up here, and get on yer back," he told her.

Then mounting her, he began to fuck her. He drove her hard and deep for several long minutes as she writhed and moaned beneath him. Finally he felt her sheath convulsing, and Sybil screamed with her delight as she bedewed the tip of his cock with her juices. He withdrew from her, still hard as a rock, and eager for more. Lily was waiting for him. Plunging into her, he used her over and over again until she too was shrieking with her pleasure. Pushing her aside finally, he reached for Sybil again.

"Do my ass," she begged him. "Yer so big. I want ye in my ass!" She rolled over into a kneeling position, her buttocks elevated high for him.

He obliged, but was careful as he entered her. He quickly found she was as easy to access there as her sheath had been. She had known more than one cock in her ass. He pumped her with slow, long, majestic strokes of his cock as he grasped her hips to hold her steady. Finally he felt his own release coming, to his great relief. He loosed his juices into her, and she moaned, "Jesu! Jesu! Ye know how to give joy, laddie."

The rest of the night progressed in similar fashion. The two sisters were insatiable in their lust for a male partner. They had no qualms, and would do anything he asked as long as he satisfied their needs. He was astounded at his own strength, considering the past few months. But then he was obviously a lustful man himself, and his needs had been suppressed these past months with his illness. He was obviously at his full strength once again. Servicing these two wenches for the ten days would take a great deal, but he knew he was a man of his word. Besides, he still needed to know more of the state of Scotland before he struck out for Edinburgh again.

None of them arose from their communal bed before midday the following noon. But once up, the sisters went about their duties as if nothing extraordinary had happened. Fin, on the other hand, felt as if he had been dragged across the moors by a team of wild horses. He knew if he was going to survive Lily and Sybil, he would have to be the master of them both. Once awake, that early afternoon they had both dressed quickly and left him. It had given him time to look about the chamber and see if there was someplace he might secrete his cache of coins. A loose board just beneath the bed proved the perfect place. He then dressed himself and went to find the sisters.

"We're low on wood," Lily said as he entered the common room of the cottage.

"I'll fetch it for ye," he told her. "Where's yer sister?"

Lily shrugged. "If ye want to be alone with me ye can," she said seductively, coming over to him and her hand going to his crotch to fondle him.

He removed the hand firmly. "Behave, lass," he said. "I'm fair worn-out with the two of ye. I'll get the wood. Ye find Sybil. I would speak with both of ye."

There was a neat pile of wood on one side of the large cottage. He gathered up several big pieces and brought them into the common room where both sisters now waited for him. Setting the wood down, he turned about and said, "Ye both seem to have a great appetite for cock, my lasses, don't ye?"

They giggled at him.

"Yet I am but one man. I'm worn-out with yer lustful games of last night," he told them. "For the rest of my term of servitude, I'll take one of ye into bed with me each night. Ye'll alternate with each other. I'd like to live long enough to get home to Edinburgh," he said to the pair.

"But last night was such fun," Sybil said, pouting.

"Indeed, lass, I cannot recall ever having had such a night," Fin admitted. "But yer father's price was that I service ye for ten days. He did not say how, just that I do it. If ye would both be well fucked in that term of days, then ye must do as I say. Which of ye is elder?"

"I am," Sybil said.

"Then tonight ye'll be the one sharing a bed with me," he said. "Now, where is yer da?"

Lily laughed. "He's gone off to visit a lady friend for a few days," she said. "He said he could hear us all the night long, and it made him randy for a woman of his own."

"Then until he returns," Fin told them, "I am the man of this house, and ye'll obey me, and do my bidding."

"And if we don't?" Lily said mischievously.

"I'm not above smacking bottoms," Fin answered, and they both giggled.

Parlan Fife remained away for almost the entire ten days Fin owed him for his passage across the border river. Fin didn't blame him at all, for he imagined that living with Lily and Sybil when they were in need of a man to assuage their lust wasn't easy. As Fin had spent the winter nursing a dying old woman, Parlan Fife had spent a winter with two randy young females in need of a strong male cock. Fin hoped that by the time he left them to travel onward, the two sisters would be satiated for at least a few weeks.

His time in the cottage took on a sameness. Each day he did the household chores that needed doing for the two sisters. They seemed to have a flock of sheep they tended to, which was obviously what helped to supplement their income. He helped them with the animals too. When night fell, and the meal was over, the three children were put to bed. They were good bairns, and gave no trouble. Then he would take either Lily or Sybil into the big bed to pleasure the night long while the other sister slept in the little chamber with the bairns on a pallet.

Fin was not sorry to see the ten days coming to an end. His own months of long-enforced celibacy had been broken by the sisters, and his lusts were more than satisfied for the time being. He was ready to be on the road again, and another bit of his memory had bloomed. He had a devoted servant named Archie, and Iver was a man-at-arms.

Parlan Fife returned smiling and looking pleased two days before Fin was to depart the cottage. He announced to his daughters that he was marrying his Katie at midsummer, and that the cottage was now theirs. "Yer both more than old enough to manage on yer own," he said. "It's unlikely either of ye will wed. A man doesn't want a wife whose road has been so well traveled as yers has been. We'll not be far away if ye need us, my daughters." He turned to Fin. "Well, ye look as if ye have survived these two."

"I have," Fin admitted. "But I'll be on my way the day after tomorrow."

"Ye've kept yer agreement," Parlan Fife said. "I've no complaints, although I imagine the lasses will."

"I suspect if one, or both of them, took up yer ferry boat, they might get more traffic," Fin suggested.

The ferryman nodded his head in agreement. "What do ye think, lasses?"

"I know if I saw a pretty girl on the other side of the river offering me a ride, I would surely take it," Fin told them.

"Ye can have the boat too," Parlan Fife said generously to his daughters.

"Lucky old sot," Sybil said that evening as she and Fin recovered from a bout of eros. "Katie is a widow, and her farmer husband left her rich. The land was his, no overlord's. She owes allegiance to no one. I wonder if he can get a bairn on her?"

"Ye and yer sister will be fine without him," Fin assured her as he played with one of her large breasts. He kissed the nipple lightly.

"Stay with us," Sybil said.

"Nay," he told her. "I have to get to Edinburgh."

"Why? What's there? A wife? A pretty woman?" Sybil queried him. She was curious, for Fin had not spoken of himself at all.

"My house. My servant who may think I'm dead," Fin answered her. "I need to get home and pick up my life again."

"As what?" she pressed him.

"I'm a soldier, lass. I hire myself out to anyone with the coin to pay," Fin said.

"With a baby for a queen, I can promise ye there will be a war. Whether it is between England and Scotland, or just between the powerful men seeking to control the little queen, I know not. And France will be involved too, for the widowed queen is French, and a member of the royal family. The French will seek to protect both King James's widow and his surviving child. I know there will be a conflict, may God help us all. And that's how I earn my living—fighting other men's wars."

These were things he knew about himself, and about the world in which he lived. Some of them he had never forgotten in those months since he had awakened in Old Mother's cottage. Other things had come back slowly over the months since the battle at Solway Moss. He sensed there was more, but he could not remember what. He hoped that reaching his house in Edinburgh, and finding Archie, his servant, as well as Iver, the man-at-arms, would help him to recall what it was that he was forgetting. It had to be important or it would not be tugging at the edges of his memory and niggling him so.

He spent his last night in Parlan Fife's cottage with Lily to amuse him. It seemed fitting that since she was the first of the sisters he had enjoyed, he should also end his visit with her. As Sybil had, she begged him to stay with them; yet when the morning came, he rose, dressed himself, and reached beneath the big bed to lift the loose floorboard to retrieve his little purse. He checked and was relieved to find all the coins there. Fin had no doubt that had his cache been found, they would have stolen it. He tucked it in his jerkin.

When he came out of the bedchamber, the sisters fed him a good breakfast of hot porridge, fresh bread, butter and jam. Sobbing, they kissed him good-bye, but they saw he had a two-day supply of food wrapped in a napkin they tucked into the sack he carried.

He waved farewell to the three bairns. They were quiet little things, and he had barely seen them in the time he had been with their mothers. The thought suddenly struck him. Did he have bairns? If he did, could he have forgotten them so easily?

"Follow the path," Parlan Fife said, pointing out a barely discernible track to Fin. After a few miles ye'll come to a road. Turn right, and ye'll find yer way to Edinburgh if ye follow it. Beware of raiders. There seem to be more out this year than in the past, and while ye haven't a horse, they'll steal anything they can lay their hands upon."

"Thank ye," Fin told the man.

Parlan Fife laughed. "Thank ye! I was able to finally get away from those two long enough to settle things with my Katie. Jesu and his Blessed Mother keep ye safe, Fingal Stewart, and get ye home to Edinburgh. Ye should reach it in a week or less."

Fin nodded, and turning, set off down the narrow path. He had no idea what awaited him, but he sensed with growing urgency that he needed to get to Edinburgh.

Or was it Edinburgh where he was needed? Was there someplace else he needed to be?

Chapter 13

⌒

$\mathcal{L}$ ord Hay was quite surprised upon reading Edmund Kerr's directive. "How the hell did ye manage this, Ewan?" he asked the younger of his two brothers.

"Lord Kerr dreams of controlling the entire Aisir nam Breug," Ewan Hay answered his elder. "He thinks by using me to assert his authority he can have it all. I told him I only wanted Mad Maggie."

"Ye do," his elder sibling said knowledgeably.

"Aye, I'll make the bitch my mistress," he said, "but I want the power that comes with controlling the Aisir nam Breug."

"And ye think Fingal Stewart is dead? That old Dugald Kerr will let you just march into his keep and take over?" Lord Hay said. "If ye do, yer a fool."

"If Maggie's husband hasn't returned by now, he's dead," Ewan responded.

"He could be a prisoner," Lord Hay reminded his brother. "Maggie has two sons who will take over the Aisir nam Breug one day. And she's breeding once again."

"Children sicken and die," Ewan said. "Even kings lose their infant children. If I put a male bairn in her belly, I'll want him to be the heir."

Lord Hay sighed, but then he considered that if Fingal Stewart didn't return, Maggie Kerr had to have another husband. If that happened, he would see Ewan married the woman. As long as his brother understood living with her put his very life in danger, then let him try to mount her, to get her with child. But to inherit, that child had to be legitimate. It was worth the gamble, and if Ewan succeeded, Lord Hay would have him off his hands, which was all to the good.

"I'll give ye thirty men. 'Tis more than enough to hold the keep against all comers. Try to befriend the Kerr men-at-arms, Ewan. Dinna throw yer weight around, and irritate their clan folk. At least pretend yer there at Edmund Kerr's insistence."

"I can handle the folk at Brae Aisir," Ewan said. "They'll have a strong master in me, Brother, and so will their bitch."

Lord Hay gave his brother thirty men-at-arms, telling his captain to part with new, half-trained lads. This way he felt his brother could not cause too much difficulty. The Hay captain did as his master requested, but he also took the opportunity to rid himself of one man among his own men who was a constant troublemaker, and a vicious bully. He appealed to the man's pride by making him captain of Ewan Hay's men-at-arms.

It was snowing the day before Christ's Mass when Ewan Hay came to Brae Aisir with his men-at-arms. The drawbridge was up, and it was almost dark when Ewan Hay begged shelter for himself and his brother's men returning from seeking survivors of Solway Moss on the border, as he claimed. The laird of Brae Aisir could hardly refuse. The lie gained him entry with his men into the keep. He strutted into the great hall with the air of a conqueror, his own captain, Bhaltair, by his side.

"I won't say yer welcome," Dugald Kerr told him, "but the laws of hospitality demand I shelter ye and yer men. Did ye find any survivors in yer travels?"

"Nay, but I did have an interesting visit with yer kinsman, Edmund Kerr," Ewan replied. "He sends ye his regards. He is concerned that with Lord Stewart dead, ye and yer asset are without suitable protection at this end of the Aisir nam Breug."

Maggie came slowly into the hall, and seeing Ewan Hay, spit a soft curse. "What are ye doing here?" she demanded of him.

"Edmund is worried about us," Dugald Kerr said dryly.

"He needn't be," Maggie said. "And even if he actually was, what the hell do ye have to do with it, Ewan Hay?"

"I am appointed by yer kinsman to oversee this portion of the Aisir nam Breug and maintain its safety," Ewan Hay replied with a smirk.

"Edmund Kerr has no authority over us," the laird said in a hard voice. "He is English. We are Scots, and my lands are in Scotland."

"The battle at Solway Moss has changed everything. Lord Stewart is among the dead. Ye have no one to champion ye, and yer kinsman knows that wars between kings have never before affected the Aisir nam Breug. He also knows yer without proper male authority. Rather than send one of his own sons, an Englishman, he sent me, a good Scot, that yer clan folk not be offended," Ewan said.

"We have no need of ye," Maggie told the man in a hard, cold voice. "And my husband is not dead. We are waiting for a ransom demand from England. But before Fingal Stewart came to Brae Aisir, my grandfather and I managed very well. We do not need an overseer now, and we certainly do not need ye! I dinna care if it's snowing. I want ye gone on the morrow!"

"Madam, ye are not being given a choice in this matter," Ewan Hay answered her. "Yer grandfather is a feeble old man. Yer a woman with a big belly, and two lads to care for, and whether ye like it or nae, this is best for ye all. Edmund Kerr's interest in the pass may not be as large as yers, but it is still considerable. The king is dead. The queen struggles to maintain her daughter's best interests. King Henry senses a weakness in Scotland. The Aisir nam Breug must be kept safe."

"And we will keep it so," Maggie told him.

"Ye, madam, will do as yer bid," Ewan said. "And ye will remember yer place, which is not to tell the men what they should and shouldn't do. Perhaps ye managed to get around yer grandfather, and yer husband, but ye will nae get around me. Now leave the hall. I have business to discuss with yer grandsire that does not concern ye."

To everyone's surprise Maggie turned about and walked from the chamber.

"Ye see, Dugald," Ewan Hay said, "ye just need to be firm with her."

"Ye pompous fool," the laird said. "Ye cannot even begin to imagine the enemy ye have just made. Before she simply disliked ye. Ye've turned that dislike into hatred."

"She's just a woman," Ewan Hay responded.

"She's Mad Maggie Kerr, and ye'll live to regret angering her," Dugald Kerr told the young man. "And in future ye will address me as *my lord*, and not by my Christian name. I am yer elder, and ye will respect that I, not ye, am the master of Brae Aisir. I want ye gone on the morrow."

"Aye, yer the laird of this place. *For now*," Ewan Hay said boldly.

Dugald Kerr smiled grimly. "Jesu help us all! Ye really are a fool, aren't ye?" Then he called out. "Busby! See Master Hay and his people are suitably housed, and bring me a whiskey." He did not offer Ewan Hay refreshment of any sort but turned his back on him, not speaking again that evening.

Upstairs, Maggie began to marshall her forces. "Keep the children from the hall unless I instruct ye otherwise," she told their nursemaids. "Grizel, keep the maids from the hall. Tell Busby to use only the men for service. I don't like the looks of the Hay captain, and as the captain goes, so go his men. Find Clennon Kerr and Iver Leslie and bring them to me. And let me know when my grandfather comes up from the hall."

"At once, my lady," Grizel replied, and she ran off to do Maggie's bidding. When she returned, however, she brought disturbing news. "I've spoken with the nursemaids, and gave Busby yer orders, my lady, but Clennon Kerr, Iver, and our men have been locked in their barracks on the orders of the Hay captain."

"How many men are in their quarters?" Maggie wondered aloud. "I know some of the lads went into the village to celebrate with their families. Find Busby, and tell him I need to see him," Maggie said to her serving woman.

Grizel nodded grimly, and hurried off. It was almost an hour before she returned with the keep's majordomo, Busby.

"Bar the door," Maggie said as they entered her chamber.

Grizel did as she was bid, and then said, "I'll see his lordship's door is both locked and barred too."

When all had been done, Maggie spoke. "It is apparent to me that Edmund Kerr has made an arrangement with Ewan Hay to attempt to steal Brae Aisir for himself. Of course, Master Hay will believe he can outfox my wily uncle, and keep the prize for himself. Lord Hay has obviously decided to gamble on his younger brother's success, for how else would he gain thirty men-at-arms? How many of our men have been trapped in their quarters, Busby? Do ye know?"

"No more than fifteen, my lady. The others are in the village," Busby said.

"Get word to them to remain hidden there, and say I charge them to keep the village safe from Hay and his men," Maggie instructed. "Can the men trapped be freed?"

"Indeed they can, my lady. Their quarters are built against the keep wall where the wall is steepest on the hillside. There is a narrow window in that wall. A man could ease himself through that opening and climb down."

"Tell Clennon and Iver to take the men remaining, and do so,"

Maggie said. "I want them hidden and ready to fight. Not boxed up, and vulnerable to being killed. And best they go tonight while it's snowing so the remaining storm will cover their tracks. Is there any way to hide their means of escape?"

"I'll ask them to attempt to do so, my lady," Busby said. "They've raised the drawbridge, and now man the gates themselves."

"What happened to our lads there?" Maggie asked, concerned there be no death.

"Hay's men threw them outside and bid them begone," Busby said, a small smile upon his face. "It was not very wise, for they will have gone to the village and warned the others of what is happening."

"I want no premature assaults," Maggie said. "Hay has successfully taken the keep by means of a foul lie, but he will not hold it. However, I need time to consider what must be done and how to do it. Tell Clennon Kerr our men are to remain hidden until I call for them to come to my aid."

"Very good, my lady," Busby replied. "Shall I tell the laird what ye have done?"

"Where is he?" she asked.

"Still in the hall," Busby responded, and again a hint of a smile touched his lips. "He will not relinquish it to the Hay fellow, my lady."

"He will go to bed in his own time," Maggie said. "When he does, send someone to me to let me know. I will speak to him then. In the meantime, keep him calm. Once it becomes apparent that the barracks are empty, perhaps we can get some of Hay's men to take up residence there and get them out of the house at least. Feed them but not lavishly. Just enough to keep Hay from whining, and doing something foolish. As long as he is well fed he is unlikely to complain. Go quickly now, Busby, before the glow of his victory wears off and Hay considers any more mischief tonight."

"Where shall he sleep, my lady?" Busby asked his mistress.

"Give him the best bedspace in the hall. One near one of the hearths. He cannot come above for these chambers are for the family only. We have no room," Maggie replied. "I will keep my husband's chamber locked until he returns home. Go now." As Busby hurried from his mistress's chamber, Maggie turned to Grizel. "Have you told Archie yet of this incursion?"

Grizel nodded. "Aye, and, of course, he would try to get up and fight the battle himself. I've been sleeping in his bed with him to be certain he needs naught in the night. I can keep him calm and quiet, my lady. But ye should go and speak with him, for he will take it more kindly if ye do."

"After the house quiets," Maggie said.

Busby finally helped her grandfather up from the hall, assuring Ewan Hay that he would return immediately to see to his comfort. He settled the old laird in his chamber with his manservant, informed Maggie that her grandfather was upstairs, and then hurried back to the hall.

"Have ye prepared me a chamber?" Ewan Hay demanded of the majordomo.

"My mistress has ordered that ye have the best bedspace here in the hall," Busby responded. "The one nearest the large hearth. Ye'll be warm and comfortable, sir."

"A bedspace? I am now master here, and I expect a chamber!"

"Sir, Dugald Kerr is the laird and master here," Busby said politely. "There is no chamber for ye. This is not some great lord's house. There is a chamber for the laird, one for the mistress and her husband, and another for the bairns. Ye are a gentleman and cannot dispossess them. My lady has requested that ye be placed in the best bedspace we have to offer ye. With yer permission, I will see it is prepared now." Busby bowed.

Ewan Hay was aggravated. He was to be the master of this keep, and should not have to sleep in the hall with his men. Still, the servant appeared to be telling the truth and was being most deferential towards him. Worse, he was correct. If the only chambers on the upper floor were for the old man, his granddaughter, and her children, it wouldn't help his cause to force one of them to give up his chamber for him. Not that he cared what anyone thought, but his brother had advised him to at least try and keep the peace at Brae Aisir. Ewan Hay capitulated. "Very well," he said sourly. Soon enough he would be sleeping in Maggie's bed and teaching the bitch how to behave with her man.

It snowed for the next three days. Father David was unable to get up to the keep to celebrate Christ's Mass. Maggie appeared in the hall only long enough to inquire if the men in the barracks had been fed. Ewan Hay said they would be fed when the snows ceased. Maggie departed the hall smiling to herself. The longer the storm lasted, the longer her men had to hide themselves in the village. She had no doubt they were long gone from the barracks building, but Ewan Hay wouldn't know until the snow stopped.

On December twenty-eighth the morning dawned clear, but gray. Maggie returned to the hall demanding her men be fed, but Ewan Hay said if they wanted to eat they could dig their own way out of the stone quarters, and across the courtyard. Then he laughed nastily. Maggie turned to go.

"Stay!" he commanded her. "I would have yer company."

"But I do not wish yers," Maggie answered him, her back still towards him.

"Ye had best get used to me, my border vixen, for I am here to stay," he said.

"Ye'll remain till ye die, aye, I'll agree to that," Maggie told him. "But I dinna have to bear yer company. What have ye gained? Yer trapped in this keep even as the rest of us are. Now feed my men. After three days without food they should be too weak to battle with yer men." Then she left the hall.

After another day Ewan Hay became concerned that no one from the barracks had come forth. He had watched as his men had gathered up the few men-at-arms in the keep and shut them in their stone quarters. He had actually been surprised at their small numbers, but he assumed Lord Stewart had taken a large force with him to impress the king, and lost them along with his own life. Well, so much the better. He could hold this keep.

Then Ewan noted that there was no smoke coming from the barracks' chimney.

He ordered his men to dig a path to the barracks and break into it. The snow was heavy, and it took several hours before the narrow path reached the thick wooden door. Bhaltair, the Hay captain, lifted the bar from the door, expecting to find the entry locked from the inside. It was not, and he opened it easily. He stepped cautiously into the large dark chamber; the fire in the hearth was out, the few candles set about having burned down to hard puddles of melted wax. He quickly looked about. The cots were empty. The barracks were empty. But it couldn't be. He had watched as the Kerr men-at-arms were marched into this building. There was no way in or out of this structure except the door. And the door had been fixed with a heavy wooden bar.

He shouted for a lantern; when it was brought, he moved farther into the chamber, seeking some other way out. The floor was hard-packed earth, and had not been moved or dug. There were no windows that he could see. Fifteen men had been in this place four days ago. They could not have simply vanished. Or was there magic at work here? He had heard it said that the mistress of this keep was rumored to be a witch. How else could the missing men be explained away? Exiting the barracks, he ran to tell Ewan Hay of what he had discovered.

As Ewan Hay listened to his captain's tale, his face darkened with rage. "Busby!" he shouted, bringing the keep's majordomo running. "Find yer mistress, and tell her I would see her in the hall immediately!" he said.

Busby did not delay. He hurried upstairs to find Maggie. "They've discovered the barracks are empty, my lady. The Hay is furious, and wants ye down in the hall at once," the majordomo told Maggie.

Maggie smiled a cat's smile, and following Busby, went down to the hall. She had barely entered the room when Ewan Hay was shouting at her.

"What mischief have ye done, madam? I demand answers!"

"Answers to what, sir? Obviously something is wrong, but unless ye tell me what it is, I cannot reply with any clarity," Maggie answered him crisply.

"The men in the barracks," Ewan Hay shouted.

"Aye? What about them?" Maggie responded. "Have ye at least had the decency to feed them yet? We dinna practice cruelty here at Brae Aisir."

"I cannot feed them!" Ewan Hay said angrily.

"You cannot feed them? Why can you not feed them?" Maggie demanded of him.

"Because they are not there!" he roared. "The barracks are empty; yet I saw those men marched into it with my own eyes. But when we opened the door just a little while ago, the chamber was empty, the fire in the hearth gone cold, the candles burned to stubs!"

"Ohh, villain!" Maggie cried. "What have ye done with my men? If ye have killed them, ye will pay for it, I promise ye!"

Her outrage was magnificent to behold, Busby thought as he stood quietly, watching as his mistress put the Hay on the defensive.

"What have *I* done?" Ewan Hay roared. "The question is what have *ye* done, madam? I have done nothing but lock yer people away.

Now they are gone, and it is certain that ye had something to do with it!"

"To my knowledge the barracks have a single door and no other exit," Maggie replied. "Yer men had the watch, for ye imprisoned mine. And I have not left the house since ye came. Again, question yer men to see if I did for I have been in my chamber upstairs much of the time since yer incursion into my home. Ye have murdered my men, and now ye wish to place the blame on an innocent woman to cover yer crime. Shame, sir, shame!" Maggie said. "There is not one of those men I did not know, and now they are foully murdered by ye and yer men. Unarmed. Helpless. May Jesu have mercy on ye, Ewan Hay, for given the chance I shall not," she wept. Then Maggie turned and left the hall, her shoulders shaking in apparent grief, but she was laughing so hard she feared he would discover her subterfuge.

Astonished, Ewan Hay watched her go. He was still faced with the problem that he had placed into confinement fifteen men who were now no longer there. "Bhaltair!" he shouted to his captain.

"I'm here, my lord," the man answered, stepping forward. He was a short, stocky man with a bald pate and small dark eyes. His face had suffered through many fights. His large wide nose had been broken several times as had his jaw, which was slightly skewed. One of his cheekbones had been smashed practically flat. He was a rather fearsome-looking fellow with a short temper, and he took his position as Ewan Hay's captain very seriously.

"Question yer men," his master said. "See if the lady has been outside of the house since we came. And see if yer men took it upon themselves to slaughter the Kerr men-at-arms, though where they would put the bodies I don't know."

"They could be underneath the snow," Bhaltair said, "but that our lot isn't experienced enough to have done something like that, nor do they have the stones for it. Yer brother gave ye a bunch of untried and lazy weaklings, but I'm getting them into shape for ye, my lord," he said, flattering his master shamelessly.

My lord. Ewan smiled. Here was a man who respected him and his position. "Do what ye must, but I want them in prime fighting condition by the time the snows are gone. Edmund Kerr believes I am his pawn in this matter, but I am not. I have but used him to gain access to Brae Aisir, and now I have it. But I must hold it. And until the Kerr clan folk accept what has happened, we must be vigilant at all times."

"Understood, my lord," Bhaltair said. "I will go and question the men now."

But none of the Hay men-at-arms had seen the lady of Brae Aisir leave her home since their arrival. And all swore innocence in the matter of the missing Kerr men-at-arms. Upon reflection, Bhaltair, who despite his rough appearance was not a stupid man, though he was superstitious, realized that until this morning they had all been penned in the hall waiting out the storm. He could not hold his men responsible for the disappearance of the Kerrs. But they were nonetheless gone. Only witchcraft could have accomplished such a feat, he decided.

But Ewan Hay did not believe in witchcraft. He went to the barracks himself to inspect them. He had had the chamber well lit so he might see what Bhaltair had obviously not. He looked up the chimney of the hearth, but there was no evidence of disturbance in along the sooty walls. He walked with his eyes down upon the floor seeking something that would indicate an exit. But the hard earth showed no outward sign of a trapdoor leading to a tunnel. He was almost ready to give up when he found the narrow window. Its wooden shutter was blackened with age and to the quick glance seemed a part of the stone walls. The window, however, was barred.

Ewan Hay removed the bar, opened the shutter, and looked down.

There was no sign of human traffic on either the sill or the ground, which was about eight feet down, but Ewan was certain this was the means by which the Kerr men-at-arms had escaped. It would not be difficult to get the bar to fall back into its place when the shutter was pulled closed from the outside, provided it was rigged properly to do so.

He had been careless, Ewan Hay realized. He knew little about the keep; before he imprisoned the Kerr clansmen, he should have inspected it more carefully and herded his prisoners into the keep's cellars where there would have been no access to escape, or at least a less easy escape. He couldn't continue to be so negligent and feckless if he expected to hold this keep against the English Kerrs. They would leave him be for the winter he could be certain. But once the snows melted and the pass was open to traffic again, Rafe Kerr was sure to come on an inspection.

He would have to keep Lord Edmund's heir as his prisoner until he could make the greedy Englishman see reason; that he, Ewan Hay, was now master of Brae Aisir, and he didn't intend relinquishing it. Brae Aisir was after all in Scotland, and he was a Scot. He would need allies, however; men he could call upon to defend his rights from the English Kerrs. And that would mean making Mad Maggie his wife, not his mistress. She was the key to seeing him made legitimate in the eyes of their neighbors. He didn't intend letting that border vixen escape him this time.

Maggie was content for the moment that Ewan Hay could do little harm. Once a path to the village was opened through the snowbanks, she sent all the maidservants from the keep. The Hay men-at-arms were a rowdy lot, and some of the lasses in service were young and apt to be foolish. Grizel, of course, remained along with the men servitors. Her grandfather was not pleased by any of what was happening, but he was afflicted by his annual winter ague coupled with a stiffness in his limbs that tended to cripple him. Maggie's two sons, Davy and

Andrew, had taken to being with their great-grandfather, and following him wherever he went, as their nursemaid had been sent away with the other female servants but for Grizel and the cook, Maudie, who kept to her kitchen, directing the young lads now replacing her kitchen wenches.

Maggie herself had returned to the hall as Ewan Hay had sent his men to inhabit the barracks formerly possessed by the Kerr men-at-arms. Once they had eaten in the evening, they stacked the trestles on the side of the hall and disappeared. Ewan had managed to convince Bhaltair that there was no witchcraft involved in the escape of the Kerrs but only their own carelessness and the Kerrs' quick thinking.

The winter deepened, and the snows continued. Maggie grew larger with her coming child. She sat by one of the hearths sewing and wondering where her husband was, why he had not returned, why there was no ransom demand. She would not accept that he was dead. She knew she would feel something if he were dead, and she didn't. As long as there was winter, they were safe; Ewan Hay could do nothing in the winter. But once the winter ended, if Fingal didn't return home, Maggie found herself fearful for what might happen. Of late Ewan Hay had attempted to charm her as she sat in the hall.

"The bairn must soon be due," he said one late-February day. "Will it be another lad, do ye think?" He attempted a smile.

Maggie looked at him bleakly. "It will be what it will be, sir. Only God knows."

The longer he stayed, the more she hated this intruder in her home.

"Ye did not answer my question," Ewan said. "When will ye birth this child?"

"When is not yer concern," Maggie answered him rudely. "The bairn will come when it comes, and not a moment before. Why do ye care?"

"I am but curious, madam, nothing more," Ewan replied. Then he changed the subject completely. "When does the pass usually open again?"

"When the snows are gone completely," Maggie said. "Once the melt begins, and we can enter the pass safely, we patrol its length each day until we are certain it is clear. I will be brought the reports," she told him.

"Nay," he responded in a hard voice. "The reports will be brought to me first. Because I am ignorant of the pass, I will confer with yer grandfather until I am sure of what I am doing. Yer responsibility is to care for yer bairns and prepare for yer marriage to me as soon as possible."

"Marry ye? Yer mad, Ewan Hay! Raving mad! I have a husband. His name is Fingal Stewart. I need no other husband but him," Maggie said, and the child in her womb stirred restlessly. Her hand went immediately to her belly to soothe it.

"Madam, sooner or later ye must face the fact that Lord Stewart did not come home after Solway Moss. No ransom demand came to Brae Aisir. If one does not come in the spring, and yer husband does not return home by then, ye must wed me," Ewan Hay said. "God's foot, madam, yer place is here in the hall with yer bairns, not out riding the Aisir nam Breug like some clansman."

"I will do as I damned well please!" Maggie told him angrily.

"Nay, ye will cease being a border vixen, and become a good border wife," Ewan said. "With our king in his grave, and a wee bairn on the throne, ye may be certain the English will be at our doors come summer. The traverse must be protected, and no woman is capable of such a task."

"I'll not wed ye," Maggie said quietly now. She didn't want the bairn disturbed again, and all the shouting was indeed distressing it.

"Ye have no choice. I need the cooperation of yer clansmen, and I cannot gain it unless ye are my wife. Stewart may have gotten bairns on ye, but yer still Dugald Kerr's heiress in the eyes of yer Kerr clan folk," Ewan Hay said.

Maggie grew pale with his words. He was right, damn him to hell. But if, God forbid, she had indeed been widowed at Solway Moss, she had no intention of remarrying, let alone marrying Ewan Hay. He was a coward, and she despised him. "I will never wed ye, and the sooner ye understand that, the better it will be for ye, sir."

"Ye'll wed me," he told her with a nasty smile. "Ye have yer bairns to consider, Maggie Kerr, and if there is one thing I have learned in my weeks here, it is that yer a good mother. Ye'll not allow anything to happen to yer lads. Fight me on this, and I'll send them through the pass to be fostered by yer greedy English kin."

"If ye think my uncle would harm my sons, yer wrong, sir. I know how Edmund Kerr thinks. He would wed the little daughter his mistress gave him several years ago to David and raise him to do his bidding, or try," Maggie countered.

"And if he turned the lad English, then it would be the fine Scots sons ye'll give me who inherit Brae Aisir, and not Fingal Stewart's lads. Yer clan folk would give their loyalty first to a good Scot, and ye know it," he matched her.

"Fingal Stewart is not dead," Maggie responded. "He will come home, and he will drive ye from Brae Aisir if I don't do it first."

Ewan Hay laughed. "Let him try and I will slay him," he said boldly.

They had two heavy snows in the first half of March. The pass would open late.

Finally as the month began to draw to its end, the hills began to quickly show signs of spring. The white snows and the gray melting began to give way to the open earth. The hillsides gave off a hint of hazy green. Ewan Hay came into the hall on the last day of the month to learn that Maggie had gone into labor in the night. The keep was oddly silent. Old Dugald sat at the high board after the morning meal playing the board game of Hare and Hounds with his two grandsons. Grizel entered the hall with another woman.

"Who is this?" Ewan Hay demanded.

"The midwife," Grizel told him bluntly.

"Is she all right?" he asked.

"She's laboring to bring forth a bairn," Grizel replied, and then hurried on with Mistress Agnes up the stairs.

"Why does she need a midwife?" Ewan asked Dugald Kerr. "She's had two bairns before this one being born."

"She's not some animal giving birth," the laird said irritably. "Every birth is different, ye dumb clot." He turned back to his game.

The main meal of the day was served. The laird, Ewan, and the two little boys ate at the high board. This was a rare treat for the two brothers who usually ate in the kitchens with Maudie. At one time, their nursemaids had eaten with them, but now they were gone. The laird directed his great-grandsons in their table manners and in how to properly use their napkin. Ewan noted that the laird was extremely fond of the two little lads. He could use that as a weapon to force Maggie to the altar, for he knew she loved her grandsire dearly and would do whatever she had to to see him happy.

The afternoon wore on. The days were noticeably longer now. The hall was silent. The laird had fallen asleep in his chair by the hearth. Davy and Andrew had disappeared. The dogs sprawled about lazily, following their master's example. Ewan Hay was bored. He decided to ride out and see how the melt was progressing. When he returned an hour later, the hall remained exactly as he left it.

"Busby!" he shouted, and the majordomo was at his side almost immediately.

"Has the lady birthed her bairn yet?"

"Not yet, sir, but Grizel tells me it will be quite soon," Busby answered. "Is there anything else, sir?"

"Get me some wine!" Ewan snapped. He was irritated, and he didn't know why.

Busby brought him a large silver goblet studded with green agate. It was filled with a rich red wine, the pungent aroma of which filled his nostrils. Ewan took the goblet from Busby and drank deeply of it. The damned servant annoyed him, and yet he had done nothing since Ewan arrived that should irritate him. He was polite—deferential to a fault—and Ewan wondered why. The other servants practically ignored him, avoiding all contact with him until spoken to, at which point they answered him, but no more than that. And the old witch who looked after Maggie made no secret of the fact she could barely tolerate him at all. He'd send her packing when he married Maggie, and he would put in her place some buxom little thing he could swive when his wife's moon link was broken.

He hadn't had a woman since he arrived at Brae Aisir. Maggie had swiftly sent all the young female serving wenches back to their family cottages in the village as the snows began. And the clansmen kept a close eye on their women whenever the Hay men-at-arms came into their midst. Of late, however, Bhaltair had mentioned that Brae Aisir had a whore who was willing to make herself available for a coin or two. He shouted for his captain, and questioned him further.

"Ye said there was a whore in the village. Where is she?" he demanded.

"There are two, but one will only service the lads whose wives are big in the belly," Bhaltair replied. "The more willing one lives on the edge of the village where the Aisir nam Breug begins and ends. Her name is Jeannie."

"Take me to the more reluctant whore," Ewan said. "If she will take a cock, she cannot be fussy about the cock she takes. Come with me, and we'll make an evening of it. This enforced celibacy is not to my taste."

The two men departed the hall, and taking their horses, rode down to the village, stopping at the cottage Bhaltair said belonged to Flora Kerr, the widow. They entered, startling the woman, who was kneading bread for the morrow. Her pretty, plump hands were covered with flour. Flora knew instantly what they wanted.

"I serve only the lads whose wives are with child," she quickly said. "You will find what you seek at the end of the lane, sir."

"But I don't want the well-traveled cunt of the village whore," Ewan told her. "My captain and I deserve something finer, Flora Kerr. It is Flora, isn't it?"

Flora nodded.

"Do ye know who I am, Flora? I am the new master of the keep, of Brae Aisir itself. Ye dinna want to displease me now, do ye?" Ewan smiled at the woman, but his eyes were cold, his tone menacing.

"Sir, I am not a common whore. I give of myself for the women's sake," Flora said in a trembling voice. "I take naught for my service."

"I am pleased that ye are not common," Ewan said, stepping up to her, and quickly putting a restraining arm about her waist. "Ye will serve me, Flora Kerr, and tonight ye will also service my captain." He thrust a hand into her blouse, his fingers closing about a very plump breast.

"Please, sir," Flora began, and then she cried out, for he had cruelly pinched the nipple of the breast he now was holding.

"Say *aye, my lord*, Flora," he told her in a hard voice. "My cock needs to sheath itself in ye, and I should far prefer to use my energies in fucking ye than restraining ye."

"*Nay!*" Flora cried out, and tried to escape his grasp, but Ewan Hay slapped her so hard her head spun. Bhaltair stepped behind the woman, putting his arms about her in a hold so tight she could barely breathe. He yanked her up, and Ewan Hay, releasing his burgeoning cock from his breeks, ripped Flora's skirt off, flinging it aside as he pushed her petticoat up, grabbed her kicking legs, pulling them about his torso, and pressed himself into her. Flora screamed and fought him.

It was but the beginning of a long evening for the poor woman. After Ewan had eased his lust once, he and his captain ripped Flora's remaining garments from her so they might have the freedom to ravage her without hindrance. Both men had her several times before leaving the cottage to ride back up to the keep. Before they departed, Ewan Hay placed a coin on the table where Flora Kerr had been kneading her bread earlier.

"For ye, sweetheart," he said, smiling at her.

The naked and bruised woman looked at him with angry eyes. Then picking up the coin, she flung it at him. But he only laughed.

As they rode, Ewan Hay said to his captain, "I shared her with ye tonight as a mark of my favor. Yer not to go near her again. Relieve yer itch with the whore at the end of the lane. Flora Kerr is mine from now on. She has spirit." He absently rubbed his arm where she had bitten him. He liked that she had fought him so vigorously, and he realized he felt much better than he had earlier.

"Thank ye, my lord, for the favor," Bhaltair said. "I'll not touch the wench again."

In the courtyard the two men parted, Bhaltair going to the stone barracks before making his evening rounds to check on his men. Ewan Hay, however, reentered the hall to be met by Busby. "Well," he demanded of the majordomo, "has she spawned her brat yet, or is she still in labor?"

"Her ladyship has just given birth to a daughter, sir," Busby said.

"I'll go see," Ewan Hay replied.

"Sir, my mistress does not want ye in her chamber. She is with her family now. Please, sir, to respect her wishes. The bairn is new and fragile as all new bairns are. This is not a time for visitors. On the morrow I'm certain she will see ye."

Ewan laughed. "She'd sooner see me in hell," he said, "than in her chamber. Take the lady my congratulations, Busby. I will see her at a time of her choosing, I know." He was in too good a humor right now to want to fight with Maggie.

"I will convey your felicitations, sir," Busby said, which he did.

"Thank ye for keeping him away," Maggie said. She was exhausted, pale, and her hair hung wet and lank. She had birthed her sons with relative ease, but this lass had been difficult. The bairn had a head full of black hair like her father.

"Does the wee lassie have a name yet, my lady?" Busby asked as he smiled down at the swaddled infant who now lay sleeping in her cradle.

"Annabelle," Maggie said. "She is Annabelle Mary Stewart."

"A fine name indeed," Busby said, and then he left her.

"Archie wants to see the bairn," Grizel said.

Maggie nodded. "Let him come, but be careful. I would not put it past the Hay to sneak up the stairs after he told Busby he wouldn't."

Grizel nodded.

Fingal's personal servant had returned to Brae Aisir grievously wounded. Only Grizel's skill and devotion had kept him from losing his arm, but he would never be able to fight with it again. They had kept him hidden above in the servants' attic for all these weeks. Maggie was fearful if Ewan Hay knew who he was, he might harm Archie. The little man had healed slowly, and he was well enough now to be secreted with the other men in the village. She would send for him very soon.

Archie came quietly into Maggie's bedchamber with Grizel. He went straight to the cradle, looked down at Annabelle Stewart, and pronounced, "She's her da's lass, and there's no mistaking it, my lady." Then he drew a long breath and said, "I'm going back to look for him. I would have never left him, but they took me away by force."

"Nay," Maggie said. "It's too dangerous for ye to go into England now. Ye would not know where to seek him now. The ransom request is certain to come soon, Archie. When it does, then ye will take it to the English and bring my husband home."

"How will ye manage a ransom with the Hay in our midst?" Archie asked.

"We do not retain all of our coin here in the keep," Maggie told him. "We store a great deal of it with a goldsmith named Kira in Edinburgh."

"Aye, his lordship has his monies with Kira as well," Archie said. "Let me go to Edinburgh as soon as I am strong enough to ride, which will be soon. That way I'll be ready to collect the ransom from the Kiras and ride down into England. I'll stay in my lord's house, and ye can send to the Kiras, who will notify me. We'll save a great deal of time that way, my lady, and I'll be out of the way of the Hay. Ye'll have difficulty enough getting the ransom paid if he is watching yer every move."

"I've already told the village to watch for a messenger. We will stop him there, and the Hay is not likely to know at all. Let him think Fin has been killed, and he can steal what belongs to the Kerrs with impunity."

"Be careful, my lady," Archie said. "Yer playing a dangerous game with this fellow."

"I know," Maggie said, and sighed. "Sometimes I am afraid, Archie, but then I remember how much Grandsire, my lads, and all of Brae Aisir depend upon me. I will be glad to have my husband home again."

The birthing by its length had worn Maggie out. She slept soundly for several hours. While she had turned her sons over to wet nurses, this small daughter of hers nursed at her mother's breast from the beginning. It was also a way of keeping Ewan Hay away from her in these first weeks. Annabelle was baptized immediately. Unlike the elder of her brothers who had a king and a queen for godparents, the little girl had Grizel for her godmother, and Dugald Kerr for her god-father. David Kerr was relieved to see his new great-niece was healthy and sturdy. So many newborns weren't.

Ewan Hay was pleased with how easily and quickly Maggie had re-covered from her difficult labor. The wench had birthed three healthy children. He had high hopes that the fourth child she bore would be his son. On the day six weeks later that Maggie was churched by Fa-ther David, Ewan Hay spoke to the priest.

"Her husband is dead. Her children are fatherless. The English are already raiding, and the Aisir nam Breug must have a strong defender. You must marry us as soon as possible so the Kerr clan folk will accept me as their new lord."

"I will not wed ye to her until she agrees," the priest said. "The marriage is not a legal one without her consent or that of her grand-sire. My brother will not give it to ye without her agreement. Why are ye in such a hurry, Ewan Hay? If Fingal Stewart is indeed dead, my great-niece will need time to mourn. We will keep the traverse open whether ye be wed to Maggie or not. We are loyal Scots, Ewan Hay."

"I want her," Ewan Hay said. "I have always wanted her."

"Ye have been patient," the priest said. "Be patient for a small while longer."

Chapter 14

〜

M arie de Guise was angrier than she had ever thought she could be. But she masked that anger very well. She hadn't wanted to marry and leave her beloved France, or her young son. But Scotland's king had wanted another royal French wife.

Marie de Guise was French, and she was a royal. She was widowed. There was no one else in France suitable enough for such a grand match. She had begged her father to refuse King François's request. The king conveyed the lady's reluctance to the Scots ambassador. Then James Stewart had written her a beautiful letter begging her to reconsider, and if she would not, to at least direct him in his search for a queen. The old alliance between Scotland and France must be kept strong.

She had liked her new husband from the beginning of their relationship, but she found he could be moody as so many Scots were. She was not as fond of many of the rough Scots lords, although none of them had been aware of it. She sought out men of intellect who might be of use to her husband, and perhaps even to her. She steered James as best she could without being obvious, and she had done her duty, though in losing their two little sons it had come to naught.

Despite her loyalty to France, she had not been certain that poking at the English lion was a wise thing. But her husband was a man of principle, and he held to the old alliance. France and Scotland had been bound together for years. France had given James not one, but two queens. A brief foray into northern England to publicly affirm the faith of Holy Mother Church and to show King Henry that Scotland was not to be trifled with was all he had planned. He owed the pope that show of faith for the pope's financial generosity to James Stewart. He hoped the threat of a Scots invasion would take the pressure off France, now engaged in another war. That it had not worked out that way came as a complete shock to James Stewart, for the Scots and the English had been having these forays for centuries.

After the disaster at Solway Moss, the king fell into a deep depression. Returning to Edinburgh, he ordered a defense of the Borders immediately. Then becoming quite ill, he had retired to his beautiful Falkland Palace. His doctors sent the queen a message that the king was ill from eating shellfish. She had been at Linlithgow for her lying-in, and she could not go to him. Marie later always wondered, had she been able to go, whether she could have drawn him out of the darkness into which he had fallen. Instead, to her disappointment, she had given birth to a daughter.

When word of his daughter's birth was brought to James Stewart at Falkland, it was the last straw. A son might have brought him out of his depression. Instead he declared, "It cam wi' a lass, and 'twill go wi' a lass." After that he spoke no more, and refused to even acknowledge his priests. His handsome face to the wall, James Stewart died six days after his daughter's birth, leaving Scotland once again in the hands of an infant monarch.

And Marie de Guise was furious at the selfish self-indulgence of her husband that had now left her alone in a cold, gloomy country. She would have to rally from her childbed as quickly as she could to defend the rights and person of her infant when at this point all she wanted to do was gather up petite Marie and return home to France.

But her daughter was now the queen of this cold, gloomy country. Marie de Guise was determined that this last child she had been able to bear her husband would survive to adulthood and rule with glory. Now, however, the young dowager queen would have to gather allies to protect her and her petite Marie.

The first order of business was to have the infant baptized. It was quickly done a day after her father's death at the kirk of St. Michael's near Linlithgow. At that point a struggle had begun for custody of the new queen. Two parties emerged, one led by the leading Roman Catholics of the land; the other by the leading Protestants. Cardinal Beaton produced a will allegedly signed by the king on the day of his death, which set up a regency council consisting of the cardinal himself; James Stewart, the Earl of Moray, the late king's half brother, and the little queen's uncle; the Earl of Huntly; and the Earl of Argyll. The man next in line for Scotland's throne, the Earl of Arran, was ignored.

The Scots nobles favoring England, however, rallied under the leadership of the late king's hated stepfather, the Earl of Angus, Archibald Douglas. Angus had been in exile in England since 1528. Now he returned, a large purse from King Henry in his possession, which allowed him to influence many. Cardinal Beaton was arrested and accused of forging James V's will. Talks began to investigate the possibility of a marriage between the English king's son and heir, Prince Edward, and the infant Scots queen.

It was an alliance that actually made sense. Mary Stewart had a claim to England's throne by virtue of her paternal grandmother, Margaret Tudor. An eventual marriage between these two royal children might have led to a peaceful union between the two lands. Unfortunately, England's king was a bully. He began making demands that could not, would not, be met. He wanted Scotland's alliance with France repudiated. He wanted Edinburgh, St. Andrew's, Dunbar, Tantallon, Dumbarton, and Stirling castles turned over to the English. But most impossible of all, he wanted the little queen sent to be brought up in England as soon as she could be weaned. That he actually believed any, let alone all, of his demands would be met was astonishing.

The Scots attempted to negotiate these terms. No castles would be turned over to England. The little queen, who had spent her first nine months at Linlithgow, was now moved to the more fortified Stirling Castle where she was crowned in the Chapel Royal with a gold bracelet of her mother's while seated in Marie de Guise's lap. She would remain in Scotland, which would maintain its independence. Two more treaties were attempted. Neither could be agreed upon, and Henry Tudor's bullying continued.

The two political factions were actually moving closer to each other courtesy of Henry Tudor's intractable attitude. A possible marriage was discussed between the Earl of Arran's son, also an heir presumptive, and baby Mary. Cardinal Beaton returned as Scotland's chancellor. Arran was made regent, and Marie de Guise was appointed head of the sixteen-member advisory council. Henry Tudor was not pleased by this turn of events. He wanted Scotland's queen for his son. He began what was called his *rough wooing* of Scotland, and the Borders became a powder keg.

Once Archie was finally healed and strong again, Maggie and Grizel managed to slip him from the keep one morning, sending him out in a cart taking manure from the stables to fertilize the fields. It did not occur to the Hay men-at-arms that the cart returned with one man, and not two. Maggie had arranged to have a horse provided for Archie in the village. Carrying a letter of instruction to the Kiras and a few coins in his purse, Archie rode to Edinburgh. Upon his arrival in the city, he learned that the English king had in an effort to gain favor with Scotland released without ransom a number of nobles. They had just been brought to Edinburgh. Archie knew if his master was among those men, he would first go to his house beneath Castle Hill. He hurried to reach his destination.

As he turned into the lane where Fingal Stewart's house was located, he saw a tall thin man slowly making his way on foot down the little street. From the back, there was something familiar about the man; yet Archie did not remember his master being so slender. The man stopped before Fingal Stewart's house. His face was turned in silhouette. Archie stared hard. The face was gaunt, but it was familiar. "My lord! My lord!" Archie called, kicking the horse into a trot to reach his master. Yanking his animal to a halt, Archie jumped from its back. "My lord! Yer alive, praise be to Jesu and his Blessed Mother Mary!" He grabbed Fingal Stewart's hand and shook it heartily, tears visible in his blue eyes.

Fin looked at the little redheaded man who was practically dancing a jig in the street. The little fellow seemed to know him and had addressed him by name. Who was he? Was he the man called Iver? *No!* He was Archie, wasn't he? "Archie?" he said.

"Aye, 'tis me, my lord, come from Brae Aisir to see if I could find ye," Archie said. "Aah, the mistress will be so happy to have ye home. She never gave up hope!"

Fingal Stewart sighed. "Archie," he said, "I barely know ye, as memory has failed me since the battle. But tell me, who is Iver?"

"Why, my lord, Iver is yer captain," Archie said. Then he reached for a key hanging from his belt, and opening the door to the empty house, ushered Fin in.

Reaching the hall, Archie was relieved to find a pile of fuel, which he used to start a fire in the hearth. "Are ye hungry, my lord?" he asked. "Ye look painfully thin to my eyes."

Fin nodded. "Aye, I am hungry," he admitted.

"I'll go right to the cookhouse two streets over," Archie said, "and get us something to eat, for I'm hungry myself. Will ye wait here for me, my lord? I'll not be long, I swear it."

Fin nodded again. He wanted to walk about this house, for to his relief much of what he had seen so far was familiar. He had been born in this house, he realized, and grown up here. "Aye, go and fetch us something to eat, Archie, and then I shall tell ye of my adventures these past months."

Archie ran from the house and to the cookshop where he obtained a dozen hard-cooked eggs, a large rasher of bacon, a loaf of fresh bread, and a quarter of a small wheel of cheese, to which he added a covered container of ale. He paid for his purchases with a coin from his carefully concealed purse and hurried back to Lord Stewart's house. He found his master dozing by the fire. Archie was very disturbed by how thin and pale Lord Stewart was. He had always been healthy and strong. Right now he didn't look up to the task of taking on even a coward like Ewan Hay. What had happened to him? Had he been in an English prison?

The serving man brought plates and cups from the sideboard and set out the meal.

Then he woke Fin, and seating themselves at the board, the two men ate. Archie noticed that his master ate slowly and that his appetite was not what it had formerly been. This, he knew, was the result of a poor diet over the past months. Finally Archie could no longer contain himself. "What happened to ye, my lord? Where have ye been?" he asked. "I would have remained with ye on the battlefield, but Iver would not allow it."

"Ye were wounded grievously," Fin said slowly. "I began to remember more when I saw yer face. Yer left arm?"

"Aye, healed now, but it will ne'er do battle again, I suspect," Archie said. "It stiffens, especially in cold wet weather."

"But can ye still sew a fine seam?" Fin asked him.

"Ye remembered that?" Archie chuckled. "Aye, I can still play the tailor for ye, my lord, and from the looks of what yer wearing, I had best see to something more suitable before we return home to Brae Aisir."

"Brae Aisir?" It had a sweet sound to it, but he could not quite remember.

"I'll explain, but only after ye tell me what happened to ye," Archie said, attempting to keep his master from being diverted.

"After ye were taken from the battlefield I fought on, but an English horseman rode at me, and I had but a moment to duck his blade. It caught the side of my head, and the blood obscured my vision so that I lost control of my horse, and fell and hit my head, I recall. When I came to, it was almost night, and the scavengers were among the fallen. My boots were being yanked from my feet, and my family's signet ring from my finger. I attempted to fight off the thief, but I was still weakened from the loss of blood. He gave me a hard smack upon my pate. I drifted in and out of consciousness for I don't know how long. I was obviously picked up from the battlefield, and when I came fully conscious again, I found myself in a tiny cottage with an old woman.

"She had seen me being carried along with the other prisoners and swore that I was her son, Bobby, come home from battle. She was so insistent that I was her lad that they let her have me. She nursed me back to health, and while I knew I wasn't her son I could not at that time recall who I was. I spent the winter in that cottage with Old Mother, as I called her. Bits and pieces of my memory began to return slowly. My name. And I had dreams of a man called Iver, and then of ye." Fingal Stewart smiled weakly.

"Old Mother grew ill with the approach of spring," he continued. "I could see she was dying, and as she did, her mind, confused until then, gained clarity. She knew I was not her son who went off to fight at Flodden years ago and never returned. I remained with her until the end and buried her respectfully. As I was now dreaming of this house, I knew I must get to Edinburgh where perhaps I might gain some answers. It was here ye found me this morning just arrived." He left out his sojourn with the Fifes.

Lord Stewart's tale had been fascinating, and it certainly explained why no ransom demand had come to Brae Aisir. Now it was Archie's turn to help his master regain his full memory. "Ye asked about Brae Aisir," he began. "'Tis where ye have made yer home these past few years. Yer wife is the heiress to Brae Aisir. Ye have two fine lads, and a wee lass born just over two months ago."

"She didn't want me to go," Fin said slowly. "She grew very angry, didn't she?"

"It was last summer she tried to stop ye, but before Solway Moss she was resigned to the fact ye would support yer kinsman, the king. Did ye know the king is dead, and our new queen just a six-month-old infant?" Archie asked him.

Fin shook his head. "*Ever faithful*," he said. "'Tis my family's motto, and why I insisted upon going. I remember I mocked Maggie. . . ." He stopped. "That's my wife's name, isn't it?" he said excitedly. "Maggie! Maggie mine!"

"Aye, my lord," Archie said, grinning. "'Tis yer lady's name."

"And my sons are David and Andrew," Fin replied.

"Aye, my lord, Davy and Andrew. And yer new lass has been baptized Annabelle," Archie told him.

Suddenly Fin's excitement died. "I can't remember what she looks like," he said.

"Ye will, my lord," Archie assured his master. "When we get home to Brae Aisir, ye'll remember it all. I'm certain of it."

"Tell me about Brae Aisir," Fin requested of his companion.

And Archie did. He explained how they had been sent by the king. He had Fin laughing at how Mad Maggie Kerr would wed no man who could not outrun, outride, and outfight her. Lord Stewart's eyes lit up with an obvious burst of memory that Archie's tale prompted, and he nodded. Then Archie told his master the true value of Brae Aisir and its history; about the Aisir nam Breug, and its value. Finally he said, "The lady needs to know that yer safe, my lord, for Ewan Hay has made a wicked pact with the Netherdale Kerrs. Old Lord Edmund thinks to control the entire traverse so he may enrich himself further while Ewan Hay thinks to steal it from the Kerrs, and have the lady for his own as well. He is certain yer dead. Many at Brae Aisir believe it to be true, although they will not give voice to it for fear of offending yer lady wife. And they are not yet ready to give their loyalty to the Hay. But if he makes a marriage with a woman he believes widowed, the Kerr clan folk will have no choice but to give the bastard their loyalty. Ye have to get home, my lord."

Fingal Stewart nodded. "I do," he said, closing his eyes a moment, "but how can I return to a place, a responsibility, and a woman I cannot fully remember, Archie? Weak and confused as I now am, I should not be able to defend and protect any of them. I need time, and I am safer here in Edinburgh in my own house than back at Brae Aisir. I am hardly the man who outran, outrode, and outfought Mad Maggie Kerr."

It was true, he realized as he spoke. His wounds still pained him. He had walked forever, it seemed. He hadn't had enough to eat in months, and the ten days he had spent with Parlan Fife's daughters had soothed his lust but exhausted him further. He needed a little more time to rest, to heal, to remember. And then he would return to Brae Aisir and kill Ewan Hay.

"At least send a message to the lady at Brae Aisir telling her yer alive and will return home shortly," Archie said. "I'll remain here with ye. With good food, and rest, yer memories are certain to return. Many already have. And ye'll have me to help ye."

"It's as good a plan as any," Fingal Stewart said.

"And I'll tell Boyle, yer estate agent, that ye'll not be renting the house for the interim," Archie told his master.

"Who has been renting it?" Lord Stewart was curious.

"Ye've let the agent rent it out to lords and churchmen with no homes, but business here in Edinburgh. Kira, the goldsmith, has yer funds, my lord. We can live comfortably while ye remain in the town."

Fin nodded. "Where is the queen now? Not the bairn; her mother."

"Still at Linlithgow. The wee queen has become a prize to be squabbled over by the Protestant lords and those who hold with the old faith," Archie said.

"Does Queen Marie ever come into Edinburgh?" Fin wondered aloud.

"I can listen to the gossip in the streets, my lord," Archie replied.

"I would pledge my loyalty privily, but I suspect it is better I not go to Linlithgow where I might be seen. My loyalty is to the royal bairn, and not to the factions that seem to arise in cases like this. I remember when King James was a lad being fought over. The lords were like dogs with a particularly meaty bone."

"It was not a good time," Archie agreed.

"Angus was a bad stepfather, and Lord Methven little better. Queen Margaret was not the woman Queen Marie is. This Queen Mother will not take another husband as her predecessor did."

"I believe yer correct, my lord," Archie said. "Everything she has done so far has been done with measured carefulness for her daughter."

That same day Archie went into the market to purchase parchment, ink, and a fresh quill. Bringing the items home, he helped Lord Stewart compose a brief missive to his wife.

Madam, he began, *I have just returned home from England. I am quite alive but have been unable to communicate with you until now. Archie has joined me, and we will remain here while I complete my business. You may expect me home within another month. My felicitations to your grandsire.* It was signed, *Your loving husband, Fingal Stewart.* While his signet ring had been stolen from him, he had a another seal in his house. He pressed it deeply into the thick wax he had drizzled onto the parchment.

The next morning, Archie took the tightly rolled parchment and went to the small square where men who hired themselves out as messengers were waiting for employment. He stepped up on a square stone put there for the very purpose of hiring a man. "I need someone to ride into the Borders for me and deliver this message to the lady of the keep at Brae Aisir," he called out. "There's a silver piece in it for the man I hire."

"The Borders grow more dangerous every day," someone in the crowd of waiting men said. "Just where is this keep?"

"In the mid-Borders," Archie said. "Away from Berwick and Carlisle."

"Just deliver the parchment? Nothing else?" the voice inquired further.

"Just deliver the message to the lady of the keep," Archie repeated. "Ye dinna have to wait for a reply. Just deliver."

"I'll do it." A rough-looking bearded man stepped from among the crowd. "Where's the silver?"

"Do I look the fool?" Archie said, glaring up at the fellow who stood at least six inches taller than he was. "My master is Lord Stewart of Torra House beneath Castle Hill. Come there when ye return with the name of the person at the keep into whose hands ye placed this message, and ye'll have yer coin. Here's a copper to show my good faith. Now will ye take the commission or nay? I've no time to haggle with ye. The price is indeed more than fair, but because the ride is long, my master is inclined to be generous with ye." He tapped the rolled parchment against his boot impatiently.

"Give it to me! I'll take it," the big messenger said, holding out his hand for the copper piece promised as good faith. The little man was right. The price offered was fair. He tucked the message into his jerkin for safety. Two days there; two days back, he thought. The messenger went to his horse, mounted up, and kicking the beast, trotted from the little square.

Archie hurried back to his master. The messenger returned to Edinburgh several days later, coming to Torra House for his payment. "Who took the parchment from ye?" Archie asked him as he held the coin up.

"Didn't catch his name," the messenger replied. "He came up to me in the keep yard and took the message from me. I said it was for the lady. I did my part."

Archie gritted his teeth. The messenger had been given specific instructions, but to argue with the clod would accomplish naught. Reluctantly he flipped the man the promised coin.

Chapter 15

Six weeks after Annabelle Stewart had been born, her mother was churched in the Brae Aisir chapel in an ancient ceremony of thanksgiving that celebrated a woman's safe passage through the ordeal of childbirth. In order to keep Ewan Hay from his great-niece, Father David declared the ceremony could be attended only by the women of the village. Knowing no better, Ewan Hay was forced to keep away.

It was the middle of May now, but no ransom demand had come for Lord Stewart.

Still there was gossip that King Henry had released a number of lords back into Scotland.

Archie had managed to slip away to Edinburgh to search for Fin in case he had gone to his house beneath Castle Hill first. Ewan Hay knew nothing about Archie, as Fin's servant had returned before his arrival at Brae Aisir, and Archie had been kept in a small chamber in the attic being nursed. Maggie held out hope yet that her husband would return.

But few others did. Even her grandfather believed now that Fingal Stewart had died at Solway Moss and lay in an unmarked grave. Father David had attempted to reason with Maggie, but she would not listen to his words of comfort. May came to an end, and one day a group of several neighboring lairds came to see Dugald Kerr. They would not speak with him until she had left the hall. She refused to go until her grandfather had quietly asked her to leave them.

Maggie had never refused any request her grandsire had asked of her. She curtsied to him, and walked from the hall, her head held high. But once out of sight of those in the hall, Maggie hurried to a small alcove on one side of the chamber's wall that had a spy hole. Here she could see and hear all that transpired. What she heard did not please Maggie in the least.

It was Alexander Bruce who spoke for the delegation. "Dugald, we tolerated yer granddaughter's disobedience in the matter of her marriage when she was a maid. And Lord Stewart was the perfect answer to all of our prayers. But it becomes more obvious as every day passes that Fingal Stewart is dead. We understand Maggie's grief. And God be praised that she has birthed two fine sons who seem to be escaping the rigors of childhood. Would that our late king had been as fortunate."

There was a murmur of assent from the other men present.

"But," Alexander Bruce continued, "while ye have male heirs, there is a need for ye to have a guardian watching over the Aisir nam Breug until they are old enough to do so. Aye, yer still the laird here, but yer an old man now, past seventy. What if something should happen to ye? Who will hold the pass? And dinna say yer granddaughter. Maggie is a woman with bairns to bring up. She should have no time to do what needs doing. Until his unfortunate death, Lord Stewart was that man. But Lord Stewart is gone.

"Lord Hay has spoken to us on behalf of Ewan, his brother, who came to protect ye early last winter, and has remained. The perfect solution would be for Ewan Hay to marry yer granddaughter. Yer great-grandsons would have a father to look up to, and Maggie, having proved a good breeder, would undoubtedly have more bairns, ensuring yer line for generations to come."

"What ye say has a certain merit to it," Dugald Kerr agreed, "but my answer is a resounding nay. Maggie doesn't like Ewan Hay, and she never will. I am not a man to tolerate foolishness, but a woman should at least like her husband, my lords. Maggie will find another man in time. But I cannot force her to wed a man she despises. Ewan Hay's contribution to this keep has been to ensure his own safety by ridding it of my Kerr clansmen while installing his own Hay men-at-arms. We have had to send the females in the keep—but for the cook, Maggie, and her tiring woman—back to their homes for fear of these undisciplined Hay men and their captain, and even then one among them has not escaped unscathed. If ye would aid me, my lords, then rid me of these Hays!"

"The pass must be kept safe," Alexander Bruce said.

"When did we not keep it safe?" Dugald Kerr asked him. "In more than five hundred years the Kerrs have never allowed the pass to be used for anything but peaceful travel. What has changed now that you would consider subverting my authority?"

"My lord," Ian Ferguson spoke up, "times have changed, I fear. King Henry sends raiding parties across the border from all directions in his effort to make the Queen Mother do his will, and give him Scotland's little queen. He has become ruthless in his pursuit. Ye are old and weak. What is to keep yer English kinsmen from succumbing to pressure from their king, of taking advantage of yer frailty, and letting an army through the Aisir nam Breug into Scotland?"

"The road through the traverse isn't wide enough for more than one man on horseback at a time," Dugald Kerr answered. "And the hills press the way so closely, it would be impossible to widen it. No army will come through the Aisir nam Breug."

"But if a small raiding party was allowed through," Ferguson persisted, "and they took charge of this keep, they could allow other raiders through until there was a large group bent on mayhem. Spies could use the pass to get in and out of Scotland easily."

"Spies already use the pass and probably have since its beginnings," the old laird said dryly.

"Ye've let spies use the Aisir nam Breug?" Ferguson gasped.

"Of course they have used it," Dugald Kerr said. "Are ye daft, man, that ye expect I would know a spy if I saw one? But it would stand to reason the pass is used by them. It's quick and safe, and 'tis discreet. Pay yer toll, and travel in peace is all that we require of those who use the Aisir nam Breug."

There was a long silence, but then Alexander Bruce spoke again. "Ian Ferguson has brought up a good point. Have ye ever defended yer keep against an enemy who came through the pass, Dugald Kerr? Has yer granddaughter? To my knowledge neither of ye has done so. But if this keep was attacked, it could not be defended by an old man and a young woman."

"So say ye," Dugald Kerr quickly replied. "But I believe yer wrong."

"I'm not," Alexander Bruce responded. "Ye need a younger man here with ye. The Hays have stepped to the forefront of this dilemma. Maggie must wed Ewan Hay so this keep and its most valuable asset have a defender."

"Ewan Hay couldn't defend a barn full of kittens," Dugald Kerr answered scornfully. "He's a bully and a coward. Forcing this man on us will cause more difficulties than you can imagine. My clan folk won't accept him."

"They will have to if he is wed to yer granddaughter," came the reply.

Maggie had listened to all the arguments from her spy hole. What was the matter with men that they could not believe that a woman was capable without a man to direct her every move? But if these border lords were united in their resolve, she was going to have a difficult time evading what was to her a horrific future. And she didn't trust Ewan Hay not to harm her sons once they were wed. He would want his own son to inherit. Annabelle would be safe, for he would consider her daughter something of value to be married off eventually to someone wealthy or powerful, or preferably both.

"See them wed by Lammastide," Alexander Bruce said. "This situation with England isn't going to get any easier."

"This man has not the strength or experience to defend us," Dugald Kerr protested. "And I'll not force my Maggie into a marriage she doesn't want! Get out of my keep, all of ye, and to hell with the laws of hospitality in the Borders! Begone! And take Ewan Hay with ye if ye would help me," the old man shouted.

Listening, Maggie was proud of her grandsire. He might be old, but he was still strong and determined. Their neighbors had left, but Ewan Hay had not. Having been given the tacit approval of the nearby lairds to wed her, Ewan Hay made plans to do so.

"I won't implement the marriage of an unwilling woman," Father David said. "Until the day comes that Maggie agrees to wed ye, I will not perform the ceremony."

Undeterred, Ewan Hay sent for his brother's priest, a man who was less scrupulous than Brae Aisir's cleric.

"We'll draw up the contracts," Father Gillies said.

"She'll never sign them," Ewan replied.

"Ah, my son, ye will find the means to force her to yer will as is yer right. And as soon as ye do, we'll perform the blessing. She will be yers."

Feeling more reassured, Ewan Hay sought to catch Maggie off guard. One late-spring evening, he watched from the shadows in the hall as she saw that the fires were banked without going out and that the candles and lamps were snuffed out. Then in the dim light of the low fires she headed for the staircase. It was there he caught her, stepping out so they were face-to-face.

"Get out of my way!" Maggie snarled at him.

He quickly slid an arm about her, yanking her close and pinioning her arms to her sides. "We are going to be wed shortly, madam," he said in a cold, hard voice. "I think it is time ye accepted that I will soon be yer husband and yer master." Then his hand plunged into her gown, wrapping itself about a plump breast.

"Take yer paws off me, ye damned animal. I have a husband, and I don't need another. I especially don't need ye." Maggie squirmed, attempting to break loose.

"Ye belong to me now, ye border vixen, and I'm going to very much enjoy taming ye to the point where ye will come when I call and eat from my hand," Ewan growled against her mouth. Then he kissed her, but as he did, his grip upon her relaxed.

Maggie yanked her arms up. Her hands clawed down his face. She pulled away from him, the bodice of her gown sustaining a tear as she did. "Don't touch me!" And she turned to escape him.

His face stinging from her nails, Ewan grabbed Maggie's thick plait and jerked her back. He slapped her several times. "Ye dare to scratch me, bitch?" he said angrily.

Maggie slapped him back so hard his ears rang, and he actually saw stars. "I warned ye not to touch me, Ewan Hay." Then she ran halfway up the stairs. "Next time ye attempt it, I'll kill ye without hesitation," Maggie warned him. Then she was gone.

Ewan Hay's cock was hard and aching. He would bind her to the bed on their wedding night to prevent her from using her claws on him again. Then he would run his hands and tongue all over her body at his leisure before he fucked her over and over until she would beg him for mercy. The picture in his head was so graphic he knew he would have to satisfy his lust. Going to the stables, he called for his horse. Then he rode down to the village to Flora Kerr's cottage.

He did not knock but walked directly into the dwelling, calling for her. To his surprise, the midwife, Agnes Kerr, came from the tiny bedchamber. "Where's Florrie?" he asked. "I have a great need to fuck."

"She's dead," Agnes Kerr said coldly.

"Dead?" He was astonished by her words.

"She aborted the bastard ye put in her belly, *my lord*," Agnes said scathingly. "Only that her sister found her and called for me, she should have died alone."

"She was enceinte?" He was surprised. Florrie had said naught about it.

"We have a perfectly good village whore. A willing good woman," Agnes said. "But ye could not patronize her, could ye? Ye needed to shame a respectable lass."

"She was a whore too," Ewan replied. "She willingly opened her legs."

"Flora offered a service to the men in this village whose wives were with child and could no longer have conjugal relations. She took no coin, or anything else for it. She did not want their men, or any entanglements. She had a need for cock, and they had a need for cunt," Agnes said. "But ye forced her, and then made her yer mistress. Well, ye'll not hurt her anymore," Agnes told him. "Now satisfy that bulge in yer breeks at the edge of the village with Jeannie."

Ewan Hay didn't argue. He walked from the cottage, not even bothering to even take a last look at the woman he had used for a mistress. He found Jeannie's cottage at the end of the lane, entered it, and then eased his lust on her before returning to the keep. She did not speak with him during the act, and saw him quickly off. It was obvious she knew something had happened and didn't approve of him at all. He would have to find a more pleasant and cooperative woman to be his mistress. And he'd soon have a spitfire wife, but once he got her with child she would hold no fascination for him.

The Hay priest drew up the marriage contracts between Ewan Hay and Maggie Kerr, but she refused to sign them. Dugald Kerr would not sign them. Maggie would not even come to the hall any longer. As he did not patrol the Aisir nam Breug himself, he had no idea that she was riding it. One day as she came to the border between Scotland and England she spied her cousin, Rafe Kerr, riding towards her. He waved to Maggie, and the two of them dismounted their horses to talk.

Maggie told her English kinsman of how Ewan Hay was attempting to force her into a marriage. "He thinks once he has me for a wife he will have our portion of the pass. He's already stealing from the tolls taken."

"How do ye know that?" Rafe queried her. It was just as he had suspected when he warned his father against Ewan Hay. The man was not to be trusted.

"Grandsire taught me when I was twelve years old how to manage our accounts. Of course, Ewan doesn't know that. He's taken over everything, or so he believes. But I have kept a careful tab of the traffic since he took my account books from me. And since he has left those records in Grandsire's old library, I wait until all are sleeping, and then go and check them. He has only recorded four travelers for every five who have come through, Rafe. He is stealing from Brae Aisir."

"Aye, and from us as well," her kinsman replied. "We have had complaints from several of our regulars traveling north that after they paid their toll to us, Ewan Hay extracted an additional toll at your end. He threatened to hold their cargo if he was not paid. I was coming to speak with yer grandsire about it."

"The Hay has driven our Kerr clansmen from the keep and peopled it with his own men. He keeps the drawbridge up day and night. He has no idea that I ride out, because he doesn't know about the little gate in the wall behind the stable," Maggie said.

"Grandsire has grown frail trying to maintain control. Now several of the more important neighboring lairds have come and demanded of him that I be wed to Ewan. Despite my having managed our section of the pass before, they insist a woman cannot do it. They will not support me. Instead, they say I must wed and they insist Ewan Hay is the natural choice."

"Are ye certain that Fingal Stewart is dead?" Rafe asked.

Maggie sighed. "I think I would sense it if he were, and I don't. Yet there has been no word from him, or request for a ransom." She sighed again. "I will have to kill Ewan Hay, Rafe, for I will not marry him."

"Don't use a weapon," Rafe advised. "They'll hang you for it. Poison him, and let him die a slow, lingering death so it looks natural. That is what Aldis did to my stepmother. Of course, many suspected, but nothing could be proved. Shall I find out for you what she used?"

"Aye, I would like to know," Maggie said, shocked to hear herself asking for such help. But she simply could not marry Ewan Hay. The thought of him atop her made her sick to her stomach. And too, if he got her with child, and she delivered a son, Fingal's lads would be in danger, she was certain.

"I'll not come to Brae Aisir today," Rafe said. "Having learned what I have from ye, I think it best I bring this to my father to learn what he would do."

"Rafe, I dinna trust yer father either," Maggie said candidly.

Her cousin laughed. "Ye shouldn't trust him. He wants the whole of the Aisir nam Breug for himself. He also wants one of yer lads for my half sister. But he is still the master of Netherdale. I will do my best to influence him in the right direction, but I will not deny him his rule or embarrass him publicly."

Maggie nodded. "I understand," she said. "It is not a bad idea, matching my elder son with yer half sister, Rafe. I would seriously consider it."

"I'll tell my father what ye have told me," Rafe said. Then he kissed Maggie on both cheeks. "Meet me here in another ten days, Cousin, so we may talk again."

"I will," Maggie said. Her kinsman was a good man even if he was English, and she felt a little less alone now. She rode back to the keep, leading her horse through the small door in the stone walls, then into the stables. She unsaddled the animal, storing his saddle, blanket, and bridle carefully away. Then she rubbed the stallion down, checking his hooves to be certain there were no pebbles caught in his shoes.

Finished, she went to the stable door, and peeped out to be sure she would not be seen exiting the stables. As no one was looking in her direction, Maggie slipped out of the barn and hurried across the courtyard into the house. She ran quickly upstairs to find Grizel and told her of the chance meeting with Rafe Kerr. "The Hay has been stealing from us both," Maggie told her serving woman. Then she said, "Have the lads been fed their meal yet? I promised them I should tell them a story tonight."

"They went down to the kitchens a little while ago," Grizel said. "Ye were careful, my lady, weren't ye? No one saw ye come or go?"

"The Hay doesn't keep a watch from the roof," Maggie said. "He doesn't even know we have a cannon up there for I camouflaged it after he arrived," she chuckled. "I can come and go as I please. I had best change out of my breeks, though, lest he become suspicious. Then I'll go down and fetch my sons upstairs."

Maggie changed her garments quickly, stripping off her breeks, shirt, and boots and replacing them with a medium blue velvet bodice and skirt. She undid her braid, brushed out her chestnut curls, and then replaited her hair. Slipping her feet into a pair of soft kid house slippers, she hurried downstairs to the kitchen where the cook was now preparing the meal. Looking about, she did not see her sons. "Where are my lads?" she asked the cook and her helpers.

"That Hay captain, Bhaltair, came and got them," the cook said.

"The poor bairns hadn't even had their meal yet. I was just serving it, but nothing would do but that he take Master Davy and Master Andrew by the hand and go off with them, my lady."

Maggie's heart began to hammer. She took several slow deep breaths to calm it. Then turning, she ran up the stairs, and into the hall. Her grandsire was dozing by one of hearths, an old deerhound by his side. Ewan Hay and his priest, Father Gillies, were speaking in low tones by the other hearth. Maggie went immediately up to them.

"What have ye done with my sons?" she demanded of him.

"I do not like yer tone, madam," he responded.

"I do not like ye," she said, "but I am forced to bear yer company. What have ye done with my lads, Ewan Hay? Yer captain took them from the kitchens where they had gone to have their meal. Where are they?"

"They are safe for the interim," he answered, smiling a cruel smile. He had cold blue eyes, and the look in them made her shiver.

"Where are they?" Maggie said, trying to keep her voice from shaking.

"Ye will have them back on the day we wed," Ewan Hay told her. "Until then they will live in a locked and windowless chamber in yer cellars. They will have a single candle for light. When it burns out, they will be in the dark, madam."

"They're little bairns!" Maggie said, horrified. "What kind of a man are ye that ye would use two wee lads to force me to yer will?"

"What kind of a man am I, madam? A real man, not a lass in breeks giving orders to her betters. I am a man who will not allow ye to run roughshod over me. I warned ye once that I would teach ye yer place. Now get out of the hall, and remain in yer chamber until ye are ready to obey me. Neither ye, nor yer lads, nor the old man dozing by the fire will receive food or drink until ye bend to my will. Do ye understand me?"

"If I ever considered being merciful to ye, Ewan Hay, ye have put such thoughts from my mind with yer behavior today. If anything should happen to my lads, ye will wish ye had never been born nor seen the light of day," Maggie said angrily.

"Do ye see, good Priest, what I must put up with?" Ewan said, turning to Father Gillies. "This woman does not know her place. She is well named Mad Maggie."

"I suggest a daily beating until she softens," Father Gillies said. "The Holy Bible instructs a man to beat a disobedient wife. Our laws allow it."

Hearing him, Maggie glared at the fat priest. "Ye would allow this mistreatment of innocent bairns?" she accused him. "I will be certain the archbishop of St. Andrews learns of yer manners, Priest." Then turning on her heel, she went to her grandfather and gently awakened him. "It is time to go upstairs, Grandsire," she told him.

"We have not eaten yet," Dugald Kerr said.

"We are not to be allowed food or drink until I wed this bastard," Maggie told her grandfather. "And he has locked the lads in the cellar."

"*What?*" Dugald Hay suddenly straightened up. He stamped across the hall to face down Ewan Hay. "How dare ye give such orders in my house, ye cowardly cur! And ye, Priest, will ye stand by and permit this injustice?"

"Old man, yer fate and that of yer great-grandsons is in the hands of yer granddaughter. She has been told she must wed me, but she will not. Yet she must! When the contracts are signed and the blessing given, I will release David and Andrew Stewart from their imprisonment, and all will feast in celebration of my marriage."

"My husband is alive!" Maggie shouted. "Would ye have me commit bigamy, Ewan Hay? And would ye condone the sin, Priest?"

"No one has seen Fingal Stewart in more than six months," Ewan said through clenched teeth. "There has been no demand for ransom. The man is dead, and ye are mine, Maggie Kerr, whether ye will it or no."

"Never!" Maggie shouted at him. "I will go to my grave first!"

"How long will a single candle last before yer sons are together in the dark, the sounds of the rats scuttling about them? How long can they survive without food or water? Will ye let them perish in the dark to have yer will, madam? And how long will this old man last in such circumstances? If ye have not bent to my will by morning, he will go into the darkness too! I will not allow ye to defy me! Ye will marry me, and ye will cry out my name in the throes of yer passion. Ye will give me sons. I will have the Aisir nam Breug for myself. Whether any of ye live or die is of little importance to me. The country is in an uproar. The English are raiding as they have never done so before. Ye have no one who will aid ye, for French Mary is too busy protecting her own. The monarchy is weakened now. This keep, Brae Aisir, is all mine for the taking!"

"Bring my lads from their dungeon, and I will wed ye," Maggie said. She had no choice, but she would kill him when he entered her bed, and Ewan Hay was too stupid to realize it. She couldn't allow him to harm her sons or hurt her grandsire.

"Nay," her grandsire said. "Ye'll not wed him!"

"Grandsire, there is no choice," Maggie said, attempting to reason with the old man. "Will ye let him murder Fin's lads?"

"I'll kill ye!" Dugald Kerr said, pulling his dirk from his belt, his gnarled hand raised as he came forward.

Ewan Hay knocked the weapon from the old man's hand, pushing him back so hard the old laird stumbled and fell. "Bhaltair," Ewan Hay called. "Take this old fool to his chamber, and lock him inside." Reaching out, he prevented Maggie from going to her grandfather. "Nay, madam, we have unfinished business. Am I to understand that ye will wed me of yer own free will?"

"Aye," Maggie ground out.

"Excellent," he said, and he smiled a triumphant smile.

"My sons," she said.

"Tomorrow," he told her. "Sign the contracts tomorrow, and I will consider releasing them. And then on the day after, we will go to the chapel to receive the blessing on our union."

"If I sign the contract tonight, will ye let my lads out?" Maggie asked him.

"Nay, on the morrow is time enough. Ye'll not have yer will with me, madam, as ye've had it with every other man who has crossed yer path. Now come to the high board, and we will eat."

"I'm not hungry," Maggie said, and she wasn't.

"Whether ye are hungry or not, madam, ye will sit with me at the high board," Ewan Hay told her. "Remember that from now on the comfort of yer sons' lives depends upon yer behavior towards me." He held out his hand to her.

Maggie took it, hating him with every fiber of her being as she did. Her bairns would be so frightened, she thought. She needed to go to them. To comfort them. She would find out where they were after she escaped the hall. The serving men began bringing the food to the table. Ewan Hay and his priest ate and drank heartily. Maggie tried to eat because she knew she had to keep her strength up, but right now in this company she simply could not swallow a thing. She drank a little of the wine in her cup. Finally Maggie could bear no more. She arose. "I should like to go to my chamber," she said.

Ewan Hay's fingers fastened about her wrist. He yanked her down into his lap.

"I'm not ready to part with yer company," he said as an arm encircled her waist, drawing her close. The hand that had pulled her down now released her wrist and plunged into her bodice. He fondled her breast, tweaking at the nipple, and pressed a wet kiss on her mouth. "Ye have soft skin," he then murmured at her.

"Have ye no shame?" she hissed at him. "Ye would lust openly before yer own priest? Take yer hand from my gown. We are not wed yet."

He snickered. "Gillies is already asleep, for he has no head for wine. Turn yer head and look at him. He'll be snoring any minute." The hand that had been crushing her breast now slipped beneath her skirt, and up her thigh.

Maggie gasped with shock at his lewdness. He was half drunk, and she felt the arm about her relaxing. Jumping up, she skittered away from him. "I am going to my chamber," she said.

"Let me come with ye," he begged her.

"I'll cut yer throat if ye do," Maggie threatened, and then she ran from the hall.

Hearing footsteps behind her, she whirled about and found Busby coming towards her. "The bairns?" she said to him. "Do ye know where they are?"

The majordomo nodded. "They're all right. When the Hay took the keys from me, he had no knowledge that there was a second set. I spoke with the lads, and told them 'tis a game we're playing. They have food, water, a lamp, and blankets, my lady. They are safe, and they are fine."

"I have to get my children out of the keep, Busby. I can't allow him to use them against me. I have had to promise to wed him to protect them, but if we can get them away, I don't have to keep that promise," Maggie said.

"But where outside the keep can they be safe?" Busby asked her.

"They must be taken through the pass to Netherdale," Maggie replied. "My uncle will not harm them, for they are his blood. Besides, he has it in mind that his daughter by Aldis, his third wife, would make a fine wife for Davy. Whether that ever happens is something we must leave up to the Fates, but my lads will be safe in Netherdale. Rafe, my cousin, will watch over them. He has several lads of his own."

"The night will be short," Busby noted. "Go to your chamber, my lady. I will take the lads to Clennon Kerr, and he will see them taken safely to Netherdale."

"I must see them, Busby. I must bid them farewell," Maggie said.

"Nay, my lady, ye must go upstairs, and let the house settle into its nighttime quiet. I will fetch the boys and take them out through yer secret gate into the village. I saw ye did not eat. Ye will find food in yer chamber, and Grizel awaiting ye. When it is discovered tomorrow that yer lads are gone, ye can say with complete honesty that ye don't know how they escaped, and Grizel can swear ye were in yer chamber all night."

Maggie nodded. "Tell them I love them, and to be respectful to Lord Edmund," she told Busby. Then turning again for the stairs, she hurried up to her chamber where Grizel was indeed awaiting her. "Bar my door," she told her servant. "I left him drunk, and apt to get drunker. If he comes sniffing about my door, we want it well locked and barred." Then Maggie told Grizel what had transpired, and of how the Hay was attempting to use her sons against her. "I am going to have to kill him," she said, "and if I'm caught and hanged for it, I will regret naught."

"Sit down and eat," Grizel said. "Then ye must get some sleep. Ye need to be strong, my lady. 'Twill not be an easy day tomorrow."

Maggie did as she was bid. She ate heartily, now able to swallow and enjoy her food. She slept heavily and on waking dressed in a dark green velvet gown. Then she descended to the hall. Just as she reached it she heard Busby's voice murmur, "All is well, madam." Maggie strode into the hall. "I've decided I will not wed ye."

"Ye would sacrifice yer lads to have yer way?" he asked.

"Why don't ye go and ask my sons yerself?" Maggie mocked him.

Ewan Hay got up slowly from the chair in which he had been sitting. "What have ye done, ye border vixen? *What have ye done?*" He came towards her.

Maggie stood her ground. "I have done nothing," she said sweetly.

"Bhaltair!" Ewan Hay shouted to his captain, and then he dashed from the chamber. "Bhaltair! To me! To me!"

Maggie smiled, pleased at the tone of panic in his voice.

"Have ye sinned, my daughter?" Father Gillies asked. "Should ye make yer confession to me?"

"Nay, I have not sinned," Maggie replied softly.

"Aye, ye have. 'Tis the sin of pride ye commit, my daughter," the priest said. "'Tis the sin of disobedience ye have committed."

"If seeing to my sons' best interests is a sin, good Priest, then I suppose I am guilty as ye have charged," Maggie told him sweetly.

Father Gillies's eyes narrowed, and he contemplated the woman before him. "It is neither wise nor good for a woman to be clever," he warned her.

"I will consider yer words and ponder upon them in my heart," Maggie replied.

"A good beating will take the defiance from ye," he responded snappishly. "I shall recommend to my lord Ewan that he apply the rod most strongly to ye from this day forth until yer behavior is corrected. I have advised him before to do this. Now he will."

Maggie dropped all pretenses at politeness. "The bastard hasn't got the stones to raise his hand to me, and the day he does will be his last, Priest, *and yers*. There is no holiness about ye as with my great-uncle. Yer an evil man to encourage the Hay into a bigamous marriage, and to advise him to cruelty towards bairns and women."

Ewan Hay returned to the hall in the company of Bhaltair. The

Hay captain was immediately behind Maggie, pinioning her arms to her side. His breath was foul.

"Now, bitch," Ewan Hay said, "ye will tell me where ye have secreted yer sons," and without waiting for an answer he slapped her several times across the cheek.

Gathering up as much spittle as she could within her mouth, Maggie spit fiercely at him. Then she smiled at him defiantly. "Go to hell!"

"I will kill ye if ye do not tell me," Ewan Hay said through gritted teeth.

"Nay, I will not tell ye," she said. "My lads are safe where ye cannot get at them. Even if ye kill me, ye will not have Brae Aisir or control the Aisir nam Breug."

"And Annabelle? Where is she?" he asked.

"I do not know," Maggie responded, surprised by his query. So her servants had thought to get her little daughter out of the keep too. Bless them! She had been so concerned with Davy and Andrew that she had not considered Annabelle. She had not thought her in danger, but obviously others did think her baby vulnerable.

Ewan Hay saw the surprise that Maggie quickly masked upon her face when he had asked about her daughter. So, he thought, the bitch had more allies within the house than he had previously considered. Then he had a thought. "Let her go, Bhaltair," he said. "She will indeed go to her grave before she tells us anything."

Father Gillies came to Ewan's side and whispered something in his ear.

"Fetch the old laird," the Hay said, a nasty smile touching his lips.

"My grandsire knows nothing of any of this," Maggie said as Bhaltair strode from the hall to do his master's bidding. "Do ye think me foolish enough to involve him?"

"I think ye will very shortly sign the contracts that Father Gillies has laid out upon the high board," Ewan Hay said coldly. "If ye do not keep yer word to wed me, then I will have Bhaltair slit yer grandfather's throat, madam. If ye would have the old man's death on yer conscience, then refuse me one more time."

God and the Blessed Mother! She had not considered the Hay would use Dugald Kerr against her. But then, a man who would put two little lads in a dank dark cellar chamber would probably do anything to get his way. Maggie pressed her lips together to keep from shrieking at her own stupidity. She was tired of this game he was playing! She wanted him dead. "There will be no coupling until the blessing, which will be in three days' time," Maggie said to him. "Ye will give me that courtesy, my lord."

He nodded as relief poured through him. He had beaten her! He had actually won this battle between them. In a few minutes she would legally be his. He could be gracious enough to wait three more days to bed her. Fingal Stewart had had to wait several months for the privilege of her body. Ewan Hay was no less a gentleman. Three days was not so long to wait. "Everything will be as we have previously agreed upon," he told her. "I will want the lads brought home, however."

"Nay," she said. "I do not trust ye not to harm them."

"Ye cannot keep them away forever," Ewan Hay told her. "They are yer heirs."

"I can, and I will," Maggie said obdurately.

"We will discuss this at a later date when yer in a more reasonable mood," he replied, smiling at her.

Maggie did not smile back.

Bhaltair now came into the hall, escorting her grandfather.

"Aah," Ewan Hay said, "here is Lord Dugald come to witness the signing of our union, madam."

Dugald Kerr cast a scornful glance at the Hay. "Are the bairns safe?" he asked his granddaughter.

"Aye," she told him. She said nothing more, but her face registered her fear.

He was surprised to see such an emotion in her eyes, for Maggie had never been one to allow fear to overcome her. "Ye don't have to wed the bastard," he said.

"I do," Maggie responded. "I gave my word, Grandsire, and my honor is every bit as important to me as a man's would be."

"But this man has not acted in an honorable fashion," the laird answered his granddaughter. "Ye are free to refuse him now."

"Nay," Maggie said low.

Dugald Kerr fastened his gaze upon Ewan Hay. "What is it ye are doing to coerce my Maggie into this foul union?" he demanded of the young man.

Ewan Hay avoided looking directly at the old man, but he did tell him the truth. "I have told her if she does not wed me, I will have ye killed," he responded coldly.

"Kill me then, ye dishonorable bastard!" the old laird said. "Ye discredit the name of Hay, and it will be shouted throughout the Borders to yer family's shame. Ye cannot keep such ignominious behavior a secret."

"Nay, Grandsire!" Maggie cried, her eyes filled with tears. She loved the old man so much, and his bravery almost broke her heart. "I cannot have yer death on my conscience, and even if he did what he threatens, he would find a way to make a marriage with me. Let this strife end here. I will wed him even though I believe this to be a bigamous union. Fingal Stewart is alive. He will return to me, to our bairns!"

"Are we ready to sign the contracts?" Father Gillies broke in. "The conflict surrounding this matter is certainly resolved now."

"I am an old man, Margaret Jean Kerr," the laird said. "I have lived more than seventy years, and I am content to die if it will keep ye from this man."

Maggie stepped forward, enfolding him in an embrace. God's toenail, he was so thin and so frail beneath his heavy dark velvet gown! "Ye will die in yer own time, Grandsire, and not on my account. I could not bear it. I will sign the marriage agreement." She hugged him gently, murmuring softly in the old man's ear so only he heard her. "But he will have no pleasure of me for I will kill him on our wedding night."

Dugald Kerr stepped back from his granddaughter, nodding. His pride in her was more than evident. "I am hungry," he said. "Let us do this wretched thing so we may break our fast quickly."

They stepped up to the high board where the priest had carefully laid out the parchment upon which the marriage contract was written. Maggie scanned it quickly, noting that it turned everything that was hers over to Ewan Hay.

"Will ye have yer grandsire sign for ye, my lady," the priest asked her, "or would ye prefer to make yer own mark?"

Maggie did not answer him, instead signing her full name at the designated spot where her name had previously been written. *Margaret Jean Kerr, by her own hand.*

The priest's mouth fell open, revealing rotting teeth. "Ye write?" he said.

"And I read as well, Priest," Maggie answered him. "I notice ye have given this thief everything that I possess. 'Tis hardly just, but no matter." She shrugged casually.

Dugald Kerr hid a smile, especially when Ewan Hay took up the quill to make an X where his name was already written. When the Hay passed the quill to the laird, the old man wrote *Dugald Alexander Kerr, by his own hand* where his name was written. He then returned the quill to the priest.

"It is done," Father Gillies said in pleased tones. "There but remains the matter of the church's blessing upon ye both in three days' time."

"Should ye not give me a kiss?" the Hay asked Maggie.

"Ye can wait until the blessing," she said coldly.

"Did ye make Fingal Stewart wait to kiss ye once the contracts were signed?" Ewan Hay wanted to know.

"Ye are not Fingal Stewart, nor will ye ever be," Maggie said with devastating effect. She signaled to Busby to bring the food so they might break their fast. Then she ate quickly so she might excuse herself with the excuse her household duties needed attending to, and hurried from the hall.

She found Grizel and Busby awaiting her in her chamber. "The contracts are signed, but they will not be legal. My lord husband will return."

"He may or he may not," Grizel said candidly. "But how will ye keep the Hay from yer bed, my lady?"

"He has given me three days, and we will see he keeps his promise," Maggie said. "And in three nights when he attempts to mount me, I will kill him."

"His priest will cry for vengeance," Busby said.

"There will be no mark on Ewan Hay," Maggie said. "I will drug his wine, and when he sleeps, I will smother him. It will appear he has died in his sleep. Let the priest cry foul to the high heavens. He will be able to prove naught against me. I'll not leave my bairns without their mother as much as I should like to slice the bastard to bits."

"It's a good plan, my lady," Busby noted. "Do not, however, change the coldness ye exhibit to him. If ye are suddenly sweet, and then he dies, suspicions will be raised. If yer attitude does not change, it is less likely that anyone other than the priest will cry foul. Especially if ye let the priest leave to spread his tale. And when questioned, say ye are not in the least unhappy that he is dead, but deny all culpability."

"To all except Father David," Maggie said.

"Confess it only on yer death bed," Grizel advised. "Let all believe God spoke in this matter. That no Hay should have Brae Aisir. I doubt Lord Hay will be distressed too greatly that his youngest brother has died. He gambled his sibling could take and hold this keep. Remember, other than the thirty men he gave to his kinsman, he has had no part in any of this at all. Admit ye are not unhappy that yer bridegroom is dead, and then tender yer sympathies to his family."

It was good advice that her servants gave her, Maggie considered, and she would take it. Her own thoughts were jumbled, and half confused by all that was happening. Where the hell was Fingal Stewart? She just knew he wasn't dead; he hadn't been killed at Solway Moss. She could almost sense him drawing near to her. And the fact that Archie hadn't returned encouraged her to continue to hold on to her hopes. But she dreaded the day when she must stand before God in Brae Aisir chapel, knowing her intent towards this man who had forced himself upon her. *Oh Fin,* she thought to herself. *I need ye now so desperately. I am so tired of being strong for myself, for Brae Aisir. I am willing to let you be strong for the both of us from now on. Come home, my darling! Come home!*

Chapter 16

rchie remained by his master's side as Fingal Stewart began to heal in body and mind. He saw that Fin was extremely well fed, and he was pleased to see his big frame filling out once again, his physical strength returning. But best of all without the stress of travel, and ill health, Fingal Stewart's memory had returned fully. He was eager to return to Brae Aisir and dispossess Ewan Hay from his home. He could but imagine Maggie's irritation and impatience with the fool.

Archie had told him of the messenger's error in delivering the note to Maggie, so Fin was more eager than ever to leave Edinburgh. Both men would have been relieved to know that Bhaltair, who had taken the message, had thrown it into the barracks' fire. Ewan's captain couldn't read himself, but he suspected his master wouldn't want Maggie receiving messages from anyone in Edinburgh or anywhere else. Then distracted by another matter, he had forgotten the messenger and not mentioned it to his master.

Now Fin needed a horse. His stallion had been stolen at Solway Moss. He could hardly walk back to Brae Aisir. Thinking on it, he realized that he had probably passed quite near it when he had come over the border from England. He had walked the distance once. He would not walk it again. "We need to purchase an animal for me to ride," he said to Archie one morning as they broke their fast with ham, fresh bread, cheese, and strawberries come in from the country-side that morning.

"It's a market day," Archie replied. "We can look, my lord."

The market square was a busy place. It was late June, and the sun was shining after several gloomy days. They walked past the many stalls, the vendors calling out to them as they went.

"Newly baked buns! Still warm. Four a penny!"

"Fresh milk and cream! The cow won't take it back!"

"Cockles, prawns, and mussels fresh from Leith this day!"

"Flowers! Who'll buy my flowers?"

Archie knew the dealers of livestock and horses would be found on the far side of the market square. He led his master through the shoppers until they finally found a horse dealer. The man was a gypsy with dark eyes and a cautious demeanor. "My master is in need of a horse," Archie said.

Fin smiled at his serving man, putting a hand on his shoulder. "I want a stallion. Well trained, not skittish," he told the horse dealer. "And hopefully not stolen."

The gypsy laughed, the tanned skin about his eyes crinkling with his amusement. "I sent the stolen horses over the border into England," he replied.

Fin laughed too. It was probably one of the few honest things the man had ever said. "Since I'll be riding into the Borders, I'll not want to come face-to-face with an angry former owner of any beastie I purchase from ye."

"Ye won't, my lord Stewart," the gypsy responded.

"Ye know me?" Fin was surprised.

"Mad Maggie lets us camp on her lands twice a year," the gypsy said. "We had heard ye were dead at Solway Moss. We've met briefly before, my lord."

Fin looked at the man, thought hard, and then said, "Jock, isn't it?"

"Aye, my lord, Jock it is!" he replied. "I have news that may not please ye."

"Ewan Hay is attempting to take over the Kerr holding," Lord Stewart said. "Aye, my man, Archie, has told me."

"It's yer wife he's attempting to gain," Jock said. "He is claiming they will be wed at Lammastide."

"I sent word to Brae Aisir almost ten days ago that I am alive," Fin said.

"My lord, I was at Brae Aisir four days ago. There is no word of yer survival, or that ye are safe in Edinburgh. The Kerrs' neighbors have been pressing yer wife to take Ewan Hay as her next husband. His brother, Lord Hay, has approved the match. They fear for the stability of the Aisir nam Breug without a man to manage it. They have said quite plainly and out loud that the laird is too old now to be useful. When they said it, I heard he took up a stick and attempted to drive the delegation of his neighbors from the hall. He collapsed and had to be carried away, but he did survive. The Hay would not allow us to camp on the Kerr lands this spring. Whatever help ye might need to drive him out of Brae Aisir, my people and I will be glad to aid ye. But ye must go home, and ye must go quickly lest ye lose all ye have."

"Is it not enough that the English are raiding us with impunity? Now I must start a feud between the Hays and the Kerrs," Fingal Stewart said angrily. Then he said to Jock, "Do ye have a stallion for me, man?"

"I do," the gypsy replied. "But not here. The horse I have for ye, my lord, is too fine for the marketplace. Our encampment is in a field about three miles from the city, north on the Perth road. Come tomorrow morning, and ye'll see."

"I'll be there early," Fin said.

Jock nodded.

Lord Stewart and Archie returned to Torra House.

"Is there anything to pack?" Fin asked his man.

Archie chuckled. "I've already burned what ye were wearing when ye got here," he said. "Yer wearing what ye own, but for a second shirt. I'll fold it, and put it in my saddlebag. I take it we'll purchase yer stallion, and immediately make our way home."

Lord Stewart nodded grimly. "God's foot! I'll need a saddle, and bridle for my horse. We'll have to go back to the market square, and see if we can find one."

"We passed a leather maker's stall near where Jock had his horse," Archie said.

The two men walked back to the market and found the leather maker.

"I need a saddle and bridle," Fin told the craftsman.

"I can make ye one, my lord, but 'twill take several weeks," the man replied.

"I need something immediately," Fin responded.

"Then ye don't mind something secondhand?" The leather maker was surprised. This was obviously a gentleman.

"It's either that or I ride into the Borders bareback and clutching my horse's mane," Fin said with a small attempt at humor.

The leather maker chuckled. "Actually, my lord, I have a saddle I made for a gentleman of the old king's court last year. But he never came back for it, and he paid me but a small deposit."

"I'll take it," Fin said without hesitation.

"Look first, my lord, 'tis a plain thing with no embellishments at all."

"I'm no courtier. I need nothing more than a plain saddle and bridle," Fin told the man. "Let me see it."

The leather maker turned and went into the back of his stall. When he returned, he carried with him a beautifully made leather saddle with matching bridle. "Here it is, my lord," he said, wiping it off with his apron. "'Tis a bit dusty, but fine otherwise."

Fin ran his hand over the leather. It was very finely tanned, and as smooth as silk.

He looked to Archie. "What do ye think?"

Archie nodded.

"How much?"

The leather maker named his price, but then said, "I'm deducting the deposit, for it was paid, my lord. I imagine the man who ordered it was killed in the wars last year, which is why he didn't come back."

Fin nodded. "Aye, that is possible." He turned to Archie. "Pay him," he said.

The transaction completed, the two men took the saddle and its equipment to return to Torra House. They made one stop before they departed the market square to purchase a thick square of woven wool that would serve as a saddle blanket. When they reached the house, they found Boyle, the estate agent, waiting for them.

"Ah, my lord, yer looking much better than ye looked several weeks ago when I first saw ye returned," he said. Seeing the saddle on Archie's arm he asked, "Will ye be leaving Edinburgh soon?"

"On the morrow," Fin answered him. "Ye can rent it again, minding ye keep to the same terms, Boyle."

"My lord!" Boyle attempted to look distressed. "Have I not been faithful to our agreement these past years?"

Fin laughed. "Aye, ye have," he admitted.

"I have a group of Protestant lords coming in from the north in a few days," he told Fin. "They've rested in this house before, and they sent to me this day. I'm relieved I can accommodate them once again." He bowed politely. "Godspeed, my lord. Safe home."

Then turning, he hurried off down the street.

They were gone from Torra House as the first fingers of light began to clutch at the skies above. Archie had insisted that Fin ride his horse until they reached the gypsy encampment. He walked sedately alongside his master, carrying the new saddle and bridle. Leaving the city proper, they turned north and stepped onto the Perth road. Several miles later with the horizon beginning to display a rainbow of color, they reached their destination.

The small wagons were carefully placed in a defensive circle. A communal fire blazed high in the center of the camp, which was already alive with men and women preparing for their day. Children raced about. Dogs barked. Fin was certain he heard a rooster crow as several chickens scattered in front of him. Jock came from the largest of the wagons to greet them.

"Good morrow," he said. "Yer right on time to get a good distance today. Come, and I show ye the animal I have in mind for ye. But remember, my lord, the beast must like ye or I cannot sell him to ye." He led them to the edge of the encampment where just beyond in a field a herd of horses grazed. The gypsy whistled a sharp note.

Fin watched as a black stallion raised his head from the sweet grass, and then obediently trotted over to where they stood. The horse was absolutely beautiful. He was as black as the darkest night but for a light marking on his left shoulder. The marking was small, but as it was pure white against the animal's silky midnight black hide, quite distinct.

"It looks like a comet," Fin said, noting the small round head attached to a curving tail. Reaching out, he rubbed the horse's soft muzzle.

"Ye have guessed his name, my lord. 'Tis Comet," Jock said.

Fin looked the animal directly in his liquid brown eyes. The creature had an intelligent air about him. Leaning forward, Fin blew gently into Comet's nostrils.

The horse nudged Fin back gently with his muzzle. "May I ride ye, Comet?" Fin asked.

The horse appeared to nod his head up and down. Grasping a handful of mane, Lord Stewart swung himself up onto the beast's back, and they galloped off across the field, sending the other horses scattering.

Jock nodded. "I knew it was his horse," he said to Archie. "I've raised him since he was born, and I couldn't let him go to just anyone. I've had offers, but the men were never right. Yer master is."

"Is he saddle broke?" Archie asked in practical tones. A horse was a horse.

"Aye, and I see ye've brought one along. Good!" Jock replied.

The horse was incredible, Fin thought as they galloped around the meadow. He had a smooth gait, and he wasn't winded at all when they returned to where Archie and Jock stood awaiting them. The animal had strong long legs and a broad chest. He was perfect. They came to a stop, and Fin slid off.

"If ye feel that Comet has accepted me, I would gladly have him for my own," Fin politely said to the gypsy. "He's a grand beast. I've never ridden finer."

"I can see he's yers, my lord," Jock said. "Now, there is just the small matter of his purchase. I will want a gold piece for him."

"Too much! Too much!" Archie said, glowering at Jock.

"He's worth it," Fin responded, "but I have no gold. I can give ye five pieces of silver, all true weight, none clipped."

"Comet is worth more," Jock said quietly.

"When ye come to Brae Aisir in the autumn," Fin promised, "ye will be welcomed again, and always. There will be water for ye, wood for yer fires, and hay for yer animals. In addition, I will give ye five additional silver pieces."

Jock thought for a long minute. Finally he nodded in the affirmative. He spit in his hand and held it out to Lord Stewart, who returned the gesture. The two men shook hands. "We have an agreement, my lord," the gypsy said. "Now take yer horse, and ride for Brae Aisir before another starts plowing with yer mare."

"She'll kill him first," Fin chuckled as he handed the five silver pieces to Jock.

"Aye, I believe she would, but still if ye hurry, ye can save her the trouble, and kill him yerself," Jock replied. "My wife read the cards for ye last night. Yer way is difficult, but ye'll have yer way in the end, my lord."

While the two men had concluded their business and talked, Archie had laid the new blanket across the horse's back, saddled, and bridled him. Comet danced, now ready to go. Fin mounted his new animal, and with a wave at Jock, the two men road off south for the Borders.

It was a good day for traveling, and they rode the day long. As it was midsummer, the sun did not set, nor the light fade till late. They stopped to rest the horses twice, once taking time to eat the simple rations they carried—oatcakes and cheese. Their flasks were filled with wine, and when the wine ran out, they would drink water. At first the sun was warm on their backs, but as it moved west as the hours passed, it came about to shine in their faces as they rode, and finally moved around to their right.

At twilight they found themselves shelter by a low stone wall that edged a portion of the road. They staked the horses in the field beyond to graze after watering them in a nearby stream. They ate sparingly from their food, and then slept as the summer darkness fell. When they awoke, the moon was shining down so brightly upon the road that Fin decided they might ride on. Watering the animals again, they saddled up and went on their way, heading south and slightly west.

The sun rose in a blaze of spendor. It was a fine summer's day. Hearing hoofbeats, they slipped into the shadows of a small wood to watch as a large party of men galloped by. The men bore no plaids or badges. Who knew who or what they were or where they were headed. They rode by meadows of sheep and fields of cattle. Now and again they saw a cottage or tower house in the distance. Passing men and women in the fields haying, they noticed there was always someone watching that those working be kept safe. In midmorning they stopped once again to rest their beasts and eat.

They rode on until finally it was necessary to leave the main road. They moved onto a smaller, barely visible track. They rested again, ate, rode onward. By the time the sun set on the second day, they were beginning to recognize the countryside around them. They stopped to shelter in a deserted, tumbledown cottage with no roof. Once again the horses were staked nearby.

"If my memory is functioning properly," Fin said, "we are about half a day's ride from Brae Aisir. If the weather remains clear, we can ride by moonlight again, and reach it by midmorning. We'll shelter in the village first so I may learn what is happening."

"Let me ride in before ye do, my lord," Archie said.

Fin considered and realized it was a very good idea. They ate what remained of their small rations and then slept. The moon was high when they arose, saddled their horses, and rode on. They were surprised to find they were closer than they had thought to Brae Aisir village. They arrived just as dawn was breaking. Fin waited in a small grove of trees while Archie, leaving his horse behind, walked quietly to the cottage he knew belonged to Clennon Kerr's family. He knocked softly. The door opened, and Archie stepped into the dwelling to find himself face-to-face with Brae Aisir's captain.

"Archie! Yer back!" the captain said to Lord Stewart's servant.

"Aye," came the answer. "Edinburgh is still there," Lord Stewart's servant said drolly, "and I've had incredible luck, Clennon Kerr."

"What luck?" Clennon Kerr asked.

Archie grinned. "My lord is in the wood just outside of the village. 'Tis a long tale, and his to tell, but I've brought him home safe."

"Praise Jesu and his Blessed Mother!" Clennon Kerr said. "He is just in time to prevent that cur Ewan Hay from forcing the lady to the altar."

"I thought the marriage was to be celebrated at Lammastide," Archie said.

"The Hay has grown frightened she might escape him, and several of the neighboring lairds have come to insist she wed him. They will not listen to either our laird or the lady. Father David said he would wed no woman who was unwilling. The Hay sent for another priest, a man without scruples, from Haydoun, to perform the ceremony. He tried to coerce Mad Maggie by threatening her lads. But she got them from the keep two nights ago, and Iver took them to Netherdale for safety. The wee lassie is safe here in the village. Ewan Hay couldn't tell her apart from any other bairn.

"He has control of the keep while our lads lurk in the shadows waiting to retake it, but without someone to lead them, how can they? I have not the skills for such an endeavor, nor does Iver. The wedding is scheduled for this morning," Clennon Kerr told Archie. "But the master will have to regain the keep to stop it, and the drawbridge is kept up at all times. There is, however, a secret passage that goes beneath the moat into the cellars. With Lord Stewart at our head we can regain the keep."

"Where is Iver?" Archie asked.

"Come," Clennon Kerr said. "I'll take ye to him. He's just back."

The two men left the cottage. The village was beginning to stir with women coming from their cottages to go to the fountain and fill their pails and jugs with water.

Clennon Kerr stopped to whisper into the ears of several of the women. By the smiles suddenly appearing upon their faces, Archie knew the captain was telling them Lord Stewart had survived and was back. Everything was going to be all right.

In another small cottage they found Iver. Fin's captain almost wept with the news that Archie brought. "Let us go and fetch him now!" Iver said.

The three men walked through the village onto the narrow track, and out into the grove of trees where Fingal Stewart now waited. The two captains fell to their knees, catching at Fin's big hands to kiss them. Lord Stewart urged them up onto their feet.

Then he listened as they told him what was about to transpire.

"Jock's wife was right," Fin said slowly.

"We must hurry!" Clennon Kerr said. "The tunnel may not be clear. It has not been used in many years."

"He won't attempt to bed her until tonight," Fin said quietly. "Any marriage vows spoken will be null and void, for I am her husband, and I live. I sent a message to Brae Aisir a few weeks back telling Maggie I was alive. Ewan Hay condemns himself when he thinks to wed my wife. But why would she wed him, knowing I was coming home?"

"That is something ye'll have to ask yer wife once we manage to retake the keep," Clennon Kerr said. "But Mad Maggie is an honorable woman. She will have an honest explanation to give ye, my lord. I know it."

"Gather the men," Fingal Stewart said. "It's time for us to come home."

Chapter 17

$\sim$

*M*aggie was furious with herself that she had not considered her grandfather when she had gotten her children safe from the keep. Why had she not thought to send the laird away? Certainly, it would have been difficult if not impossible to make him go, and where could she have hidden him? He would never have asked sanctuary of his English kinsman. And given the pressure their neighbors had been putting on him to force her into a marriage she didn't want, she was certain none of them would have protected him.

Now through her own lack of foresight she had been forced to sign a marriage contract, and would have to put her immortal soul in danger by killing Ewan Hay. There would have been a time when the mere thought of killing the wretch would have given her pleasure, but now it did not. Killing Ewan Hay was an absolute necessity, but it was also a sordid imposition. He was a despicable cur, but she would nonetheless feel guilt for the rest of her life for the taking of his life.

But then Maggie considered that Ewan Hay's threatening Brae Aisir was no worse than an English borderer's threatening them. She would have no hesitation in picking up her claymore and killing in that case. *But ye would do it face-to-face and not by smothering the man to death*, her conscience reminded her. She pushed the thoughts away. She had to remain strong for the sake of her own sanity, but especially for her bairns and her elderly grandsire. There would be talk, she knew, but as Busby and Grizel had agreed, it would be impossible to prove anything other than a natural death. God's disapproval of the marriage would be bruited about along with Maggie's belief that Lord Stewart lived. Although he would go to sleep in her bed, Ewan Hay would wake up in hell, where he surely belonged; yet that was nonetheless a better death than he deserved.

She avoided him for the remainder of the day, but each time she caught a glimpse of him, he was smiling smugly. She wanted to smack the smile off his face. It was the face of a spoiled boy. Her grandsire was none too pleased by what had happened.

"I should have been able to protect ye," he told her.

"I could not even protect myself," she replied. "It was the bairns I feared for, but I should have gotten ye from the keep too."

"I would have been glad to die for ye, lass," the old man told her.

"Yer the bravest man I know," Maggie told him. "But he is so determined that he would have found a way, and yer death would have been for naught. The priest is partner in all of this. He's an evil man. I want him out of the keep, but short of killing him I don't know how to get him gone, Grandsire."

"We'll find a way," the laird promised. "Jesu, I wish Fin hadn't been killed."

"He is not dead, Grandsire," Maggie insisted. "I just know he isn't!"

"Well where the hell is he then, lass?" Dugald Kerr wanted to know.

The laird would have been surprised to learn how close his granddaughter's husband actually was. The summer's day that had begun bright was now three hours later clouding over with large thunderheads gathering and racing towards Brae Aisir. In the village the men had gathered discreetly in Clennon Kerr's cottage, surprised and delighted to see Lord Stewart. Their faces were wreathed in smiles as each of them shook his hand in hearty welcome. Now their captain held up his hand for silence. The room quieted, and the men looked to Fingal Stewart eagerly.

"We must retake the keep, and take it quickly," he began. "We have two means of accomplishing this, lads. We can either try to go through the secret tunnel that travels beneath the moat; or we can wait for them to lower the drawbridge and storm the keep. The danger in this second plan is that it will alert the Hay, and my wife could be in danger. If we use the tunnel, we have the advantage of surprise. We'll be in the hall and take the house before anyone knows we're there. I want no casualties if we can avoid them."

There were nods and murmurings of agreement from the men in the room.

"The tunnel, however, has not been used in years," Lord Stewart continued. "We cannot be certain if it is even passable. Clennon thinks it opens into the cellars, but even he has never been through it to learn the truth of that. So first we must learn if we can use this tunnel, but we must hurry, for Father David has told me that the blessing of this unholy union is planned for midday."

Clennon Kerr's two oldest nephews stepped forward and volunteered to see if the tunnel was usable. Its entrance was in the hillside below the keep.

"It's well hidden," the Brae Aisir captain said. "There are several trees on the hillside obscuring the entry, and brambles and bushes have grown up about it. But ye cannot be seen from the keep walls even if the Hay thought to position men there. Don't worry about the growth. Just get inside, and see if the tunnel can be used. Here is the key that should open the tunnel door."

The two young men nodded, and then slipped from their uncle's abode. It had begun to rain, which camouflaged them even further.

They reached the hillside, and sought the small entry. The bushes were thick, but they finally located the solid, wooden door. The lock was blocked, and they painstakingly cleaned it out with a knife, then managed to fit the key into it. At first the key would not turn at all, but then slowly, patiently, they worked it, jiggling and half rotating it until the key turned suddenly and the door creaked open enough for them to peer into the old tunnel. It seemed to be clear, judging from the small distance they could see.

They squeezed past the door with the single light they had brought. Using a flint, they managed to strike a spark to ignite the oily torch. Then they began to advance forward. The tunnel was narrow. It would be necessary to go through it single file. They were surprised to see the walls were shored up with stone to prevent cave-ins, as was the low ceiling, which was just high enough to allow an average-size man to walk standing up.

Taller men such as Lord Stewart would probably have to bend slightly. The tunnel floor was set with slates. This was a structure that had obviously been built to last. The stone and slate kept it dry and reasonably rodent free.

After they had walked for several long minutes, they came to a flight of six stone steps. Holding the torch up, they were able to see another door at the top of the landing. The two Kerr clansmen climbed the steps to the door. It too had a lock, but the key from the first door would not fit it. One of the young men knelt, and drawing his dirk from his belt, put the tip of the dagger into the lock. He then began working to engage the mechanism so the lock would open for them. The other man held the torch so he might see better exactly what he was doing.

"I've almost got it, Huey," the kneeling man said. "Just a moment more." There was an audible *click*. "Aah, it's open now. Let's see where we are." He stood up.

357

Slowly, carefully they opened the door a crack. It creaked loudly. The two men held their breath, waiting to see if they had attracted any attention. Satisfied they had not, they peeped through the entry. They could see wooden shelves and the butchered carcass of a stag hanging from an iron hook.

"'Tis the cold pantry," the man named Huey whispered to his companion. He pushed the door fully open, and they stepped into the room. "We must be near the kitchen." He looked about him for an exit. Finding it, he motioned the other man forward. Opening the second door, they were faced with a narrow flight of stairs, another door at its top. They crept up to the second portal and listened; but then Huey motioned that they should descend back down the stairs. "The lord said only to see if the tunnel was passable, and to where it led. We dare not get ourselves caught, Dermid." Huey then drew a small flask from his leather jerkin and oiled the hinges of the door to the tunnel.

Dermid nodded in agreement with his companion's assessment of their situation. Then they stepped through onto the landing, making certain that the lock to the cold pantry was now open. Closing the door behind them, they descended back into the tunnel, running lightly now that they were sure of the structure and their destination. Coming out into the day again, they quickly made their way back to Clennon Kerr's cottage where their uncle, Lord Stewart, and the other men were awaiting them. It was raining heavily now, and the weather did not appear as if it would clear any time soon.

"The tunnel is clear," Huey Kerr told them. "Whoever built it made certain it would remain. We followed it through to a flight of steps that led into a cold pantry. I did not think it wise to go farther, my lord. There is a second flight of stairs up to another door. I suspect it will lead into another pantry or the kitchens."

Fingal Stewart nodded. "Ye did well, lads, and I commend yer caution. Better we not give ourselves away until we're ready to fight." He looked out at the clansmen. "And are we ready, lads?"

"*Aye!*" they roared their agreement. Outside the thunder rumbled.

Fin conferred with Clennon and Iver. "Are we agreed then that the tunnel is our way back into the keep?"

The two captains spoke as one. "Aye, my lord!" they said.

"Gather yer weapons then, men, and follow me," Lord Stewart instructed them.

They ran through the pouring rain to the hillside, where they entered the tunnel one by one. A single young lad was left outside to make certain no one discovered the entrance by chance. Once inside, the clansmen moved single file through the passageway. Several of them carried torches to light the way. Their shadows were dark and large upon the firelit stone walls. Up the stairs they climbed and into the cold pantry. Here they stopped, gathering to make certain that everyone had gotten through. Then they ascended the second staircase.

Lord Stewart put his hand upon the door's latch. The door opened slowly. Another pantry chamber greeted them. The clansmen poured into the room behind their master. At that moment the door from the kitchen opened, and the cook herself stepped inside. Her hand went to her heart in surprise. Her mouth flew open to shriek, but then she saw Clennon Kerr, her brother. He put his finger to his lips, and the cook's lips closed with a snap. When she saw Lord Stewart, her hand flew to her mouth.

Tears began to flow down her plump cheeks. Lord Stewart stepped quickly forward, putting his arms about the cook and giving her a hug.

"Thank God yer home, my lord!" she told him.

He nodded in acknowledgment. "Who is in the hall?" he asked her.

"No one, my lord. The house is empty but for the Hay, yer wife, Grizel, the old laird, Busby, and a few menservants. The rest of them are outside either in the barracks or in the courtyard, my lord."

"Bar yer kitchen door that leads to the outside," Lord Stewart instructed her. Then turning he said, "Come, lads, up to the hall with ye. The house is easily ours."

They exited the pantry, going into the kitchen. The few menservants there gaped with their surprise, but then like the cook, they quietly welcomed their master home. The clansmen now hurried up the kitchen stairs into the corridor outside of the great hall. They filled the hall, surprising Busby who, recognizing Fingal Stewart, ran forward to take up his hand and kiss it.

"Where is the Hay?" he asked.

"In his chamber dressing himself in his finery for the blessing of his *marriage*," Busby replied.

"Lock him in," Lord Stewart said. "Then go and tell my wife that her husband is awaiting her in the hall. She is to come down immediately." His gray eyes were twinkling. "Do not tell her 'tis me."

Busby chuckled. "She has no use for the Hay, my lord. I can but imagine what she'll say when I bring her such a message."

Fingal Stewart grinned. Then he turned to Clennon Kerr. "Bar the doors to the house. I don't wish to be interrupted. Time enough now to clear the riffraff from the house. Where is Father David? And this other priest Iver tells me about?"

"Both are down at the Brae Aisir chapel preparing for the ceremony of blessing," Busby responded. "Does Father David know yer back, my lord?"

Fin shook his head. "I went straight to Clennon Kerr's cottage," he said.

Nodding, Busby bowed, and then went off to fetch Maggie. He hurried up the stairs, unable to believe the sudden good fortune that had brought Fingal Stewart home in time to prevent his wife's bigamous union. Ewan Hay had several weeks prior moved himself into a small chamber upstairs, refusing to remain in a bedspace in the hall any longer. He claimed it was not fitting. It had been the small room in which the children's nursemaids slept. Busby went to its door, and quietly inserting a key from the key ring he carried into the door's lock, turned it. There had been no key in the inside lock. Ewan Hay was imprisoned until Lord Stewart said otherwise.

Then Busby went to the door of his mistress's chamber. He knocked, and being bid enter, he did, bowing to Maggie as he did. "Yer husband bids ye come down to the hall *immediately*," he said to her, struggling to keep from laughing at the look of outrage that suddenly suffused her face.

"Does he now?" Maggie responded, her tone angry. "Tell the bastard that I will come down when I choose to come down, and not a moment before. I am in no hurry to have a bigamous union blessed by that evil priest."

Grizel looked equally offended. "The nerve of that wretch to try to order my mistress about in such a scurvy fashion!" she declared.

"My lady," Busby said in a reasonable tone, for he was teetering on the edge of laughter, "do not lower yerself to his level, for ye know if ye do not come down, he will come huffing and puffing up the stairs to fetch ye. As much as we should all enjoy that, I suggest 'tis better to get this day over and done with as quickly as possible."

Maggie sighed a deep long sigh. "Aye," she said. "Yer right, Busby. I thank ye for yer sensible nature, for I am not happy this day at all." She turned about. "Grizel, get my cape, for I will need it in this rain."

"I'm relieved yer wearing that old black velvet gown," Grizel said. "If it gets wet, who will care. We can burn it tonight for I doubt ye'll want it again." She picked up a dark silk cloak and put it about Maggie's shoulders. "I suppose yer ready," she said.

"I am," Maggie agreed. "Have my orders been followed, Busby? No one is to come to the church to witness this travesty."

"Everyone is in their cottage, my lady," Busby assured her as they went from Maggie's bedchamber. As they neared the stairs, the majordomo heard a shout from the locked room.

"What was that?" Maggie asked him.

"The Hay is shouting for you from the hall," Busby said, and hurried them down the staircase. "He is surely an impatient man." He led her quickly to the great hall.

The hall was full of men, and suddenly Maggie recognized her own Kerr clansmen. They parted to make a path for her as she walked forward, and then she heard a familiar voice.

"Well, madam, ye certainly took yer time coming down to welcome me home," Fingal Stewart said. "Are ye not glad to see me?"

She stared. She grew pale. Then standing on trembling legs, Mad Maggie Kerr shouted at her husband, "Where the hell have ye been, Fingal Stewart? Have ye no idea of the misery and worry ye have put me through? The danger our bairns have been in? It's been almost a year, and not a word from ye!" And to her own horror and that of all about her, Maggie burst into tears. Seeing Mad Maggie weep was uncomfortable for all.

Fingal Stewart jumped forward, enfolding his wife in his embrace. "Ah, lass, 'tis good to see ye too. 'Tis a long story, and I promise to tell it to ye, but for now we have another matter to settle—that of yer betrothed husband." He kissed the top of her head. "What are we to do with Ewan Hay, Maggie mine?" Tipping her face up, he kissed her lips with tender passion. There would be time later to slake their longings.

She wept harder at the treasured and familiar endearment. The touch of his mouth on hers made her remember how much she loved this man. She tried to burrow into his chest. He let her weep until finally her tears eased, and she looked up at him, her eyelashes clumped into spikes, her eyes red. "Does Grandsire know yer home?" she asked.

"Not yet. I thought it better to greet ye first." He turned to Busby. "Go and fetch the laird, and tell him I'm home. I don't want to shock him."

Busby hurried off.

"Where is the Hay?" Maggie asked her husband.

"Busby has locked him in his chamber," Fin answered.

"Then that was the shouting I heard as we came downstairs. Busby said the Hay was shouting at me from the hall." A small watery giggle excaped her. "Can we leave him there forever, my lord?"

He laughed wickedly. Her suggestion had a certain merit to it. "I'm afraid we must return him to his brother if we are to keep the peace with Clan Hay," Fin said.

Maggie continued to snuggle in his arms. "He threatened our wee bairns, Fin. He locked our lads in the cellar without food or water, and but a single candle. He said he would not let them out until I wed him. But I got them away to Netherdale. Our daughter, however, is safe in the village. Then the cur put a knife to Grandsire, and he threatened to kill him if I did not sign his damnable wedding contract. I had no choice."

"The blessing today would have made it seem all was legal," Fin said quietly. "What did you mean to do tonight when he planned to bed you, Maggie mine?" He looked down into her face, which he now held between his two big hands. His gray eyes were serious and thoughtful.

"I prepared a strong sleeping draft for his wine," Maggie explained to her husband as she looked up at him. "Two or three sips and he would have been asleep. Then I was going to smother the life from him with a pillow. He would not have been able to fight me, and it would have appeared a natural death. Some might have been suspicious, but I intended shouting to all who would listen that it was God's judgment on Ewan Hay for marrying a woman whose husband still lived, for I never gave up hope, Fin, that ye were alive, and would come home to Brae Aisir, to me, to our bairns, one day. I told everyone that you were not dead, but they would not listen. Even Grandsire was beginning to lose hope. But I didn't!"

Dugald Kerr now came into the hall, going directly to Fin and shaking his hand. "Ye'll have an explanation for yer absence, I'm certain," he said. "But thank God ye've returned home, and just in time."

"I'll tell the tale later in the hall for all to hear," Fin promised the old laird. "For now we must deal with the impatient bridegroom who will be surprised to find his bride's husband has returned home even as she told him I would. Busby, release the Hay. Tell him naught but that Maggie is awaiting him in the hall."

"At once, my lord," the majordomo said with a small smile. Then he went off to unlock the door of the chamber where Ewan Hay was residing. He could hear the pounding and the shouting as he climbed the stairs. His smile grew wider as he reached the door and heard the rather colorful language the Hay was now using. Reaching for the keys, Busby found the correct one, fitted it into the lock, and then opened the door.

Ewan Hay jumped back startled, his hand going to his belt, but seeing Busby, he began to shout. "Who the hell locked me in here? Did no one hear me calling?"

"I believed the chamber empty," Busby lied. "I would have thought ye had moved yer possessions to the master's bedchamber by now. The lady is awaiting ye in the hall. I regret the weather is most foul today, sir."

"*My lord*, ye fool! Ye will address me in future as *my lord*," Ewan Hay said through gritted teeth. He pushed past Busby and descended the stairs. Shortly the marriage contract signed recently would be blessed by the priest, and then she would be his. She had wanted no celebration. He had seen the pouring rain from his own windows. Good! He would not wait until tonight. They would come back from Brae Aisir chapel, and he would take her to bed immediately. God only knew he had waited long enough to fuck her. But first he intended taking a thick hazel switch to her buttocks and whipping her until she begged him for mercy. He would curb her defiance immediately. In the next few hours he would teach her obedience to his will, and she would never disobey or challenge him ever again.

He had used the hazel switch to good effect on Flora Kerr so that she had ceased fighting him each time her came to her cottage. Instead, she went to her bed immediately, lay down, and pulled her skirts up so he might take his pleasure of her. He would miss that willingness to obey him, but he would choose another lass in the village to service him when his wife was with child, or when he grew bored with her. He had no desire to use the village whore his men-at-arms used. He wanted a mistress who served him only—a wench who could be taught to obey.

Ewan Hay was so caught up in his thought that it wasn't until he was gone several feet into the hall that he realized it was filled with men-at-arms. And they were not his men. Then at the end of the hall he saw Lord Stewart with the laird, and Maggie. "Yer dead!" his voice croaked. Then Ewan Hay turned to run, only to be stopped by a large hand that clamped onto his shoulder. He recognized the voice of Clennon Kerr, who growled in his ear menacingly.

"Ye canna go yet, sir. My lord wishes a word with ye." The captain half dragged the Hay the length of the hall to stand before the high board.

"I understand ye intended forcing my wife into a bigamous union,"

Fingal Stewart said. He stood, his big palms flat on the board's surface as he leaned forward to look down at Ewan Hay.

"*Yer dead!*" the man before him repeated, but his tone was less certain now.

"If I am, 'tis a ghost with whom ye speak, Hay," Fin said. The creature before him was contemptible. A coward, a bully, and worse, a fool. He slammed his hand down hard on the high board. "Do ye believe me to be a ghost, Hay?" The look of fear upon Ewan Hay's face caused Lord Stewart to wonder if the man would shame his name further by soiling himself.

"Nay! Nay! I don't think ye a ghost," Ewan Hay babbled. "But ye were dead! Few survived Solway Moss. There was no ransom demand. Ye had to be dead!" He was going to pee himself, he thought, struggling to gain a mastery of his emotions, his fear.

"So without waiting for some sort of confirmation of my fate, ye marched yerself to Brae Aisir and attempted to take over Dugald Kerr's keep and responsibilities," Lord Stewart said. "And ye tried to take my wife. I must tell ye that I value her far above the Aisir nam Breug, Hay. Had ye harmed Maggie, my bairns, or Dugald Kerr, ye would have faced being hanged at the crossroads for yer insolence."

"I thought ye were dead!" Ewan Hay cried out. "I'll fight ye now, Fingal Stewart!" They weren't going to kill him.

"*Fight ye?*" Fin laughed scornfully. "Yer a coward, Hay. I won't engage ye in battle. Instead, I'll send ye back to yer brother with my compliments, although I doubt he'll be particularly glad to see ye at this point."

"The other border lords wanted me here," Ewan said.

"They wanted a man younger than our laird, and they didn't trust my wife to do what needed to be done," Fin replied. "By tomorrow those nearest us will know I have returned, and they will spread the word farther abroad. They have no rights to decide anything with regard to Brae Aisir, or the Aisir nam Breug. Not one of them will protest against me. Now one of the servants will go into the courtyard, and call yer captain to ye. When he comes, ye will tell him to gather yer men, and ye will leave Brae Aisir immediately. Do ye understand me?" Fin stared hard at Ewan Hay.

The man nodded.

"I'll go, my lord," Busby said, and hurried out.

"Be careful of the fellow," the laird warned. "He's a dangerous sort, and no more to be trusted than this fool standing before us."

Bhaltair came into the hall, and seeing it filled with Kerr clansmen, stopped where he stood. "My lord?" He looked to Ewan Hay, puzzled.

"Gather yer men," the Hay said. "We are leaving Brae Aisir now."

"But, my lord, yer wedding?"

"The wedding has been called off," Fingal Stewart said. "The lady's lawful husband has returned to claim her, and to claim the keep. Will ye argue the point with me? Or will ye do as ye have been bid?"

Bhaltair looked at the tall man standing behind the high board. He recognized him as a hardened soldier, a man not to be trifled with, and Ewan Hay wasn't worth getting killed over. It had been a different thing when the pickings had seemed easy and simple, but not now. Completely ignoring Ewan Hay, Bhaltair bowed to Fingal Stewart, giving him a sardonic smile as he did so. "I will gather the men immediately, my lord," he said.

Lord Stewart nodded. "My men will help ye," he said. "Clennon Kerr, take those ye need and see the Hay men-at-arms are escorted from the keep. The Hay will join them as soon as they are all mounted." Fin knew as long as he held Ewan Hay in his custody,

Bhaltair and his men would cause no difficulty. If anything happened to Lord Hay's youngest brother, they would have to answer for it, and Lord Stewart's word would be taken long before theirs would.

Ewan Hay continued standing. No one invited him to sit. Finally he asked the question he had been dying to ask since he had entered the hall and found Lord Stewart and his men. "How the hell did ye get in here?"

"That shall remain my secret," Fin told him. "Possibly 'twas magic, or possibly God so disapproved of what ye were doing, he aided me."

"The drawbridge is up," Ewan Hay said. "I've always kept it up."

Fin laughed. "Afraid of yer neighbors? Or to keep me out?"

Ewan Hay flushed. "Ye were dead," he muttered.

"Nay, I was not," he said.

"Then why didn't ye return?" Ewan Hay wanted to know.

"That is a story ye'll not be here to hear when I tell it tonight," Lord Stewart said.

"If ye've come back without a ransom, then yer siding with the English, as many of the lords captured at Solway Moss are. King Henry sent them back with gold in their pockets, and instructions to influence French Mary to give our little queen to him for his son to marry one day. Yer a traitor!"

Fingal Stewart's stern face grew dark with his anger. "Do ye truly wish to die, Ewan Hay?" he asked the man. "I am no traitor. I have no English gold in my pocket. I am a Stewart, kin to our late King James."

"Ye think being the king's kinsman exempts ye from disloyalty? What of Angus and Arran and the others who have more often than not betrayed the royal Stewarts?"

"But my branch has never betrayed any Stewart king," Fin replied quietly. "*Ever faithful* is the motto of the Stewarts of Torra. And we have been. *And I am!* Should ye ever suggest again that I am not, I will kill ye where ye stand. Today I have returned home to Brae Aisir and retaken the keep without casualties. I am of a mind to be merciful, Ewan Hay, to ye and to yer men. But disparage my honor and my name again, and it is my sword that will pierce yer cowardly black heart!"

At that moment one of the Kerr men-at-arms returned to the hall. He bowed to Fingal Stewart. "The Hay men-at-arms and their captain are outside on the other side of the drawbridge, my lord. They but await the Hay to join them."

"Take him, and put him on his horse. Have Clennon Kerr bring him to the Hay captain." He turned to Ewan Hay. "Do not come back. My mercy is now at an end."

Ewan Hay said nothing further. He turned and followed the Kerr man-at-arms from the keep's hall. It was some time before Clennon Kerr returned to report that he and his men had escorted the Hays several miles beyond the village, putting them on the road that would take them back to Haydoun. He also reported that the rains had stopped and the sun was reappearing.

Dugald Kerr chortled. "God is smiling on Brae Aisir now that Fin is safe home. We must spread the word about this day. I'll dispatch messengers to our near neighbors. And ye must fetch my great-grandsons home. And wee Annabelle. Ye've not seen yer daughter yet, Fin. She is a bright and bonnie bairn, born the last day of March. She looks like Maggie looked when she was that age, but she has yer coloring."

"We'll fetch the bairns in a day or two," Fin said, looking at his wife. "I would like a few days with Maggie, Dugald."

The laird's eyes lit up, and then he chuckled. "Aye," he agreed. "I'll not argue ye on this, my son."

Maggie blushed at the look in her husband's eyes.

"Yer dressed in black," he said.

"Ye didn't expect me to celebrate a marriage to that coward, did ye?" she replied sharply. "I intended burning the garment afterwards."

"Would ye really have killed him?" Fin wanted to know.

"Aye, I would," Maggie said, her gaze steady. "I would harm my immortal soul by doing so, but rather that than have him touch me, or give me a child I should have had to tear from my womb. Ye are my husband, Fingal Stewart, and had ye indeed been killed at Solway Moss, it would have made no difference to me. I am yer wife. I would have never taken another again to wed."

He stood close to her, his hand caressing her face. How could he have ever forgotten her for even a moment? "I love ye, Maggie mine," he said, "and I promised ye I would be back." Their lips met again in a sweet kiss.

"And I knew ye would not break that promise to me. Not once did I believe, or even sense ye were no longer among the living, Fin. But it grew so difficult, and then no one would listen to me. Then the Hay arrived and took over the keep. The neighboring lairds began demanding that Grandsire marry me off to him. Father David refused, for he knew I was unwilling. So another priest, not so scrupulous, was found. It was so difficult, Fin, and I was beginning to grow weary, but never would I have given in to Ewan Hay."

"I know," he reassured her. "Yer Mad Maggie Kerr; not some frail creature all sighs and swoons."

"But what kept ye from us, Fin? Why did ye wait so long to return home?"

"Today is Midsummer's Eve," Fin said. "Let me tell my tale tonight as we all celebrate about the Midsummer fire. It is an amazing tale, Maggie mine."

Father David rushed into the hall. "Praise be to God!" he shouted, clapping Fingal Stewart upon his broad back. "Welcome home, lad! Welcome home!"

Fin burst out laughing. "Ye have no idea how great a part God played in this, good Father, but I'll be telling the tale tonight."

"Where is that toad of a Hay priest?" Maggie wanted to know.

"They took him with them when they rode through the village," Father David replied. "It was not a pleasant departure. The villagers threw the contents of their night jars on them as they went."

The laird and Fin burst out laughing, and even Maggie was forced to giggle.

"I hope most of it hit the Hay," she said.

"They did save the best for him, and for his priest," Father David admitted. "I must remember to preach a sermon on charity this Sabbath." But he was smiling as he said it, and a small chortle escaped him.

"Come," Maggie said, taking her husband's hand. "We must go into the village so they may see that ye are truly home again."

"I should rather take ye to bed," he whispered in her ear. "It has been close to a year since I've made love to ye, Maggie mine."

She blushed, then smiled at him. "Aye, but I think our pleasure must wait until nightfall, for there is much we must do that our clan folk feel settled and safe again. Only ye and I can do it, my husband."

"Change yer gown, for I would not go into the village with ye in that black crow's garment," he said.

"Ye must wait in the hall," she said with a small smile. "Grizel, come with me."

Maggie hurried from the great hall of the keep, and upstairs to her bedchamber. "What shall I wear for him?" she asked her tiring woman.

Grizel thought a moment. "Wear something simple. A skirt, a blouse, a bit of yer Kerr plaid. Tonight ye can wear the claret red velvet gown I made for ye last winter."

Maggie quickly donned a dark green skirt and a white shirt that laced up the front; then she drew her green Kerr plaid shawl about her shoulders. She had pulled off her stockings and boots. She wanted to be the Mad Maggie of old, bare legged, and barefoot. She loosened her hair from its plait and tucked a small dagger in her wide brown leather belt. "I'm ready," she said, running from the room and back down into the hall.

"I'm ready, Fingal Stewart. Are ye?" she called to him.

He turned from her grandfather, and saw the girl he had raced that day almost six years ago. He grinned. "Aye, Mad Maggie Kerr, I'm ready," he said as he came to join her. Then together they walked from the keep, across the bridge, and down into the village where their clan folk waited.

They came forth from their cottages, smiling and greeting Maggie and Lord Stewart warmly. Maggie stood back, letting her husband play the primary role. He greeted men and women by name. He asked oldsters about their health and aching joints, sympathizing with an understanding nod of his head. He teased the young girls, who giggled and blushed with his compliments. He joined in a game with the men and boys that involved kicking a stuffed sheep's bladder from one end of a field to another. The darkness had lifted with the exit of the Hay and the end of the storm.

It was traditionally the longest day of the year. Dugald Kerr came from the keep to join Maggie and Fin. The clan folk were relieved to see their old laird, for he had been virtually imprisoned in his keep for several months. Maggie left her men together and walked to the tollgate. A small party of merchants was preparing to exit. They were arguing with the gatekeeper. Maggie went to see what the difficulty was.

"I'm telling ye," the gatekeeper said, "ye paid yer toll when ye entered the Aisir nam Breug. Now if ye were entering here, and not exiting ye would pay a toll. But one toll is all ye pay for one trip."

"But," the man in charge of the merchant train said, "when we came up from England in April, we paid at both ends."

Maggie stepped forward. "It's all right, Allen, I'll handle this," she said to the gatekeeper. "Sir, unfortunately while the old laird of Brae Aisir was recovering from a winter illness, and my husband was away, a dishonest man was put in charge here. When it was found out that he was forcing tolls from travelers come up from the south, he was dismissed. Can ye recall what ye paid when ye last traveled through the pass?"

The merchant named the charge.

Maggie turned to the gatekeeper. "Allen, give the gentleman the amount he has named," she said. Then she spoke again to the merchant. "The Kerrs of Brae Aisir have held this pass with their English kin for centuries. We are honest folk. I am sorry ye were cheated. Here is yer toll returned to ye. It will not happen again. And when ye return south this time, yer trip will be free."

"Thank ye, good lady," the merchant said. "We could not bring our goods to Edinburgh and Perth were it not for this safe traverse. I should not want it said that I spoke treasonably, but King Henry is not a happy man right now."

Maggie laughed. "I know," she said with a small smile, "but somehow we shall all survive these monarchs and their quarrels, eh?"

The merchant nodded, and then, signaling, he was on his way again.

Maggie turned to her gatekeeper. "Refund any tolls charged when they should not have been," she said. "Why didn't ye come to me, Allen?"

"The Hay removed me from my position," Allen answered her. "He replaced me with one of his own men. Since no one from the village could come or go into the keep held by the Hays, I had no way of speaking with ye, my lady."

"How long did this go on?" Maggie wanted to know.

"Since the pass opened again this spring," Allen told her.

Maggie walked back through the village and up the hill into the keep to find her Fingal and her grandsire. She told them what Allen had told her, what the merchant party had told her, and what Rafe Kerr, her cousin, had said when she had seen him recently.

"'Twas a quick and good thought," Dugald Kerr said, "to refund that traveler his coin, lass. Hay would have destroyed our reputation had he been allowed to continue. It will now be known that the Kerrs are once more in charge."

"Stewart-Kerrs," Fin said quietly.

"It pleases me ye would add yer proud name to ours," Dugald Kerr said, smiling.

"With yer approval, of course," Fin told the old man. "The Kerr name should remain connected to the Aisir nam Breug."

Maggie's eyes grew moist. As proud as she was of her family's name, she knew that Fin was equally proud of his family's name, and his descent from a king of Scotland.

It was a generous gesture he was making. "Thank ye!" she told him.

"In the months that I was away from ye," Fin told her, "all I wanted to do was get home, Maggie mine. I own a house in Edinburgh where I was born and raised, 'tis true, but Brae Aisir has been the only real home I've ever had. That is thanks to ye, and to ye, Dugald Kerr. I have always felt welcome here."

"Hush now, laddie," the old laird said, wiping a tear from his own eyes. "Of course ye were welcome from the moment ye arrived. Did I not see a husband for my lass in ye when ye came to me with yer command from the king to wed Maggie?" He chuckled. "I knew ye were the one, and ye were."

"I could have outfought him if ye had not given the match to him just because I fell," Maggie teased her grandfather.

"Ye were on both knees and could hardly draw a breath," Dugald

Kerr said dryly, his brown eyes twinkling. He had always been proud of Maggie's fine spirit. "And Fingal was too much of a gentleman to want to blood ye. Of course I called the match. He was worthy of ye when none of the others had been, including that cur Hay."

They all laughed. It had been just a few short years ago and so much had happened since then. Scotland was never as secure as when it had a king on the throne.

"But what kept ye away from us, lad?" the laird asked as he had earlier.

"Tonight," Fin promised once again. "I will tell my tale about the Midsummer fire for all our clan folk to hear."

Maggie left her men folk to go to the kitchen now, and see if there was still time to set out a small feast for the villagers this night. The cook, however, now that the Hay had been driven from the keep, had taken it upon herself to bake enough fresh bread for all. She had sliced cold meats, arranging them upon platters. She had geese and capons roasting upon several spits in her huge hearth. There were several baskets of strawberries, and tiny crisp sweet wafers. Seeing it all, Maggie laughed.

"Did ye at least wait until he was marched away?" she asked the cook.

"I began the moment our clansmen went up the stairs to the hall," the cook replied. "With the young lord leading them, I knew the Hay would be either hanged or driven off within a very short time. I would have hanged him myself from the chimney in Flora Kerr's cottage."

"Grandsire did not wish to begin a feud with Lord Hay," Maggie said, "but if it had been up to me, I would have hanged him too! I doubt Lord Hay will be pleased to see his brother back."

"From the first time he came to Brae Aisir, the Hay lusted after ye, my lady. He'll not cease wanting to have ye, or wanting Brae Aisir's riches until he's dead. Mark my words, my lady. The Hay will cause us trouble once again. Ye'll eventually have no choice but to kill him."

Maggie had an uncomfortable feeling the cook was right. As long as Ewan Hay lived, he would seek to take what wasn't his. "Have the men put everything out on the trestles when they're finally set up outside of the keep. And tomorrow fetch back the lasses who were yer helpers from the village," Maggie told her.

"I will, my lady, and be glad to see them. Lads in a kitchen are not to be borne," the cook declared, "and they've been little help to me."

"Don't forget to come up from yer kitchens and join the rest of the clan folk when all is set out," Maggie reminded her.

The cook bobbed a curtsy. "I will, my lady."

Chapter 18

ᴄᴏ

The trestles from the hall and their benches had been brought out and set up on a level piece of land on the far side of the drawbridge. The food was brought forth, and the clan folk from the village came to celebrate the Midsummer holiday, and especially the departure of the Hay and his men. Throughout the late afternoon, men, women, and children had gathered wood for the great fire that would finally be lit at the moment of the sunset. Both men and women brought good-size pieces of wood, and the pyre grew and grew. The little ones found sticks and bits that they added, dashing up to the great pile to fling them on it with shouts of glee.

To the west, the skies finally began to glow with the coming sunset. A wash of orange was streaked with crimson and edged in gold. Small dark purple and pale pink clouds seemed almost stationary in the pale blue sky, its edges trimmed in palest green. The sun sank lower and lower. Torches were lit, and everyone stood poised for the blazing orb to sink behind the now-dark hills. No one spoke. They were surrounded by silence.

Then the old laird of Brae Aisir stepped forward and thrust his torch into the great pile of wood. Maggie and Fin followed. On all sides of the pyre, torches were thrust into the wood. The Midsummer fire caught. It blazed high into the night, and the clan folk cheered.

Finally, when the fire was burning well, the laird called for silence, inviting his guests to seat themselves on the benches.

"My grandson will now tell his tale of Solway Moss, and why it took him so long to return to us." Dugald Kerr sat down next to his granddaughter.

Fin stood upon one of the trestles in their midst so he might be seen. His deep, almost musical voice carried to all the tables. He told them of the battle, and how because a spy among the Scots had warned the English, the attack, which should have been successful, turned into a rout. He told them of how many of the king's lords would not fight for James V. Too many of them remembered Flodden when so many of Scotland's first families had lost all of their adult males.

"Many of these lords embrace the new Protestant faith," Fin explained. "They felt the king went into England for the pope's sake, not Scotland's."

There were some small murmurings among the trestles, but Maggie didn't know if they were in ageement with the king or those who espoused the new faith. Times were changing in Scotland, and men preaching the new religion had come through the Aisir nam Breug ready to lead Scotland away from the Catholicism of its ancestors. While there were some things about the church that chafed at Maggie, she wasn't certain she was quite willing to give up one faith for another. God was God, and Jesu, Jesu.

Fin continued telling them of the battle. He explained that when he had seen how things were going, and that there was no hope of the Scots' prevailing, he had sent his own men away. "I remained for the sake of my kinsman, King James, may God assoil his soul. I fought on until I was injured." He explained to all his fascinated listeners that the blow to his head had taken his memory from him, a condition worsened when he was struck a second time after having awakened to find scavengers stealing his boots, among other things.

He told them how he recalled nothing else until he found himself upon a stretcher, and an old woman shrieking for all who could hear that he was her son, Bobby. "Finally the officer in charge had them carry me to her cottage," Fin said. "I suppose they thought I would die, so they let the old woman deal with it if she wanted me."

Lord Stewart continued on with his tale. He told his listeners that while he could dredge up no memory of who he was, or where he had come from, he knew for certain he was not the old woman's son, Bobby. But Old Mother—he never learned her Christian name—nursed him back to health over the next few weeks. The winter had now set in, and because he had no idea of who he was or where he belonged, he remained with her. Then his memory began returning in small bits and pieces. He dreamed of a man named Iver, and then of one called Archie.

"I had no idea who they were," Fin told his wide-eyed audience, "but I realized I must find them. But then Old Mother grew ill. I remained to nurse her, and I buried her when she finally died." At that point, he explained, she realized that he was not her son. Her son had gone off to war almost thirty years prior and died at Flodden among the English dead. More of his memory returned. He knew he owned a house in Edinburgh, and he realized he had to get there if he was to unravel the mystery of who he was.

"It was there I found him standing before the door of his house," Archie broke in.

"Aye, he did," Fin said. "And thanks to being with my old friend and retainer, the rest of my memory was restored over the next few days. When I finally remembered, Archie told me of the troubles here at Brae Aisir with the Hay. We rode for the Borders, arriving in the village a few days ago and driving the Hays from the keep. That is the tale of why it took me so long to return home and why no ransom demand came for me."

"Ye didn't remember *me?*" Maggie was glaring at her husband, and a ripple of laughter arose from the clan folk around them.

"To my discredit, Maggie mine, I did not," Fin admitted candidly.

She threw her silver goblet at him, but he ducked, avoiding another injury to his head. The clan folk roared with laughter as Fin leaped from the trestle, grabbing his wife, whom he turned over his knee. He smacked her bottom twice, then tipped her back onto her feet and kissed her long and passionately.

"Yer a fool, Fingal Stewart!" Maggie shouted at him, breaking away from his embrace and dashing off into the darkness.

He followed after her shouting, "Come back here, ye damned border vixen!"

Dugald Kerr smiled, watching them go. He wondered if they would return to the keep tonight or settle their silly differences in the heather. He drained his own goblet down; then turning to Clennon, Kerr said, "Take me in, man. The night air, for all 'tis summer, is making my old bones ache. I need my hearth."

Fingal Stewart found his wife quickly, for she made no effort to hide as she crashed down the hillside in her temper. Catching up with her, he pulled her into his arms again. "If I promise never to forget ye again, will ye forgive me?" he asked, and he kissed her on the very tip of her nose.

Maggie didn't struggle. Her outrage was gone as common sense had set in. Still, she would not allow him to believe he could wheedle her so easily. His arms felt wonderful about her—making her all warm and safe. "Yer a great fool," she repeated. "How does a man forget a woman he says he loves? Have ye stopped loving me?"

"Nay, I love ye now more than I ever have, for I could have lost ye,

Maggie mine. Had my memory not been restored to me, I would not have known where to come home," he told her. He looked down into her face. "I loved ye yesterday. I love ye today. I'll love ye tomorrow and forever," he promised her. "I always knew something was missing," he told her. "There was always something I was struggling to recall."

"No more wars!" Maggie said sternly.

"No more wars," Fin promised her. "James Stewart is dead, and my first loyalty is now to ye, to our bairns, to Brae Aisir. I'll fight only in defense of these lands. The French queen knows little of me. She has a coterie of great lords squabbling to rule for her daughter. Marie de Guise is a strong woman. She'll struggle with every bit of her being to see that the little queen is safe. Remember her powerful kin in France, her brothers, François, the duke de Guise, and Charles, the cardinal of Lorraine. And for all the reformers, Scotland is still a Catholic land. Our biggest worry must be the English king, for I heard in Edinburgh that he wants our little queen as a bride to his son and heir, Prince Edward. Many favor such a match."

"I don't want to talk politics tonight," Maggie said boldly.

"Ye don't?" he teased her softly.

"Let's go home, my lord," she invited him.

"Ye wouldn't rather remain outside tonight?" he asked her.

"Nay," Maggie replied. "While this should not be a night for raiders for the moon is dark, and most celebrate this night, I shouldn't like to be caught outside my walls if someone decided to come calling uninvited."

"Yer a practical woman," he chuckled.

"Ye'll like my bed better than a rocky hillside," she promised him, taking his hand to lead him back up the hill. The Midsummer fire still blazed, but the trestles and benches were even now being carried back into the house as they walked slowly together across the draw-bridge. The laird was nowhere to be seen.

"Let me make certain he is settled," Maggie said as they climbed the stairs together. "Then I'll come to ye." Giving him a quick kiss, she turned to the door to Dugald Kerr's bedchamber.

But Fingal Stewart reached out to draw his wife back to his side. "Listen," he said softly. "I believe yer grandsire is well settled, Maggie mine."

She listened, and then blushed furiously. From her grandfather's bedchamber came several easily identifiable sounds; the bed ropes creaking rhymically, the happy giggles of a woman, and the satisfied grunts of the man laboring over a woman. "God's toenail!" Maggie whispered. "He has a woman in there with him." Then she chuckled. "The next time he pretends to be frail to gain his way with me, I shall remember this."

"He's setting us a proper example," Fin murmured in her ear as he drew her into her bedchamber. Shutting the door, he backed her up against it, his big body pressing into hers, his mouth seeking and finding her lips. His hands came up to undo the laces of her shirt, pushing it back over her shoulders. His fingers tore at the fabric of her chemise as he kissed her over and over until his own head was spinning with the sweetness she was returning. His hand clasped about her waist, lifting her up so his mouth might clamp about the nipple of a breast. He groaned as his nose pressed against the silken flesh.

His lips! Holy Mother Mary, she had missed his lips! His mouth was big, but his lips were long and shapely. They knew how to give a woman pleasure so sweet that she would not care if death overtook her at that exact moment as long as his lips remained on hers. She gave herself over to his foraging mouth, kissing him back again and again until she was dizzy with the sweetness herself. When he had lifted her up to take her nipple in his mouth, Maggie gave a distinct cry of pleasure.

"Oh God," she gasped, "I've missed ye so, Fingal Stewart!"

He suckled on the nipple but a moment before setting her back on her feet. Maggie's legs felt like jelly, but she managed to retain her balance by clutching at him. As if guided by another, she tore at his shirt, ripping it open and licking at his flesh with long strokes of her wet tongue. His fingers found the tie holding her skirt up. He pulled it open so that the skirt fell to the floor. Her fingers found the buttons to his breeks, and undid them, pushing them off and over his hips. He ripped the remainder of her chemise away. She reached for his cock, finding it engorged and ready for play.

"*Here!*" he said, his hands beneath her buttocks as he lifted her up.

"*Now!*" she acquiesced, her hands guiding him.

He thrust hard, groaning as the heated silken walls of her sheath swallowed him whole. How long had it been? He struggled to control his unfettered lust.

She wrapped herself about him, legs around his torso, arms encircling his neck. "Oh Fingal!" she breathed hotly into his ear as his thick length filled her. She hadn't realized until now how much she had missed this passion between them.

He began to move upon her, driving back and forth into her, but despite his great need, he found he wanted more and more of her. Holding her tightly in his arms, he turned and walked across the chamber to lay her upon the bed. Her legs fell away from him as he set her down, but reaching for those legs, he drew them up and over his shoulders. Then standing over her, he began to piston her once more with long deep strokes of his cock over and over and over again until they were both almost unconscious. Maggie screamed softly as each delicious thrust brought her closer and closer to perfection. Fin groaned at the incredible sweetness the possession of her body gave him. Finally he could contain himself no longer. His juices burst forth, sending them into a paroxysm of ecstasy that left them totally exhausted as incredible pleasure flowed through them.

Withdrawing from her, Fin fell facedown onto the bed, where he lay for some minutes. Finally turning over, he gathered her into his arms, breathing slowly, his face in her scented hair. He felt her hands caressing him gently. Together they fell into a contented sleep. When they awoke shortly before the early dawn, they were still where they had fallen earlier, and chilled by the night air. They crawled beneath the coverlet, Fin drawing Maggie against him, his hand clasping one of her plump breasts, her bottom pressed into his groin.

He awoke upon his back with the sun up and shining into the bedchamber to find his wife straddling him, playing with his upstanding cock. Maggie smiled wickedly down into his face; then without a word she raised herself up to sheath him. "I have always enjoyed a brisk ride in the early morning," she said mischievously.

He grinned back, reaching up to take her two breasts into his hands so he might fondle them. "How alike we are, Maggie mine," he said.

"Yer content to be my stallion?" she asked, jogging just slightly.

"I expect to see ye ride me at a full gallop, madam," he told her.

"Gladly, my lord," Maggie said.

Then she rode him hard until he rewarded her with his tribute, but not before turning her over onto her back, reversing their positions, and galloping her all the way home. They fell away from each other, gasping, and laughing.

"Oh, Maggie mine, how I love ye, lass!" he told her.

"And I love ye also, Fingal Stewart." Then she grew serious. "Ye'll keep yer promise to me? No more wars?"

"No more wars, love. I will only take up my sword in defense of Brae Aisir and what is our own," he promised her. Then he sealed his promise with a deep kiss.

Maggie could have let him go on kissing her, but she didn't. "We have to get up," she said to him. "There is much for us to do today.

I want to send a message to Netherdale that we are coming to fetch the bairns."

"Aye, we'll go tomorrow," he agreed as he climbed from their bed. "I'm a selfish man, and I want one more day with just ye alone, wife."

"Now that ye have yer memory back," she teased him.

"Will ye never let me forget my sins, madam?" he asked, smiling.

"Nay, never!" she told him, and then Maggie laughed aloud.

Two perfect summer days in a row were a gift. Fingal Stewart and Maggie rode out after their morning meal with a party of their men-at-arms to explore their lands, making certain that the Hay was gone from them and that all was as it should be. They were relieved to find no trace of Ewan Hay, but disturbed to discover that a flock of sheep in the summer meadows had disappeared. At first there was no sign of the shepherds or the dogs, but then they found them in a wooded copse. Men and dogs had been slain.

The clansmen gathered up their kinsmen, returning to the village so the shepherds might be buried properly and mourned. The canines were buried where they had fallen.

Maggie shook her head. "I did not think raiders would strike on Midsummer, and without a bright border moon."

"They were probably killed at dawn or close to it," Fin said. "Neither dogs nor men were quite cold yet."

"Our location has usually kept us safe," Maggie said sadly.

"We need to get our bairns home," Fingal Stewart said.

"I dispatched the messenger," Maggie told her husband. "We go tomorrow."

They departed before the sun was even up the next day, but the coming day was already bright. They had not yet reached the border when they saw Rafe Kerr riding towards them with a man-at-arms. Each man carried a boy before him on his saddle. The two lads waved and called out to their parents.

"Rafe!" Maggie waved a welcome. "Ah, how good ye are, Cousin. Ye didn't have to bring the boys. We were happy to come and fetch them."

"'Twas better I brought them, and quickly," Rafe Kerr told her. "Da was of a mind not to let them go. Aldis took him off to calm him. He grows stranger as each day passes, Maggie. This obsession to control the whole of the Aisir nam Breug is a sickness with him, and it grows stronger. I'll do my best to keep him under control, but beware." He held out his hand to Fin. "I'm glad to see ye returned safely."

"He lost his memory for a time," Maggie told her cousin. "Imagine forgetting me! I am not certain I can forgive such an oversight."

Rafe Kerr laughed. "Aye, Cousin, I can't imagine such a thing." He winked at Fingal Stewart. "I hope ye've chastised him properly for it." He lifted David Stewart from the front of his saddle and handed him to his father as the man-at-arms passed Andrew to Maggie.

"Ye came home, Da! That poxy Hay said ye were dead, but Mama said nay," Davy Stewart told his father. "Our mama never lies," Davy confided to his companions.

"Did ye kill the Hay?" Andrew asked.

"Nay, lads, we sent him back to his brother," Fin told his boys.

Davy and Andrew looked disappointed.

"Yer da was very brave and captured the keep right out from under the nose of the Hay," Maggie said. "When we get home, I'll tell ye all about it," she promised. She looked to her cousin again. "Thank ye, Rafe."

He nodded.

"We were raided last night in the far summer meadows," Fin told Rafe. "Two shepherds and their dogs were killed, and a flock of sheep stolen. There will be more raids back and forth, I'm certain. Keep a watch."

"The sheep can be replaced," Rafe said, "but the men and dogs can't." He shook his head. "It's going to get bad. The travelers are falling off, which is always a warning sign of trouble. The gossip I'm garnering says that King Henry will have your little Queen Mary for his son, Prince Edward. He'll not take no for an answer either."

"French Mary, I suspect, plans a French marriage for her daughter. The French king's heir is available. She will hold to the auld alliance, Rafe."

"God help us all here on both sides of the borders," Rafe Kerr said.

They parted, Maggie and Fin taking their sons home again. Their daughter had been brought up from the village by her new wet nurse while they had been gone. Annabelle Stewart was now almost three months old, and Fin was enchanted with this petite black-haired replica of his wife. The news Rafe had passed on to them troubled him. As he held the tiny girl in his arms, he felt more strongly than ever the great responsibility that Brae Aisir was. He couldn't fail his family, his clan folk, or the laird.

The news as the summer progressed grew worse. The peace treaty that had been drawn up between England and Scotland lingered, waiting to be signed. A second treaty that would send little Queen Mary to England as Prince Edward's bride when she was ten, and he fifteen, also waited for signatures. But Henry Tudor's arrogance was badly eroding the pro-English faction in Scotland. Any child produced by a marriage between Mary and Edward would inherit Scotland's throne. The English king was not treating Scotland as an equal, but rather as a vassal state.

Cardinal Beaton, released from confinement, welcomed back from voluntary exile in France the abbot of Paisley, who was the Earl of Arran's bastard half brother, along with the Earl of Lennox. The pro-French faction grew stronger with the return of these two men. Feeling more secure than she had in months, the Queen Mother removed her infant daughter from Linlithgow to the better-fortified Stirling Castle protected as they traveled by twenty-five hundred horsemen and a thousand men-at-arms on foot.

On the ninth of September 1543, little baby Mary, seated upon her mother's lap, was officially crowned queen of Scotland.

The year came to a close, and the English parliament had not ratified the peace treaty between the two countries. Nor had they confirmed the marriage agreement that would unite the two countries. It was at this point the Scots, directed by Cardinal Beaton and the Queen Mother, suggested that the queen, now a year old, be wed to the twenty-six-year-old Earl of Lennox, who now stood second in line to the throne behind the Earl of Arran.

At Brae Aisir, other than a few more raids that summer that were beaten off, the countryside was quiet as it waited for Henry Tudor to retaliate. The Earl of Arran, the little queen's heir, was not pleased at the thought of the Earl of Lennox marrying her. Nothing, however, came of the suggestion. The Borders lay waiting for what would come next in this drama between their rulers.

The autumn and the winter came. Annabelle Stewart was toddling all over the keep after her brothers. Both Davy and Andrew could now ride by themselves. Fin was surprised to one day come upon his wife teaching their sons the rudimentary uses of a sword. The boys had been outfitted with wooden swords just their size. He watched fascinated as they parried and thrust.

Seeing him watching them Maggie called out, "Ye'll soon have them to teach yerself. I thought it was time they started learning. After all, they don't live in Edinburgh." And she grinned at him.

"Tell me when ye think they're ready for me," Fin said.

"Watch me, Da!" Davy called, waving his wooden sword.

"Nay, watch me!" Andrew cried.

"I'll watch ye both," Fin told them, and he did.

Spring returned again and with it began Henry Tudor's *rough wooing* of Scotland's queen. Prince Edward's uncle, Edward Seymour, the Earl of Hertford, came into Scotland with sixteen thousand soldiers, landing his men on the beaches of the Firth of Forth. A second English army even larger than Seymour's crossed over the River Tweed, advancing forward and destroying everything in its path.

Newly planted fields just showing green growth were trampled over. Livestock was wantonly slaughtered or taken to feed the two vast armies. Farms and villages were burned to the ground, their inhabitants—men, women, children, the aged—murdered. The women as usual suffered the worst for the unfettered rape that was permitted by the English commanders.

Nothing in the path of the English invaders was spared, including the church. Along the border were some of Scotland's greatest abbeys—Kelso, Dryburgh, Melrose, and Jedburgh. All were sacked and then burned to the ground; the monks slaughtered without mercy. Edinburgh's port of Leith was in ruins. Edinburgh was attacked, and part of the city burned for two days. The castle itself could not be taken, but the English sacked both Holyrood Abbey and its adjoining palace.

Marie de Guise quickly had the little queen moved from Stirling north into Perthshire. They took up residence in Dunkeld Castle. The English who had been advancing on Stirling stopped upon learning their quarry had escaped them. They returned to England, leaving the southeast of Scotland in shock, mourning, and ruins.

Word of this tragedy was slow to reach Brae Aisir, but the lack of traffic both ways through the pass told them that something was very wrong. Fin doubled the watch and kept the cattle and sheep nearer to the keep as the summer progressed. Not until late July when a member of the Kira banking family came from Edinburgh to go south to England did they learn the extent of what had happened.

They were not located on the south side of the city, which had suffered the most damage, he told them. "Thank God for the Aisir nam Breug," he said, "for I need to get to London to inform our family there of what has happened here. We must remain open for our clients, of course, but it is dangerous now, and likely to become more dangerous."

"It's begun, and God help us all now," Fingal Stewart said. "We may not escape the ravages of the war that is not really a war. I will have to keep the drawbridge up now as the Hay did. It's becoming too dangerous to leave it down."

"No one has attacked us," Maggie said.

"There is war all around us, Maggie mine," he told her. "We cannot wait for an attack to come, but we must be ready when it does, for it surely will."

And for the first time in her life Maggie Kerr was afraid. But she was not fearful for herself; she was fearful for her two sons, her daughter, and the new bairn she suspected she was carrying. If Master Kira was to be believed, the English had spared no one, even the littlest of children. The thought of their coming to Brae Aisir sent an icy shiver through her. She went to the keep's little armory, and taking down her claymore, she began to carefully hone its dulled blade to a fine sharp edge. If the English came to Brae Aisir, Mad Maggie Kerr would be more than ready.

Chapter 19

c᷍ᗡ

$\mathscr{E}$ wan Hay had returned home to find the older of his two
brothers not particularly welcoming.

"Ye had yer chance," Lord Hay told him. "'Tis over
now."

"Her husband returned," Ewan whined. "What the hell was I supposed to do?"

"Aye, her husband came back, but ye were outmaneuvered. I'll wager ye still haven't figured out how he got into the keep. There was probably some secret entry, but ye made no effort to befriend the Kerrs. Instead, ye walled yerself up with yer own men and gained no allies," his older brother said. "Yer a fool, but then I always knew it. There's nothing for ye here at Haydoun."

"Where am I supposed to go?" Ewan demanded. Curse Mad Maggie Kerr and her husband. They had brought him to this ruin. He'd have his revenge on them somehow.

"Go to England," Lord Hay advised.

"*What?*" Ewan Hay was astounded by his brother's words. "Why would I go to England?" he demanded to know.

"For the coin they will put in yer purse, of course, ye donkey," Lord Hay told him. "King Henry is determined to have our queen for his son. There is a strong pro-English faction here in Scotland. They are being paid in hard coin to support this marriage."

"And how would ye know this, Brother?"

Lord Hay smiled archly. "Ye could become one of what the English call *assured Scots*, Ewan. Seek out the Earl of Hertford, and tell him yer my brother. That I sent ye to him. Ye'll be welcome, and I'm certain yer firsthand knowledge of the Aisir nam Breug will be a great interest to him."

"Can I take Bhaltair, and my men?" Ewan asked his brother.

Lord Hay shrugged. "If ye can pay them, they're yers," he agreed.

And so Ewan Hay had taken his captain along with their men-at-arms and gone over the border into England where he found he was indeed welcomed by the English. He took part ravaging the Borders in that terrible summer. He did not, however, reveal his knowledge of the Aisir nam Breug right away, gaining a reputation as a ruthless fighter and a reliable ally instead. There would come a time when his information would garner him more than just gold. And he would have his revenge on the Kerrs of Brae Aisir. He was learning to cultivate patience.

And Ewan Hay was in good company. Matthew Stewart, the Earl of Lennox, second in line for Scotland's throne, defected to England, pledging his allegiance to King Henry. He also turned over Dumbarton Castle and the Isle of Bute for English bases. The king made him his lieutenant for the whole of northern England and for southern Scotland. And then the handsome twenty-seven-year-old earl was married to Henry's niece, Lady Margaret Douglas, daughter of Henry's late sister, Margaret Tudor, by her second husband, Archibald Douglas, the Earl of Angus.

This betrayal, however, but strengthened the Queen Mother's position. The common folk praised her desperate defense of Scotland in the name of their little queen.

Her closest adviser, Cardinal Beaton, was blamed for the terrible destruction of the southeast. They threw stones at him when he rode past in the streets. The common folk didn't know that the cardinal was a great diplomat. They only knew he lived like a king, had several mistresses, and had fathered more than twenty children. Scotland had burned while the cardinal had feasted with his noble whores. And the English kept badgering the Borders, keeping the Scots busy defending themselves while King Henry waged war with France, whose Scots allies were unable to aid them.

An invasion was being considered into the southwest of Scotland. Ewan Hay at last saw the opening he had been awaiting. His reputation allowed him an audience with the Earl of Lennox. Matthew Stewart was a tall, handsome man whose wife had just given birth to their first child, a boy they named Henry in honor of her uncle. He waved Ewan Hay into his presence with an impatient hand from the chair where he was sitting.

"I am told ye would speak with me," the earl said.

"I am told yer considering an invasion of the southwest," Ewan replied boldly. "I may have some information that could be of use to ye, my lord."

Lennox did not invite Ewan Hay to sit down. "Speak," the earl instructed him.

"Do ye know of the Aisir nam Breug, my lord?" Ewan asked.

"I do not," the earl responded.

"It is a narrow pass going through the border hills that has been controlled by the same family for centuries. The Kerrs of Netherdale control the section of the traverse that runs through England. The Kerrs of Brae Aisir manage the portion that is in Scotland. It is tradition that the road is used only for peaceful purposes, families, messengers, merchant trains. Neither side has ever deviated from this unspoken rule."

"Are ye suggesting that we take our army through this pass, Hay?" the earl asked.

"Nay, my lord, for it it too narrow," Ewan said.

"Then what is the point of yer tale, Hay?" Matthew Stewart asked impatiently.

"If ye would allow me and my men to take the Aisir nam Breug, and its keep at Brae Aisir, the pass can be used as a safe and swift passage for yer messengers in and out of Scotland. As for the Netherdale Kerrs, Lord Edmund has always wanted to control the entire traverse himself. Promise it to him as a reward when King Henry has Scotland beneath his boot. I know Lord Edmund, and I can get him to cooperate with ye."

"And in exchange for this ye will want?" The earl was no fool. Anyone who brought him information like this wanted something substantial in exchange.

"The keep at Brae Aisir," Ewan Hay said.

"Whose is it now?" the earl asked.

"Dugald Kerr is the laird of Brae Aisir. He has a granddaughter who is his heiress, and she has a husband and several bairns. The husband is loyal to the Queen Mother, and to the little queen."

"You would drive them out of their home?" The Earl of Lennox wondered what the real purpose of Ewan Hay's offer was, but then he decided he didn't care. He was planning a campaign into Aye and Renfrew eventually. A safe passage for messengers through the Borders would be a great advantage to him.

"I would hold the keep for ye, my lord," Ewan Hay said.

Matthew Stewart laughed sardonically. "Ye have my permission then to forge an understanding with this Lord Edmund Kerr first; and then take the keep at Brae Aisir for me. Since its inhabitants have an unwavering loyalty to their child queen, do what ye will with them. I don't care. Just make the keep and this passage secure for me."

Ewan Hay bowed to the earl. "Ye have my word on it, my lord," he said as he backed from the earl's presence. Hurrying to find Bhaltair, he told him that the Earl of Lennox had chosen them for this assignment. "Gather the men! We ride for Netherdale on the morrow."

Bhaltair grunted in acknowledgment of Ewan's words. Then he said, "We had best find out the secret of how Fingal Stewart got into the keep without coming across the drawbridge. Then we can use that same route. Ye'll not take the keep by riding into it."

"How are we supposed to learn *that?*" Ewan said irritably. Why was Bhaltair always trying to spoil his plans?

"We could take one of the tower men and torture him until he revealed the secret," Bhaltair said. "The men in the village obviously knew."

"Aye," Ewan Hay said. "Yer right." Now why hadn't he thought of that? "But I'll have to convince Edmund Kerr into cooperating with me first."

"Ye'll lie to him, of course," Bhaltair replied. "Will ye promise him Brae Aisir?"

"Nay, but I'll promise him all the income from the pass. I must hold the keep at Brae Aisir for the earl," Ewan Hay answered.

Bhaltair laughed cynically. "Ye'll be holding the keep for King Henry," he said bluntly, "but I know 'tis because like so many other good Scots, ye believe a marriage between the little queen and King Henry's heir is a good and godly thing."

"One day yer careless talk will get ye killed," Ewan Hay said irritably.

"I'll gather the men and have them ready to ride tomorrow," Bhaltair replied, ignoring his master's remark. Aye, he'd die one day, but not at Ewan Hay's hand.

Ewan Hay had managed to retain twenty of the original thirty men his elder brother had given him. A man possessing twenty soldiers and a captain was considered valuable. It took several days for the Hay and his men to reach Netherdale Hall. They rode in on a rainy night, glad to have reached a warm hall. Edmund Kerr was suspicious. He knew what had happened at Brae Aisir the previous year.

"What do ye want?" he demanded of his guest, waving him to a place at the high board. He gazed at the Hay's men as they seated themselves at the trestles below the salt. A quick glance told him they were fewer than they had been. Lord Edmund nodded to a servant to fill his guest's goblet with ale and place a trencher of rabbit stew before him.

"I come from the Earl of Lennox," the Hay began.

"Indeed, and what does that Scot want with me?" Edmund Kerr's tone was not particularly friendly, but he was curious.

"King Henry's nephew by marriage has a proposition for ye, my lord," Ewan Hay said in a bland and polite tone. "One that will serve us all."

Rafe Kerr sat at his father's right hand, listening silently. Whatever it was that the Hay had to say, it did not bode well for the Kerrs on either side of the border, he was sure.

"Say on, Hay," Lord Edmund responded, and his eyes narrowed as he sat back in his chair.

"The Earl of Lennox would like me to take the keep at Brae Aisir for him. I will then remain to govern the keep in his name. In exchange, ye will be allowed to collect all of the tolls," the Hay said.

"Except for those ye steal at the other end," Lord Edmund replied.

"Nay, only ye will collect the tolls. My function is to provide the earl with a safe passage for his messengers, and a secure refuge in the Borders for his allies in Scotland whenever they need to meet."

"How long will he want Brae Aisir?" Lord Edmund sought to know. "This warring will end sooner or later. Some of the high and mighty will forgive one another, or will be forgiven by the Queen Mother, who is grateful for allies, and some will return home. Others will exile themselves into England even as Angus did. Those ordinary men among us on both sides of the border will be left to gather up what remains of our former lives. We will be judged by our associations, Hay."

"King Henry will be very grateful for yer aid," Ewan Hay said.

"King Henry wouldn't know me from a wart on his bottom," Lord Edmund said pithily, causing Rafe to smile. "He knows naught of me or mine."

"But the Earl of Lennox does, and this earl has King Henry's ear, my lord," the Hay reminded his host. "Ye could find yerself created Baron Kerr."

Edmund Kerr laughed aloud. "An empty title costing the parsimonious Henry Tudor nothing but a piece of parchment upon which the words will be written."

"Then what do ye want?" Ewan Hay asked.

"I want all of the Aisir nam Breug for the Kerrs of Netherdale. I want David Kerr for my daughter's husband," Edmund Kerr said. "If ye can promise me those things, then I will help ye attain yer goal so ye can stand in high esteem with the earl."

"I was only authorized to allow ye the tolls collected," the Hay said.

"Ye think to have Brae Aisir for yerself, Ewan Hay, but I am no fool. Ye may hold the keep for the earl until the mighty stop their haggling over the Scots queen. But there is no need for ye to retain it after the settlement that will eventually come. It is Kerr land, not Hay land. Now, what will ye do with Fingal Stewart and my niece? And of course old Dugald will not give in to ye so easily."

"I mean to slay Lord Stewart, and take his wife for my mistress. Once I would have wed her, but no more," Ewan Hay lied to the Lord of Netherdale. He would find another priest lacking scruples and force the widow to the altar. Then her sons would meet with a tragic accident. It would be his children who inherited Brae Aisir, not Fingal Stewart's and certainly not the grandchildren of Edmund Kerr. But right now he would tell his host whatever it would take to gain his alliance.

"If ye will guarantee me Brae Aisir after ye have finished with it, I will help ye," Edmund Kerr said.

Rafe Kerr listened to his father, appalled. The familial relationship between the Kerrs of Netherdale and the Kerrs of Brae Aisir had always been stronger than politics and kings. It was the Aisir nam Breug that mattered; that, not the fortunes of the mighty, came first with the Kerrs. However, Rafe wisely held his own counsel and kept silent. He had thought his father had given up on his craving to control the entire traverse, but it had obviously become a desire that Edmund Kerr could not control or let go.

Ewan Hay remained at Netherdale Hall, now an honored guest. Rafe listened as Ewan Hay outlined his plan. He knew how Fingal Stewart had regained the keep, for Maggie had told him when the three had met in the pass one day. Early one morning as the sky began to lighten, Rafe Kerr wrote a note to his cousin on a miniscule piece of paper, folded it into a tiny scroll, and fitted it into a little metal cylinder, which he affixed to the leg of a pigeon he took from the dovecote. Releasing the bird, he watched it as it soared into the skies above Netherdale and then turned north. This was a means of communication used by the Kerr families in times of emergency, and this was certainly an emergency. He wished the bird Godspeed and silently prayed it would reach its destination without being hunted down by a hawk.

Several hours later the pigeon reached the dovecote at Brae Aisir. Fortunately, it was seen by little David Kerr, who ran to his mother saying, "Mama, a bird has just come into the cote. There is something on its leg."

Maggie ran to the dovecote, and peeping inside, saw the bird among her own. Reaching in, she drew the pigeon out, unfastened the cylinder, and then set the creature back among the others. Hurrying to the house, she called to David, "Go and fetch yer da."

The little boy ran off. Going into the hall, Maggie opened the cylinder, carefully drew out the little scroll, unrolled it, and spread it out flat upon the high board. The message was written in tiny letters, but she could read it.

Hay here. Assured Scot. Wants keep, pass, for Lennox.

Seeks secret entry. Will kill to learn it. What to do?

The message was signed by Rafe Kerr, her cousin.

Fingal came into the hall. "What's happened?" he asked her.

Maggie pointed to the message, and her husband read it slowly. Finally she said, "I am so tired of Ewan Hay, Fin."

He nodded his agreement. "Tell Rafe to somehow give the information to the Hay," he said. "We'll barricade the far end of the tunnel so there is no way he can enter the keep. And once Hay and his men are halfway down the tunnel, we'll roll boulders in front of the outside entrance. With both ends of the tunnel tightly sealed, Hay and his men will die down there. After a few months, we'll open the passageway up again, and give the bodies a Christian burial," Fin said.

"If I didn't think we might need the tunnel again someday, I would suggest we flood it when they are down there," Maggie said fiercely.

"It's obvious that the Hay told the English about the Aisir nam Breug, but if he doesn't return to his masters, they will probably forget all about it. They probably wanted the convenience of a discreet refuge to meet with their assured Scots on this side of the border," Fin said, "but I don't believe it's very important to them, as many of those men are borderers and have nearby homes."

"I'll let the pigeon rest the day, and send it back with our reply just before dawn tomorrow," Maggie told her husband, and he agreed.

At Netherdale, Rafe Kerr watched the next morning for his bird to return. He prayed that none of the Hay's men would notice the avian. His prayers were answered as he saw the pigeon swoop down from the sky and dance into its cote. He hurried to get the capsule, and taking it to his own apartments, he opened the cylinder, spread the parchment out, and read the following message:

Find a way to tell the secret. We'll end this. Maggie

Rafe smiled, then tossed the tiny piece of parchment into the fire in his hearth. He watched as it burned to ash. Then he sought out one of the housemaids he knew to be totally trustworthy. "I need yer help, Glenda," he began. Then he explained to her what it was he wanted.

Glenda listened, then said, "I'll do it. One of the younger lasses might grow frightened and give it all away. The Hay has been casting about for a bedmate, for he is a lustful man. Better me than an untried maid. Give me a few days, my lord."

"I won't forget this service," Rafe told her.

Glenda laughed. "Ye've always been more generous than yer da," she said dryly.

That evening when Ewan Hay entered his bedchamber, he found a maidservant bent over while tending to the fire in his hearth. "Well, well, what have we here?" he purred.

The servant straightened, whirling about, a startled look upon her face. "Oh, sir, forgive me," she said. "I meant to be gone, but the fire was stubborn and would not catch properly." She curtsied to him.

She was very pretty, he considered, with large pillowy breasts, yellow hair, and big blue eyes.

"And is the fire as it should be now?" he said, smiling at her.

"Aye, sir." She curtsied again. "Is there anything else I may do for ye, sir?"

"Give me a kiss," Ewan Hay said.

"Oh, sir, 'tis very naughty of ye," the maidservant told him. But she did not go.

"Tell me yer name," he said, stepping to block her route to his door.

"Glenda, sir," she half whispered.

"I am a guest in this house, Glenda, and I believe yer master would want every effort made to make my stay a pleasant one." Reaching out, Ewan Hay put an arm about the servant and drew her close.

"Ohh, sir!" Glenda sighed, and she appeared to grow weak in his embrace.

He leaned in to give her a kiss. Her mouth opened beneath his, her tongue seeming to welcome his tongue. She was quite proficient at kissing, he quickly discovered. Reluctantly leaving her lips, he said, "I think ye may be a very naughty lass, Glenda. Are ye naughty?" His other hand fondled her covered breasts.

She giggled again. "Some say I am naughty. Others call me generous, sir." She pressed herself against him, looking up into his face. "Which would ye like me to be?" she asked him, her eyes wide, her mouth pouting suggestively.

"*Both!*" he told her. He could feel his cock already straining to be released. "Now ye tell me what ye would like me to be?"

Glenda reached down to stroke the thick hard ridge in his breeks. "Tireless, sir," she whispered to him. "Or do I presume too much, sir?"

Ewan Hay grinned wolfishly at the maidservant. "I'm going to fuck ye," he growled at her fiercely, pushing her onto the bed, pushing up her skirts, and falling atop her. He found her entry immediately and was as good as his word.

But Glenda's mother had been the Netherdale village whore, a position now held by Glenda's older sister. Glenda, however, wanted a more respectable life. She had an aunt who was a servant at Netherdale Hall, and her aunt had gained her niece a position. Having grown up in her mother's cottage, Glenda knew well how to tease a man into his best performance. She praised the man now using her, encouraged him to heights he had never before known or even imagined, stroked his vanity by shrieking with apparent delight at his prowess. And when he lay exhausted, she arose, straightened her garb, and left him.

Ewan Hay's itch had been but lightly scratched. His eyes now constantly swept the hall looking for Glenda. Catching her in a corridor the next day, he put her against the wall and used her vigorously. When he had finished he told her, "Ye will come to my chamber tonight and stay with me. I have a yearning to see ye naked."

"I'll try, sir," she promised him, and then waited until very late to finally go to him. Without his even asking, she stripped off her garments, laying them aside, and stood silently, turning slowly, so he might view her to his pleasure.

Ewan Hay almost moaned aloud at the lushness of the girl's body. His manhood grew stiff beneath the bed coverlet. He beckoned her into the bed, flinging back the covering so she could see he was quite naked, and ready for her. Ewan Hay felt out of control with this female. He had never been so lustful in his life. He took her once, and it simply wasn't enough. She brought him some wine from the bedchamber sideboard. He did not know she had laced it with certain herbs that would help him regain his strength sooner and keep him that way longer. He had his way with her a second time.

Afterwards Glenda looked up at him with her blue eyes. She smiled saying, "Oh, sir, I have never before known such a lover as ye are!"

"I am frankly surprised the old lord, or one of his sons, hasn't taken ye for a mistress," Ewan said with candid observation.

"Oh nay, sir! I am not that kind of a girl," she protested. "But last night when ye . . . when we . . . Ye are the first man I have not been able to resist, sir."

"Ye weren't a virgin," he said.

Glenda laughed. "I should hope not! I am seventeen after all, but I am not a wanton with the lads, sir. Every lass has a tumble beneath a hedge or in the hay now and again, but only some become familiar to all. Most of us do not. But ye, sir. Yer gentry, and ye still wanted me, and have treated me with kindness.

"I have a half sister who married into Brae Aisir village, and she has not been as fortunate in her husband as I have been this day with ye. Her husband is a rough man-at-arms, and sometimes beats her. She came recently through the pass for a visit, and said he has been in a much better mood since his master returned, and they recaptured the keep. Have ye heard the tale, sir?"

"Nay," Ewan Hay said. "I have been in England fighting with the Earl of Lennox. Wasn't this keep defended?"

"Aye, sir, it was, and the drawbridge was up. But those attempting to steal the keep from its rightful owners did not know about the secret tunnel that leads beneath the moat, and up into the kitchen pantry. That's how Brae Aisir's rightful lord regained his property. He came through using that tunnel in the hillside beneath the keep. And the victory put my brother-in-law in an excellent mood, so he allowed my half sister to come home for a visit," Glenda said. Then reaching up, she pulled his head down to hers and began kissing him with expert and tempting lips.

Ewan Hay almost jumped from his bed in delight. Now he knew how he could enter Brae Aisir's keep and retake it for the Earl of Lennox. But first he needed to slake the lust building up in his body again. With his new knowledge, he might linger another day enjoying Glenda's extraordinary charms. And when he had settled himself back at Brae Aisir, he would send for her. The thought of having the servant girl and Maggie Kerr both in his bed at the same time was more than exciting.

Glenda let him have his pleasure of her body one more time, and then the wine she gave him this second time held a sleeping potion. She waited until he was snoring loudly, and then dressing quickly, the serving woman left the bedchamber to hurry to find Rafe Kerr. Though it was past midnight, Rafe had lingered in the hall. His wife was with child for a fifth time, and she could not go to sleep if he was in their bed. So he waited. When Glenda hurried up to him, he said softly, "What news?"

"The secret's out," she replied with a mischievous grin. "He may linger a day to prepare, but before he fell asleep, he told me he would be leaving Netherdale Hall shortly."

"Can ye continue to give him what he wants so he does not grow suspicious?" Rafe asked her. "Ye've done so much, I dislike asking."

Glenda shook her head. "Nay, my lord, I will do what I must for Netherdale."

Rafe released two pigeons at first light. He could not take the chance that the message to Brae Aisir not be received.

Maggie had put a watch on the dovecote. In midmorning a man-servant brought her a message capsule. Opening it and unrolling the bit of parchment she read:

The bait has been taken. He leaves tomorrow. Be ready. Rafe

"Are we ready?" she asked her husband after reading him the message.

Fin nodded in the affirmative. "The rock is all in place, ready to seal the opening. Come, and I will show you how we have blocked the pantry door."

They descended to the kitchens, through a pantry, and then down another small flight of stone steps into the cold pantry. The door that had once led into the tunnel was no longer visible at all. Fin pointed out to her where it had once been.

"We removed the staircase from the tunnel to this level," he explained. "Then we sealed the door with wide strips of iron the blacksmith forged for that purpose. Then we closed the door off with stone on both sides. They cannot reach the door now, and if they somehow managed to get up to where it was, the door is secured by two stone walls and a wall of iron. Finding their exit gone, Hay and his men will return to the entry to find it blocked, thus preventing their escape."

"What if they send someone through to reconnoiter?" Maggie asked.

"Then we will drive them into the tunnel before sealing it. I think, however, that not realizing we know he is coming, and knowing we used the tunnel in recent months, Ewan Hay will march straight into our trap, Maggie mine. His reputation is one for violence, not tactical skills," Fin responded.

"So in a few days this should all be over," Maggie replied.

"For us hopefully, but not for the Borders," Fin said.

"How will we know when the Hay comes?" she asked.

"The watchtower guards will notify us. A lantern signal will be sent from tower to tower to tower. The last tower will send a man with the warning."

Towards dusk two days later, a man-at-arms came from the last tower to warn them that Ewan Hay and his men were even now coming to the end of the Aisir nam Breug. Strategically placed men observed as the Hay's men stopped just short of the pass's end to dismount to lead their horses to a small wooded copse where they tethered them. Then the invaders came stealthily and on foot, circling around the village, for their purpose was to enter the keep, and take it, not battle the village.

While the residents of Brae Aisir had been advised of the impend-ing attempt to retake the keep, they kept to their cottages as if it were an ordinary evening. If they saw a shadowy figure flit by behind their dwellings, they pretended not to notice at all. The Hay and his men crept up the hillside and after an hour or more of searching, found the entry behind a thicket of bushes. Darkness was about to fall as they discovered the door pulled easily open, and stepped into the mouth of the tunnel to light their torches where they would not be seen by accidental eyes.

"I think ye should send two men through to make certain the tun-nel is clear," Bhaltair advised the Hay.

"Nay, 'tis not necessary. They used the tunnel but recently," Ewan Hay replied. He was eager to regain the advantage he had lost to Fingal Stewart; eager to see the look of astonishment and then fear on Maggie Kerr's face when she saw him returned. He would have his revenge on them both. Tonight after all was secure, he intended having Fingal Stewart brought to the hall bound securely to watch while Ewan Hay raped his wife on the high board, and then allowed Bhaltair the same privilege. This time there would be no escape for the Kerrs of Brae Aisir or Fingal Stewart. And the Earl of Lennox would reward Ewan Hay generously for the capture of this keep, and the Aisir nam Breug. "Forward, men!" he instructed, actually leading the way for the first time. His torch cut the darkness as he hurried into the depths of the tunnel, and Bhaltair and the others came at a trot behind him.

When the sounds of their voices had faded, shadowy figures crept from the surrounding brush. The door to the tunnel was quietly closed, and then locked. Then the large boulders that had been dis-guised with greenery were slowly pushed into place until the old oak door was no longer even visible. There was not the tiniest crack or crevice available where the light might shine through. Ewan Hay and his men were firmly and solidly trapped in the tunnel. They would not ever escape.

Reaching the end of the tunnel, the invaders found nothing. There were no stairs leading up to a door. They could not even discover where a door had been. They wondered whether they had taken a wrong turn and missed another arm of the tunnel, but retracing their steps, they discovered the tunnel was but a single extension. Panic ensued. The men broke ranks, racing back to the tunnel's entrance, only to discover the door closed upon them, and worse, it seemed to be locked tightly.

They attempted over the next few days to remove the door's lock and hinges, but when they finally succeeded, they found themselves facing a wall of black stone. They would die within the darkness as their torches were slowly extinguished. Some of the men began to pray. Bhaltair sat down stoically to await his eventual death. Ewan Hay cursed and howled with both his fear and his fury at having once again been defeated by the Kerrs. When he finally lapsed into hysterical babbling and weeping, Bhaltair beat him into silence. He might have cut his throat, but Bhaltair decided that would have been too merciful a death for Ewan Hay. He would suffer with the rest of them.

The Earl of Lennox was on the move, coming into the southwest of Scotland to pillage its towns and villages, and burn its harvests so that the clan folk would starve in the coming winter. A small party of soldiers came to Netherdale Hall, seeking to use the Aisir nam Breug.

Rafe Kerr refused them. "The traverse is only for peaceful travel, my lord," he told the nobleman who captained the soldiers.

"We were told the pass would be available to us by the Earl of Lennox," the nobleman said. "He sent one of his assured Scots to take the keep on the other side of the border several weeks back."

Rafe shook his head in apparent puzzlement. "We did not see such a man, or even hear of such a happening. Our Scots kinsmen hold the other end of the pass, and I know they are still in control of their keep, for I spoke with them just a few days back. It is our custom to inspect the Aisir nam Breug together monthly, my lord. Mad Maggie Kerr, my cousin, and her husband, Fingal Stewart, were with me. If their keep had been taken over, they would surely be either dead or fled from Brae Aisir."

"Ye deal with these Scots?" the nobleman asked, surprised. "Do ye not realize there is a war between England and Scotland?"

"My lord, these are the Borders. The Kerrs of Netherdale and the Kerrs of Brae Aisir have held this pass for peaceful travel for several hundred years. Not even King Edward the First, called the Hammer of the Scots, could change the loyalty that exists between our two families. We are not people to be involved in politics. We keep a safe route between our two countries open in order that families, peddlers, and merchant trains can pass through unscathed."

Edmund Kerr had listened as his son dealt with the English war party. Why was Rafe lying about Ewan Hay and his men? He was wise enough, however, to wait until the English had departed back to the Earl of Lennox for further instructions.

Rafe, however, seeing his father's face, did not wait to be asked. "The Hay and his men are dead. The Kerrs protect their own."

"We had a chance," Edmund Kerr said angrily, "a chance to control the pass alone, and ye spoiled it?"

"Did ye really believe Hay would give it all to ye, Da? If he had been allowed to succeed, he would have taken it all for himself. He would have used the pass for war. The Kerrs have kept the Aisir nam

Breug free of war for more than five hundred years. That has been its value to both families. If ye let one small war party through it, every raider in the border will want to use it, and if ye say them nay, they will take it from us." Rafe was growing angry. He slammed his hand down upon the high board where he and his father were seated. "Nay, I tell ye, old man, nay! I will not allow ye to besmirch the honor of the Kerrs in yer foolishness and yer greed. 'Tis time for ye to spend yer days in Aldis's bower. From now on, the decisions for this family will be made by me, and not ye. And before ye start making idle threats, know that my brothers are in agreement with this."

Edmund Kerr grew almost purple with his fury. He opened his mouth to shout at his son, but no sounds came forth. His eyes bulged from their sockets as he stood, only to collapse back into his chair unconscious.

"Have ye killed him?" Aldis, his third wife, asked of Rafe.

"I think not," Rafe answered her, signaling to their servants. "Take Lord Edmund to his bed," he told them. "I think he's suffered the effects of being overthrown in his own house, Aldis. Go and care for him now, for he will need yer love to sustain him."

"Of course, my lord," Aldis replied. She arose and curtsied to Rafe politely, then turned to leave the hall.

"Will yer brothers really support ye?" Rafe's wife seated on the other side of him asked. "All of them?"

"They have no choice if they wish to remain here at Netherdale," Rafe said. "I have seen that each of them has a house and a wife who brought a good dower. I have encouraged them to pursue their own interests. There is not one of them who wants to deal with the responsibilities of Netherdale or the Aisir nam Breug. I am the lord here now, and I will see my brothers remain in their own places," he told her. "Hopefully we are finished with this war, and will be left in peace."

But Rafe Kerr's wish was not to be granted. A messenger from the Earl of Lennox arrived several days after he had sent away the war party. The earl still wanted the use of the Aisir nam Breug for his messengers, and he was willing to offer a large bribe to both the Kerrs of Netherdale and the Kerrs of Brae Aisir. Rafe sent the messenger back with a promise to quickly consider it and discuss it with his Scots cousins. Then he rode through the pass to Brae Aisir to tell Maggie and Fin of recent events.

"Ye know the history of the pass, Cousin," Maggie said to him. "Ye know what we must do."

"Aye, it would seem we have no other choice at this juncture," Rafe agreed.

"What must ye do?" Fin inquired of them.

"In the time of King Edward the First, there were those who sought to use the pass for war. We could not allow it, for our reputation was one of peaceful and safe travel," Maggie said. "So we blocked the pass. It was several years before we were able to unblock it, but the Aisir nam Breug was not used for warlike purposes then, and we will not allow it to be used that way now."

"We are in agreement, then?" Rafe said.

Maggie nodded.

"If the pass is closed to all travel, then yer income is cut off," Fin said.

The cousins nodded. "Aye," they said together.

"Can ye survive?" Fin asked. He had not until this moment realized the depth of familial loyalty between the English Kerrs and the Scots Kerrs. It was going to be difficult for both families until the border wars were ended, and the Aisir nam Breug could be opened once again, if indeed it ever was.

Rafe nodded. "We will survive," he said. Then he turned and

walked over to where old Dugald Kerr sat by his fire. "My lord, will ye approve this action?"

"What of yer father?" the laird asked.

"My father is no longer in charge at Netherdale," Rafe said quietly.

"And ye can defend yer holding from him?" the laird inquired.

"Aye! My brothers are behind the decision. My father has not been well for some time. He lost his sense of honor. Had he not been ill, it should never have happened."

Dugald Kerr nodded. "Very well then, I approve the action that ye and Maggie mean to take. Do it tomorrow as ye return. Have ye stopped the northward flow of traffic?"

Rafe nodded.

"And we'll let no one going south through after today," Maggie said.

Rafe Kerr remained the night at Brae Aisir. The following morning, he rode out with Maggie to the border within the pass that separated the two nations. Maggie had insisted upon going alone with her cousin, but she knew Fin rode the hills above the traverse watching her. A good quarter mile from the border, Maggie dismounted her horse and tied its reins to a gorse bush. Rafe galloped ahead, riding over the invisible line to tether his mount a quarter mile into England. Walking, the cousins reached the spot where the great stone thistle and its matching rose were set in the hillside. They climbed their respective hillsides up to the large markers.

"Ready?" Rafe called to Maggie from across the divide now separating them.

Maggie nodded. Then she raised up the panel in the front of the marker to let down a rain of large stones and small boulders into the pass even as Rafe Kerr did the same. The rocks rumbled down the hillside, loosening more rock and dirt as they fell. A cloud of dust arose up from the pass, turning the air briefly brown. Then it dissipated in the cool, damp autumn air along with the thunderous sound the stones had made.

A light rain began to fall. Maggie gazed down. The Aisir nam Breug was well and thoroughly blocked. It would remain that way until the day came that it was once again safe to open it up to peaceful travel. The English would not attempt to unblock it, for it was far too tedious a task and would take quite a long time. Raising her head, she looked across to Rafe. He nodded, satisfied; then smiling at her, he saluted Mad Maggie Kerr with an elegant bow and a charming grin.

"Farewell for now, Cousin," he called to her.

"Farewell, Rafe," she called to him, and then she added, "Ye'll surely go down in the family history as the most honorable among all the Kerrs on both sides of the border."

And she gave him a brilliant smile before they both turned away.

Maggie climbed down the side of the hill even as she knew Rafe was doing right now. She walked slowly back to where she had tethered her horse and, mounting it, rode back to Brae Aisir. Fingal Stewart met his wife as she exited the Aisir nam Breug.

"'Twas not easy to do what ye did," he said.

"We are honorable folk, we Kerrs," she said.

"Do ye think the traverse will ever be opened again?" he asked her.

"I don't know," Maggie admitted, "but the Kerrs of Brae Aisir have had a long and glorious history keeping the Aisir nam Breug safe. Whether we will ever do so again, I do not know, Fin." A single tear slipped down her cheek. "'Tis the end of an era for us," she said.

"And the start of an era for the Kerr-Stewarts of Brae Aisir," he told her. Then Fingal Stewart surprised his wife, reaching out to lift her from her horse to bring her to sit next to him on his stallion. He smiled into her startled face, then bent to give her a deep, hungry kiss. Holding her close, he kicked his mount into a gentle canter. "'Tis not the end, Maggie mine," he said, whispering the promise into her ear. "'Tis but a glorious new beginning!" And it was.

Afterword

The Border Wars, often known as Henry Tudor's *rough wooing* of Scotland's little queen for his son and heir, lasted between 1544 and 1549. The strife peaked with the Battle of Pinkie on the tenth of September 1547. The English took over a great deal of southern Scotland after Pinkie. The wars finally ended two years later in September 1549 when the English were forced to withdraw entirely from Scotland, as their forces were needed elsewhere. The new French king, Henri II, Scotland's chief ally, had laid siege to English-held Bologne.

Although Henry VIII had died in January 1547, the new king's uncle, Edward Seymour, now the Duke of Somerset, was the protector of the realm. He was as eager for a match between his young nephew, Edward VI, as Henry had been, which meant there was no change in England's policy towards Scotland. The brutality of the Border Wars, however, had united Scotland firmly against England.

With the death of François I, Henri II came to the throne in France. His closest advisers were the brothers of Marie de Guise, Scotland's Queen Mother. Because of the English, the little queen had spent her early years being moved from one castle to another. She had survived chicken pox and the measles. Now in June 1548, the five-year-old queen, formally betrothed to Henri II's son and heir, the dauphin François, was taken to France to be brought up with her future husband.

In her greatest sacrifice, Marie de Guise elected to remain behind in Scotland to protect her daughter's interests. As her daughter's regent, she ruled with equanimity. The Reformation came to Scotland, and Marie de Guise practiced open tolerance, allowing the pastors of the Protestant pursuasion to preach openly and without hindrance. When King Edward VI died, his sister Mary Tudor took England's throne and began a ferocious persecution of the Protestant faith. Marie de Guise offered sanctuary to those persecuted Protestant English ministers.

Sadly, all her good work was for naught because most of those holding high office in Scotland at that time as well as the army were French. An anti-French sentiment began to arise, and leading it were those very Protestant churchmen and lords Marie de Guise had protected. However, the dissidents represented Scotland and a cry for freedom from the French. The Queen Mother was French despite all her years in Scotland. Her popularity began to disappear. She died in June 1560.

In England, Elizabeth Tudor, the Catholic Mary's Protestant half sister, now sat on the throne. She watched with careful eyes as her fabled beautiful cousin, the elegant and sophisticated eighteen-year-old Mary of Scotland, now a widow, returned home to rule. But that is a different story for another time.

As for the Aisir nam Breug, it was never reopened, and in the years that followed, its existence was completely forgotten. Scotland and England entered a different era. With the death of Elizabeth I, Mary Stewart's son, James VI of Scotland, became James I of England. The few roads running through the Borders were now as safe as any of the many roads in the two united kingdoms, and the families at Brae Aisir and Netherdale survived for many generations to come.

About the Author

_____

Bertrice Small is a _New York Times_ bestselling author and the recipient of numerous awards. In keeping with her profession, she lives in the oldest English-speaking town in the state of New York, founded in 1640. Her light-filled studio includes the paintings of her favorite cover artist, Elaine Duillo, and a large library. Because she believes in happy endings, Bertrice Small has been married to the same man, her hero, George, for forty-seven years. They have a son, Thomas, a daughter-in-law, Megan, and four wonderful grandchildren. Long-time readers will be happy to know that Nicki the cockatiel flourishes along with his housemates: Finnegan, the long-haired, bad, black kitty; and Sylvester, the black-and-white tuxedo cat who is the official family bedcat.